Advance Praise f[...]

"In this gripping, tension-filled sto[...] choices that one woman was forced to ma[...] her dream for a better life. As with many courageous acts, contro[...]y follows our heroine, and for that reason alone, book clubs will find much to discuss here."

—Kathleen Grissom, *New York Times* bestselling author of
The Kitchen House

"Tanabe weaves a tale rich with historical detail and heartbreaking human emotion that demonstrates the complex and unjust choices facing a woman of color in nineteenth-century America. That so many of the questions explored by Tanabe about race, gender, ambition, and privilege still resonate today makes this novel required reading."

—Tara Conklin, *New York Times* bestselling author of
The House Girl

"A thrilling and foreboding tale about social and racial rules in nineteenth-century America . . . Tanabe's narration is reminiscent of novels of the 1890s, with dialogue that is spot-on for that era. The compelling story covers a shameful time in American history, and is unrelenting in its tension and gripping detail."

—Anna Jean Mayhew, author of *The Dry Grass of August*

"The true story of Anita Hemmings comes to life in vivid detail in *The Gilded Years*. Hemmings's gut-wrenching decision to pass as white in order to obtain an education is a poignant journey, and Tanabe's lyrical style is sure to keep readers turning pages."

—Renee Rosen, author of *White Collar Girl*

"*The Gilded Years* really brought home the horrific limitations and choices that were faced by black people post–Civil War, even in the supposedly more enlightened north. . . . That the story is based on true people only added to its richness."

—Laila Ibrahim, author of *Yellow Crocus*

Praise for *The Price of Inheritance*

"Readers will find plenty to savor . . . Carolyn is a winning character with a quick wit, and the opulent environs she inhabits are definitely worth a visit."

—*The Washington Post*

"A compelling novel of financial and emotional high stakes."

—*In Touch*

"Tanabe's absorbing novel blends equal parts mystery, wit, and romance."

—*Booklist*

"A deeply enjoyable and riotously funny takedown of the high-stakes New York art world and its most glamorous and illicit auction houses. Tanabe focuses her shimmering humor and laser eye on the dangerous lengths the very wealthy will journey to own a costly piece of history. Lushly detailed and ambitious in scope, *The Price of Inheritance* is rich in romance, war stories, and betrayals. A priceless read by a writer of immense talent."

—Amber Dermont, *New York Times* bestselling author of *The Starboard Sea*

"This absorbing, quick-turning story takes us behind the doors of the big auction houses, into the homes of the art-collecting elite, and onto the international marketplace with sure-handedness, and in fascinating detail. Tanabe writes with passion, intelligence, and a lot of wit, and the book is insanely difficult to put down."

—Jessica Lott, author of *The Rest of Us*

"Tanabe pulls off a triple coup: she gives us a juicy insider's look at the high-stakes auction business, a late coming-of-age (and enticingly New York) love story, and a truly suspenseful mystery that crosses borders from Rhode Island to Iraq."

—Allison Lynn, author of *Now You See It*

"Karin Tanabe weaves a tangled web of romance and intrigue, while exposing the underbelly of the art world. This smart and captivating read will have you turning pages faster than you can say forgery."

—Emily Liebert, author of *You Knew Me When*

Praise for *The List*

"A biting, hilarious send-up of D.C.'s elite."

—*People*

"Former *Politico* reporter Tanabe's roman-a-clef is a hilarious skewering of digital journalism—and how news is tweeted and blogged at a dizzying pace by armies of underpaid and overworked twentysomething journos— as well as a smartly paced and dishy debut, part political thriller, part surprisingly sweet coming-of-age tale, and part timeless ode to dogged reporters with good instincts and guts of steel."

—*Publishers Weekly* (starred review)

"A contemporary, politically astute novel that is both wickedly humorous and enticing . . . [with] complex characters, an intriguing plot, and tightly brilliant execution. When word gets around about *The List*, readers will clamor for their copy and devour this book."

—*New York Journal of Books*

ALSO BY KARIN TANABE

The List

The Price of Inheritance

THE GILDED YEARS

A Novel

KARIN TANABE

WASHINGTON SQUARE PRESS

NEW YORK   LONDON   TORONTO   SYDNEY   NEW DELHI

W

Washington Square Press
An Imprint of Simon & Schuster, Inc.
1230 Avenue of the Americas
New York, NY 10020

First Washington Square Press trade paperback edition June 2016

For information about special discounts for bulk purchases, please contact Simon & Schuster Special Sales at 1-866-506-1949 or business@simonandschuster.com.

The Simon & Schuster Speakers Bureau can bring authors to your live event. For more information or to book an event contact the Simon & Schuster Speakers Bureau at 1-866-248-3049 or visit our website at www.simonspeakers.com.

Manufactured in the United States of America

10 9 8 7 6 5 4

Library of Congress Cataloging-in-Publication Data

Names: Tanabe, Karin, author.
Title: The gilded years: a novel / Karin Tanabe.
Description: First Washington Square Press trade paperback edition. | New York : Washington Square Press, 2016.
Classification: LCC PS3620.A6837 G55 2016 | DDC 813/.6—dc23 LC record available at http://lccn.loc.gov/2015037370

ISBN 978-1-5011-1045-0
ISBN 978-1-5011-1046-7 (ebook)

For the VCVG—with love

There were in her at the moment two beings, one drawing deep breaths of freedom and exhilaration, the other gasping for air in a little black prison-house of fears.

—EDITH WHARTON, *The House of Mirth*

THE GILDED
YEARS

CHAPTER 1

As the electric trolley turned the corner onto Raymond Avenue, the driver sang out, "Vassar College!" The elongated vowels of his coarse New York accent reverberated off the walls, though every woman sitting on the wooden seats was already poised to disembark. Anita Hemmings smiled at two freshman girls who looked at once delighted and struck by nerves, and walked down the steps to collect her suitcases. Her trunk had been sent ahead and would be waiting for her in the school's congested luggage room, then brought up to her quarters by a porter.

The New York town of Poughkeepsie had boasted a trolley only since 1894. In her freshman year, Anita had arrived with her cases in a shaky horse-drawn tram, dusty and soot-colored, and painted with the words HUDSON RIVER R.R. DEPOT and a large gold number four. But for the past three years, Vassar students had pulled up in the efficient trolley, and she couldn't think of a better way to approach the Lodge, the handsome, red-brick gatehouse that served as the campus's entrance and guard post. Anita glanced up at the clock atop its simple façade, centered above four long windows. It was almost five o'clock. She had left Boston at just past seven in the morning and hadn't encountered any other Vassar girl until she changed trains in Albany. Now she was just steps away from her favorite sliver of the world, the college where she would reside for one more year.

Anita had never lived in a building that could be described as handsome until she went off to school, first in Massachusetts's Pioneer Valley, then at Vassar. Her hometown of Boston was crowded with elegant structures: stately brick houses you could stroll past, imagining the favored lives transpiring inside. But she had never had more than a glimpse of their sumptuous interiors. Here, on the vast expanse of land Vassar occupied a few miles from the gently curving Hudson River, every inch was hers—shared with 522 other girls, but still hers.

In Boston's Roxbury neighborhood, Anita, the oldest of four, shared a small, red-brick row house with her parents; her brothers, Frederick and Robert; and her sister, Elizabeth. It was indistinguishable from its squat neighbors, with a roof that leaked and too few rooms for six. She knew every vein of Roxbury, every needy character in the quarter, and was keenly aware that her friends at Vassar had not grown up in such a place.

"Is that Anita Hemmings?"

At the sound of her name, she turned to see the alabaster face of Caroline Hyde Hardin. The puffs of Caroline's dress sleeves were bigger than last year's, and she wore the trumpet-shaped, S-curved skirt that had become even more in vogue over the summer. Anita fretted for a moment over her travel-weary appearance, but her tension vanished as she was enveloped in a welcoming hug.

"Caroline!" she exclaimed, as her friend stepped back and wiped strands of red hair from her face. It was September 18, but the day was thick with the dense heat of a mid-July afternoon.

"I could tell it was you," said Caroline. "You walk so elegantly, even when you're laden down. Where is Mervis to help us?" she said, looking around for the porter everyone preferred.

"He's just assisting with the trunks of a few other girls who came on the earlier trains. He'll be back down," Anita said, smoothing her light summer dress and taking Caroline's hand, unable to hide her pleasure at being back on campus. "Oh, how I missed this beautiful place," she said, nodding toward the ivy-clad, Renwick-designed Main Building.

The circle in front of Main was crowded with carriages, tired horses, and girls bidding their families goodbye while vying for help with their boxes and suitcases. Before Anita and Caroline had arrived at Vassar as freshmen in 1893, Main had a regal entry with a double staircase leading to an impressive second-floor door, but a long annex had been added to the center of the building that year, courtesy of the school's favorite trustee, Frederick Ferris Thompson. The students called it Uncle Fred's Nose or the Soap Box, for its ample use of white marble. It now housed the ever-expanding library, where the students spent many an evening trying to push to the top of their class.

"It's enormous, but it does look smaller every year, doesn't it?" said Anita. "Perhaps because we've become more comfortable here."

She was right on both counts. The building, built to mimic the Tuileries Palace in Paris, was monumental in size, with five floors crisscrossed by halls twelve feet wide and almost two hundred yards long. On the roof were six thousand feet of lightning rods to help prevent the incessant threat of fire.

Caroline and Anita headed inside and were greeted by a chorus of delighted voices.

"Where did you spend your summer, Anita?" Caroline asked before they were both absorbed into the feminine gaggle.

"Nowhere exotic, I'm afraid. I was just home in Boston and then on Martha's Vineyard again. My usual summer holiday in charming Cottage City. At home I tutored Greek to several girls preparing for Vassar's entrance exam. I hope some will be freshmen next year, though I believe a proficiency in Greek and Latin is less important than it used to be."

"Isn't that refreshing to hear? I am wretched at Greek. That class on Thucydides and Pausanias last spring tied my brain into knots, though not yours." Caroline spread her arms as if she were about to clutch the building and let them drop when several families saying farewell to their freshmen moved by.

"Were you back in the Middle East, Caroline?" Anita asked, fixing her grip on her small bag.

"Oh, yes," she said. "For most of the summer I was in Syria, then we spent some time exploring Italy and France. I wanted to spend more time in Venice, which is just the most enchanting place on earth, a world floating on water, but Father had me working in his school for most of June and July. Lessons in Christianity, lessons in biology, lessons in just about everything. But August was so dreadfully hot that we had to leave."

Caroline's father ran a large school in Syria, and she had an abundance of captivating stories about her childhood there. Anita had been nowhere but the American Northeast and clung to Caroline's tales as if they were Scheherazade's.

"Are you rooming with Elise Monroe again, Anita?" asked Caroline, waving to a friend who had just entered the building.

"No, didn't you hear? She's left school to be married."

"Has she!" said Caroline, her attention fully on Anita. "Is she marrying the Browning boy? The one who was such a star at Yale?"

"The very one. He's from Washington, and they're to be married there just before Thanksgiving."

"Congratulations to the soon-to-be Mrs. Browning, then. Though it's sad that her parents didn't let her finish up one more year here. She was so strong in drama. Such a knack for comedic delivery. I'll miss her in the hall plays."

Anita nodded in agreement and the friends meandered through Main, heading up to the senior hall on what everyone called the third floor, though it was the fourth story of the building, a floor above where they had roomed the year before. They took the stairs, as the elevator had a line down the hall.

"If Elise is gone, then who is your roommate this year?" asked Caroline, taking a piece of paper from her case with her room number on it. "Or do you have a single, too?"

"No, I'm rooming with Louise Taylor, from New York."

Caroline looked at Anita with surprise. "Louise Taylor! As in Lottie Taylor? I never thought she would be short a roommate. How did that happen? Isn't she rooming with Dora Fairchild again? They have for two years now. They're awfully close."

"Dora stayed on in London, it seems, after her summer travels," said Anita. "Much to the shock and disappointment of Lottie. Kendrick informed me of everything just a few weeks ago. I thought I might be placed in a single in Strong Hall, but I don't mind."

"You've already communicated with Kendrick? Aren't you the lucky one," said Caroline of their admired lady principal.

"Do you know Louise well?" Anita asked, trying to catch her breath after the climb.

"Lottie?" said Caroline, in a suddenly serious voice. "I would say we're friends, even close friends, but in truth I know her just like everyone knows her."

Anita looked questioningly at her classmate, hoping she would say more.

"Well, I know of her money and her palatial house in New York," said Caroline, picking up on Anita's curiosity. "It's right near the Vanderbilts' on Fifth Avenue, you know. Of course you do. It *was* the talk freshman year. She's also very close to the Rockefellers. Bessie Rockefeller Strong, who was a special student here in the eighties and is Mr. Rockefeller's eldest, is a mentor to her. Or so they say. Bessie is the one who suggested Vassar to Clarence Taylor, Lottie's father. Lottie is also friendly with Consuelo Vanderbilt. She was a guest at her wedding last year to the Duke of Marlborough. You know, the one held at St. Thomas' Church that the papers made *such* a fuss about."

She looked at her friend to see if she was still listening and saw Anita's eyes were wide with fascination.

"You saw the pictures, I'm sure. The *New York Times* even ran that ridiculous piece on the luxury of her trousseau, paying particular attention to her intimate wears. I don't think the whole of America needed to read about the lace on her ivory corset covers, though it was all quite an affair. People lined up for days in front of St. Thomas' to get a glimpse of her. Consuelo and her swanlike neck. Not Lottie. She was inside the church along with her parents and her very handsome brother, now up at Harvard. A towhead like her. He's been on campus before. Younger, but not young enough for it to matter. So I know quite a bit about that, and I know the rumors of what happened between Lottie and

Lewis Van de Graff, of the Philadelphia Van de Graffs, at Harvard last year. Everyone here says she's very fast. But I don't really know her as a best friend would, though I'd like to. We're both in Philaletheis, though I'm Chapter Beta and she's Chapter Theta."

Caroline put her hand on the wooden rail and exhaled loudly, as if she was surprised by her own knowledge of Lottie Taylor. Caroline and Lottie had been members of Philaletheis together for three years, the college's exclusive dramatic society and oldest club, but rooming with a woman once described as a speeding locomotive with hair by the Harvard senior class president was another thing entirely.

"I'm sure you two will get on," she concluded. "She's just . . . quite a girl. Yes, that's a good way to put it. She's quite a girl."

Anita had known that Lottie's family was well-off but could not visualize to what extent. Caroline uttering Lottie's name in the same breath as John Rockefeller—who had funded the school's first separate dormitory and was funding a new academic building to break ground that year— was constricting her breathing even further. And then there was Consuelo Vanderbilt. All the Vassar girls followed her doings, but Caroline had said Lottie actually attended her wedding. Anita's starched traveling dress suddenly felt very tight. She put down her bag and reached up to loosen the stiff lace collar.

"Anita, are you unwell?" asked Caroline.

Anita flushed in embarrassment and bent to pick up her things. "I don't know what came over me. It must be this awful heat. I feel a bit faint."

"Come, let's walk down to senior hall and get settled in," said Caroline, taking her arm. "Those stairs were dreadful.

One of the maids can fetch you something cool to drink. Of course it's the heat. They need to open some of these windows and circulate the air." Caroline said as much to one of the young maids, and the two moved away from the other girls still greeting one another as if they'd been off fighting a war, rather than just separated by a summer vacation.

As they walked to the seniors' area, Anita thought about her idiocy in agreeing to share rooms with Lottie Taylor. She didn't want to be housed with anyone prominent, anyone who might attract attention. She needed a nobody from nowhere so she could keep walking quietly through the crowd of Vassar women, well liked, but not too well liked; active in school, but not president of any esteemed club; smart enough, but not first in her class—nothing that would make her shine too brightly or fall too hard. She wanted to be smiled at and then quickly forgotten.

"I'm here in room eighty-nine," said Caroline, as they reached it. "Will you be all right to walk to yours?"

"Me? Oh, yes, I'm feeling much better now. Just a quick spell. I'm in room twenty-one, right in front of the art gallery," said Anita, pointing down the hall. "I'll see you at dinner, Caroline."

"You're in twenty-one?" said Caroline, looking down at the hallway's double marble staircase near Anita's room. "But that's the very best senior room, with a perfect view of the Lodge. How did you draw that one? Oh, never mind," she said, smiling and opening her door. "Lottie Taylor," she whispered.

Caroline was in a single, a bedroom without a parlor, and a less desirable view.

"I'm so happy to be back, aren't you?" Anita said, watching her friend walk into her bright, sparsely furnished room.

"I am, too, Anita. There's no place I love more."

The girls bid each other goodbye, and Anita turned the corner toward her room, opening the oak door with her free hand.

"Just leave it by the desk closest to the window, please," she heard a voice say at once. Anita saw Lottie, her back to the door, trying to nail a square of ornate silk fabric above their parlor window.

"I'm sorry," Anita replied. "You must be waiting for your trunk." Lottie turned to look at her with a nail in her mouth and nearly dropped the hammer. She took the nail out and gave her an apologetic smile.

"You're Anita Hemmings! And you must think me the rudest girl in the world. I'm sorry I didn't turn around. I thought you were Mervis with my things."

"It's nothing at all," Anita said, walking into the already heavily decorated room. "I saw Mervis downstairs, but I'm afraid he's extremely busy. I'm sure our trunks will be brought up soon. Though I think they'll have to be attended to by someone else. Every senior girl in Main seems to be after him." As with most of the accommodations in Main, Anita and Lottie had a set of three rooms with two bedrooms and a large shared parlor.

"Fine, fine. I'm in no particular rush," said Lottie brightly. "I have all the accessories I need to get our parlor in order right here." Both girls looked at the floor of their square room, which was covered in fabrics and paintings.

Lottie paused her chatter as she stepped down from her chair. In her white dress, with her blond hair pinned to her head and the dying evening light creating a shadow behind her, she looked as if she had flown down from somewhere much finer, somewhere celestial.

"Look at you, you're even prettier than everybody said," she pronounced, approaching Anita. "I remembered you, of course, but we didn't overlap much in classes, did we? You're very Greek and Latin, I hear. I like Asian history and the sciences." She extended her hand, then held Anita by the shoulders as a mother might do to a child who had just come in from playing outside.

"Just look at your hair," she said excitedly. "Straight and dark like an Indian's. I'm very jealous. My life's desire is to be able to tame this top," she said, tilting her head. "My mother tried, my maids tried, all in vain, I might add. When I was fifteen, my parlor maid burned about half of it off. I wore many hats that year."

"I hate hats," Anita said, laughing.

"Oh, me too," Lottie said, smiling with her. "So old-fashioned. If it were up to me, I would spend the entire day lounging in my golf costume. I do love golf. A modern woman's game. Or I'd be totally nude like the French."

She looked at Anita's surprised face, enjoying her reaction. "You're going to be an awful lot of fun to shock. That's apparent already, and it's scarcely been five minutes. We need to shake a little of that puritanical Boston out of you before the semester's end or we won't have any fun at all." She spun around the room, already comfortable in her roommate's presence.

"Did you know a princess lived in this room? A real one. Sutematsu Yamakawa. Or Stematz Yamakawa, as she was known here. She now holds the title of Princess Oyama of Japan. Vassar class of 1882 and the very first Japanese woman to receive a college degree. Ever. You've heard the stories about her, have you not?"

Anita shook her head. She was familiar with the exotic name, but it was clear that Lottie knew the better stories.

"A woman of legend," Lottie declared. "President of Philaletheis. President of '82 her sophomore year. Third in her class. And such penmanship. I've seen her letters, barely an inch left without text, and she still keeps in contact with her professors. She married the Japanese minister of war. Isn't that charming? War is so dramatic, it's hard not to be taken with it. I curse the world that I wasn't born before the Civil War. I would have been so good at it. Well, at being supportive. As for Princess Oyama, I hear her husband is afraid that she'll divulge national secrets, but I'm sure she'll remain tight-lipped. I plan on meeting her one day quite soon so I've been practicing my bow. The royals expect you to bend at a full forty-five-degree angle."

Anita had no idea where one heard that a princess might pose a threat to Japanese national security, but she didn't doubt Lottie.

"I can't even recount to you the lies I had to tell to secure us these rooms," said Lottie, fluttering her eyelashes as if she'd been caught in a rainstorm. "I made up a whole to-do about not being able to sleep unless I could see straight down the dusty drive to the Lodge. Then I added some nonsense about extreme claustrophobia and an incurable passion for the architecture of James Renwick. But it was worth it, I'm sure you'll agree."

Anita looked at her in awe and nodded.

"I'm simply enamored with Japan. This school is so backward not teaching the Asian languages," said Lottie, looking wistfully at the room's décor, most of it picked up during her travels in the Orient.

"Caroline Hardin will teach you off-color words in Arabic if you bring her molasses candy," Anita offered.

"Caroline can eat all the candy she wants. Arabia does not interest me. The art is poor, and there isn't enough fish to eat." Lottie sucked in her cheeks and pursed her lips, making little underwater noises. Anita wasn't sure which world

Lottie had sprung from, but she was already convinced it was one she wanted to be a part of.

"Oh, look, our rocking chair from Uncle Fred," Lottie said, running her hand over the curved chair that was paid for and placed in every dormitory room by the prominent trustee. "I used to sit in mine all the time last year when I'd had too much to drink. I'd just collapse like a rag doll and sleep it off."

"Do you drink often?" her roommate asked, hoping she didn't sound prudish.

"Anita, dearest. One has to live a little, don't you think?" Lottie looked up with her pale, heart-shaped face, which clearly favored mischief over morals.

"Of course," Anita replied hastily, though on campus she was noted for her reserve.

"With your beauty, you are destined to live a dramatic life," said Lottie, putting her hand on Anita's chin and studying her face. "Living, *really* living, is awfully entertaining. We'll do a lot of it this year, I promise you." She peered around the room at the wall hangings she had put up before Anita's arrival. In between the draped blue silk was an exquisite kimono, hand-painted with a mountain scene and cascading pink cherry blossoms on the back.

"Let's tack this cloth to the wall by that kimono," Lottie said, reaching for a few yards of fabric and picking up a scroll painting of evergreen rice paper with her other hand. "The maids go on about cluttering up the room like this, because dust gathers or some nonsense, and they're worried we'll burn the whole place down when it falls into the oil lamps, but I don't care. I am not living in bland quarters. My mind won't expand. And for me to keep up here, my mind needs a lot of expanding."

"I like what you've done with it so far. It's much more

striking than my parlor room last year," her roommate said. Their room looked like a fourteen-by-fourteen-foot advertisement for luxury travel to the Orient.

Lottie let the fabric drop and admired her work.

"Well, as I said, I am besotted with Japan at the moment. I traveled to Tokyo and Kyoto in July and August with Father, and it was majestic. I can't even begin to describe the people. So slight, so diminutive and elegant. They walk on wooden shoes, can you imagine? And they wear long silk kimonos and the food is beautifully presented. Plus the fish! You haven't eaten a fish until you've eaten a raw Japanese fish. I know it sounds dreadful, but it's just the opposite. And then of course there is the actual art. The paintings and calligraphy, the woodblock prints. My father bought an original Hokusai, whose work is causing a sensation in Paris. His name will make it to America soon. We're behind, of course. Isn't that always the case? I tried to bring the print here, but you can guess how that conversation terminated. I'm going to sail to Japan again after graduation. Father promised me I could, as long as I'm chaperoned. I want to go all over the Orient. You should accompany me. We'd have a magnificent time."

Anita knew that within days of graduation, she would have a sensible teaching job or a scholarship to another school. And not one across the Pacific Ocean.

"It sounds splendid," Anita said noncommittally, diverting the conversation from any future plans.

"I am so taken with Orientals," said Lottie. "They have the most marvelous features." She picked up the hammer and headed to the wall above the ornate lacquer tea table, delivered from overseas just that morning.

"You don't mind, do you?" she asked, after she had already put the first hole in the plaster.

"Not at all," Anita answered honestly.

"I told Father that I was going to marry the future emperor of Japan, Crown Prince Yoshihito," she said with her back turned and a nail between her teeth again. "And he said he would shoot me first. He meant it, too. He has several guns and a terrible temper." She spat out the nail so she could be better heard. "It's not like I said I was going to run off with a despondent railroad worker with an opium pipe. A sensitive man, my father, but a real modern person despite it all. I forgave him because he's originally from Pittsburgh, and people from Pittsburgh are natural brutes. It's a good thing my mother was born in New York or I would be an absolute lost cause and never get invited anywhere of note. Mrs. Astor has a real disdain for people from Pittsburgh."

She looked around the room again and jumped onto the small green velvet couch.

"Come, Anita, let's tack this all up to the walls and make this room look like a palace." She grabbed her roommate by the hand and handed her a small nail and the hammer she had been using. "You try this. I'll wield my Latin dictionary. It will have the most use it's had in years. Just be mindful of the noise because if Mervis hears us, we're sure to get fined."

"Fined?" Anita asked, crossing to the opposite wall.

"It's worth it, don't you think? I was fined at the start of every semester last year, but we can't be expected to live in some desolate chamber. How will we learn anything? You should have seen my parlor as a freshman. That was the year I was absolutely taken with the French Revolution. This year's décor will be decidedly cheaper, as the Japanese really do have a simpler aesthetic. Plus, if my father doesn't receive fines from the college, he will think I'm in ill health and have lost my spirit. This," she said, motioning to the room, "is in everybody's best interest."

The roommates finished tacking up the silk just as Mervis came in with their trunks, grunting about the walls. Lottie smiled sweetly and told him to make out the bill to Mr. Clarence Taylor, then she sent for a maid who helped the pair put away their dresses.

"I'm starving," Lottie declared after she had placed her silver hairbrush on the table by her bed and her silver inkstand on the writing table. Anita had done the same in her room with her modest belongings.

"How about we walk over for an ice cream at the Dutchess? Is there still time to get a leave of absence to go to town?" Lottie asked.

"I believe the Dutchess is closed now. It's nearly six o'clock," Anita replied, looking at the gold clock by Lottie's bed. "The dinner bell will ring soon."

"Not those awful bells," said Lottie, sticking her tongue out like a gargoyle. "Isn't it horrible that we have to run around listening to the cling clang of old bells? The rising hour bell, the dinner bell, the chapel bell—I feel like the Hunchback of Notre Dame."

Anita laughed and said, "You don't look it."

"Really?" Lottie said, puffing up her cheeks. "I feel quite like a French hunchback today. I hate the sleeves on this dress," she added, trying to pull them up at the shoulder. "I told my seamstress in Paris to make them bigger, but she's so conservative and her answer to everything is '*Non, ma chérie.*' Not shockingly, she makes my mother's day clothes, and I tend to hate my mother's day clothes. For eveningwear I much prefer the House of Worth, but Mother said I wasn't allowed to train up in my Lyon silk. Anyway, you should go on. I know you were voted class beauty as a freshman. Don't try to deny it. And I heard all about you and your big, beautiful brown eyes from a few of my Harvard acquaintances, too."

Anita's surprised look caused Lottie to elaborate. "I said *acquaintances*, Anita. Don't tell me you believe all of that gossip. One little dalliance during the Harvard-Yale game as a sophomore and I'm a scorned woman. Vassar girls sure can talk. I don't have a flaxen-haired daughter hidden in a convent in Switzerland, if you happen to be wondering."

"I hadn't heard that one," Anita replied, thoroughly entertained.

"Well, I don't. What I do have is a younger brother in his junior year at Harvard, and he told me that you were quite the talk of the school after our Founder's Day dance last spring. Many Harvard men in attendance, if you remember. Yes, I launched an inquisition on you, Miss Hemmings."

It was unfortunate that Anita hadn't done the same.

As Anita contemplated what rooming with Lottie Taylor would mean for her final year at Vassar, she heard a light knock on their parlor door.

"Come in!" bellowed Lottie in her low, raspy voice. Anita speculated that Lottie's voice was half the reason so many rumors circulated about her. There was something quite intoxicating about it.

The door opened slowly, and a tall girl bounded in, earning smiles from both roommates. Belle Tiffany, an alto in the choir and the Glee Club, was one of Anita's closest friends.

"Belle Tiffany! Look at you," said Lottie. "See, I'm rooming with your old friend Anita Hemmings. The beautiful girls with the soaring voices. What will I do with myself around both of you? I need to develop a skill. I'm a terrible disappointment."

"You're exceedingly rich," said Belle, looking at the decorated walls. "And I suppose you're amusing, too."

"That's true. I am awfully funny," said Lottie, hopping onto the couch again. "Matthew Ellery, Lucy Ellery's brother up at Harvard, he was my Phil date last year, and he said I was the most entertaining girl he had ever known. Then he said men aren't supposed to be fond of girls who favor humor over femininity. But then when I laughed and said I found the whole thing quite amusing, the beast leaned over and kissed me. And I mean kissed. Not just with his mouth, with his entire body, especially the middle. If we hadn't been clothed, who knows what would have happened?"

"Lottie, stop trying to shock. We're seniors now. We're immune to your alarming ways," said Belle.

"Speak for yourself. I'm sure I'll make Anita Hemmings faint before the semester is over. Besides, do you want me to graduate without so much as kissing a few Harvard seniors?"

"Most say you've done quite a bit more than that," teased Belle.

"Belle, don't start rumors. Even if they are true," said Lottie, catching a glimpse of herself in the mirror propped on her dressing table. "And Anita, try not to look as if you're going to wilt. I'll burn your books if I have to—it's our last year here, and I won't spend it stuck in Uncle Fred's Nose reading *Beowulf*."

"You read *Beowulf* as a freshman. You aren't required to read it again," said Belle. "And have as much fun as you want, Lottie, just remember that you should graduate like the rest of us or your father will write you out of his will." Belle winked at Anita. "Lottie's father is a major financial supporter of women's education. He was asked to be a trustee, but he said not until his daughter had graduated. Did you hear that, Lottie? Critical detail, *graduated*."

"Belle, hold your judgment until we've reached the finish line. I'll graduate. Maybe not with the highest honors, but I will. You'll both just have to help me."

When the roommates came back from dinner that evening—where they were happily assigned to a senior table with Caroline, Belle, and Belle's roommate, Hortense Lewis—Lottie boiled water for tea with lemon and Anita lit a lamp between them.

"I do miss electric lamps," Lottie said, watching Anita fiddle with the gas. "I was getting rather used to them and look at us now, back like moths to a flame."

"Do you have electricity at home?" Anita asked, trying to make the gas stream stronger. Her own house in Boston only had gas lamps, and a very limited number at that.

"Oh, yes, my father had every lamp installed with electric wiring, though some chandeliers are constructed for both gas and electricity. It's glorious. You just use a switch, on and off. One day we'll have them here, but not for years and years. We'll be long gone by then, living our extraordinary ordinary lives."

"Caroline Hardin told me you were rather exceptional," Anita said, sipping her tea. She stood up to open their large parlor window, as the heat of the day had burned off and the air from the river had turned in their direction.

"Caroline Hardin did? My favorite Syrian redhead?"

"The very one."

"And what do you think of that?" said Lottie.

"I think Caroline Hardin is usually right," she said diplomatically. Lottie twinkled a smile, the dimples on her face looking more pronounced in the lamplight.

The two prepared for bed under walls draped in silks and kimonos and pictures of Kyoto. Somewhere, tucked in among the Japonisme, was Anita's small photograph of a

statue of the Greek goddess Artemis, taken in the Louvre
and given to her by one of the Harvard seniors Lottie mentioned. It seemed somehow fitting that her contribution to
their rooms was so small. The Lottie Taylors of the world
were always the ones to have an enormous impact.

CHAPTER 2

On their second afternoon on campus, Anita's roommate found her on the path to Main after her physics class in the Vassar Brothers Laboratory. Lottie slid next to her and took her by the arm.

"You are coming to the first meeting of the Federal Debating Society, aren't you?" Lottie said. "I know you were a member last year, and I've decided to join up this semester. Be more academic and all that."

"I was planning on it, after choir practice," Anita replied. "We have the vocal and violin recital on the twenty-fifth and we're singing at the Christian Association Reception on the first of October."

"That is ever so much trilling. We should have you give private concerts in our room with that voice of yours. You and Belle, though you take the lead, since you're the coveted first soprano. We could fleece the freshmen and then spend all our earnings in New York. You will come down to New York with me, won't you?"

"Of course I will," said Anita, trying not to sound too thrilled. If Vassar was her most cherished place, then New York City, which she had visited twice, was what she dreamed about.

"Good! It's all settled. First we'll go to the debating society meeting, then we'll put in with Kendrick for a weekend when we can go down. You'll love my family. I don't most of the time, but most others seem to."

"Lottie!" Anita said, stopping midstep.

"I know, I'm shockingly honest," she replied with an impish smile. "Such an unfeminine trait. But being feminine is a great annoyance most of the time. What is your family like? Are they as outrageous as mine?"

"I doubt it," said Anita, growing uneasy at the mention of her relatives. "They're rather serious. Very intellectual. Yours sound more entertaining."

"We do excel in the social arts, especially my mother. You should meet her; she measures the distance between teacups with long mahogany rulers and likes there to be fireworks for every occasion. Recover from the common cold? Fireworks. Home before the rain? Fireworks. You'll see. Now go sing, and meet me in the J Parlor for the meeting. And beware, Father says I win every argument because I can talk past the limit of most human vocal chords."

"I should be thrilled to hear it. I'll see you there at four o'clock," said Anita, back on the dusty path to Main.

After choir, Belle walked Anita to the debating society meeting and headed alone to the library. Anita promised to come and read Greek with her afterward and opened the door to the ornate, gold silk-lined parlor, one of her favorite rooms on campus, saying hello to two sophomores. Lottie was already present and waved her in. Anita sat down next to her and they greeted the other girls they knew.

"I hear you're rooming with Lottie Taylor," whispered Gratia Clough, a girl who had been in debating since freshman year. Anita shot Lottie a glance, but she was deep in conversation with her back to the pair. "You're the lucky one. You'll get to stay at her house in New York. I heard it's magnificent. Dora Fairchild used to make the trip down with her. She even spent Christmas there sophomore year as she didn't want to travel home to Georgia. You'll tell me all about it when you go, promise?"

"I promise," Anita whispered, already savoring the prospect.

Medora Higgins, the newly appointed debating president, stood up, called for silence, and launched into a recollection of the outstanding debates conducted by last year's seniors. Lottie leaned over and pulled Anita's ear.

"Do you bicycle?" she whispered. She offered her a shortbread biscuit, but Anita shook her head no and watched Lottie insert the entire thing in her mouth.

"Hardly," Anita whispered back.

"Oh, no. We have to change that at once. You'll adore flying on two wheels. I'm wonderful at it now, though I was miserable for my first few rides. I fell flat on my face and nearly broke a tooth. Tricycling was the thing here in the eighties, but now, I assure you, it's bicycling. Mastering it is a bit like the French tongue, painful at first but then you're off and it's *une très belle vie.* I'll teach you. I have a bicycle here already; it's an Orient bicycle from the Waltham Manufacturing Company in Massachusetts. The very best. It weighs a mere twenty-two pounds, has a pneumatic saddle and a very effective dress guard. I'll have Father send me another, then we can ride to the farm. Do you have a bicycling costume?"

She looked at Anita's blank face.

"Of course you don't. Why would you if you don't have a bicycle? I daresay it's almost as fun as an automobile. I did that this summer, too."

"Really? You were in a horseless carriage?" Anita whispered. Hearing that, Gratia leaned over to listen, too, as

Lottie was the only person either of them knew who had even ridden in an automobile.

"Oh, yes, one day they'll be everywhere. That's obvious. My father loves modern contraptions, so we took the train up to Michigan to view one. They're very impressive, but I'm quite convinced they'll explode past a certain speed and then there goes your new motoring outfit, and perhaps your head. For now, it's all about bicycling, ladies. I'll bring several more to school. The ones from Orient or Keating, in New York, are only one hundred dollars. We have to go on many rides before the cold settles in, because after that it's just skating. But it doesn't feel like that's going to be anytime soon, does it? It's absolutely sweltering in here. I swear old President Taylor has the building heated already. He'll fry us into working."

"Lottie Taylor," said Medora, stopping her speech.

"I'm sorry, Medora," said Lottie, pursing her lips. "I did so want to make a good impression during our first meeting, but there is just so much to say on the subject of debate. It impassions me. I couldn't hold my tongue."

"I'm happy you're so enthused about joining us this year," said Medora. "Since you're clearly the most passionate person in the room, why don't you and Anita Hemmings share the first debate? You can have something prepared by Friday, can't you?"

Lottie glanced at Anita apologetically. "Of course, Friday, though Anita does have an awful lot of singing to do between now and then. The school's most talented soprano. We don't want to put too much on her dance card at once."

"I'm sure Anita can handle it all," said Medora, looking haughtily her way.

"It's no trouble, Medora," she replied. In truth, Anita rather shied from debate. The prospect of taking part in the year's first debate terrified her, but it was much in vogue on campus, so she had debated for all three years, even if it meant heart palpitations and locked knees when she stood behind the podium.

"What topic would you like us to fight like savages over?" asked Lottie.

"Plessy versus Ferguson," said Medora, returning Lottie's smile.

"Delightful," said Lottie. "I'll take Plessy, and Anita can argue Ferguson." Anita nodded, then turned toward the wall of wide glass windows that overlooked the walkway to the Lodge, letting the sun create spots in her vision.

Plessy v Ferguson: the Supreme Court case over separation versus equality between races. Anita remembered the man's face. Plessy. Homer Plessy. A shoemaker from New Orleans. Pale-skinned, yet Negro. Guilty, but only because he admitted his crime. And made an example of, forever.

With Plessy's image burning in her mind, Anita's anxiety began to mount. At Vassar and well before, she had always acted with deliberate decorum—reining in her words, declining to speak out, repressing herself. But could she now? She tried to blink away the image of the man's face, but it stayed with her, a line drawing that had been printed again and again in the *Boston Daily Globe*. Anita had survived lengthy discussions of the trial in class, endless talks about justice since the Civil War, but no one had forced her onstage to speak alone on the matter. No one had compelled her to take one side instead of another.

She could not protest. So she sat, nodded again, and went through the motions she had perfected through so many years of practice. And inside her thin shirtwaist, her heartbeat took off like a deer in the woods.

"Is that topic even worth a debate?" said a voice suddenly. It came from directly behind Anita. The roommates both turned to see Sarah Douglas, a senior from North Pleasureville, Kentucky, and president of the school's Southern Club. "This is Vassar, not an abolitionist meeting. Shouldn't we debate something more relevant?"

Medora, who was from Ticonderoga, New York, merely smiled politely and said: "It was the most-talked-about Supreme Court case of the year, Sarah. I think that makes it important enough to debate here, don't you agree? This is an esteemed debating club, not the school's floral society, am I correct?"

Sarah shrugged, and because Medora was the president, which meant she was going to win that or any other argument, the topic turned to which other issues of the day were worthy of dialogue.

For the last half hour of the meeting, Anita sat as if someone had nailed her to her chair and taped her mouth shut. She was afraid of what she would do or say, so she said nothing. She was still sitting there rigidly when Lottie alerted her that the meeting had been adjourned. They stood up together, said goodbye to the other girls, and headed down the wide hallway. It was then that Anita realized that from the nape of her neck to the back of her knees, she was covered in a slip of sweat.

"Can you believe Sarah Douglas speaking out at the meeting the way she did?" said Lottie, when they were a few yards from the parlor. "I know I uttered a few words out of turn, too, but I'm much more agreeable than she is and no one seemed to mind when I did. But then Sarah had to carry on with that nonsense. I do not care for her jejune opinions, not one bit. And she's very set in her ways, that one. Her grandfather was one of the wealthiest slave owners in South Carolina before the war. Rumor has it they owned two hundred slaves, can you imagine? But the war hit them hard, as did the hurricanes in '93, and the family moved to Kentucky. Brought their belief system up with them, too. I'm surprised her parents let her come up here at all. The wicked North. She rooms with Alice Sawyer from Jacksonville."

"Oh, Alice," said Anita, thinking of the quiet brunette with the beautiful dresses who had sat next to her in French class the year before. "She's a lovely girl."

"Lovely!" said Lottie. "Maybe if you're Bloody Bill Anderson she's lovely. She's the one who told the story about the Negro children being used for alligator bait down in Florida. She swears up and down that it happens. Calls them pickaninnies when she tells the story. She said the mothers are given two dollars and their children may or may not come back alive after being tossed in a swamp to lure the animals. Something about their black skin that attracts them, she said. Tourists are captivated by it."

"That cannot be true," said Anita, horrified.

"It is Florida," said Lottie, with big eyes. "Who knows what happens in that uncivilized swamp country. But of course, she loves boring old mouse-faced Sarah Douglas. Five girls from the South in our year, and two are rooming together. Certainly not a coincidence. Sarah's father even fought in the war, under P. G. T. Beauregard, defending Charleston in '63. I suppose he did a decent job, as the city is still standing. But don't get her talking about all of that because she will never cease. She speaks about her father like he's the unacknowledged fourth member of the Holy Trinity."

Lottie pulled another shortbread biscuit out of her bag and popped it in her mouth. Like an animal hunting its prey, she required constant refueling and was forever grazing on delicacies her mother sent up from New York. "Was she in the club last year?" she asked, her mouth full.

"Yes, but she didn't attend many meetings," said Anita, thinking back.

"I hope the same can be said for this year. I find her very tiresome."

"Did your father fight in the war?" Anita asked, just the slightest hesitation catching in her voice.

"No. He was too young, I suppose. But I assume he would have if he were older. For the Union. Like I said, Pittsburgh. Did yours?"

"No. For the same reason. He was eighteen when the war broke out, and I suppose he felt too young."

"And what does your father do now?" asked Lottie, pausing between snacks. "He's a lawyer of sorts?"

"That's right," Anita said, spinning the line she had first used freshman year. "He's a lawyer in Boston."

"No wonder you're so intelligent," said Lottie, sighing. She had been put on academic probation her freshman year and still showed signs of the shock. "Though I still plan on beating you flat in that debate. I excel under bright lights. Even if they are powered by gas." She rolled her eyes and took Anita by the arm. "I knew we'd get along, Anita Hemmings. I think I'm glad Dora decided to stay in Europe, after all. It's nice to have a change for our final year, don't you think?"

"I do," Anita replied honestly. Unfortunately for Lottie, Anita couldn't let her best her in the debate. Not on this topic, and certainly not in front of Sarah Douglas.

For the next four days, Anita ignored her studies of the artistry of the Virgilian hexameter for Professor Macurdy's Greek class. She also put aside her physics, Latin, French, and ethics. She attended choir practice, sang with the Glee Club, went to nightly chapel exercises, took her meals, and did the mandatory physical exercises in Alumnae Gymnasium, but otherwise, she slept, ate, and studied *Plessy v Ferguson*.

As she pored over the case documents from the past spring in the J Parlor after dinner on Thursday, Medora walked by her table, leaned over, and turned down her burner, which she had cleverly rigged to increase the stream of gas.

"As seriously as I take it, the Federal Debating Society is not worth the risk of carbon monoxide poisoning, is it, Anita?"

Anita looked up at Medora standing above her, and turned the gas a pinch lower. "I suppose not. I just want to do a respectable job in the opening debate for the year. Set a precedent for excellence. That's what Lottie said we should do, and I agree."

"I suppose rooming with Lottie Taylor does mean a lot of 'that's what Lottie said we should do,'" said Medora. "Between us, I heard that Dora did fall for London during her tour this summer, but that another reason she stayed was that she wanted to return to school and not live under Lottie Taylor's nimble little thumb. She intends to reenter Vassar next fall."

"Is that so?" Anita asked, thinking that Dora had seemed happy during her first three years at the college.

"That's what they say," said Medora, motioning to the other girls in the parlor. Medora prided herself on being the sort of college girl who refused to gossip, unless it was for the right cause. "I don't know how much I believe," she added. "People delight in gossiping about the seniors, and if you're going to pick one to whisper about, I suppose you would pick Lottie Taylor as she's the richest—and loudest—girl in school. If we go on as we do about Lottie, imagine what it was like for Bessie Rockefeller or the Japanese princess. A tunnel of never-ending hearsay, I imagine."

Imagining life for a Rockefeller or royalty was not something Anita was in a position to do.

"You'll do well, Anita," said Medora, looking down at the papers on the desk. "You always do. Though I must say Lottie did you a favor choosing *Plessy*. The court went Ferguson, and I imagine our girls will, too. I'll see you tomorrow," she said as she left to study elsewhere.

Anita returned to her notes. As the affirmative speaker, she had to open the debate. She was terrified her voice would quaver, that her conviction would come off as fabricated, and that with one short sentence, everyone would know. They would know everything. She pushed her fear to the far-off recesses of her mind and looked down at her writing table, drumming her fingers quietly to calm down. A moment later, Belle Tiffany came into the room and placed a hand on Anita's shoulder, causing her to shudder in surprise.

"Did you skip the swimming tank today, Anita?" she said, laughing. "You look like a racehorse training to win Saratoga." She bent down and looked at Anita's papers.

"*Plessy versus Ferguson*," Belle said, dragging out the words. "I remember that in the newspapers. What a bore. Are you sure you want to debate for another year? You should join guitar and mandolin club with me. You're in every other musical organization. Why concern yourself with all this propaganda? You know the whole thing *was* planned. A New Orleans citizens committee pressured that Negro man Plessy into declaring his race in the white car. He certainly didn't appear Negro—from the pictures I've glimpsed I remember there was blond in his hair—but that was part of their act, I suppose. Aren't there more pressing racial matters than this? I read that there will be more lynchings of southern Negroes in the nineties than in all the years combined since the Civil War. I imagine the coloreds down there care more about keeping their necks from snapping than if they can sit in a white train car. Which side are you arguing?" she asked, looking down at the newspaper in front of her.

"Ferguson," Anita said, inching the paper down. "I'm arguing pro the Separate Car Act in the state of Louisiana."

"You were lucky in that coin toss, then. You wouldn't sound convincing arguing the other side, and neither will Lottie." She read aloud over Anita's shoulder. "The Jim Crow Car Case is what the papers all called it, from Salt Lake to Boston and way down South."

Anita read along with her, her hands moving nervously.

"Anita!" Belle exclaimed, suddenly taking a step back. "You just spilled your ink everywhere!"

Right over the article, a puddle of black ink was sinking through the thin newsprint into her cotton writing papers. Anita quickly picked up the inkpot but dropped it again when she realized it was staining her hands.

"Your hands, Anita!" said Belle, moving Anita's papers. "Don't touch another thing. You'll get ink on your white dress. I'll fetch one of the maids to help clean this up."

A moment after Belle left the room, Anita did, too. With her black-stained hands, she gathered her papers and rushed down the stairs and out the back of the building toward the farm. Once on the path, she forced herself to walk. If she ran the mile up Sunset Hill to the farm, everyone she passed would wonder why she was moving with such haste.

Anita leaned down, wiped her stained hands on the grass, and continued along the path. Belle would worry when she returned with the maid, but she would suppose that Anita had gone to clean up. And when she was not in her room when she checked, she would presume Anita had gone elsewhere to study. Anita's dress stuck to her back, and she could already smell the fetor of animals in the barn. If the professors knew the truth, she thought, if President

Taylor knew, she would be more welcome there, with the cows and the swine, than she was sharing rooms with Lottie Taylor.

Anita had decided on Vassar long before Vassar had decided on her. And here she was, standing above the stately campus, living out her nearly unattainable dream. Nearly.

But at times it was achingly hard. She wiped her hands on the grass again, the lines on her palms still caked with iron gall ink, then dipped them repeatedly in the small stream on the approach to the farm. When they were as clean as nature could make them, she sat down, removed her pen, ink, and the rest of her paper from her bag, set it against her writing board, and started a letter.

> *My Dear Mother,*
>
> *I know there are women much stronger, much smarter than I who were not granted the opportunities I was, but I think God may have been mistaken this time around. I am not formidable and bright, as you always said. I am weak. I am breakable. I fall apart under duress.*
>
> *I have a recurring nightmare in which I'm attending Sunday chapel, and the guest minister, President Taylor, and the entire student body have all been informed. My secret has been passed along in little hurried whispers from pink mouth to pink ear, followed by gasps, worry, dreadful embarrassment. Because all of a sudden, every single one of them knows that I, Anita Florence Hemmings, am a liar. I am not just of French and English descent, as I wrote on my application, I am also a Negro. The only one ever admitted to Vassar. I am alone and suddenly hated. Reviled. Looked upon as something to be pitied and ostracized.*
>
> *I tell myself, when I wake up shivering in my nightdress,*

that it's only a nightmare. I am still a student at Vassar—this is still mine. So I let myself become comfortable, convince myself that I am the same as everyone else here, and that's when terror creeps in. When it happens—a remark, a reading assignment about the war, a comment about the inferiority of Negroes—I feel my bones cracking because I've let my defenses down. I've been caught by surprise. I've let myself become too *comfortable.*

Do you remember when I was at the Prince Grammar School and I came home to tell you that I was at the top of my class, the very first? You and Father weren't surprised at all—even though you had scarcely attended school, even though I was the first Negro girl admitted and one of the only Negro students in all my years there. You knew Frederick and I were going to carry ourselves forward, despite written and unwritten rules that seemed to keep us from moving anywhere but down.

Your words carried me here, Mother, but I'm walking unsteadily today. Can I make it through one more year pretending I am just like them? Please tell me I can. I know you cannot write to me, but please tell me through your prayers.

While you and Father serve people, clean up after their easy lives, I stand in my room and call for the janitor. I ring for a maid to help me button the dress we sewed together, with your savings. I laugh and dine and study with women who come from the best families in the country. White families. But what if they knew, Mother?

Sometimes my dream is not that I'm in chapel, but that I'm standing in my best shoes on the edge of a bluff, one of the dusty, orange ones that we've seen pictures of out west. I know that the slightest breeze will knock me over, but I dare to stand there anyway. Suddenly, I feel a woman's small hand push with great force on my back and I speed through the air before hitting the ground with a tremendous sound. I lie there, dead. They send for you and Father, and then they know. I'm a dead Negro who learned Greek and Latin, and who, for three years, was a promising student at Vassar College with an alarming secret.

Mother, tomorrow I will be arguing the pro-segregation side of Plessy v. Ferguson *in my debate society. I have to smile widely and devote every ounce of my intellect to winning the argument that separate but equal is the right way to live. I have to be the most convincing voice in the room—the alternative is a risk I cannot take. I must read all I can about the ruling in Louisiana. I must explain with conviction why seven white Supreme Court judges determined that Homer Plessy's 13th and 14th Amendment rights were not denied when they forced him out of the white car. I must declare that separating races is what God intended and that white and colored should never be forced to sit together in a train car. And if not in a train car, then certainly not in a classroom, or a dormitory room. What I am arguing is simple. One drop of Negro blood taints a person. Plessy did not belong, and neither do I. No Negro belongs in a white train car, and they don't belong at Vassar College, either. But I do belong, don't I? Pray for me, Mother, and I will do the same for you.*

With all my love,
Anita

As soon as she had finished, Anita ripped the letter into pieces, tiny shreds of paper covered in incriminating words. She held them in her hand, then let them fall into the clear, cold stream.

Anita watched the bits of pressed cotton until they had

sunk to the bottom, turned to pulp, the ink washed away and her secret with it. When she finally heard footsteps behind her, she turned to see Belle, her face cloaked in concern.

"There you are, Anita! Is anything wrong?"

Anita stood, deliberately smiling.

"No, Belle," she said calmly. "Everything is perfect."

CHAPTER 3

K neeling next to her bed, Anita closed her eyes and squeezed her eyelids so tightly that the pressure made her face quiver. But this was a prayer that she needed to shut out the world for.

As she had done on Friday in front of her peers, she recited the passage she had memorized from the *Plessy v Ferguson* court document. "Under the Louisiana statute, no colored person is permitted to occupy a seat in a coach assigned to white persons, nor any white person to occupy a seat in a coach assigned to colored persons. If a passenger insists upon going into a coach or compartment not set apart for persons of his race, he is subject to be fined or to be imprisoned in the parish jail."

Anita had been voted the victor in the debate, but Lottie had shrugged it off good-naturedly, congratulating Anita on her evident passion. It was the outcome Anita needed, and that she had earned after her hours of fervent study. In the days that followed, the torment she had felt making her hateful case was starting to ease, but the one image she knew she would never erase was of Sarah Douglas nodding in agreement with her. The audience was supposed to stay neutral, listening to both sides until the very end. But Sarah was apparently incapable of neutrality on such an issue.

Lottie had delved into the argument of what constitutes a colored person and noted that Plessy had only one-eighth African blood, nondiscernible in his appearance. It was an argument Anita stayed far away from, as she considered her own origins. Her mother's mother had been a Negro slave, impregnated by a white man. Her father was born from a similar forced union.

Anita's father was ten years older than her mother and hailed from Harrisonburg, Virginia, eight miles north of Bridgewater, where her mother was born in 1853. His mother's name was Sarah, born without a last name. Like Anita's mother, he had never known his father.

Anita felt no softness in her heart for those white men, except that they had created her parents, who had, in turn, made her. And when she went to Vassar, she felt a small debt to them for the light skin that made it possible for her to attend. Like Homer Plessy, if Anita never told anyone she was a Negro, they would never guess.

Her thoughts were interrupted when Lottie opened the door to her bedroom and found her on her knees, her chin pressed to her chest.

"Anita!" Lottie said, rushing into the small room. "This is no time for prayer. You can reflect during chapel this evening. We have a grave situation upon us." Anita stayed on her knees and turned her eyes to Lottie. Her roommate was a person who seemed more beautiful when life was frantic, as if she couldn't fully shine in a state of boredom or routine.

"Anita, please! Cease your praying and listen to me," said Lottie, sitting on the bed. "I have very upsetting news."

Now worried, Anita stood up. "I'm sorry, you just startled me. I didn't expect you back. Do you not have a Philaletheis meeting?"

"Oh, do I?" said Lottie, with a glance at the wooden clock propped by Anita's bed. "I suppose I do. Well, I can't arrive at this hour, so I might as well be absent. Plus, as I said, something terrible has happened, and I'm quite rattled."

"What is it?" Anita asked anxiously. *It was about her. It had to be about her.*

Lottie threw herself down and covered her eyes with her hands.

"The Harvard-Yale game is not being played this year," she groaned. "Canceled! Just like it was last year. Can you believe it? Two years in succession. It's inhumane. We are being robbed of a collegiate tradition. It's unpatriotic."

"Oh. Is that the terrible news?" Anita asked, removing Lottie's small hands from her face.

"Of course that's the terrible news!" she exclaimed. "Four years of our college career and only able to attend two Harvard-Yale games, and as freshers and sophomores, at that. Not to mention that Harvard lost both of them, the first an absolute slaughter!"

"I'm glad that it's nothing graver than that. Illness, death, or even worse."

"Scoff at me," said Lottie, sitting up and perching herself on her elbows. "But I know you took in the game as a sophomore. I have it on record."

"You have a lot of spies at Harvard," Anita said, her breath regulating again. "It sounds like a volunteer army."

"Don't I?" Lottie said, looking around Anita's sparsely decorated bedroom. "I need to train up to Cambridge and greet them all, or they'll forget I exist. There's been such a drought of social events, and I am certainly not waiting for

Phil Day in December to socialize with our nation's finest college men."

"Lottie! The way you say that is shocking," Anita said, lying back on her bed, too. She took one of her plump, cotton-wrapped pillows and placed it under her head. On Lottie's bed, one small wall away, all the pillows were covered in lavender silk.

"Isn't it?" Lottie said proudly. "But it's more shocking for a girl to have to wait three months for male company. That's why I'm proposing we go to Harvard this weekend for the Harvard-Williams game on Sunday. That one they actually have a chance of winning, as those Williams boys are the size of beetles this year. We can stay at an inn in town and visit my dear cousin Lilly, who lives in Cambridge, the day before the game."

Before Anita could protest about work or cost, Lottie threw her arms around her and said, "Say yes, Anita, please? Do say yes. Father will pay for everything. He has been pestering me to check on my brother John anyhow, and we can be back to Poughkeepsie by Sunday evening. We won't even have to crawl in a window or poison the Lodge watchman."

Anita looked at her with narrowed eyes.

"Very well, perhaps, more realistically, it will be late Sunday night, or early Monday, but it will be in time for classes, I promise," Lottie implored. "We will be granted a leave of absence, I'm sure of it. Just say yes, Anita, I beg you. It won't be any fun if you're not with me. Please don't make me attend alone, or with some dreadfully bland girl. That would be such a waste of a memorable weekend." She pouted her lips and blinked until her eyes watered, and Anita couldn't do a thing but say yes.

As the roommates were packing their dresses on Friday to travel to Boston early the next morning, Lottie turned to Anita and said, "Anita, forgive me. I've been too excited about the football game to think correctly. We're going to take a train that terminates in Boston. Shall we stop in to see your family? We don't have much time, but if we are to visit my cousin Lilly in Cambridge, then of course we must call on your family."

Holding her white day dress in her hand, Anita let her arms fall, and the dress fell with them. Lottie bent down and picked it up for her.

"No, we will not have enough time for a visit," Anita said, turning away. "And I just said goodbye to them two weeks before. I would much rather spend the day in Cambridge with your cousin."

"Are you certain? I don't mind a slight detour."

"We can make the trip up another time. I'm sure there will be many more reasons to visit Harvard as the year progresses."

"I certainly hope so. They hold two formal dances a year," said Lottie. "And attending a football game in the fall guarantees an invitation."

"Then I can't decline, can I?"

"Most certainly not!"

The girls agreed that when they arrived Saturday, they would take a carriage straight to the inn and rest, dine in Cambridge, and spend the morning on Sunday with Lilly after an early church service. Lottie and Anita were not the only girls from Vassar making the journey up for the first Harvard football game of the fall, but they decided not to group with any of the other Vassar students, wanting no distractions during their first trip together.

"You'll simply fall in love with Lilly," said Lottie, as their train glided from Albany to Boston. They had spent an hour on the platform waiting to change trains and head east and were just starting to recover from the heat. Inside the car, the bulbous lamps embedded in ornate metalwork were not helping. "She's a real beauty, Lilly is. Everyone was always going on about it when we were children, and you can imagine how that made me feel. I won't pretend I wasn't elated when she didn't pass the Vassar entrance exam. She was one year ahead of me at the Brearley School. She had her share of admirers at that time, but I'm happy to report that her grades were not near the top of her class. But don't take that to mean that I was jealous of her. She's really a lovely girl. You'll see. I'm so very fond of her."

"Lottie," Anita said, watching her friend's gloved hands fidget with everything in reach. "You're a very pretty girl, too. Sometimes I think you're simply unaware of it. And you're an awfully entertaining person, which I think is more important."

"Aren't you lucky, rooming with a comedienne?" Lottie said happily. She looked out the window at New York turning into Massachusetts and said, "Anita, I am well aware that I have a flair for the dramatic, but one thing I know about is people. I can see which girls cause men to turn their heads and which do not. You, Lilly—you're the kind of women men fall for. I'm a good-enough-looking girl, but I'm no great beauty."

"I think you're mistaken," said Anita, surprised by her roommate's harsh judgment of herself. Anita guessed she was quoting an overcritical mother.

"Let's not analyze it too closely," said Lottie. She leaned back on the green velvet seat and ran her hands down the carved wooden armrests. "Let's just remember that we are young and intelligent and not so bad to look at. This weekend will be memorable, so let's bask in it. It's our last year, and I'm already feeling painfully sentimental. It's my nature."

Anita smiled at her, sharing that part of her nature.

"If your cousin did not pass the Vassar entrance exam, did she attend another college?" asked Anita a moment later, watching a porter bring lunch to the travelers ahead of them.

"Did I not tell you?" said Lottie, flagging him down and ordering them rare steak and potato soufflé. "She's at Radcliffe now. Class of 1899. She prepared for the exam up north so she's behind me now. And the girls don't live on campus at Radcliffe, so I'm in the habit of saying Cambridge. But we are to visit her on campus tomorrow."

"She's a student there? Presently?" Anita repeated, her voice rising with every word. "We are going to visit her at Radcliffe?"

"Of course!" said Lottie, laughing at Anita's disquiet. "Is that all right?"

It was anything but. Anita knew only one girl at Radcliffe College—Gertrude Baker, class of 1900, a dark-skinned Negro from Cambridge. She had known her for many years, and if they encountered each other on campus, it was highly likely that she would acknowledge Anita like an old friend.

Anita knew that traveling to Harvard with Lottie had its risks, with Frederick at school in nearby Boston and the rest of her family in the city, too, but she would never have accepted the invitation if Lottie had uttered the word *Radcliffe*.

"Yes!" Anita said, trying to lighten her tone. "That sounds wonderful. A day on the Radcliffe campus. I just wasn't aware. That seems like a very pleasant way to spend the morning."

Anita turned her face away from Lottie and rested her head against the thick glass of the train window. How could she have been so impetuous, saying yes to Lottie's invitation without considering whom she might see? Running into Gertrude could be her ruin.

Anita thought of her years at the Prince Grammar School in Boston, then at the Girls' High School. At both she was enrolled as a Negro student. She was at the top of her class, and she was a Negro. At Dwight Moody's Northfield Seminary, the boarding school she attended to prepare for Vassar, she had passed as white. Her roommate there was Elizabeth Baker—or Bessie, as she was known—her closest friend and Gertrude's older sister.

Bessie, too, was a light-skinned Negro, a quadroon, and she could have passed as white, like Anita, but she chose not to. On Anita's application to the school, she had asked to room with Bessie, and because Mr. Moody's academy was different from most, and because her request solved the school's problem of where to house Bessie, the girls were placed together without question.

Bessie was now attending Wellesley College as a Negro student, where the color line had been broken in 1883, but Anita had no communication with her during the school year. They did not exchange letters because Anita was terrified to have Bessie's name appear anywhere on her correspondence. The Vassar students had too many friends at Wellesley, and everyone there knew the name Bessie Baker. Anita was able to see her occasionally during the summers and other holidays at home, but only when she was with the Negro community, never as a white Vassar girl.

But Gertrude did not resemble Bessie. She was much darker.

When the train pulled slowly into Cambridge, expelling steam as it braked, Anita's nervousness stayed with her. She didn't know what it would feel like to be close to Boston in the company of someone so removed from her own domestic life, and the fear of crossing paths with Gertrude only heightened her uneasiness. She had decided that if she saw her on campus, she would have to turn and flee, praying that Gertrude, who knew of her situation at Vassar, would understand and not follow her.

They headed to their hotel, the Magnolia Inn, and Lottie spent the hour they were at tea telling Anita whom she should bother speaking to at Harvard the next day and who was a waste of breath.

"The men from the Middle West are the kindest, which of course bores me, but that might sit well with you. You have to leave me all of the men from New York. It's states' rights," she said. Anita promised she would ignore the Empire State, and they changed and headed to dinner in town.

"Thank goodness for hansoms," said Lottie as the hotel doorman helped them into the carriage. "The restaurant's not far, quite close to the campus, but it is still too hot to walk, I'm sure you agree."

There were hansoms all over Boston, just as there were in Cambridge and New York City, but when Anita returned home, she was never allowed to hail one. They charged seventy-five cents an hour, far too much. But Lottie had been opening her little purse since they left Poughkeepsie, insisting that because the trip was her idea, it would cost Anita nothing. "Father is practically forcing us up here," she said as Anita tried to purchase them refreshments at the Albany train station. "Save your money for school." Lottie might not have known how little money Anita had, but she was used to the fact that she was always the richest person in the room, unless a Vanderbilt was about.

As they finished their dinner of lemon-glazed chicken with morels and Lottie settled the bill, a fashionably dressed woman approached their table with her husband, looking unsure at first, but then rushing toward them as Lottie glanced up.

"Is that Lottie Taylor?" the woman asked. She had the arm of a slight, elegant man in a white vest and dinner jacket, though he moved considerably more slowly than she did.

"Nettie!" exclaimed Lottie, standing up. "Nettie DeWitt. But of course, you live in Cambridge now, don't you?" They exchanged greetings, Nettie pushing back her high-crowned velvet hat, and Lottie introduced her friend. "Miss Anita Hemmings," she said as Anita rose. "My roommate at Vassar this year, and the reigning class beauty."

"That's apparent," said Nettie, taking Anita's hand. "It's lovely to meet you. I'm a Vassar girl myself, but before you both arrived on campus. I'm a proud member of the class of '92. Such an old girl now."

"Nonsense," said Lottie, interrupting her. "You only missed us by a year, and you still look like a freshman, with a good seamstress."

Nettie waved away the compliment, her thick, sable hair bobbing as she moved. "You were always a delight, weren't you?" She turned to Anita and said, "Lottie and I grew up around the corner from each other in New York. I remember her when she was a three-foot terror. I'm still terribly bitter that she was able to stay in the city and attend Brearley while I was shipped off like a parcel with legs to Emma Willard in Troy."

She turned her wide eyes back to Anita and asked, "Where did you prepare for Vassar, Anita?"

"I'm from Boston, and I stayed in the state. I went to Dwight Moody's Northfield Seminary. It's very far north, on the Vermont border."

"Dwight Moody's? That's an awfully liberal place, I hear," said Nettie. Had even one other girl from her time at Vassar prepared at Northfield? "Students from far-off reaches of the globe, of all creeds and colors."

"It was quite modern in that sense, but deeply religious," Anita replied, hoping to protect her beloved school. "Everyone certainly left a committed Christian."

"Of course, of course. You ladies and your religious educations."

"Nettie! You sound like a heathen," said Lottie, laughing.

"Blame my husband," she said. "He may be a Harvard English professor but lately he's also become a naturalist or a nationalist, or something like that. Isn't that right, dear?" she said, turning to nudge the silent man behind her.

"My husband, Talbot Aldrich. I'm Nettie Aldrich now. I've abandoned the Dutch."

"A pleasure to meet you both," said Talbot. His passive face suggested that he was quite used to standing behind his wife.

"Will you be attending the Harvard game tomorrow?" Lottie asked Talbot. "My brother John is in his third year at Harvard. We're here on Papa's orders to make sure he isn't failing out or ruining lives. Last summer he threatened to elope with one of the maids. You can guess how that was taken."

"It's a good thing you're here," said Nettie, laughing with Lottie. "Are you, or we, attending the game, Talbot?" she asked her husband.

"Afraid not, my dear. The last time we took in a game, you complained from the first moment about the weather and we left after twenty minutes."

"That's right," said Nettie. "I just remembered that I detest football. Barbaric sport. But have a grand time, you two, and please call on me the next time you're in Cambridge. We'll be here for simply ever as Talbot is such a to-do at

Harvard now. Running his whole department. Number 7, Brattle Street. Nettie Aldrich. Don't forget the Aldrich or you'll never find me!" She waved goodbye, showing off the Belgian lace pulled tightly over her hand.

"But you must have heard stories about Nettie," said Lottie, as the girls left the building in another hansom. "She was a terror at Vassar. She somehow skated by and graduated—she is awfully bright—but she's a monster."

"Monster? How exactly?" Anita asked, already learning to be skeptical of Lottie's colorful language.

"She loves a prank. Really, she once found herself stranded on top of Main with her dress caught on the bell. And in the rain. She's legendary."

"I have a feeling they'll say the same thing about you one day," Anita said.

"We shall see," said Lottie, closing her eyes. "The worst fate I can think of is not to be talked about."

That, Anita was sure, would never be a problem for Lottie Taylor.

CHAPTER 4

The next morning found them leaving their hotel by carriage for Radcliffe. Lottie had cabled her cousin to say they would arrive at nine, after attending the 7:30 A.M. church service in town.

"Have you visited Radcliffe before?" asked Lottie as the carriage wound its way to the small campus.

"On one occasion," said Anita, trying to calm her palpitating heart. "When I was home from Northfield. But it was just a brief visit. And in vain as I already intended to take the entrance exam for Vassar."

"Me, too. I was sure, even as a child, that there would be nowhere more splendid than Vassar."

As a child, thought Anita. It was when she knew, too.

When she was ten years old, and already a very promising grade school student, Anita had overheard a white woman at her Episcopalian church telling the Reverend Phillips Brooks that her daughter was graduating from Vassar College in the spring. Other Trinity Church parishioners had overheard her and had gathered around to hear the story, as a woman pursuing higher education in 1882 was extremely rare. Vassar had been founded only twenty-one years earlier but already the women who had converged spoke about it as if this woman's daughter had obtained a golden ticket to heaven. She called Vassar the most exclusive and the best school for women in America, and everyone around her agreed. So that was the way Anita first viewed a Vassar education, as something that could make well-to-do white women beam with pride and envy.

The same summer, following worship at Trinity, Anita met the daughter in question, a confident fair-haired girl named Cora Shailer. Anita came down from the seats in the back upper gallery, which were free of charge and where the colored members of the congregation were relegated to, and walked to the first floor, where wealthy white parishioners rented the pews. She hovered on the edge of the group of women who had gathered after the service to hear about Cora's time at Vassar. Halfway through her stories, Cora had seen Anita and smiled familiarly.

"Anita Hemmings, I remember you," she said with a welcoming expression. "Do you remember me?" she asked.

Anita nodded yes, not because she remembered Cora, but because she had been imagining her for many months.

"I've heard you're a bright girl," she said in the same kind tone. "You should attend Vassar in a few years." She smiled again as the older women looked down at the young girl, all unaware that Anita was colored. "Keep it in mind," said Cora before launching back into the gossip of her college days.

From that moment on, Vassar never left Anita's thoughts.

She had always loved her studies and the way her parents beamed at her when she came home happy and with perfect grades, which was in part due to their reverence for learning. Anita had begun grammar school later than most, as her parents had waited to send her until there was a place open for a colored girl at the Prince School on Newbury Street in affluent Back Bay. They thought, even when Anita was young, that she showed too much intelligence to be just another face at the poorly funded schools in Roxbury. And their foresight had paid off.

It wasn't until five years after the conversation in church, when the dream of Vassar was still very much alive in Anita, that she became aware that her race would keep her from gaining admission, even if her character and intellectual capacity were worthy. She was, without question, her grammar school's most promising student, and because of her academic standing, she had grown quite close to her teachers, and felt more kinship to them than to her peers. It was in this phase of intellectual curiosity, a year before she entered the Girls' High School, that she spoke to someone other than family about Vassar.

It was her seventh-year teacher at the Prince School, a stern yet well-meaning woman from a long line of Bostonians, who listened to Anita as she disclosed her desire to attend Vassar with the intention of becoming a teacher herself. With remorse, she informed her dedicated pupil that attending Vassar was out of the question for a Negro woman and urged Anita to consider Wellesley or the newly founded Radcliffe College.

Shocked by the news, as Anita had thought Cora knew the truth about her race, she shared the brutal admissions policy with her mother. The following Sunday, Dora Hemmings confided in her close circle at the church. Her extremely bright daughter had had her dreams stamped out. It was within that supportive community that a young woman named Margaret Marshall—Mame to her friends—pulled Anita aside after worship and told her that of course there was a way. Very light-skinned herself, she recounted to Anita how she had passed as white to attend the good grammar and high school down in Christiansburg, Virginia, walking ten miles a day and lying to everyone about her race so that she could learn to read and write, unlike her siblings.

"Passing to continue your education, to better your mind at the best school in America is not something you should look at shamefully. It is not an escape," Mame had said while speaking to Anita in private. "People may try to scare you, carry on about psychological repercussions and betrayal, but I do not regret what I did. To live life without the Negro marker by your name, even for a short period of time, can expand your world. It's something you should consider, Anita."

In the community of Roxbury, where the complexions ranged from dark to light, the subject of passing was often heard in conversation. Some believed it was the ultimate sin against the Negro race, and others—those who had relatives who had passed or had passed themselves—saw it as an occasional necessity. "They make us pass," Mame had said. "If they would give us good schools, any rights at all, then we wouldn't even have to consider it, would we? People escaped slavery through passing, saved their own lives, the lives of their families. It's not all just a traitor's behavior to live an easier existence. Anita, please heed my advice: do not waste your strong mind because some might disagree with the practice, might chastise you. When one passes for a higher purpose, it's worth it. Go on and prove to those Vassar women that we can be them, too."

At fifteen years old, Anita hadn't fully understood the strength of Mame's words or the varying perspectives of her community on passing, but she was no stranger to the concept, having often been mistaken as white when she was without family or friends in Boston. And she knew stories of women who had passed to improve their positions in the world, and had heard them labeled as weak, as defectors, but it was the first time she ever considered passing herself. For education, thought Anita, it felt right.

When she shared Mame Marshall's idea with her parents that evening, an idea that she had quickly embraced, they agreed. A Vassar education was worth lying for.

Anita still held that conviction close to her heart and she let the powerful memories accompany her as she and Lottie approached the school. The hansom soon deposited both women in front of Fay House, the building that housed every aspect of life at Radcliffe. With its mere three floors, it resembled an elegant but diminutive family mansion more than it did their college's soaring Main Building.

"We're to go to the reception room, and one of the maids will send up a visitor's card," said Lottie.

"Just like at Vassar," Anita said, looking all around her for Gertrude's recognizable face.

"Not quite. The girls do not reside on campus here, no exceptions, but Lilly promised she would be in the library studying. She's doing so on purpose, I'm sure, to appear as diligent as possible." Lottie paid the carriage driver and they walked into the building, past the Radcliffe girls, who looked nearly identical to the Vassar girls—the same capriciousness, same chatter, same airs of privilege and intelligence.

"Miss Louise Taylor to see Miss Elizabeth Taylor," said Lottie to the woman monitoring visitors that day. She handed the young woman her card and explained that Lilly was her cousin.

"Of course, miss," she replied, and left to fetch Lilly from the third-floor library.

"It's pretty here," said Lottie, looking up at the ceiling. "Is it prettier than Vassar, do you think?"

"Certainly not," Anita said, looking around her at the small single staircase. "Not even a fair competition."

Suddenly, they heard Lottie's name called out in a high, melodic voice. They turned to see Lilly approaching, all smiles and with the same blond curls, deep blue eyes, and cherubic features as her cousin.

"Lottie and Anita!" she said, stretching out her arms. She gave the Vassar girls each kisses on the cheek, her plaid taffeta dress swishing against them, and took their hands. "I'm so happy you're both here! Lottie warned me that you were the prettiest girl at Vassar, Anita. Isn't she brave to room with you?"

"Oh, that's not—" Anita tried to protest, but Lilly stopped her.

"People see what they see, Anita dear." She smiled, and Anita was happy to note that she shared her cousin's gaiety.

"Are you two really going to that brutish football game today?" Lilly asked as she led them out of the parlor.

"I take great delight in a football game," said Lottie. "I've always enjoyed the display of athleticism that comes with the sport. But it's more than that. There's something very democratic about it. Not just a bunch of silly rich people who have more money than hair."

Lilly and Anita laughed, because it was obvious that almost everyone Lottie knew had more money than hair.

"Shall we do a tour of the campus?" asked Lilly, steering them toward the second floor. "You've visited Radcliffe, Anita?" she asked, her cool blue eyes admiring Anita's striking face.

"Yes, she has," answered Lottie for her roommate. "She's from Boston."

"Oh? I wasn't aware. We girls are often making trips to Boston. Is your family there?"

"Yes," said Anita, quickly peeking into a nearby parlor, looking to change the subject. "What a splendid room," she said. "The Corinthian columns are very elegant. Beautiful acanthus design."

"Why, yes," said Lilly, with a look of surprise at this sudden interest in architecture. "We are fond of our parlors." Lottie glanced in and asked Lilly how much time she spent inside.

"Are you asking me how well I'm doing in school, cousin? Wondering why I'm loafing about in parlors and not upstairs in the library?"

Lottie laughed and put her arm around her cousin's cinched waist. "Obviously, Lilly. You're no stranger to me. I know your love of lazing about."

"I'm doing just fine," said Lilly. "Aren't you kind to inquire."

Lottie did a little curtsey and took Anita by the arm. They both followed her charming cousin through the building.

Anita, pretending that she wanted to see every inch of the structure, kept turning around, looking this way and that, but they were able to complete their visit of the public rooms without glimpsing Gertrude.

"I need some air," said Lottie, yawning as they ended their tour. "Let's go outside and see if it has cooled off at all. One would think we'd stop suffocating by early October."

The three young women walked down the hill from Fay House, toward Cambridge Common, enjoying the slight breeze. Lilly introduced her cousin and Anita to several of the girls they passed, animatedly relaying the gossip about each one after they had bid them goodbye.

"Hollis Kelly: so poor at French that it sounds as if her tongue has been split like a lizard," said Lilly, speaking louder than she should have been. She nodded to two more girls after giving them a warm hello and introducing her guests. "Alice Truman: her father was flush with money out west, but he died in a mine collapse and the family went bankrupt. An estranged uncle has to pay for her schooling now. The other is Edna de France: Be sure to look at her from the side as she walks away. Her nose is so hooked she can hang a coat on it."

Lottie made a face at her cousin. "It's no wonder you always got along so well with my mother," she told her.

As they looped back to Fay House, Lilly slowed her steps and whispered something to her cousin. Anita stopped behind them, her body stiffening as they spoke, then Lilly turned back to her and said, "Anita, up ahead of us is Alberta Scott. Did Lottie warn you about her?"

Anita looked at Lottie, who shrugged and said, "I forgot she was here. We don't have that concern at Vassar."

"She was the first," said Lilly in a whisper, and suddenly Anita knew. She was speaking about a Negro.

"She was the only one until another came this year, a Gertrude Baker in the class of 1900. And now that they've made their little point, I pray they are done admitting them," said Lilly. "It cheapens the school. Of course, neither of them resides near anyone we're acquainted with or engage with us outside our classes, so I suppose it could be even more inappropriate. I hear there have been several of them at Wellesley. And this Alberta Scott, the first one to arrive, she's very dark. In the evening all you can see of her are those bulging white eyes. You know the type. She's class of 1898, but they admitted her accidentally, I'm sure. Unfortunately, we haven't been able to get rid of her."

Lottie turned and looked ahead. "She's stopped walking. She's just standing there in the middle of the road."

"Let's cross the lane so we don't have to walk by her. It makes me very uncomfortable. She has a smell about her that isn't quite right," said Lilly, her face pinching in disgust. "They all do, don't they? Especially when it's warm outside. Virginia Bloomingdale had Greek with her last year and had to sit right next to her. Imagine. And Virginia is from Atlanta. The poor girl barely made it through class. Her father wrote letters to the president to protest, threatened to pull Virginia out of school, but the administration wouldn't listen. They even went so far as to say there would be more admitted in the years to come, so perhaps it wasn't an accident after all. Now Alberta is still here and Virginia is not."

It took Anita a moment to follow Lottie and Lilly across the street so they would not have to pass close to Alberta. She took a few steps, careful not to look back at Radcliffe's first Negro student. She had been so scared at the prospect of running into Gertrude that she had not even considered the possibility of seeing another Negro on campus.

Anita had never lost sight of the fiction she was living at Vassar. The *Plessy v Ferguson* debate and discussions about the Jim Crow laws were just recent reminders. Her freshman year, she had been in a hall play and blackened her face with makeup to play a Negro woman along with ten other girls, who declared it all great fun. She had listened to southern girls talk about the former slaves who were still on their properties, sharecropping cotton to survive. Some spoke more highly of their dogs. Anita had overheard two sophomores dismiss the Negro as mentally, physically, and spiritually inferior and had stayed silent, she had repeatedly read the word *nigger* in the school newspaper and ignored it, but she had never felt shame the way she did when she crossed the street to avoid Alberta Scott. She wanted to be the person who did not cross the street, the person who instead went right up to her. She wanted to say, "You, Alberta

Scott, are a Negro at Radcliffe College, and I, Anita Hemmings, am the only Negro at Vassar College."

But Vassar was not Radcliffe.

"Anita. Anita?" said Lilly, looking back at her. Anita realized that she had stopped walking and that her eyes were still fixed on Alberta's slowly disappearing form.

"I'm sorry," she said to Lilly. "I was lost in thought."

"It's jarring, I know," said Lilly. "Did Lottie not tell you about her and Gertrude? Negroes at Radcliffe. It's disgusting. I can't imagine their grades are up to snuff. They don't have the same capacity for learning as we do. I've read studies on their minds. They are built for labor and breeding. Though I wish they would stop the latter. Many of the girls here think differently, but then again, it's Massachusetts, isn't it? Easier to brainwash the women of New England."

"Lottie did not tell me," Anita said. "But please don't worry, Lilly—"

"No wonder you're in shock. Come, we'll linger a bit here, and she'll most likely be off campus by the time we arrive at Fay House. She doesn't spend much time inside with us, especially during the weekend. She just comes for classes and then heads back to that Negro family she lives with on Parker Street."

"She lives with a family?" Anita asked.

"Of course," said Lilly. "We may have made the mistake of letting her in, but the school knows well enough that no girl, even the most northern, would want to reside on the same block as her. Girls would drop out of school by the dozen if that were the case. The other one, Gertrude, still lives with her family on Museum Street in a Negro neighborhood, I'm told. But you might know better, Anita, about which streets to avoid in Cambridge and Boston?"

Anita shook her head no.

"All this bores me," said Lottie, letting out a yawn and stretching uncouthly. "Black, white, green, why bother about all that? Let's have an ice cream before Anita and I head off to Soldiers Field. And we must have time to fix ourselves. I am not setting a foot on Harvard campus with my hair out of sorts. And Anita can't, either. She has a reputation to uphold since she waves the flag of beauty for all the Vassar students. Is there a maid here who can help us?"

"Of course," said Lilly, determined to show them that Radcliffe was everything Vassar was, despite having Alberta Scott and Gertrude Baker in its classrooms.

When they reached Fay House, all three of them stopped midstep when they saw Alberta standing outside the building next to the front entrance.

"How presumptuous!" exclaimed Lilly. "She is perfectly aware that if she lingers there, we have no choice but to walk right past her. It's too hot to make our way around to another door."

"Lilly, I don't see the need to find another entrance. Let's just go indoors. If I don't have something cool to drink, I'll throw a fit," said Lottie.

"Lottie is an expert at fits," said Lilly, before they all marched single-file through the door, Lottie in the lead.

When Anita passed Alberta, she tried to catch her eye, to show compassion in her face, as she didn't dare utter a word. She wanted Alberta to see in her something different than the Taylors, but Alberta did not look in her direction.

Inside the entrance hall, Lottie leaned against the carved wooden wall and turned to Lilly, all thought of Alberta forgotten. "Lilly, are you sure we cannot change your mind?" she said. "Won't you please come with us this afternoon?"

"Absolutely not," said Lilly. "Sitting outside in an unruly crowd does not appeal to me. I'm not sure it's proper."

"Which is exactly why it's amusing," said Lottie.

As the two went back and forth on the merits of attending a football game, Anita watched as Alberta struck up a conversation outside with a fair-haired girl in a simple white shirtwaist. Suddenly both of them broke out in laughter, their voices loud enough to be heard through the front door. Lilly leaned back to look at them, too.

"Not this again. That awful girl is Anna Lowe. Look at her speaking to Alberta as if she's a white woman. I should go out there and tell Alberta that she can try all she wants, she'll remain a dirty-faced Negro, even if Radcliffe makes the mistake of conferring a degree on her." Lilly looked away but spun around again when she heard Anna laugh. "Anna's family is Quaker," Lilly spat out. "Her grandfather was a vocal abolitionist during the war. Alice went to one of those public schools full of diseased coloreds. She's used to being surrounded by them and speaks to Alberta, and now Gertrude, shockingly often. She's on some sort of awful crusade. Such an embarrassment."

Lilly turned back to Lottie, who had glanced at the pair without much interest. Lottie looked off toward the rooftops of Harvard in the distance and changed the subject back to the afternoon's game.

Anita could not pull her gaze from Alberta and the willowy girl who was speaking to her directly in front of the Fay House doors. The smoldering shame she had felt in crossing the street was now burning in her face and she was about to turn away when she saw the girl take her ungloved hand and reach for Alberta's.

"Will you both excuse me for one moment?" Anita said to Lottie and Lilly. "I'll be just a minute." She left before they could answer and walked quickly into the building, desperate to find a corner where she could be alone. She needed to fall apart, just for a few minutes, so that she could show self-possession through the day ahead.

She realized she was alone in the wide hall and put her hand on the wall to steady herself. There she was, barely able to stand, half-dizzy with shame, and the Quaker girl was outside laughing with, *touching*, Alberta Scott. Anita felt herself completely undeserving of what she had. She knew from the girl's face that she wasn't speaking to Alberta out of obligation, but because she desired to, because they were friends. She rushed to the stairs Lilly had guided them up earlier and turned a corner, hoping to find a powder room. Three more corners and two hallways farther on, she found one near the visitors' parlor.

She stared in the mirror, chastising herself for her weakness. She knew she could have been like Alberta or Gertrude and Bessie Baker and attended a school where there was no need to deceive the world. But she did not make that choice. She chose instead to be America's most educated coward.

She reached for a towel and wiped her face, wondering how she would explain her appearance to Lottie and Lilly. So many tears were running down her cheeks, she knew her face would be swollen.

Turning away from the mirror, she examined the window. It was separated into rectangular panes of glass divided by a thick iron grid. Without giving it any further thought, she hit the bottom pane, closest to the latch. It cracked into several shards and fell to the floor. She leaned down, stuck one in her right palm, and dragged it across. She took the towel she had used to wipe her face, wrapped it around her bleeding hand, and walked to the door. Now her tears needed no explanation.

CHAPTER 5

My apologies for our tardiness. Anita cut her hand opening a window at Radcliffe. I had to save her," Lottie told her brother, John Taylor, when she and Anita sat down next to him on the Harvard bleachers. He had the same big curls and bright eyes as his sister and cousin, though nearly two heads taller.

Lottie looked at the score and smiled back at Anita. "Oh good, it's still nil-nil. And here I was worried we missed something."

"I'm terribly sorry," said John, concern shadowing his handsome face. "Are you all right, Anita?"

"It's nothing at all. Just bad luck," Anita said. "I was opening a window to get some air, as I had come down with a bit of a headache, and the pane shattered. Your sister did save me," she said, holding up her bandaged right hand. "She and your cousin Lilly brought me to the infirmary, where the doctor applied pressure and this not-so-handsome bandage."

She lowered her hand and sighed at the unfortunate timing of it all.

"If it wasn't for me and my swift thinking, she probably would have bled to death," said Lottie, arranging her dress around her. "Radcliffe clearly has inferior windows to Vassar. Now, tell me everything about your Harvard life, my dear brother. I'm to give Father a full report when I return to Poughkeepsie. Five pages at least."

John grinned at both of them and said, "You can tell Father that I just met a lovely Vassar girl who hails from Boston named Anita Hemmings and that we're going to be married at once."

"Pay no mind to him, Anita," said Lottie, grimacing at her brother. "He knows he's far too young for you, and not even close to handsome enough, but he'll happily flirt anyway. I'm afraid it runs in the family. We're natural flirts."

"One of our only talents," said John.

Lottie nodded in agreement and clucked at her little brother to act with decorum. "Now, John, you are aware that we are going to have to move out of these dreadful seats straightaway. Where are the seniors sitting? That's where we want to sit. We traveled all the way from Poughkeepsie, spent a harrowing night in town, and Anita sustained a near-fatal hand injury. Our time is precious."

"You can see the game perfectly well from here," said John, indicating the men in crimson and white running on Soldiers Field.

"The game!" said Lottie, throwing her slender arms around her brother's broad shoulders. "We didn't come to watch the game. What's a football game good for if you're not securing a date for the Phil Day dance?"

"This should be suitable enough for you," said John pointing. "We're right on the fifty-yard line."

"I demand that we move," said Lottie, standing up and blocking the view of the spectators above them. "Or I'll tell Father that you're drinking heavily, running around with unsavory women, and working little."

"That sounds close to the truth," said John, looking around for new seats.

"Ah, this will please you, dear Lottie. Five rows down and to the right are Porter Hamilton, of the Chicago lumber Hamiltons, and Henry Silsbury, former star left tackle for this illustrious institution. He graduated last year, but he's still a big man in Cambridge. He was all-American his senior year. Passable placement for you, my discerning one?"

"That will do," said Lottie, with a smirk, tugging at John's suit jacket. "And you know just as well as I do that Henry and I are dear, dear friends. We're practically engaged."

"Naturally," said John.

As the women stood up, Lottie whispered to Anita, "By practically engaged, I mean that I had one dance with him at Founder's Day last year. His palms sweat like a goldfish, from what I remember, but he's dashing all the same. And terribly strong. He practically dragged me across the parlor floor like a fraying mop during the quadrille. It was more of a float than a dance." She winked at Anita and they headed toward the men, pushing their way through the bleachers with a flurry of apologies.

When they were near, Henry turned to the group and smiled. It took him a moment, but by the time they reached him and Porter, who was transfixed by the Harvard offense, recognition had lit up his face.

"Hey, Taylor," Henry said, standing up to shake John's hand. "Joining us?"

"I am, if you don't mind," said John. "But don't worry, I know my place. I've brought very pleasant company along to make up for my undesirable presence. Henry, I believe you've met my sister, Lottie? She's a senior at Vassar. And this is her roommate, Anita Hemmings."

Henry greeted them warmly, then kicked his friend. Surprised by the leather-shod toe that bruised his shin, Porter looked up quickly, realized his rudeness, and jumped to his feet.

"My apologies, everyone. I'm not even the one who played for Harvard, and I am entranced by this still-scoreless game. But that is no excuse. How are you, Taylor?" he said, looking to him to introduce his companions.

"Well, well. I'm well," said John. "This is my sister Lottie and her roommate, Miss Anita Hemmings. They're up from Vassar to join us in all of this."

"Fine idea," said Porter. He turned around after tipping his hat hello and told his side of the bleacher to push down so the three could join them. Catching his friend's eye, he added, "Anita, why don't you sit by me? I believe Lottie and Henry already know each other."

Lottie smiled approvingly, and Anita stepped over a bleacher with the help of Porter's steady hand. Anita may have had no idea who the Chicago Hamiltons were, but Lottie certainly did.

"It's Anita Hemmings, is that right?" said Porter, moving over so he wasn't touching her.

"Yes, Hemmings," Anita answered, embarrassed by her bandaged hand.

"I believe I know someone who was in love with you once," Porter said, flashing a grin. "Though, come to think of it, he probably still is. I'll rephrase. Anita Hemmings, I know someone who is desperately in love with you."

"Who is that?" said Lottie, leaning over Henry and letting her arm brush his knee.

"Miss Taylor, I simply can't say," Porter replied. "We Harvard men have bonds of silence which will never be broken."

"Fine, then," said Lottie. "Be a bore. And tell him to join the line. Anita is highly sought after. Class beauty and all."

Henry whispered something to Lottie that made her blush and the rest pretended not to notice.

When Williams failed to score a touchdown, the group resumed their chatter and the men traded opinions on the game. But while Anita was engaged with the others, Porter leaned toward her and said in a soft voice, "I'm not going to tell you my friend's name, if that's acceptable to you."

"Of course," she said, turning to him. He was good-looking in an arresting way. Classically handsome, she thought.

"But I want you to know that I'm doing so for selfish reasons."

He looked at her directly, and she quickly averted her gaze, not knowing how to respond and surprised at the jolt of excitement she felt.

She pleaded with her brain to come up with the perfect quick-witted response, something that seemed second nature to Lottie, but all she could do was look at the floor until someone on the field saved her. Harvard had their first touchdown. The group of five jumped up and cheered as one, the din from the band egging them on.

"Did you see that run?" Henry said to Porter.

"Just the end of it," Porter commented. "I was looking at something even more appealing."

Henry climbed onto the bleacher to cheer, launching into one of the school's many songs. John and Porter joined in, and Lottie caught her roommate's eye and flashed her a brilliant smile. Anita had never met a girl who fed off the attention of men quite like Lottie Taylor.

Anita watched as Porter boomed out, "Fair Harvard! Thy sons to thy Jubilee throng!" and he broke out in a laugh when he caught her looking at him, and couldn't remember the next line. "Anita Hemmings, your disapproval is distracting me," he said. "I should know better than to sing next to a beautiful woman."

Lottie whipped her head around at Porter's compliment.

"Can't you hold a tune, Porter?" she asked as Henry sang off-key at the top of his lungs, jumping on the bleacher next to them. "Miss Hemmings sings like an angel."

"I do quite well, Miss Taylor," said Porter. "And if Miss Hemmings sings like an angel, she also looks like one."

"You have a very nice voice," Anita responded back, her pulse taking off with every compliment. "And loud."

"Loud?" he said loudly. "I'll show you loud." He hopped on the bleacher with Henry, and the two of them shouted the rest of the song as if they had been drinking the day away.

"I see Mary Hurlbut and Persis Breed three rows down and to the left," said Lottie when they all came up for air. Anita looked down and saw the two sophomore girls who lived a floor below them in Main. They were sitting with a group of Harvard men who were doting on them as much as Anita and Lottie were being doted upon. "But I'm going to pretend I don't see them because I'm content just like this."

Anita smiled at her and didn't have to say anything, because it was obvious she was happy, too.

Even though she knew she could never do anything more than casually speak to a Harvard man—never engaging too much, never promising to see him again—Anita was reveling in every minute of her conversation with Porter. He was distinguished, with trim brown hair, the clean-shaven face of a school boy, and startling green eyes, but there was a lightness to his personality that Anita liked immediately. She felt thrilled just to be standing next to him.

The game ended as a 6–0 win for Harvard, with the

touchdown that inspired Porter and Henry to bellow the school song left as the only one of the day. It was nearly four o'clock when it all ended and Lottie and Anita had to rush to the station to make their five o'clock train to Albany.

"Let us away, ladies," said John, tipping his hat to the girls. "Bid these fair gentlemen goodbye."

"Goodbye, fair gentlemen," Lottie and Anita chorused.

"But you can't expect a simple farewell to be sufficient after the wonderful day we've all spent together," said Henry, eyeing Lottie like a prize he was planning on collecting. "John, please let us accompany these ladies to the station. I promise that we will see them safely on board." Porter nodded his agreement.

John, clearly not wanting to be shut out of the fun, and aware of how much more popular his older sister was making him, started to create a high-spirited fuss.

"I promised our father that I would make sure Lottie and Anita were on the train, properly boarded, and I couldn't let the old man down now. I'm afraid I can't leave them in your hands, good sirs."

Lottie snickered and said, "Well, then, just come on, all of you. We can keep this celebration going until the train whistles and Anita and I are carried away to New York."

Exuding good spirits, the five of them boarded the electric trolley to the station.

"I don't remember all the Vassar girls being as pretty as the two of you," said Henry, from his seat behind them in the trolley, where he had an uninterrupted view of the napes of their necks.

"Do you even remember dancing with me at Founder's Day last year, Henry?" asked Lottie, with an air of studied nonchalance.

"Do I even remember?" said Henry, acting slighted. "I've only been thinking about it every hour since then."

"Funny, as I've never received as much as a one-line missive from you," Lottie said. "But it's not bothering me. I get ever so much mail. Bags of it. The maids can barely carry it in as it is."

"You can burn all of that rubbish and just read my letters from now on," said Henry.

He was quickly distracted by a group of Harvard students on the trolley who wanted his expert take on the game. All were convinced that despite the presence of Edgar Wrightington and Norman Cabot—the two players with the best chances of going All-American in '96—if Henry had still been playing, Harvard would have scored more than one touchdown.

At the station, John caught up with Anita after the three men had walked the women to their platform.

"Anita Hemmings, have I already lost you to Porter Hamilton? Should I tell Lottie to alter her letter to Father? Is our engagement off?" he said in his good-natured Taylor way.

"I'll write that letter if you'd like," said Porter, catching up. "Anita, you must know a girl for John. A senior like you certainly can't be pulled in underclassman directions. It's just not what is done in our world."

The men gave the ladies' luggage to one of the porters, and Lottie waved at Mary and Persis, who were waiting for the same train.

"Actually, John," Anita said, "I'm sure your sister would be more than happy to introduce you to Mary and Persis." She nodded in the direction of the two girls. "They're sophomores, and if I had to guess, are probably already distressed about whom to invite to the Phil Day dance in December."

"Excellent!" said John, casting a glance at them. "Now that you've rejected me, I need someone to give my heart to. Or maybe a few someones. I'm only a junior, after all. I might as well allow all Vassar women an even chance."

He caught up with his sister and after she delivered a quick lecture on why his plan was piteous, she walked him over and introduced him to her schoolmates.

"Anita, say flattering things about me to Lottie and I'll be forever indebted to you," said Henry, while the other three stood at the opposite end of the platform watching John flirt with the underclassmen.

"I'm happy to," said Anita, politely. "But she seems quite embittered that you danced with her at Founder's and never penned her a letter."

"Last year's Founder's Day at Vassar? You have to have a little compassion for me, Miss Hemmings. I was a senior and we football boys got our hands on so much to drink before that dance that I wasn't sure if I was dancing with men or women. I honestly don't remember dancing with her at all. She's Lottie Taylor. I would have remembered."

"Should I believe you?"

"Of course you should!" he said, looking at Porter for help.

"Don't believe a word he says, Anita. Henry is a natural-born liar."

"You're a turncoat, Porter Hamilton," said Henry, laughing, as Lottie and John returned.

"Anita, you should expect to see me on the Vassar campus quite often this year," John announced. "I just proposed marriage to both of those fine young ladies. And while neither of them has accepted, I'm sure one of them will crack soon. I know how to make a woman's heart swell."

"I have no doubt," Anita said drily.

As the Albany train's heavy engine roared to life and the group were saying their goodbyes, Porter put his hand on Anita's gloved one and said quietly, "I hope you don't think John is the only one you'll be seeing on Vassar's campus. I would like to spend the day with you again. Soon. Would you make time for me if I came to Poughkeepsie?"

Against what she knew she should do, what she had to do, she said yes. Yes to everything.

CHAPTER 6

I think I'll marry Henry soon after graduation," Lottie declared, pushing away her chemistry notes. She wrapped her burnt-orange shawl around herself. In her hair was a sizable ostrich feather.

"What about the future emperor of Japan?" Anita asked. The roommates were sitting in the library whispering over the oil lamp they were sharing. Lottie was trying to focus on chemistry, while Anita was attempting her most difficult Greek translation yet.

"Oh, the crown prince!" said Lottie, too loudly. She put her hand over her mouth and whispered back. "I'll have to send him a letter to explain my dilemma."

"Are you going to invite Henry to the Phil Day dance?" asked Belle from one table over. Lottie's courtship with Henry was much more interesting than the Latin that Belle was studying.

"I most certainly am," said Lottie, peering around the book stacks for eavesdroppers. Lottie loved an audience, even in the library. "Though he's graduated from Harvard, he's only one year out, so he won't feel out of place at Phil. And he's still quite the football star. Everyone knows who

Henry Silsbury is, just like everyone knows who Porter Hamilton is . . . but for different reasons."

She looked meaningfully at Anita, prompting Belle and her tablemate Caroline Hardin to look over, too.

Anita gave them nothing but an indecipherable smile, and they went reluctantly back to their work. Lottie placed two monocles on her face, both crystal-clear glass wrapped in tortoise shell. Her friends all looked at her in disbelief and broke the silence of the library again.

"They make me feel more intelligent," Lottie declared, tapping them with the emerald ring she was wearing on her left hand. It was in the shape of a chrysanthemum, a flower used as the imperial seal of Japan. "Plus, I think I look like a snowy owl, and who doesn't appreciate a snowy owl."

"A snowy owl? You just look like a madwoman," said Belle.

Lottie ignored Belle, and said something about the pure agony of not being allowed to do round dances at Phil that year, but Anita refused to engage her and they were all quiet for the next hour.

"That settles it," said Belle abruptly, turning to Anita again. "I'm bursting at the seams with curiosity. So I'm having a midnight whist party in my room tonight and the topic of conversation will be your trip to Harvard and how you bewitched Porter Hamilton."

Anita froze. The thought of her friends firing questions at *her*, rather than Lottie, set off a wave of panic, compounded by the fact that Belle's room was next to that of Sarah Douglas, who would certainly drop by.

"What a brilliant idea," said Lottie. "I am not in love with your neighbors, especially Sarah, but I'm sure I can tolerate her if Caroline and your ever-so-kind roommate Hortense Lewis are also present."

"Of course I'll be there. And I want to hear all about you and Henry, too, Lottie," said Caroline.

Lottie and Anita were tasked with bringing tea, and Anita nodded, her neck feeling unsteady and weak, as she realized she could not decline.

"I have a heap of exquisite teas from Ceylon," said Lottie, "wrapped up in a Persian green box with pink tissue paper lined with flecks of gold. But maybe I won't be able to find them and will have to bring champagne instead."

"President Taylor is going to execute you before the year is over," said Belle. "And if we are ever caught, I am blaming you for everything."

"Certainly," said Lottie.

Anita wasn't worried about Lottie's love of imbibing; it was Sarah Douglas she feared.

Anita was restless in her last class that day, which was advanced Latin literature taught by Miss Franklin, a young professor with a Ph.D. and whom Anita greatly admired. She planned to return to her room by way of the library so she could complete her Latin and Greek work and have time alone to think about the evening's late event. She needed to come up with short rote answers to the girls' excited questions. She wouldn't touch the alcohol that Lottie would certainly bring, and she would encourage her roommate to carry on about Henry, as she was sure to spin a story full of embellishments that centered on herself.

Anita had been in the library for just a few minutes when Anna Post, a senior from Oswego, New York, hurried over and sat down next to her at the wooden table.

"Anita, you are being beckoned to the visitors' parlor," she whispered. "The maid on duty was sent up for you, but Lottie said you weren't in and that the maid should try the library. But then another visitor came and the maid couldn't come tell you, so Lottie sent me instead. She said it would be rude of her not to entertain your visitor herself."

"Who is my visitor?" Anita asked worriedly.

"Your visitor is Mr. Hamilton," said Anna, making an obvious effort to sound calm. "Porter Hamilton." Any male visitor at Vassar was a source of gossip, but a senior from Harvard with a reputable last name and a handsome face was sure to cause a flood of it.

"He's here? At Vassar? To see me?" Anita asked, suddenly a jumble of terror and anticipation.

"Yes. He's waiting in the visitors' parlor with Lottie."

"Oh no! But, Anna," Anita said grabbing her skirt, "I must look a terrible mess."

"You look beautiful," Anna said. "You always look beautiful. But if it suits you, we could slip up to my room by way of the back stairs and we could freshen you up there. You can borrow one of my silk dresses. We'll call a maid to change you quickly."

"Are you sure he won't see us? What if he was accidentally escorted upstairs?"

"That would never happen," said Anna. "Come, I have a perfect dress for you. It's a two-piece, made from woven blue and black striped silk. Very heavy, very elegant. And my rooms are closer than yours."

"That sounds too much, Anna. Don't you think?" asked Anita, looking down at her old cotton shirtwaist, slightly yellowed with age.

"No, it will be marvelous on you. It has lace-edge cuffs, a perfectly done high collar with a white pleated jabot, and is Paris made. It might be a bit big in the waist, but I can pin it quickly. You'll look so lovely." She took her hand and they hurried upstairs, collecting one of the maids as they went.

By the time Anita came down to the parlor, she did not

look much like the girl who had been wearing the same dresses for three years at school, but rather someone Porter Hamilton might be used to associating with. She had the look of Anna, or Lottie. And to him, that's who she was, a high-born Vassar woman, with every privilege available to her.

"Anita!" said Lottie, before Porter could. He stood up next to Lottie and walked over to her.

"I hope you haven't been waiting long," Anita said hurriedly. "I was in search of a book in the library and Anna had a difficult time locating me. Please accept my apologies." She thought she had never seen a man look better than Porter Hamilton standing in the visitors' parlor, his single-breasted cassimere suit cut perfectly for his tall frame, his derby hat clutched to his side.

There were three parlors on the ground floor, all of them allotted for visitors, the first for administrative visitors and the second for the students' visitors. The third, which had unglazed windows as the other two did, and was a favorite spot for the college gossips to lurk around, was for the sole use of engaged students and their fiancés. Anita was assuaged that Porter had not made the mistake of entering that one.

"Not at all," said Porter. "You hadn't any idea that I was planning on coming. And Miss Taylor has been wonderful company."

"Wonderful company who will be leaving you now," said Lottie, taking her roommate's arm. "Anita, if you don't make it to Belle's card party tonight, we shall all understand. We'll miss you terribly, but we'll make do. I'll simply have to lead the entertaining. Monocles for all."

Anita thanked her, and Lottie executed a formal Japanese bow and left her with Porter, though Anita imagined she was just around the corner listening with Anna.

"I brought you flowers, Miss Hemmings. Anita," Porter said, holding out a bouquet. "Many of the Harvard men told me to bring daisies, which they claimed is the official flower of Vassar College, but those seemed too simple for a first formal meeting. I then considered red roses, but they seemed quite the opposite, too correct. So I chose pink. Pink roses. Softer than red, and more in keeping with your personality, I believe."

"They are perfect. And perfectly me. Thank you, Porter," said Anita, bringing her nose to them and inhaling the scent.

"At what time is your card party this evening?" asked Porter. "I promise not to keep you."

"It's not until midnight," said Anita.

"Ah," he said, breaking into a laugh. "I am sure I will be able to return you safely to your room before midnight."

He looked at Anita and blushed. "Not to your room, of course. I meant to say, right here. To this very respectable public parlor."

"How about some air?" Anita suggested before Porter's embarrassment overwhelmed him further. "Shall we walk outside? That is, if you've already placed your name with the maid?"

"Yes, I have registered. Lottie assisted me." He cleared his throat, nervously. "A walk sounds perfect," he added. "You may not believe me, but I haven't spent much time on your campus. I came to a Phil Day dance as a sophomore, but haven't returned since."

"I don't believe we met then," said Anita, remembering herself at the dance two years before. She had been asked by several men for a place on her dance card but had declined almost all.

"We did not," said Porter, his eyes fixed on her arresting face. "I would have never let you go."

Anita, discomposed, turned quickly away, and they headed out the back door of Main near the clamorous heating plant. As soon as they made their way down the stairs, Porter stopped on the path and turned to Anita.

"I'm sorry I didn't write to tell you I was coming to campus. I was afraid you might encourage me not to. I felt—after meeting you last weekend—I felt that I had to come. And right away. I hope you're not angry with me and that you might have some time for me today. Not just a few minutes, but hours. Though I do not want to impose on you or your day."

"I'm very surprised to see you," Anita said candidly.

"But are you *happy* that I came?" he asked, putting his hand on her cheek.

She didn't jump, as she thought she might the first time a man touched her face. Instead she breathed in the feeling it gave her, the loop of pleasure it sent through her body, and said, "Yes. I really am."

"I'm so glad," he said, and they walked in silence toward the observatory. As they approached, Anita gave him a brief history of the domed building, a Main in miniature, citing the achievements of Vassar's great astronomer, Maria Mitchell.

"The distinguished Miss Mitchell was a professor here for twenty-three years," she concluded. "She used to throw a dome party every year for the senior class, just the women and the telescope, celebrating the sky. I imagine it must have been lovely."

"I'm a vocal supporter of women's education," said Porter. "I'm from Chicago, which is the Wild West compared to New York, and my parents are very modern. My mother always says she wished she had the opportunity to attend a women's college. She's very involved with suffrage now, which is great mental stimulation for her, but even without a college education, she's more intelligent than the rest of us. A quality I appreciate."

"So few women attended college in your mother's generation. I suppose it's still that way," Anita said. "I believe only three percent of Americans are in college at all."

"But here you are," said Porter. "Extremely smart and intimidatingly beautiful."

"I can't agree with either of those statements," Anita replied, her face burning up to her ears. "But I am happy here."

"I can see that," said Porter. "And now I want to know why. Now that we aren't surrounded by Harvard men, and Lottie Taylor, tell me everything there is to know about you."

"Everything about me," she said slowly.

She couldn't tell Porter anything about herself. She couldn't tell him that her mother ran a boardinghouse in Cottage City every summer, or that her father had recently begun working two jobs, as a janitor and a coachman, cleaning up after and transporting white wealthy Bostonians. She couldn't announce that she lived in the city's Negro neighborhood or that she had never left the state of Massachusetts until she was an adolescent, and still had not traveled beyond the Northeast. Was she supposed to talk about her profound fear that she would grow so comfortable at Vassar that her secret would burst out of her like a sneeze? That she would accidentally mention something about her background, her education, her family that would expose her true origins? Or should she admit that she was not supposed to be speaking to him at all? That he should stay away from her, because she was the thing the world reviled most: a Negro woman?

Instead, Anita looked up at his handsome face, smiling

when she saw the freckles on his short nose, and said, "I hope to be a professor after years more study. I'd like to teach Greek, perhaps even here, as I am happy at Vassar and very afraid to leave."

They walked away from the building, past the museum housing the hall of casts, the art gallery, and the museum of mineralogy and toward the school's stone western wall. Beyond that was the large lake across Raymond Avenue, the one the girls skated on when the water froze and created beautiful white veins on the surface.

Porter let Anita lead him around the campus and inquired more about her future plans, asking why she hoped to teach.

"Nearly forty percent of the students who graduate from Vassar go on to teach," she explained. "There are not many other professions open to women, are there? When I first applied to the school, I had my mind set on being a high school teacher, perhaps at the school where I prepped for the entrance exam. But living here, meeting female college professors, being exposed to their levels of learning, I changed my mind. I can't imagine another school as invested in women's education as Vassar. It's not just a finishing school masquerading as a college. The expansion of a woman's mind is the primary goal here, and the curriculum is just as vigorous as at a men's college. They want us to be intelligent, academic women first, and everything else comes second, quite the opposite of the priorities in the outside world. I feel like I've come alive here, Porter," she disclosed, surprising herself with the fervor in her voice. "I feel safe, and if I could hold on to that feeling forever, well, I would be very fulfilled."

"That sounds like a realistic goal," said Porter, watching her face become beautifully animated.

"I hope so," she replied. "Though I must confess, a small part of me still dreams of becoming a Greek translator, or perhaps an archaeologist, but I don't think those are possibilities for someone like me."

"Someone like you?"

"Female."

"I am awfully glad you're female," he said as the stone gate at the corner of Raymond and College View avenues came into sight. "And you shouldn't be scared to leave Vassar, as beautiful as it is. You're going to do wonderful things when you graduate, I can tell. And Vassar will be right here waiting for your return."

"I hope so," Anita said, thinking how much she liked being gated inside the Vassar world. "If I could just make it to Greece one day—to see Delphi, the Temple of Apollo at Bassae, the city of Rhodes—that would be a dream. If I have to leave Vassar, I'd like to see a little more of the world than Boston and Poughkeepsie."

Porter nodded. Anita guessed, from his expression, that he had already been to a great many places, but instead of boasting about his travels, he told her about his life in Chicago and his plans to work for his father's lumber company after graduating from Harvard.

"You would fall under Chicago's spell, Anita," he said. "The population has tripled since 1880; skyscrapers are rising up everywhere. There are languages spoken that you can't identify, people from all over the world, growth in every industry. It's fascinating. It doesn't have the trappings of the East Coast, the separation of the classes, the races, old money, new money. If you are industrious there, the world is open to you, you can make something of yourself."

"If you're an industrious man there," Anita corrected him.

"Yes, that's true," he said. "If you are an industrious man. Which I am. I know my father has already done very well for himself, but I want to do even better. I don't want to be known as the son of. Rather, I want my father to be known as the father of."

Anita beamed at his ambition and pointed to a stretch of wall where they could sit together.

"I'm excited to return next year," said Porter after he had laid out his suit jacket for Anita to rest on. "A great many Poles work for my father. I've been trying to learn the language at Harvard from some of the janitorial staff, but I'm not proving to be much of a linguist, unlike you. Still, Chicago, it's the future of America. So many people say we will never meet the standards of New York, but it's exactly the lack of those standards that makes it so exciting. There's a freedom to the city. It's because of that, the fact that there are so few conventions to be broken, that I plan to return."

"It all sounds wonderful," Anita replied. "I don't know much about it. We have a few girls here from Chicago, but they don't speak about it quite the way you do."

"You should speak with my mother. She likes to think of herself as the unofficial mayor. She'll lead the suffrage movement for the whole state of Illinois soon."

Anita nodded, thinking about her own mother, who had attended school for just two years in Virginia before the Civil War.

Despite that, Dora Hemmings knew what education meant for her children. Ever since her two eldest had shown academic promise, she and her husband, Robert, had lived frugally and saved for their children's studies. The tuition at Vassar was four hundred dollars a year. The Massachusetts Institute of Technology, where Frederick was a senior, was similarly expensive. Though younger than Anita, Frederick had not prepped for the entrance exam after high school and found himself entering college the same year as his sister. But unlike Anita, he had been awarded several scholarships, as he was not attending the school under false racial pretenses. The institute accepted Negro students, and Frederick was able to study chemistry. Anita never spoke of her brother, and the few times she had been forced to, she used the story that he was a white student at far-flung Cornell University. He, like Anita, was poised to graduate in the spring.

She thought of what her mother could have done if she'd had the opportunities Porter's mother had. Would her mother be a voice for suffrage if she was not supporting an overworked husband and working herself? If she were able to pass for white? Anita liked to think that she would be.

"Anita," said Porter, looking down at her. "You look pensive. Are you sure it's all right that I'm here? Am I making you uncomfortable? Or, perhaps, you don't have an interest in seeing me past one afternoon. Maybe I interpreted the day differently than you. I just—"

"No, Porter," she said, interrupting him. "I'm very glad you came to Vassar. I shouldn't be as glad as I am. It scares me quite a bit. But I'm very pleased you're here."

And with that reassurance, he leaned down and kissed her. The first kiss of her life. As his lips met hers, she stopped thinking of herself as Anita Hemmings the Negro—Anita Hemmings the liar, the coward, the dreamer—and let herself be simply Anita Hemmings, a girl being kissed under the pine trees on a beautiful autumn day.

CHAPTER 7

Anita's first three years at Vassar had been a spiral of in-
tense academia, but the fall of her senior year marked
an unexpected turn. A pile of elegant letters from Porter
Hamilton sat on her desk, their arrival now the pinnacle of
Anita's day. She did not stray from her classes or activities,
remaining the top student in Greek and lead soprano in the
choir and Glee Club, but the world felt as if it had suddenly
tilted. College ticked on, but because of Porter, and Lottie
too, Anita was enjoying Vassar more than she ever had.
Everything seemed more vibrant, alive, and full of possibilities.

But even more, she appreciated the sense of safety she
felt with Lottie and Porter in her life.

Their friendship gave her a feeling of immunity. Having
two such prominent people around her, she thought, meant
her secret was safer, as if being associated with a Hamilton
and a Taylor had whitened her even further.

"Anita!" shouted Lottie, causing Anita to spin around in
the warm water she was immersed in. Lottie, Caroline, and
Belle had burst into the Alumnae Gymnasium swimming
room, where Anita had just completed a lesson.

"The sophomores have changed their plans and are planting the class tree today," exclaimed Lottie. "Those little fresher spies are positive that they're planting on Friday, so the sophomores are going to blitz them and do it today. Get changed quickly. We have to head to the laboratory and help them. I've never seen a freshman class with more spies than 1900!"

"But I thought the sophomores were going to do it very late? Everyone said two o'clock in the morning," Anita said, struggling to clamber out of the swim tank with her long wool bathing suit sticking to her body.

"Not so," said Lottie shaking her head. "I am the tree master at this school. Not one freshman was at our ceremony, remember?"

"Of course," said Anita, who had been quite unaware that the successful staging of their secret tree ceremony had been Lottie's doing.

"Come on, Anita!" said Belle, unfolding a towel for her friend and walking with her to change. "We have to help the poor sophomores. As a class they really lack the deceit and trickery of 1897."

Anita, the most deceptive of all, changed quickly, stepped around the girls flocking upstairs to Philalethean Hall for play practice, and followed her friends to the Vassar Brothers Laboratory.

There were many traditions the Vassar classes took very seriously, and one of the most important of those was the planting of the class tree. It was done during sophomore year, at a secret time on a secret day, and the role of the freshman class was to try to foil their plans and attend the ceremony. The sophomores would go so far as to perform mock ceremonies with sickly trees and post notices around campus advertising fraudulent times and days. But this sophomore class had proved itself insufficiently cunning and now needed senior assistance to thwart the freshmen.

"We are to distract those nosy 1900s so the sophomores can make it from Strong Hall to the lake," said Lottie.

"And how will we distract them, fearless leader?" asked Belle, raising her skirts slightly and trotting alongside Lottie. Belle was tall and athletic, a star on the class of 1897 basketball team, but her appearance-consumed mother refused to buy her clothes conducive to movement.

"Bicycles," whispered Lottie, with big, enchanting eyes. "The answer to every problem is bicycles. A life on wheels for all! I even bought a special hat for the occasion." She reached into her bag for a straw hat with a straight brim and a navy blue ribbon tied around it. "One cannot be duplicitous without the right headwear."

Belle, Caroline, and Anita stopped, looked at each other's bare heads, and all reached for Lottie's hat.

"You three leave the duplicity up to me!" Lottie said, guarding it. "I just need your help pedaling. So much pedaling until we emerge with legs like gladiators."

The four of them walked past the laboratory to a wide space where several cherry-red bicycles were set upright. Five girls, all freshmen, were already inspecting them.

"Are these yours?" asked Flora Dean, the freshman class treasurer, who had come to Vassar all the way from California. She looked at Lottie, the person everyone knew as the most likely to own the nicest things.

"Why, yes, they are!" said Lottie, so gaily that Belle shot her a look warning her to tone it down. "We're having our October meeting of the Vassar chapter of the National Ladies Bicycling Club today, and you're just in time."

The freshmen swallowed Lottie's plot like a piece of warm French cheese. Lottie immediately hopped on one of them and started circling round the freshmen, even managing to pedal without holding on to the handlebars.

"Lottie! You will break all your teeth!" cried Caroline.

"Never!" screamed Lottie before falling off. She stood up unconcerned, wiped her dress, and motioned for the others to join her. Anita, who had never ridden a bicycle, merely sat on the seat of one and posed the way she had seen it done in pictures.

"I'm the president of the bicycling club, and today is the day when the freshmen can join up," Lottie explained. "You should round up your friends and become a part of Vassar's most exclusive society."

At the prospect of being in a new club founded by Lottie Taylor, the girls ran off to Main and Strong and came back with a large group. Lottie spent the next hour attempting to do tricks with her bicycle, only falling on her head one more time, but managing to keep a great many freshmen entertained. With all the commotion centered far from the stretch between Strong and the lake, the sophomores were able to plant their tree in peace.

At dinner that evening, Lottie, Caroline, Anita, and Belle were hailed as heroes by the sophomores. Lottie stood up on her dining chair to curtsy, her ostrich feather tucked into her coiffure, despite the loud exclamations of horror from the lady principal.

"We really should consider hiring a mute lady principal," Belle whispered. "This one makes such a racket."

Though the girls feared the lady principal, as she was in the habit of criticizing their table manners, and chided them when they did not wear plain dress, they also recognized her as the president's closest aid, and the person who set the character of the college. She served as confidante to many of the underclassmen, but by the time the women had reached their senior year, they did their very best to avoid her and her observant eye.

"Ladies, I am going to be president of this school one day," said Lottie, stepping back down. "And the first thing I will do is make the position of lady principal redundant. The second thing I will do is devote less money to ridiculous trinkets like this spoon holder," she said holding up the small silver utensil. "Does every girl really need a spoon holder in college?"

"I'm quite attached to my spoon holder," said Belle, clutching it in her hand and looking fondly at the silver and china room, which was connected to the dining room. "Don't take it away."

"Spoon holders or not," Anita broke in, "a very good president you would make."

After dinner and chapel were over, the girls retired to lounge in the senior parlor, still relishing the privilege of having their own class-dedicated space, redecorated, as was done every year, just for them.

"Lottie!" said Lillian Lovejoy, who lived in their hall and was sitting on a small divan near the Steinway piano surrounded by four other girls. "And all the Gatehouse group, just in time. Come and sit with us. Annie Chase's mother sent her the funniest little newspaper clipping."

Anita was one of four girls from Massachusetts in the senior class, as was Annie Chase of Fall River, a few hours south of Boston. Anita had kept her distance from Annie and the other Massachusetts girls during her three years at Vassar, not wanting to speak about the state she'd seen so little of or have them inquire about her life in Boston. Anita was sure they would have family in the city. That was why her first friend at Vassar had been Caroline Hardin. Anita deemed Syria a safe distance from Massachusetts.

Lottie crossed to the group, treading lightly on the Oriental rugs that had just been placed artistically around the room, and the rest followed.

"My mother cut this out of the *New York Tribune* because she saw the word *Vassar* in it," Annie said. "She was traveling through New York calling on a Vassar graduate at the time, so the coincidence had her in a frenzy. You should see her letter that accompanied it. It's eight pages long."

"She'll spare you that horror," said Lillian, lifting up the clipping to show the newcomers a photograph of a small Negro child. "It's all about a woman who adopted this funny little Negro baby and plans on sending it to Vassar in twenty years time."

"Here, hand it back to me," said Annie. "I'll read it aloud." She sat up straight and waited until Lottie and Caroline had moved behind her for a better view of the photo.

Anita stayed standing, staring at the group, until she felt Belle's hand tug her to the floor with the others.

"The headline is 'MRS. GRANNIS'S PICKANINNY WAIF MAY GO TO VASSAR.'" Annie looked at the picture again, holding it close to her nose. "Now isn't that extraordinary? And the article goes as follows. 'Little Christian League Woodwea [*sic*] is the adopted daughter of Mrs. Elizabeth B. Grannis of No. 33 East Twenty-Second Street. Christian League, or "Tummy" as she is familiarly called, is a genuine little pickaninny, as brown as a mud pie, with the bow legs and kinky head of the typical African baby. She is just three years old and a tot of many accomplishments.'"

"Black as the night sky is more like it," interrupted Lillian from her perch next to Annie.

"The storyteller is still telling, Lillian," said Annie, tapping the article with her index finger.

"Did that woman really name her child Christian League?"

said Gratia Clough, laughing loudly. "Is she unsound? I understand one's devotion to one's religion, but this woman has an air of mental illness. Little Christian League's skin color is the least of her problems."

"Tummy is not much of an improvement," said Lillian. "Sounds like me after two plates of dessert."

"The storyteller is still telling!" said Annie again. "How do these professors keep you all quiet?" She took up the paper and read faster. "'Dressed up in a fantastic colored garment and a Fourth of July cap made of flags, she sang and danced before the mirror, lost in admiration for her own reflection, and looking much like an organ grinder's dancing monkey. She chats volubly, or, as her adopted mother exclaimed enthusiastically, '"She's a fine linguist and I'll match her physically and mentally with any child of her age in the country."'"

Annie stopped reading and looked up. "It does go on a bit but the most fascinating excerpt is at the end. The child's mother mutters on about sending her to the best kindergarten and then closes with this remark: 'I shall teach her to be above all snubs that may be offered on account of her color. I expect to send her to college, and I mean that she shall have the best advantages—go to Vassar, perhaps.'"

"Such lofty ambitions," said Belle. "With that ghastly name she's destined to do missionary work in Africa. Not that there's a thing wrong with that," she said, smiling at Caroline.

"I don't know," said Lottie, taking the paper from Annie. "It all sounds very bold of this woman, this Elizabeth Grannis. And I do admire daring people."

"You know who would not appreciate it if you adopted a Negro waif? Your mother," said Belle.

"Yes, Mrs. Taylor nearly faints when I give the street

children a few coins. I don't think she could stomach me bringing one in for tea. Or life."

"I don't think anything of it," said Gratia, standing up and moving to the piano. "Why shouldn't she be raised just like any other child and attend Vassar one day if she passes the exam? I'm sure the world will be a much different place in fifteen or twenty years. Personally, I have always believed in the equality of the races."

"I tend to agree," said her friend Marion Schibsby. "In fact, I hope she does make it here. I'll certainly come back to see that." Marion was from Omaha, Nebraska, and lacked some of the rigid views of the girls who had grown up on the East Coast. "I think it's up to women like us, educated women, to lead the charge in changing the perception of Negroes, especially Negro women. To call this poor child an organ grinder's monkey is just not correct. That newspaperman should be ashamed of himself. Talk like that is much of the reason that prejudices against the colored race exist."

"She is black, isn't she," said Caroline, leaning down to look at the photograph. "A coal black. The natives in Syria aren't near as black. And some of them have glorious green eyes. The children especially can look quite captivating."

Anita knew she should have commented on the child's skin color, like Caroline, or said something disparaging to join the conversation. She surely couldn't say anything audacious, as Marion had.

"Even though this was in a New York paper, all our mothers will probably read it eventually and send it our way," said Annie. "They are so involved in our Vassar lives."

No, thought Anita, my mother knows almost nothing of my Vassar life, except that I always behave with self-restraint.

Later that October evening, in their silk-draped parlor,

Anita and Lottie were discussing their afternoon adventure with the freshmen when a maid brought in a letter.

"I'm sorry, Miss Hemmings. I hadn't seen it in the messenger room this afternoon," she said apologetically in her thick Hudson Valley accent. Anita took it and thanked her, ripping it open and throwing the envelope down quickly. It was from her brother Frederick.

"It's not from Porter. My brother is coming to visit me tomorrow," she said to Lottie, who had come over and was peering at the top of the letter with interest. Anita normally would have lied to her, as she avoided all conversations about her family, but Lottie would have torn it out of her hands if she hadn't told her more as she read.

"Anita!" Lottie exclaimed, "You have a brother and you haven't said a thing about it? You're a devil! How old is this mysterious brother and is he as striking as you are? If so, I'm joining you for lunch in town, and I won't take no for an answer."

"What happened to handsome Henry?" Anita asked, angry with herself for opening the letter in front of Lottie and displeased that the maid had delivered it so late in the day. Anita couldn't afford to make any missteps, and with Frederick, there were ample chances for error.

Lottie walked over to the window, looking at the light from the Lodge spilling into the night. "What happened to Henry is that I haven't received a letter from him since the football game, so I suppose he has already forgotten about little old me down here in Poughkeepsie and has fallen in love with another." Lottie put her hand to her head and collapsed to the floor in a mock faint. She turned upside down so that her legs were high and exposed.

"I've heard this is a sexual position in India," she said, wiggling her feet.

"Lottie!" Anita said sharply. "Do not speak like that."

"Why not? Perhaps if I had at Harvard, Henry would have written."

"But you're still set on marrying him?" Anita asked.

"Of course!" Lottie said, jumping upright. "He's such a brute, it's hard not to be in love with him. He has a peasant-like quality that I really do find charming. I think it's from all that football. But he's not a peasant, he's from a very good New York family, which makes him a contender. I'll get him to look my way eventually. If he doesn't like this version of me, then I'll just reintroduce myself as someone else entirely. Men are awfully simple creatures. Can you imagine, I have them all figured out and I'm only twenty-two? What will I do with my time from now on?"

The next afternoon, when Anita was walking back to her room after Latin class, the halls feeling much colder with the fall peaking in the valley, one of the maids stopped her again.

"You have a note from a visitor, Miss Hemmings," said the maid, bending her covered head. "He is visiting from Cornell University and left word with the gatekeeper at the Lodge. Frederick Hemmings is his name."

"Yes, Leticia. Thank you. He is my brother," Anita clarified.

"Very good, miss," the maid said, handing Anita the note. Written in Frederick's neat hand was a letter asking his sister to meet him at the Smith Brothers restaurant on Market Street. Frederick had come to Vassar twice in the years before to check on Anita, but he had always been careful not to step on campus, always leaving a note at the Lodge instead. Anita glanced through the hallways around the parlor to make sure that Lottie wasn't lurking about, and when she confirmed she was alone, headed to town.

Though Anita, at twenty-four, was Frederick's older sister, he knew under what guise she was attending the college, and like the rest of her family, worried about her constantly. Despite his concern, he never stayed at Vassar long. The two knew the way a small community talked, and Frederick had darker skin than Anita. It was not dark enough to attract real attention, as both their parents had light complexions, but they still took every precaution they could.

Anita walked the few blocks to Smith Brothers, across the street from the large Nelson House Hotel, and saw Frederick in a far seat, barely visible in the window. He looked handsome and self-assured, his wavy hair neatly parted in the middle, his tailored suit new. Anita paused on the street in her simple brown school dress to enjoy the sophisticated figure he struck. Frederick saw her from the window and smiled brightly, nodding his head toward the door and standing as she came inside.

"Frederick! I'm overjoyed to see you," she said, embracing him. "How was the train journey down?"

"Anita, I'm so relieved you received my letter," he said. "I sent it rather last minute, and I was afraid I'd beat it to Poughkeepsie. I should have sent a telegram, but I didn't think to until I was on the train. I so wanted to come see you before the weather changed and before midsemester exams."

"It's no trouble at all. Your timing is wonderful. I was just beginning to get homesick. Did you take an early train?" she asked.

"No, I came down yesterday and spent the night in the little hotel, Dudley Cottage, on Raymond Avenue. I didn't want to bother you until morning."

"You're never a bother, Frederick. I'm so happy to see you," Anita said, her face alight. She knew this was the one conversation she would have all semester in which she could speak freely. She wanted to fully enjoy it.

"Are things going smoothly at school?" asked Frederick. "Are you still happy here?"

"I am," Anita replied. "I have a new roommate this year. Louise Taylor. Perhaps you've heard of the family. They live in New York. One of those big families that the papers make such a fuss about. 'Big' as in wealthy, not 'big' as in numerous."

"Taylor. Of course I know the name," said Frederick. "And that is going well?"

"Surprisingly, yes," Anita confirmed. "We attended the Harvard-Williams football game in September, and her father paid the fare for our journey. It was wonderful."

"You traveled to Cambridge with this Taylor girl?" Frederick tensed, and he leaned toward his sister with a stern expression. "I don't like that, Anita. Not a good decision at all."

Anita knew exactly what he meant. Do not travel to places where you interact with white men. Avoid forming close relationships of any kind. Be friendly, but do not be anyone's friend, especially not someone like Lottie Taylor. Frederick had always been more cautious than his sister when it came to interacting and befriending those outside the Negro community. His slightly darker skin, the fact that he had never passed as white for more than a few days, his reality of being a Negro student in a white world, and his naturally circumspect character meant he never dared take the risks his sister did. And he did not approve of her behavior when she acted in a way he wouldn't.

"It all went well, Frederick," she said sweetly. "I promise. Lottie would have thought me rude if I didn't go to Cambridge with her. And we had a lovely time."

"I should trust your judgment," Frederick said, taking a sip of his strong English tea. "But in this case I cannot. Please don't do something like that again. Stay on campus. Don't attend any more events with her. Certainly do not travel to New York with her, or become acquainted with her family. Keep a distance. Your work could suffer because of these unnecessary social commitments."

Anita nodded in apparent agreement.

"And how are things for you? At school? You look very well," she said, quick to change the subject.

"They're going fine. My classes are challenging, but as they should be. That's what we've worked so hard for, isn't it?"

"Absolutely it is. And at home? How is everyone?"

"Everyone misses you," said Frederick, his expression softening at the mention of family. "Mother worries about you, of course. And Father more than he will admit. He's added additional employment, more janitorial work, at night, just for this last year while we finish our schooling. He comes home very late, almost one in the morning most days. I can see the exhaustion becoming a part of him, bending his spine. He tells me not to be concerned, but I am. He's a slight man to begin with, and all his work is so physically demanding."

"Another employment?" said Anita, thinking about her already overworked father, tears forming behind her eyes. "I wish he wouldn't. I can take on additional tutoring hours. It doesn't pay very well, but it would help. Or perhaps I can find something more lucrative in town."

"No, Anita, you do not have time. You do enough already. He'll be fine for one more year, and so will you."

"I will be, Frederick," said Anita, knowing full well that her schedule did not allow for anything but the occasional tutoring. "Things are different this year. They're better."

"I'm glad to hear it," he said pushing his biscuits around his plate with a small fork. "I'm quite jealous that you are away, while I'm still in my childhood bedroom with Robert. I'm too old to be there with him, but I don't have a choice, do I?" He did not. The Institute of Technology had very limited campus housing, and the only living quarters, the residential fraternities, did not allow Negroes.

"It certainly isn't fair," Anita said, "but sometimes I wish that I was in your position. Being here, even though lately I've been quite happy, I have moments of crippling exhaustion. Just remembering to be this version of Anita Hemmings, it wears on me at times."

"I understand, but please don't yearn after my position," Frederick said. "Yes, there are men who are kind to me, but there are many who are not, who are hateful when they see me in classrooms." Anita thought of Lilly Taylor's words when they saw Alberta Scott on the Radcliffe campus, and the memory caused her stomach to flip.

"Of course," she said apologetically. "I forget sometimes, and I shouldn't."

Frederick sighed, refilling her teacup. "It's just different. I know you have your own challenges."

The siblings looked at one another: two driven, intelligent people living lives dictated by educational institutions and their rules. Frederick could attend school as a Negro but suffered from the racism that went with it. And Anita managed to attend school as a white student while never being allowed to break from her charade. She smiled at him, wishing he could stay with her for more than a few hours. When they were growing up in their small row house, they had always been a pair, studious from the start, sharing one singular goal: a college diploma.

"You will come home when you graduate, won't you?"

asked Frederick. That had always been the family's expectation, and Anita knew it.

"I suppose so," she said, reluctantly. "Though, if possible, I would like to continue my schooling." It was a dream that in recent months had crystallized for Anita, and finally seemed attainable. "I would like very much to be a professor, hopefully here."

"In Greek?" he asked.

"Yes. Maybe Latin as well. And Professor Macurdy, our Greek professor, said there might be an opportunity for me to go to Greece to study at the American School of Classical Studies at Athens after I graduate. Many of the other girls will be in Europe—"

"That is not something you can do," said Frederick, bluntly. "Even if there was a scholarship to be had, Anita, that kind of attention would not be something you would want to bring on yourself."

"And what is it that I want to bring on myself, Frederick?" she asked, trying to keep her voice down despite her rising irritation.

"A nice quiet life," he said. "Stability. But anonymity. We've always said, after you came here, there was a certain way you had to live, and gallivanting around Europe with Vassar graduates, even if it is a continuation of your schooling, is not a possibility."

"I'm doing everything that has been asked of me," Anita replied. At times she detested her brother's levelheadedness. He didn't know what it was like to be at Vassar, to be treated like someone special, with an entrée to the intellectual world, and then be unable to pursue any path because in nine months time she was required to start living a small, anonymous life.

"It is not what others ask of you, but what you ask of yourself, what you have always wanted," Frederick retorted.

"Our parents are supportive. I am supportive. But remember, the driving force behind the educational career of Anita Hemmings has always been Anita Hemmings."

Anita glowered at her brother, but she knew he was right. She had decided on Vassar for herself years before, the day she heard it mentioned in church. No one had suggested it to her.

"I know how hard you've been working, how modestly you've been living," said Frederick. "But it can't be something that just ends when you graduate. It has to always be like this. You simply can't excel past a certain point, and you are fully aware that Vassar is your limit in this world. I appreciate your desire to attend graduate school, to become a professor, but it's not a safe route for you. Teaching at the grade school or high school level like you always planned is much more sound."

As Anita turned the negative thought over in her mind, the door opened and Lottie burst in, every patron in the restaurant turning to look at her. She was powdered and perfect and obviously ready to play the starring role of the afternoon.

"Anita! There you are!" she boomed. "I was strolling down Market Street with every intention of purchasing a new Paul E. Wirt Fountain Pen and perhaps some more Lautier's Quintessence of Violets, when whom do I see through the window but my beautiful roommate and the handsome man I assume is her brother?"

Quickly catching Anita's eye, Frederick stood up and offered his chair to Lottie.

"Yes, I'm Frederick Hemmings, Anita's brother. You must be Miss Taylor. I'm very pleased to meet you. My sister has been talking unremittingly about you, and I insist that you join us."

"Well, if you insist, it would be rude to decline," said Lottie, taking Frederick's chair. "And call me Lottie, please. Everyone does. Except my younger brother John, who calls me things I won't repeat in polite company."

Another chair was brought for Frederick, and he ordered Lottie Darjeeling tea and a variety of afternoon desserts. Frederick, like his sister, knew to spend money only when someone important was looking. Frugality was imperative, except when a point had to be made.

"So your sister did mention me, after all. I'm glad," said Lottie, taking Anita's hand. "She is my very best friend. Did she tell you we were barely acquainted until we became roommates, but now we are inseparable and I'm sure will always remain so?"

"She's very lucky," said Frederick.

"Oh, we both are, Frederick. We're the happiest seniors in Main Building." She set her teacup in front of her daintily and placed her lace-covered hands on each other. "Now tell me, Frederick. What is Cornell like? Is it a horrible place? Very liberal, isn't it? Is it true you attend classes with women?"

"Classes? Yes. There are female students, though not many, and while they have far more stringent housing rules, and many focus their studies on home economics or teaching, they do take several classes with the men." Frederick was an expert on Cornell, even though he had never seen Ithaca.

"Do they now?" said Lottie, lighting a cigarette. Smoking was something she did when she seemed bent on shocking. "I should love that. How lucky they are to take the same lessons as male students, not frittering away their time on classes like hygiene. I assume you are not required to take hygiene at Cornell?"

Frederick looked at her with a certain admiration and laughed. "No, that we certainly are not."

"I'm glad it's only the students of women's colleges who have to deal with such frivolities. Why should one engage in an extra science course when they can study hygiene? Every single freshman has to take the wretched class here, mind you, lectured on the subjects of dress, exercise, bathing, food, work, and rest. You'd think every woman would have learned how to take a bath and cut a steak by the time she was twenty-odd. And my anatomy is not as foreign to me as all these dear professors would like to think." Lottie's cigarette went out and Frederick leaned over, close to her, and relit it. "Now tell me, Frederick," Lottie purred, "are you here to check on Anita? Word travels fast, does it not? I imagine she's already the talk of Cornell, too."

The Hemmings siblings looked at Lottie as if her hat were on fire.

"And why would Anita be the talk of Cornell?" asked Frederick. Like his sister, he was clearly trying to keep his composure, but Anita knew where Lottie was headed and there was no way she could stop her.

"Well, if she's not already, she will be soon. At least among the girls," Lottie said mischievously. "Gossip does make it to Ithaca along with all those blizzards, does it not? Yes, I'm sure it does, and this will travel up there posthaste." She beamed at Anita and put her hand on Frederick's. "Your beautiful sister happens to have the undivided attention of Porter Hamilton, of the very well-to-do Chicago Hamiltons. Lumber millionaires. He was absolutely smitten with her at the Harvard-Williams football game, and he's already called on her once at Vassar."

"And did my sister see him at Vassar?" said Frederick, without looking at Anita.

At Frederick's change in tone, Lottie checked Anita's expression, but Anita was sitting motionless, praying for Lottie to stop speaking.

"Well . . . she did," said Lottie, with less zeal. "But he came unannounced. No letter or telegram. He just tromped into the visitors' parlor and demanded to see her. Demanded in a gentlemanly fashion. Your sister couldn't leave him there to rot, now, could she?" said Lottie.

"No, I suppose she couldn't," said Frederick, lowering his voice.

"My, my," said Lottie, fanning herself with a linen napkin. She placed one of her monocles on her left eye for effect. "Who knew Anita had such a protective brother? It might not be much fun for her, but I find it charming. I appreciate a man who looks after his family. But as someone who knows a bit about these things, let me tell you, Frederick, that Porter Hamilton isn't one to be worried about. If he's showing interest in Anita, he's serious. He hasn't flirted with anyone the past three years, besides a dance or two. And his family is very highly regarded in Chicago. I'd say he's one of the most eligible men at Harvard in the class of '97, so you can't be too cross with your sister."

"My sister is here to study and graduate as close to the top of her class as she can," said Frederick, putting down his cup with a rattle. "But no, as you say, I can't be too cross with her."

Lottie, thought Anita, would never have any idea how angry Frederick was with her at that moment, for she, Anita, had done the unthinkable. She had let a reputable white man become interested in her, and then had encouraged him by seeing him a second time. She knew that as soon as she was alone with her brother, he wouldn't be able to hold his tongue, and she would have to listen because he was right. She couldn't see Porter again. That's what Frederick would tell her. And she'd been aware of that from the beginning.

"Let's leave all this talk of romance alone, shall we?" said Lottie, with a sympathetic glance Anita's way. "Tell me more about Cornell, Frederick."

"It's frigid half the year," he said, his tone light again. "What else interests you, Lottie?" he asked. "Politics?"

"Domestic policy tends to bore me," said Lottie, nodding yes as Frederick offered her more tea. "I'm more interested in foreign policy. If I could, I would go straight into the Foreign Service and work as a diplomat in Asia. We, as in the country, have an envoy extraordinary in Japan now, one very lucky Edwin Dun, and he is but a rancher from Ohio, of all places. Can you imagine, of all the men to represent the United States in a country newly open to foreigners, they choose a rancher. It's ghastly."

"Lottie is very taken with Japan," Anita explained to Frederick, happy at the turn the conversation had taken.

"Now, I don't speak the language yet, but I *have* visited and can say, 'This fish is delicious' in their dialect: '*Kono sakana wa oishii desu,*'" Lottie went on. "Father has started frantically collecting the art. He's excellent at staying ahead of the movements in the art market. 'Respectable for a man from Pittsburgh,' he always declares when assessing his collection, and now, it's nothing but Japanese art for him. He even sold a small Thomas Cole and replaced it with an intricate woodblock print of naked courtesans doing the most shocking things. When I first saw the print, I held it upside down, but my father assured me that the woman in the center was supposed to be in such a position. They call them geishas there. As you can imagine, my poor mother was beside herself."

Lottie proceeded to elaborate on what was and was not in vogue in the art world, to which Frederick nodded politely, as he did when he knew nothing of a subject.

When Lottie's disquisition had run its course, she put both her hands on the table and said, "Well! I think it's time I left the Hemmings siblings to themselves. Thank you for letting me impose on your tête-à-tête. I hope I wasn't too much of a bore. I so wanted to meet you, Frederick. I knew Anita would keep you hidden away if I didn't do a little spying on my own. That's just her style, isn't it?"

Anita opened her mouth to protest, but Lottie winked at her. "Don't take offense, my dear, we can't all be the hurricane. You're more of a light drizzle." She looked at Frederick and said, "Will you be a gentleman and escort me back to campus? Anita, you don't mind, do you? It's just a few steps."

"I'd be happy to," said Frederick, before his sister had time to answer. "Anita, will you order more Darjeeling? I'll return shortly."

Lottie beamed at her friend and went off with Frederick. Anita ignored her brother's request and ordered a root beer. She wanted to follow them and listen to every word, but she knew it wasn't necessary. Frederick was more careful with her reputation than she was.

When he returned, as Anita knew they would be, the first two words out of his mouth were "Porter Hamilton."

"Anita, I don't even have to say it, do I?"

"Of course you don't, Frederick," she said, refusing to look at him.

"I hope this disaster isn't out of hand yet. Tell me it hasn't gone far."

"Far?" she said. "I've only seen him twice. Once at Harvard and once here."

"And there haven't been letters?"

Anita looked away.

"There can't be any more, Anita," he warned, his voice stern with anger. "You are conscious of that. It's very dangerous. And weak on your part. You are fully aware that you can't behave this way."

"Fully aware," she mumbled.

"You could ruin everything you've worked for. You can't form relationships, even friendships, with anyone. You've known that for three years and now you decide to abandon caution? In your very final year? What has possessed you to act that way?"

She sat up and lowered her voice. "Frederick, I mean no disrespect, but you have no idea what the position I am in is like."

With a nervous glance at the other customers, Frederick settled the bill and motioned for his sister to finish her root beer and leave the restaurant with him.

They walked outside into the brisk October air, down Raymond Avenue to a quiet corner a few paces from campus. Frederick gazed around to make sure there was no one nearby and suggested they walk a bit farther.

When they hadn't passed another person for several minutes, Anita said as quietly as she could, "Frederick, you will never fully understand my situation. You, as a Negro, can speak to women like us and no one will condemn you. I can't converse with Negro men, and I can't speak to white men, either. I can't make white friends, nor can I make colored friends. Bessie Baker is at Wellesley, and I don't dare send her a letter in fear of having to acknowledge that I know her. Here I am white, Frederick, just like every other student. And I have to act that way. I need to dance with white men at proms, I need to be civil to my white roommate. I need to keep up the act that I have been keeping up successfully for three years. You are allowed to have your own identity. I have to create mine."

"I have an identity that keeps me completely excluded from my peers," said Frederick, raising his voice. "I don't room on campus, and you know why. I do not have friendships with other students. They do not invite me to football games or their homes. Some of them flinch when they have to work in the laboratory with me. It pains them to be near me. Embarrasses them. It's only when I'm out of Boston, out of our Negro world, that I know what it's like to be treated the way you are treated here every single day."

"You speak as if it's a gift!"

"It is a gift," said Frederick, pitilessly. "Do not ruin it for yourself. Do not see Porter Hamilton again. Do not write to him. Do not dance with him. Do not enter a room that he is already in. Excise him from your life immediately."

Anita didn't respond, and they walked in silence, in anger, until they were close to campus again.

"I didn't come here to scold you, Anita. I came here to make sure you were continuing to do well. To see you."

"You saw me," she replied. "And I'm glad you came, Frederick, but I've been handling myself here for three years. I think I can manage for nine more months."

"I am sure you can. Just remember, you are not allowed the same luxuries as every other girl here. You can never let your guard down. Don't let the affections of Porter Hamilton undermine all of your hard work."

"I know," Anita snapped. "Frederick, I know."

She thought of her conversation on campus with Porter and how progressive he was. He wasn't like the white men Frederick knew, or the men they read about. Porter's parents, the city where he lived, and the new ideals that some Americans had begun to believe had shaped him into the kind of man she knew Frederick would approve of if he would only broaden his position.

But she did not want to let Frederick's disapproval stop the movements of her heart. After all, her brother would not return to campus again that year, but she was sure Porter would.

When Frederick had collected his things from the hotel and boarded the crowded streetcar for the rail station, Anita walked back to campus and up to her room. Lottie was sitting at her desk, writing a letter.

"It's to your brother," she said, without turning around. "He's dashing, isn't he?"

"Is he? I have a lot of trouble thinking about him as anything but my younger brother."

"He doesn't look much younger. He has quite a mature face. A wonderful jawline."

"I'm just one year his senior," said Anita, walking over to try to read Lottie's letter. "But that shouldn't make him any more striking."

Lottie turned around. Her hair was down and falling in big curls around her shoulders. She looked like everything Anita was not. "Anita, he certainly is striking. Just like you. It's those hypnotic Hemmings eyes. You should be forced to wear eyeglasses. How are the rest of us to keep up?" She turned back to her letter when Anita sat down. "It would be rude of me not to write him something about how lovely it was to make his acquaintance, so I'm doing so before I forget. Not that I would forget. You aren't upset, are you?"

"Of course not. I'm glad you could meet."

"So am I," said Lottie, folding her paper and reaching for an envelope, which she had Anita address. It was the fashion for the women to have their own stationery pressed before they arrived at the college, with a gold-embossed vc, their class year, and a poignant Latin phrase underneath. Lottie had already gone through fifteen sets in three years.

Anita folded the blanket on their little velvet divan and went into her bedroom. From the window, she could see girls coming in for the night, walking toward Strong Hall, happy and laughing. She hadn't exaggerated her words to her brother. She had flourished at school for three years, trying desperately to be another Vassar girl amid the throng. But now she had Porter Hamilton; she was no longer part of the throng, and she could never go back.

CHAPTER 8

By November, the cardinal leaves of autumn were browning and falling rapidly, and the Vassar campus was taking on its winter appearance, crinkling around the edges like burning pages of a book. But while the Northeast was sliding into its winter silence, Anita was doing anything but. In her senior year, protected by Lottie and the storied world she represented, and with the name Porter Hamilton now linked to hers, Anita had started to shed her long-ingrained caution, despite her brother's warning. In the two months she'd been back on campus, she was quickly becoming the person she had dreamed she might be at Vassar.

Anita was still exchanging daily letters with Porter, who had yet to make another trip down to Poughkeepsie but had promised he would come for the Phil Day dance on December 4. Anita had read his letters until the paper felt thin, and then they grew even thinner from Lottie reading them, too. She often plucked them out of Anita's hand when she was done, lying down on her bed with them as if they had been addressed to her.

Porter often wrote to Anita not only of his days at Harvard, full of club activities and sporting events, but also of his Chicago life and what he was looking forward to after graduation. He wrote about riding the elevated railway system with his mother for the first time and how much they both loved it. Passionate about all forms of transportation, when Anita told him about cycling around campus on Lottie's new bicycles, he wrote back and said he could not wait to show her what a wheelman he was and that they could bicycle together not only on the grand avenues of the city but along Lake Michigan. The city was expanding faster than any other city in American history, he explained to Anita, and he couldn't wait to go back and be a big part of the reason why. Anita imagined herself right next to him, living a life marked by freedom, just like his mother had. With every letter she received, the idea of Chicago, of continuing her education there, of a life with Porter, became more vibrant, more real.

If the circumstances were different, Lottie might have been jealous of the attention Porter was paying Anita, but it was apparent that she had her sights fixed very close to her new circle, squarely on Anita's brother. Lottie brought the same passion to everything she did. So, just as she had taken to Anita as the sister she never had, she focused her romantic aspirations on Frederick. She had written him several letters, and though he had only responded to a few, Henry Silsbury of Harvard was quickly fading from the scene. He had proved to be a terrible correspondent, and Lottie had her mind set on taking Frederick to the Phil Day dance. Meanwhile, not only was Anita more than aware that Lottie and Frederick were exchanging letters; she was playing a hand in it.

Since Frederick and Anita's freshman year, the two had used a go-between at Cornell. A friend of Anita's from Boston who taught in Ithaca knew of Anita's situation and allowed Frederick to use her address. She would then forward his mail to him so that no one could discover that the white Frederick Hemmings who pretended to attend Cornell was actually the colored Frederick Hemmings who was a senior at the Massachusetts Institute of Technology.

Frederick had written to his sister and explained to her that he was responding to Lottie, as little as he could but still a few letters, and that he planned to stop as soon as he felt it was appropriate. As hypocritical as Anita felt her brother's actions were, she understood that Lottie was not someone you could handle abrasively. So the letters passed between them, and Anita did her best to keep Lottie's affections for Frederick subdued while she quietly allowed hers for Porter to soar.

With the late autumn well settled in at Vassar, the season's next excitement was the annual class trip to Mohonk Mountain House, twenty miles west, in New Paltz. This Arcadian excursion was one that Vassar students took twice during their time in Poughkeepsie, first as freshmen, then again in their senior year. The class of 1897 still reminisced fondly about their trip in '93 and they were twittering with excitement as the second outing inched closer. With Vassar's growing numbers—the class of '97 alone had 104 members—the visit had to be divided in two, half the girls traveling in October and the remaining in November. Anita and Lottie had been assigned to the November 8 trip and had been listening to the first group's highly embellished accounts of Catskills climbs since their outing on October 17.

Anita had just one class left before she could retire to her room and start discussing the next day's excursion with Lottie, Belle, and Caroline. She hurried into Professor Franklin's advanced Latin class, her surprise favorite of the semester, and set up her inkstand on the large mahogany table. Susan Braley Franklin was one of six female teachers at Vassar with a doctoral degree, something Anita had dreamed of attaining since her freshman year. The two had spoken at length about Miss Franklin's path to her advanced degree, and the teacher had seemed sure Anita could achieve the same success. But today she stopped her student as she came into the room, the first to arrive.

"Miss Hemmings, if you're not pressed, could you stay a few moments after class today? I've been meaning to discuss something with you," she said.

"Is it about my last translation?" Anita asked, suddenly panicked that her strong grade was in jeopardy.

"No, no. Nothing to be concerned about, Miss Hemmings. I'd just like a quick word."

"Yes, Miss Franklin," said Anita, trying to sound confident.

The hour-long analysis of the poems of Propertius and Catullus moved as swiftly as a frozen pond. Anita had never before had a class in which she didn't contribute one word to the discussion. She listened to Hortense Lewis speak knowledgeably about Propertius and looked on blankly as Belle Tiffany presented the influence of the Alexandrian school on Catullus's work, a summary they had written together the day before. Belle looked to Anita to share the points she crafted, but Anita's dark eyes were glassed over in distress.

After the class had concluded, Anita tried her best to appear deep into her translation of Catullus's poem 61. She hoped Belle would not linger as they often walked to the senior parlor together following class. Belle touched her shoulder as she walked out, aware of the academic trances that Anita could find herself in when it came to dead languages. Miss Franklin waited until Anita closed her book, never one to interrupt the study of Latin, then walked over and shut the door before perching herself in front of Anita's wooden table.

"Miss Hemmings, let's put away the work now. I don't want to speak to you about your Latin."

"Thank you, Miss Franklin," said Anita, packing away her translations.

Miss Franklin assumed a relaxed position, almost as if she were going to sit with her legs folded on her desk.

"Miss Hemmings, you prepared for Vassar at Northfield Seminary, did you not?" she asked. "Dwight Moody's school in Massachusetts?"

"Yes, I did," Anita confirmed, searching her brain for the relevance of that to her Latin class. Her academic shortcomings were few, and they certainly were not in the classics. "Do you think they did a poor job preparing me?"

"No, of course not," said Miss Franklin, fidgeting with the sleeve of her heavy black dress. "I don't mean to imply that at all. You are one of the strongest Latin students in '97. I do hope you'll pursue your study after graduation, if Greek does not inspire you more."

Anita nodded, to indicate that she intended to pursue one of the two.

"I just hoped to speak about your time at Northfield, as I have a very close friend working as an instructor there. Perhaps you had her as a teacher when you were a Northfield student in '92? A Miss Emma Bassett. Did you happen to become acquainted with her?"

"I did know her, yes," Anita answered. Miss Bassett had been a well-liked teacher at Northfield Seminary. She had taught Anita's class on Cicero, which she had taken along with French, geometry, and algebra for the year she was there.

"I recently met Miss Bassett at a lecture in Albany,

and we, after much discussion of the teaching of Latin at the high school level, turned to the topic of the students at Northfield. She mentioned that there was a Negro alumna, very strong in Latin, whom she is still in contact with, a Miss Elizabeth Baker, now a student at Wellesley. She was also there in '92, I believe, and the following year as well."

At the sound of her closest friend's name, Anita stiffened before making her own effort to appear relaxed.

"Yes, Elizabeth Baker," said Anita, making sure not to use her friend's nickname, Bessie, the only one Anita ever used for her. "Our time there overlapped."

"That is what I heard," said Miss Franklin. "Miss Bassett mentioned that not only did your time overlap at Northfield, but that you roomed together for a year. That you requested to room with Miss Baker, the Negro daughter of a traveling cracker salesman."

Anita felt the blood rush to her face. It was true. She had requested to room with Bessie. She'd attended Northfield as a white student, having always intended to apply to Vassar from there, but she had asked to room with Bessie and the school hadn't balked at the idea. There was no other self-described Negro woman in the class of '92, and the school authorities could not place Bessie with a white woman unless one volunteered. They were thrilled to have such a volunteer in Anita Hemmings.

Anita looked up and saw Miss Franklin's concerned face waiting for an answer. She could see clearly that Miss Franklin, a strict instructor who hailed from a small town in Maine and spoke often of growing up in a puritanical household, was very surprised to hear such an allegation. Anita considered fabricating a story, saying that the professor at Northfield was gravely mistaken. Or she could leave out large strands of the truth, portraying her time at Northfield like a moth-eaten garment.

"Miss Bassett is correct," she said, hoping her face looked as calm as her voice sounded. "I did request to live with Miss Baker. I made her acquaintance when visiting the school a year before and found her most agreeable, despite her strains of Negro blood." In truth, Anita and Bessie had been acquainted for more than a decade and had decided together to attend Northfield.

Miss Franklin started, and Anita looked out the window, wishing she were on the other side of it.

"It's very surprising," said the professor. "It's a school that admits the other races, is it not? I imagine there were other Negroes for Miss Baker to room with, instead of a white woman like you. And one choosing to do so? It's unheard-of."

"It is not unheard-of at Northfield," said Anita, thinking back on her decision to claim she was Caucasian before entering. If she had intended to apply to Wellesley like Bessie Baker, she would not have had to. "Dwight Moody, as you may know, thinks of all the races as equals. He has been a friend to the Indian and the Negro since the founding of the school. But in truth, I was fond of Elizabeth and thought her character was more important than her race, in this instance." Anita was starting to sound defensive, though she desperately didn't want to.

"That's extremely modern of you, Miss Hemmings, but dangerous, too. I dare say, if the girls here knew about it, they would be shocked. Some might even ostracize you. You are without a doubt the only girl here who has ever roomed with a Negro, even one whom Miss Bassett described as high yellow."

"I imagine I am," said Anita, thinking about her current

roommate and her roommates past. Now they, too, had roomed with a girl who could be described as high yellow.

"When Miss Bassett told me about this unique circumstance between you and Miss Baker, I was astonished, Miss Hemmings. You've always struck me as such a serious, conservative girl. Not one who would make rash, unsound decisions."

"But do you not see it as Christian charity, as I did?" said Anita, hoping to save herself through religion.

Religion had helped her many times, Anita thought to herself, remembering the note of recommendation that her Trinity Church reverend had penned on her behalf for entrance into Northfield. He, a staunch abolitionist, had been the only one she called upon to vouch for her character, and he had not mentioned her race, which allowed her to start passing for the sake of education. He, thought Anita, envisioning the tall, imposing man whose sermons she had listened to during her teenage years, was a model of the kind of charity she hoped Miss Franklin had within her.

"Of course, Christian charity," said her teacher, briefly acknowledging her point. "I admit it was noble of you, especially at such a young age. So many other women in their teens and twenties would not see such a decision as the Christian thing to do. The truth is, there are limits to everything, even Christian charity."

Anita nodded but maintained her level gaze. Miss Franklin was a kindly, idealistic person, she knew, but she was trying to understand something Anita could never let her unravel.

"I have been an active member of the Young Women's Christian Association here at Vassar, and much of my adult belief system in Christianity stems from the work of Northfield's Mr. Moody," Anita said. Her voice sounded strong, but every fiber in her body felt ready to give up. Was it possible, she wondered, that Miss Franklin had an inkling of her true identity? If she had, she would have spoken plainly, Anita was sure of it. In the lecture room, just the two of them, she would have said the word. *Negro. I think you, too, are a Negro. You are a high-yellow Negro, and you do not belong here. No sensible white woman would ask to room with a Negro, so it must be that you are one, too.* But that was not said and, Anita prayed, not thought, either.

"Do you not believe in the separation of the races, Miss Hemmings? That a Negro should move aside for a white person when passing on the street? That they should not share our facilities?" Miss Franklin asked, her fingers gripping her desk.

Anita tried to soften her expression, to imagine she was trying to fall asleep. Tension, in this case, could be the end of her.

"Elizabeth Baker was quite a different sort of Negro," she said, finally. "And so high yellow that it was easy to forget that she was a Negro."

Miss Franklin looked at her, and received dignified silence in return. It was plain that further explanation—and certainly no apology—would be given.

"That will be all, Miss Hemmings," the teacher said, looking down as though shaken by Anita's conviction. "And you can do away with that concerned expression. I won't speak of Miss Baker again."

"Thank you, Miss Franklin," said Anita, moving toward the door.

"Do you and she remain friendly?" Miss Franklin asked, delaying her.

"No, I'm afraid we don't," said Anita. Miss Franklin

nodded and dismissed her student, who rushed out the door, almost running into Lottie.

"Finally! I've been waiting here for hours. Or what felt like hours," said Lottie, pushing herself off the wall she'd been resting against. "Belle said you remained in Latin class after the bell, and I said, 'Anita Hemmings? My Anita Hemmings? Better at Latin than Agelastus? It can't be.' So I trotted over here to check, but there you were, locked behind the door like Eustache Dauger. I pressed my ear quite hard against it, but I couldn't hear a thing. If you ask me, they are going too far with these fire doors. So Anita, did you survive? Or are you failing Miss Franklin's class? Is a meeting with Prexy Taylor on the horizon?" she asked, using the students' favorite nickname for the school president.

"I made it through," said Anita, as the two walked away. "It was just a brief discussion about post-Vassar life."

"Oh, no, not post-Vassar life." Lottie put her hand to her forehead and stumbled a few steps for added effect. She'd seen it done in *An Ideal Husband* onstage last fall and had wanted to imitate it since. "Let's just ignore that there is life post-Vassar and embrace the present. And speaking of embracing, look in front of us, that is Monsieur Jean Charlemagne Bracq. The dashing love of Sarah Douglas's life."

"Excuse me?" said Anita, surprised that Lottie would speak of a professor that way but pleased that her meeting with Miss Franklin had been forgotten. Men always trumped Latin.

"What?" said Lottie, surprised in turn by Anita's ignorance of campus gossip. "Don't tell me you didn't know. She's been in love with him since he first said '*Bonjour, Mademoiselle Douglas*' to her chaste ears in French literature class. Did you never hear the rumors? They were louder than a stampeding bull last year."

"I most definitely did not."

"Anita," said Lottie, stopping in mid-dramatic step to peer at her roommate. "What were you doing for the last three years? It's as if you were locked up in the attic of Main speaking Greek to the wall."

"That's not far off, except that I was a few floors below."

Lottie resumed her steps and Anita followed, because that's what her world had become, following Lottie's confident lead.

"Personally, I would like her far better if the rumors were true, but they can't be. Sarah's not the type to even kiss before an engagement. She must just lie there, all alone, and dream about her professor like Charlotte Brontë. What a bore. Kissing men is so much more interesting than thinking about kissing men."

"You live to shock, Lottie Taylor," said Anita, her laughter with Lottie serving as a welcome diversion after her alarming meeting. Anita hurried ahead of her and said, "Maybe one day, I'll shock you, too."

CHAPTER 9

With the long-anticipated Mohonk trip looming in less than twelve hours, Anita's dramatic detention slipped even further from her mind. Lottie, meanwhile, redirected all her energy into galvanizing the fourth floor of Main for its day of freedom outdoors.

As was the custom the day of the trip, the first bell went off at 5:45 A.M. and the two girls rushed through their morning routines, piling on thick dresses and cream-colored wool sweaters with their class year embroidered on the chest. Anita and Lottie savored the moment as they dressed. They would always be '97, but their time as part of a senior class on campus was ticking quickly by.

With their clothes layered artfully and their hats pinned to their heads, they ran down the stairs as soon as they saw the wagons approaching the drive around Fred's Nose. They burst out the doors, Anita's hand grasped in Lottie's.

"Come, Anita! We need to be in the front of the wagon!" Lottie screamed. They ran, their hats tilting off their heads, tripping on their skirts like youthful tumbleweeds.

"Don't you take that seat, Mary Chambers!" Lottie warned as they joined the three other girls on the first wagon. "I've had that very seat saved in my mind since freshman year."

"You're as childish as they come, Lottie Taylor," said Mary, moving one row back, but she was laughing. Everyone trod lightly around Mary because she was class president, except for Lottie. The roommates sat snugly together, their hands tight in their laps against the cold, ready to absorb every moment of the day's promised bliss.

"I'm so happy we are not on one of the barges. This is so much more amusing, isn't it?" said Lottie, bouncing up and down as the horses twitched and whinnied in their harnesses. "We had to go by wagon again, just like freshman year."

Anita nodded, eager for the convoy to pass through the Vassar gates. She had wanted to take a barge until this moment, since she had never been down the Hudson in one, but Lottie's passionate desire to re-create her freshman experience brought Anita to her side.

"Belle! Caroline! Here we are! Join us!" Lottie cried when she saw their friends coming out the big wooden doors of Main.

"Look at the pair of you in your class sweaters!" Caroline shouted. They, too, had followed the trend and layered college clothing over their dresses. The two climbed in with the help of the driver and were soon followed by Sarah Douglas and her roommate, Alice Sawyer.

"Oh, no, no," whispered Lottie to Anita. "In our wagon? Quickly, Anita, fake a fainting spell so we can move."

"I will not," she said, though she would have loved to.

Sarah and Alice took the last row in the wagon and picked up their conversation about the Southern Club's alumnae reception, which was to be held in the J Parlor the following week.

Anita listened with a mix of dread and fascination, but Belle's melodic alto broke out, overpowering their conversation, and soon they were all screaming the school song:

"Then a cheer for the rose and the gray, despondency swift sped away, and we sing alma mater together, three cheers for the rose and the gray!"

Two hours later, their faces chilled by the November air, and with Anita having thoroughly enjoyed the wagon ride after all, they arrived at Mohonk Mountain House—the last time many of them would ever come to that beautiful slice of the Hudson Valley. They immediately recognized the familiar form of Frederick Ferris Thompson, the most popular Vassar trustee and the man who financed the trip every year, greeting them with a smile the size of a croissant.

A chorus of "Uncle Fred!" arose as the girls saluted the beneficent millionaire like their favorite grandfather.

"The ladies of '97 have arrived! And let's not forget 1900—our turn-of-the-century class! A warmest welcome to you all," he said, ushering them into the handsome building.

A light show of emotion took over Anita when she walked inside the imposing structure, thinking of her trip freshman year and how lonely she'd felt then. Her roommate that year lacked Lottie's warmth, and the two girls did very little in their shared rooms but sleep and exchange polite niceties about their studies. She had been a nervous, cautious twenty-one-year-old that first fall, but she had loved the trip to Mohonk, the rowing on the lake, hiking up Sky Top hill with a pack of girls declaiming Longfellow and Whitman and shouting out every autumnal word they could think of. But this year's trip, Anita knew, would be better because Lottie was there to breathe her exceptional version of life into it.

As the girls separated into hiking groups, Anita's thoughts homed in on a particular memory from that earlier trip. She had gone rowing in the afternoon with three girls from her hallway. She had loved the way her muscles felt as she had dipped her sturdy wooden oars in the lake, the way her dress had seemed to float around her in the narrow boat, the sound it made cutting across the water like her own private rainstorm. The girls had traded stories as they rowed and then broken out into song. Anita, with one of the best voices at Vassar, had sung the loudest, the most vibrantly. She started humming one of the songs they had shouted out that day, "Daughters of Vassar Dear."

"Why are you singing that little song, Miss Hemmings?" asked Belle, who always picked up a stray note in the air.

"I don't know," said Anita. "I think we sang it here freshman year."

"Did we?" asked Belle. "And I thought just the girls in the eighties sang that old tune."

Lottie joined them, bowing as Belle took over the singing.

"Why are you bowing at a song?" asked Belle, stopping during the chorus.

"The Japanese bow at everything," said Lottie, knowledgeably.

"You're from New York."

"But I might as well be Japanese. Unless I marry Anita's brother. He's American, I take it?" she asked with a coquettish simper at her roommate.

"Anita! Who is this brother you've been hiding?" asked Belle. "Three years in choir and Glee Club with you and not a word. I should be terribly vexed."

"No, you should not be," said Lottie. "Clearly, it was fate that brought him to me, this year."

"Well, what will it be, ladies? Are we rowers or are we hikers?" Caroline shouted.

"We are hikers," said Lottie, and Anita didn't dare argue for the lake.

She thought of how much she had loved that day in '93, how that had been it for her: Vassar would be her safe corner of the world, a place she would forever love without limit, despite everything.

The girls climbed as high as nature would allow them to go on Sky Top and looked out at the last of the fall leaves and the gentle arch of the Hudson Valley mountain range. They all stayed quiet for a moment, just letting the heavy breeze move through them, then past them, heading south.

They watched as another group of their classmates made it to the top, huddling together for warmth, acting as if there wasn't an eye on them. That's what it was like to exist in this world. It was a perfect, pellucid bubble, moving idly along. But this particular bubble only had seven months until it burst.

CHAPTER 10

Belle, play something charming on the mandolin, will you? I have a terrible, nearly incurable case of the borings."

Lottie was reclining on the parlor couch watching a pool of light flooding the window change shapes as the afternoon clouds moved in. The week after the annual trip to Mohonk seemed to stretch on for two. It was nearly a month until the Phil Day dance, and the campus ticked around the clock of normalcy from early November to early December, without a notable event to distract the students from their work. When no such distractions were provided, Lottie had to find a way to create them.

"What are the borings?" asked Belle, making no move to get her mandolin from her room. She loved Lottie, but she seldom did what she asked unless she asked twice.

"Oh," said Lottie swinging her arm over the side of the couch for effect. "It's when you're dreadfully bored and the only way out is through some*one* charming doing some*thing* charming."

"That makes perfect sense," said Belle, heading to her room for her instrument. She liked being labeled charming, especially by Lottie.

"But it can't be someone with just a splash of charm," Lottie elaborated, making up her definition as she went along. "It has to be someone who smokes charm, weeps charm, who seems to have been swaddled in it from birth."

"And preferably this charming person can also provide music," added Anita, who had been Lottie's antidote to the borings for three months now. But it was fair, as Lottie was everybody's antidote to the borings.

"I bet it helps if the person is exquisitely rich," said Caroline, lifting her head from the poetry book she had been reading aloud.

"Frightfully, frightfully rich," added Belle, coming back with her mandolin.

"Oh, no," said Lottie sitting up. "It doesn't help at all. Money does not give people charm. It usually provides them an excuse not to be charming. Not to try at all." She put her hand to her chest and said, "There are exceptions, of course."

Belle started to play the mandolin with ease, her lithe fingers moving up and down the neck of the squat instrument.

"That's wonderful," said Lottie, closing her eyes. She reached over and plucked an ostrich feather from her desk beside her—which served half as workspace and half as Lottie's personal museum—and fanned herself to the rhythm. "What is this melancholy song?"

"Bach's Sonata Number One in G Minor," said Belle and Anita in unison. Belle and Anita had always been close, having been in Glee Club and chorus together since their first year at Vassar, but they had become much more attached now that they were both Lottie's friends. The friendship that they shared with Lottie, the fact that they could spend their days together in a beautiful room with a perfect gatehouse view, made each of them feel part of something fleeting and rare.

Anita and Belle hummed along as Belle's nimble hand worked its way across the frets, each finger lifting and pressing so deftly it was easy to forget about the music and focus on the beauty of Belle's hands.

"What a world full of talent we dwell in," said Caroline. "At least for these four years."

"Is life among the natives in Syria not like this?" asked Lottie from her place of repose. Lottie, it seemed, was no longer suffering from the borings.

"Oh, but it is," said Caroline. "Belle, your playing makes me think of the nights when I'm allowed to leave the confines of my father's school and see the real Syria. The Arab world rather than the Christian one." Caroline let her head fall to the side in perfect repose while she enjoyed Belle's playing. "Though there are communities of Jews, too. There is room for all in dear old Syria."

"And they all play Bach on the mandolin?" asked Lottie, gently mocking her.

"No, of course not," said Caroline, smiling proudly to show that her one leg up on a Taylor was how much of the world she'd seen. "They play wooden flutes and crude drums and long stringed instruments that could be inspired by a mandolin but are unique to the Arab world. Some are even played with bows. But I've only seen them played by men. And they're very dusty. Everything in Syria is covered in dust. One day you will all come to visit me and I'll order up a dust storm especially for my Vassar family."

"I'll have a hat made now," said Lottie, throwing the bedsheet on her head.

"That's almost appropriate," said Caroline, laughing.

A dust storm, thought Anita. She imagined all the

people, the sights and sounds that Caroline had seen and heard in her life during her childhood abroad and through her travels. Rather than the longing she usually felt when Caroline spoke of her life in Syria, Anita thought about the world that was waiting for her after school—one full of travel, starting with studying in Greece and then a life with Porter in Chicago. She would have her own stories soon, and she would send them to Caroline in long letters. Greece would not have dust storms, but she would write of the pounding sun and the men with their wide black eyes. Yes, she thought to herself, I'll write to all three of them a year from now and say, You must all come visit me and I'll order up the bluest sky especially for you.

Anita looked out the window at the snow falling through the swirls of gray clouds, a reminder that everything that started high and holy eventually came tumbling down. But, she thought as the flakes swam past the glass, the process was beautiful. Even if she did not become a professor, even if Vassar was the apex of her intellectual life, as Frederick had said it must be, she had this, these friends, this day.

When the autumn browns began to deepen and the girls could see only tattered leaves when they looked down from the high floor, the gossip at the college turned to the Philaletheis Day dance, the highlight of each December.

Anita and Porter had been going over their plans for the dance in every letter they had exchanged since November 1.

The event was set for a Saturday, and Porter planned to take an early train to Poughkeepsie on Friday with other Harvard men. He had asked Anita if he should pester Henry about Lottie, and Anita wasn't sure how to answer.

She had her pen poised to write back, when Lottie walked into the room in a burgundy silk taffeta dress, very formal for a school day. She had just returned from lunch in town with one of her distant relations, the type of older moneyed person who would expect such dress at all times, even from a student.

"Lottie, you look wonderful in that gown," said Anita as her roommate fell onto the little divan in mock exhaustion, immediately wrinkling her dress.

"Relay that fact to your brother, would you, please?" said Lottie, taking one of her many pleated fans from her desk. "I haven't heard from him in over two weeks, and he still owes me a reply for the Phil Dance. I'd be panicked, as it's three weeks away, but I know he'll say yes."

Anita, suddenly unsettled, looked across the room at Lottie, her eyes wide and worried.

"Don't give me that face, Anita Hemmings, I know you are quite aware that we've been writing each other, and sisters always have sway over brothers, so please go ahead and sway. I know it will be a yes, though. How could he say no to a trip to see his little sister?"

"Big sister," Anita corrected her.

"Big, is it? But he's not so much younger, is he?"

"No. Just one year," she reminded her.

"Fine, then. And as I'm a youthful twenty-two, that works swimmingly." She threw the fan on the floor and stood up. "Anita, I absolutely cannot wait for Phil. It's our very last one! Then we'll never go to dances like Phil again because we will be old, wrinkled dowagers as soon as we step off campus with our diplomas. We'll be the walking dead. The educated walking dead!"

"I thought you were moving to the Orient and earning your doctorate in chemistry while eating piles of fish?"

"Am I?" said Lottie, grinning. "Oh, thank goodness. My future *does* sound entertaining. Maybe I won't run away from it, after all."

Two days later, Lottie had news from Frederick about the Phil Day dance, and it was not what anyone was expecting.

When Anita came into the parlor room with Belle behind her, both girls with songbooks and sheet music under their arms, having just finished choir practice, Lottie's face was a deep pink hue and she had a noticeable line of sweat on her forehead. Her head was hanging off the bed, her body nearly upside down, and she had the pieces of a torn letter in her hand.

"Lottie! What on earth is wrong? Are you ill? You're all red!" Belle rushed over to her bed with Anita a step behind.

"You do look ill, Lottie. We should take you to see Dr. Thelberg," Anita said. "You need a mustard plaster on your chest. I knew we should have asked the maids to take our flannels out of the catacombs before November. Do you think you can stand?"

"It's not an illness, Miss Hemmings," said Lottie in a gravelly voice. "It's so much worse." Anita looked more closely at Lottie's bed and spotted the rest of the torn-up note, instantly recognizing Frederick's even hand.

"Frederick!" she exclaimed. "Is he ill?"

"Your brother is perfectly fine, Anita. Unless you think academic probation is something to worry about. I was constantly on it as a freshman, and now I'm practically top of the class. So, yes, Frederick is thriving, but I am not! He, your own brother, has rejected me! He will not be coming to the dance, will not be my date for Phil Day, and as it's already November twenty-fifth, I won't be able to arrange another date. I will be the only senior at Phil with an empty dance card. I will die on December fourth, 1896, of public humiliation."

She hung her head off the bed again and started turning a fascinating shade of fuchsia.

Anita was furious with her brother. She had known he would never come to the dance, but was academic probation the best excuse he could conjure up? It wasn't even a believable one. Lottie had met him, and they had spoken about their shared love of chemistry and how they were both flying through with perfect grades their senior year. And now Lottie, the person most responsible for her own happiness this year, had been left devastated by his rejection.

Anita picked up the pieces of the letter, extracting the ones in Lottie's hand, and read it over twice. It was not remotely credible.

Together, she and Belle sat Lottie up on her bed. Then she attempted to salvage the situation.

"Lottie, you know you can find a date for Phil as easily as you can pick up a pen. I'm sorry about Frederick, but if he's on academic probation at Cornell, you understand, don't you? He can't leave. He is a senior. If it were one of us, we couldn't attend the dance even though it will be just downstairs."

"Yes, yes, I understand," said Lottie, "but I feel so very ill. I don't want to attend Phil my senior year with just anyone. I want to be escorted by Frederick Hemmings. This all comes as such a shock. In his last letter, he stated that he had never met a woman who wanted to be a chemistry professor and had traveled to the Far East. He said I was the most fascinating woman he had ever met! This does not bode well for my future confidence in men, Anita," she concluded.

That evening, both Belle and Anita wired their dates for Phil to inquire whether they knew a handsome senior they could bring with them for Lottie. In the next few days, both girls were overwhelmed with suggestions, which almost spurred Lottie out of her depression. The three, along with Caroline Hardin, sat up until the final bell the day after the responses arrived, eating plates of charlotte russe and debating which would be better for Lottie, a Harvard or a Yale man. They had it down to two: Harvard man Joseph Southworth from Boston and Yale man Philip Hinkle from Philadelphia. Anita lobbied heavily for Philip, as she was concerned that someone from Boston might pry into her family name, but Belle and Caroline won when they mentioned that Joseph was related to Commodore Matthew Perry, the man who helped open Japan to the West in 1854.

"How could I turn away such a man?" said Lottie. "I'm sure there are no other twenty-two-year-old girls who know as much about Japan as I do. I may have to sneak him up here to show him my collection of woodblock prints."

"Don't you dare, Louise Taylor," cautioned Caroline. "I am not going to spend the rest of my senior year crying over you when you are dismissed from college, dragged out by your little ear."

"I wouldn't dare, but it does sound agreeable," she said, running her finger over the faded blues and oranges of the works on the walls. "And I'm sure old Prexy Taylor would understand. He is an art connoisseur. Just look at the dear college's museum. There are two Durands and three oils by Frederic Church."

So it was settled. Anita wrote back to Porter and told him that his classmate Joseph Southworth had emerged the winner and that she and Lottie were both looking forward to their December arrival.

"Please know I am still brokenhearted, Anita," said Lottie, when they were alone in their parlor room that night. "And if Frederick can find a way to escape awful Cornell, I will drop Joseph Southworth immediately, even if he is related to the esteemed commodore."

"That's awfully committed of you," said Anita. "One meeting, and you're so taken with my brother. Isn't he lucky?"

"It's you Hemmings children," said Lottie, propping herself on her elbow and letting her blond curls hang dramatically over her face. "There's something quietly charming about you both. Such beautiful faces, such elegance, all wrapped up in a bewitching sort of humility. And don't say you can blame me, Anita. He's your brother!"

Yes, Anita thought, that was the problem.

The following day, Anita received a response to her latest letter to Frederick. She had been asking the maid for the mail early every day so that it was never brought to her room when both she and Lottie were there. Any letter from Frederick would have been torn out of her hand by Lottie to be delivered as a monologue.

She folded the envelope and stuffed it in the pocket of her dress. She was already wearing her heaviest, a deep blue wool and silk with a trumpet skirt and a wide shoulder, purchased with her tutoring money before her sophomore year. She walked down to the library and chose a table in the middle back, surrounded by twenty thousand leather-bound books. She took the letter out of the envelope, already planning to burn it a few minutes later, as she did all Frederick's letters.

He had always been the mouthpiece of her family. He told her what her parents were doing in their day-to-day lives—about their health, their worries—along with news of their younger siblings. But she knew that was not the subject of this letter. She would have to wait for news of her family until she returned home for Christmas. Anita lifted the page. The paper was thin and cheap, not the thick, embossed stationery Frederick had used to reply to Lottie.

Dear Anita,

By the time this letter reaches you, you'll know that I've been communicating with Lottie, but you being you, you were well aware of it already.

I often think about you there, a Vassar girl just like the others—yet not. And I forget at times that it must be extremely difficult. When I check into a hotel in Poughkeepsie as a white man, or when I'm writing to a woman like Lottie (a very rare occurrence), then I remember the difficulty. How hard it must be to constantly remain alert, to appear effortless with so much effort, to leave the reality about yourself somewhere else. Will it die, you might wonder? Will I just become this person I am pretending to be?

This is my way of apologizing. I'm sorry I was less than understanding with you when I was in Poughkeepsie last. Being a Negro student at the Institute of Technology is difficult. I attend the school, but I am not a part of it. There are teachers who try very hard to make me feel like just another student, but there are students who won't let me feel that way. I've been taken for a worker, a servant. Once a freshman from Georgia handed me his formal shoes, thinking I was a bootblack, even though I was in my nicest suit. My situation is not ideal, but I need to remember that neither is yours. I have not been wearing the mask of a white person for almost four years. And when I think about you having to do so, not just for a weekend, but always—awake, asleep, in class, with friends, with strangers—it exhausts me, and my admiration for you is renewed.

Which brings me to Lottie. It was with you in mind that I first responded to her. When you spoke of her at Smith Brothers that memorable autumn day in Poughkeepsie, you emphasized that she is a Taylor and that one cannot treat a Taylor casually. Thus, I did not. I responded to her letter, and I would be dishonest if I said I didn't feel immensely flattered by her interest in me. Frederick Hemmings, Negro student, mistaken for the bootblack, attending the Vassar Philaletheis Day Dance with Lottie Taylor. We both know my skin is noticeably darker than yours, but she did not seem to see it, and if she did, she did not care.

But the compliment didn't entirely cloud my clarity of mind. It can never happen. Only for you, when I come to Vassar, do I live a double life, and if I attempted to do so full-time, I am sure I would be caught. It is not so simple to move fluidly between the black and white worlds. Yours are in separate compartments, and only when you are home during the summers do you become you again, a Negro again. Even over the Christmas holiday, there is not enough time for you to recover your habits. You seem foreign to all of us until we have you back for months.

You are white at Vassar, and I am a Negro at MIT, and because of it, it's dangerous for me even to be in Poughkeepsie. I've visited these past three years because there was no Lottie Taylor. No one took an interest in me or noticed me off-campus with you. But she has, and it's a flattering, yet dangerous problem.

I have handled Lottie's advances as I hope you would have wanted me to. I was as polite as I felt I could be without swaying her affection further my way, but short of rude enough for her to feel disdain or anger toward me. I am hoping she will eventually feel detached enough to forget me altogether. Because that's what we need to be when we walk in and out of these two worlds, Anita. Forgotten.

She may—and part of me does hope she will—be

upset by my poor excuse for why I cannot attend Phil Day.
Please convince her that it is the case, that I have secretly
been struggling with my studies. And then find someone
she can quickly forget me for. Someone memorable.

I know you will be attending Phil, but I urge you, Sister,
in fact I beg you: Do not attend the dance with Porter
Hamilton. If he is there, grant him one dance, be civil, but
dance with other men, one dance with each. Do not show
any interest, past politeness, to anyone. You have done this
so well all your years there. Continue to do it well now.

I can imagine your face as I write this—bridling at
the unfairness of it all. But it must be, Anita. You cannot,
must not, get close to a man like Hamilton. It is the most
dangerous thing you can do. If he ever knew, Anita, if you
ever slipped and told him the truth, you would never see
Vassar again.

But I do not want to end my letter this way. I want
to say that when I spent time with Lottie and you in
Poughkeepsie, when I felt her warmth toward me and then
had it confirmed by her many letters, I felt a great surge
of pride. I wanted to be the type of man who could attend
Phil Day with Lottie Taylor. I felt what you must feel with
Porter. So it is with shame that I write what I write, but
it is because of my love that you must follow my warning.
You've known that since you were still at the Girls' High
School and said to me, "I won't be staying here long. I'll be
attending Vassar College soon." And you did.

Your brother Frederick

Anita reread the letter three times, the second two read-
ings when it was hidden in one of her Greek texts. Frederick
never used the word *Negro* in his letters. He knew better
than to write anything that would be harmful to Anita if

read by another. But this time, he had. She imagined that he was doing so as a threat, as a way to make her more fearful about attending the dance with Porter. She looked at the dangerous words on the page, then crumpled the letter, walked quickly to the new senior parlor, and let it tumble into the fire as she pretended to warm her hands. She watched as Frederick's warnings were turned to ash. In ten days' time, despite her brother's disapproval, Porter would return.

CHAPTER 11

Before the first morning bell rang on December 4, Lottie was at Anita's bedside in her nightclothes. She wrapped her silk-topped blanket tight around her, climbed on the bed and shouted, "It's Phil Day!" jumping up and down as best she could with Anita's legs in the way.

Her roommate turned groggily over and watched her with amusement. Outside the window, Anita could see that it was snowing heavily, and she was happy that her last Phil Day dance would be bathed in snow, the fairy-tale setting of the campus in early winter.

There was a serenity to four hundred acres without eligible men. There were, of course, men on campus, but besides the French professor, who had more than a few of the girls besotted, none were suitable. But everything changed on Phil Day. As the men arrived in the afternoon, their male energy upended the decorous atmosphere of Main, seeping under the windows and through door frames like steam escaping a kettle.

"I can't believe it's our last Phil Day," said Anita, pushing back her covers, as excited as Lottie. She knew that after a barely touched breakfast, girls in costumes for the Phil plays would fly through the school and there would be hours of preparations—the decorating of the boxes for the dance, and more important, the decorating of the women for the impending arrival of the men.

"Anita! Don't get nostalgic yet. What you can't believe is that the dashing Porter Hamilton is arriving in six hours. And what I can't believe is that I am attending Phil with some street urchin I have never met. Old Southpaw." Lottie pulled Anita's straight black hair. "Hand me your mirror, Anita. I know I look frightening. That Southpaw boy will scream in horror when he sees me."

"*Worth*, South*worth*," said Anita, handing her the mirror.

"Umm-hmm," said Lottie, standing up. "Say his name all you want, but all you're thinking about is Porter Hamilton. Hamilton, Hamilton. How convenient. Marry him, and you won't even have to change your monogram."

The two girls dressed quickly and hurried down to the senior table in the center of the dining hall. Breakfast was more animated than on any morning since the semester began. Even the freshmen, who didn't know what to expect past the play and the lecture, were buzzing.

"Who is giving the address this year?" asked Caroline, through bites of pancakes. The college had a passion for pancakes, and there was even a special ten-foot griddle in the kitchen to cook them on.

Belle took a bite from Caroline's plate and motioned to the servers to bring her more. Anita may have been too nervous to eat, but Belle was not. "It's a Mr. John Kendrick Bangs," she said, watching the servers bring out plates of still-sizzling bacon. "He is the editor for the departments of humor for all three Harper's magazines, including *Bazaar*." Belle was an avid connoisseur of all things print, magazines included.

"At least he won't be dry. Is he handsome?" asked Caroline.

"Extremely bald, I'm afraid. Tiny eyes like a street pigeon. A Columbia man," Belle said.

"A man's looks are not everything," Marion Schibsby chimed in from three seats down. She was promised to Jessup Platt, one of the homeliest men Yale had ever graduated. But he made up for his crooked face with his very straight bank account.

"I know what will make the occasion less dry," said Lottie.

"The bottle of gin you're hiding in your room!" said Belle, covering her mouth before the lady principal could come and scold her.

The rest of the morning and the early afternoon saw Main transformed into a den of high-pitched chatter and flying clothes. Belle, Caroline, Anita, and Lottie took over their hallway, practicing their square dances and promenades down the long space. They paused in their antics and Belle let the top hat she was wearing fall, catching it on her foot.

"Bravo, Belle!" said Lottie, applauding with her palms as she had seen them do in Japan. Behind her, a chorus of voices swelled, and she turned to see four girls floating down the hall on a similar cloud of excitement.

"Hide, ladies!" Lottie hissed. "It's the grandmothers club. Look at them, and your eyes are guaranteed to burn right out of your skull."

"Oh, it's the Society of the Granddaughters," Caroline said. "They must be getting ready in Emma's room."

Mary Baille, Elizabeth Bishop, Emma Baker, and Clara Tuttle were the four members of the class of 1897 who were part of the exclusive Granddaughters club, open only to girls whose mothers had graduated from Vassar.

"Do you know what that club's motto is?" asked Lottie, after the group had passed without greeting them. "'The condition of your birth is the measure of your worth.' Have you ever heard such nonsense?"

"Of course we've heard it," said Anita. "They've been chanting it since we arrived. And don't be too spiteful, Lottie. They would gladly give up being a Vassar Granddaughter to be a Taylor."

"Aren't you sweet," said Lottie, stealing the top hat from Belle and bowing to Anita. But Anita was right. Although Lottie may have been the first female Taylor to go to Vassar, she certainly wouldn't be the last, and one day there would be buildings boasting her name, just as Strong Hall had been named for Bessie Rockefeller Strong. Yet Lottie was always quick to skewer elitist behavior, and Anita suspected that even if she were eligible for the Granddaughters, she would shun a club with such an arrogant motto.

After the girls were satisfied with their steps and had lamented again the ban on round dancing, they separated and went back to their rooms to dress.

"Only an hour until Porter and what's-his-name arrives!" shouted Lottie, throwing every single dress that felt like silk or sateen onto her bed. "I hate your brother for not coming, Anita, hate, hate. How could he let his grades drop when he knew something as important as Phil Day was on the horizon!"

"I can't imagine," said Anita. "I'm sure he truly regrets it."

"He should," said Lottie from inside her closet. "I plan on looking sensational this evening. And so will you. The two prettiest square dancers there ever were. When will this school modernize? No one has ever ended up with child after a night of round dancing. Not right away, anyhow." She emerged with her hair unfolding onto her shoulders, pins sticking out in all directions.

"Clearly, something needs to be done about this," she

said, pointing to her head. "Is there a maid available? I'm going to run down and see."

The college, not individual girls, employed the maids at Vassar, but on a day like Phil, it did not seem like it.

With the help of two of the older maids, who lived above the girls in the fifth-floor attic alcoves, Anita and Lottie, who were both petite and could easily exchange gowns, dressed in two of Lottie's finest, a navy blue organdie and silk with two layers of ruffles at the base of the skirt for Anita and a daring, Grecian-cut white sateen dress for Lottie. Very few had yet dared to wear artistic dress at Vassar, though a few rebellious society women had done so in New York City.

"Look at the asymmetrical himation," Lottie said, fingering the smooth fabric draped dramatically over only her left shoulder. "I am in love with this gown." She started curtseying to imaginary men and introducing herself to the air.

Anita would never have dared wear such a modern, figure-revealing style, but Lottie lit up with even more confidence in it. "Tell me you at least have a corset on under that thin fabric," Anita said, as her roommate wiggled in places she shouldn't have been able to.

"Of course I do," Lottie said, tugging at her waist. "These corsets are becoming so long we will all look like Egyptian mummies soon. Hand me that little bag, will you, Anita?" she said, nodding to the divan. "It has my Duvelleroy fan inside." Anita passed it to her. Last month the roommates had read in the latest issue of *Harper's Bazaar* that a Duvelleroy fan cost as much as four hundred dollars, an entire year's tuition at Vassar. "I have to bring it along or I won't be able to hide my mouth and gossip the night away. And since I'm stuck with old Southpaw instead of the dashing Mr. Frederick Hemmings, what choice do I have?"

Just before four o'clock, Anita and Lottie gathered with

Belle and Caroline, and all four descended the stairs to the ground floor to meet their guests in the three visitors' parlors. As they were the only place in Main where the students were allowed to greet their male visitors, the rooms, and the areas around them, were seething with men.

"Where is that hunchbacked Southpaw fellow?" said Lottie loudly, scanning the visitors. She stopped and laughed, leaning back in her curve-exposing dress. "Why am I surveying the room? I don't even know what old Southpaw looks like."

At that moment, a striking man in evening attire approached Lottie and bowed. "Very pleased to meet you," he said. "*I* am old Southpaw."

"Oh dear," said Lottie. "How did you know me?"

"I do hate to be the one to tell you, Miss Taylor, but your likeness has been in the newspapers quite a few times," he said, handing her a bouquet. "I don't think there is a man on the East Coast under the age of fifty who doesn't know your beautiful face." He bowed to her, all the while keeping his dark eyes on hers. "The name is Old Southpaw, and I am at your service."

While Caroline and Belle laughed along with Lottie at Joseph's routine, Anita looked for Porter, who quickly emerged from behind Joseph Southworth as he was charming Lottie.

Seeing Porter again, everything Anita had felt before multiplied like blood cells. He moved closer to her, and she watched his eyes go from her hair, to her dress, and up to her face before pronouncing her name.

"Anita. I'm so glad I'm here," he said, kissing her right hand just above her glove.

"I am the one—" Anita began quietly, and then stopped, feeling no need to finish her sentence.

Once Belle and Caroline had found their escorts, Arthur Martin and Raymond DeGroot, both Yale men, the group was complete and Joseph finished his story. Still addressing Lottie, but speaking loudly enough for them all to hear, he said, "You, Miss Taylor, fixated on the Orient as you are, will be most pleased to know that I am secretly Japanese. My mother hailed from Kyoto, a geisha who died in childbirth. But I pray you, do not tell a soul. I know that you, Louise Taylor, the empire of Japan's biggest American fan—besides my late esteemed relation Commodore Perry—will keep my secret safe."

"Why would you ask me not to tell a soul but then say such a thing in front of my friends?" Lottie asked.

"I've always believed that if you tell a secret out loud, there's more of a chance that someone will keep it, as they can talk it over with their intimate friends. If you confide in just one person, they'll tell everyone in town."

Anita felt an inward frisson of dissent.

"I don't believe you," said Lottie, her pink mouth turning up, "but I think we'll get along just fine." She took Joseph's arm and guided the group toward the chapel for the afternoon's first event, the annual lecture.

"You should believe me. It's true," said Joseph, positioning his tall, thin frame in the window light. "Just look at my face."

Anita watched as Lottie examined the wings of his white collar standing up against his elegant neck, his high cheekbones, and small nose. Her roommate suddenly seemed to be finding Old Southpaw much more interesting.

"How are the top brass at the college? Expect a lot out of you?" Joseph asked the girls when they were all sitting in their senior seats in the chapel waiting for Mr. John Kendrick Bangs to begin his oration.

"Only the very highest success or a magnificent failure will satisfy them—mediocrity is the one unpardonable sin," Lottie replied.

"Aren't you a clever girl?" said Joseph, beaming at his prize.

"Clever, nothing," said Belle, leaning over to Anita. "That's a line from the *Three Girls at Vassar* books. At least she can memorize."

The two exchanged a smile and listened to the buzz in the audience. It felt almost cruel to force a room of young people bursting with repressed sexual energy to calm themselves for an hour-long lecture. But since they had all been raised to act with decorum when required, they maintained their composure not just for the lecture, but through a concert of Hungarian music, dinner, and two Glee Club performances—which Anita and Belle slipped in to join—until the dining room and college parlors finally opened for the evening at eight o'clock.

As usual, boxes for the girls and their guests had been set up in the two parlors to make promenading and socializing easier, and refreshments were served in the faculty room. The dancing took place in the enormous dining room, and though the faculty tried to prevent it, promenading took place down the halls. Fifteen dances were planned that year, though the student government had lobbied desperately for twenty.

When Anita's group of eight entered the dining room, they stopped short.

"We are in the Orient!" said Lottie, delightedly. The whole room was decorated with silks and paintings done in the Asian style.

"Are you behind all this, Lottie?" asked Caroline, motioning to a drape of muted gold and blue printed with cranes.

She picked up one of the paper parasols in the entry and twirled it.

"I'm not," said Lottie. "But I am not the only one captivated by the Orient. It's quite in vogue now. Haven't you read about the Japonisme movements in Paris and London, Caroline? It took a great while, but it finally trickled over here."

"You were the one to bring it over, of course," said Joseph, already comfortable teasing Lottie.

"Me?" said Lottie, flattered. "You might say that I did. At least on campus," she continued, plucking the parasol from Caroline's hand. "Come, we might need this later to fend off all our suitors. I am sure our box will be overflowing."

"Someone stop Lottie before she bounds in," said Anita, as her friend appeared ready to sprint into the dining room. "They are announcing our guests this year."

This was a new custom for the class of 1897's last Phil Day, and Anita had been anticipating it since the plan was announced. She had been playing with the way her name would sound with Porter's for the last few weeks, mumbling it under her breath as she walked to class: Anita Hemmings and her escort, Porter Hamilton.

"Look," said Caroline as they approached the door. "They are using colored ushers to announce the guests. Such a nice addition. For our first three years we had to do without them and walk in without so much as a nod," she explained to her escort. "It was such confusion."

"They do add a touch, don't they?" said Belle. "And all so alike in their tailcoats. Like African statues."

"I'm glad they're announcing guests," Porter said to Anita. "I've often said our names aloud together, myself."

As the girls straightened their dresses and fretted over each other's hair, Anita thought of Belle's words. "All so alike." She looked at the colored men, standing tall and proud, yet so deferential in their white waistcoats and black tails, and thought about how rare it was to see a black face on campus. She couldn't help but think of the Negro rag song "All Coons Look Alike to Me." Though she listened mostly to classical music, the song was one of the biggest hits of the year and unavoidable at many of the girls' card parties, where it played on phonographs from cylinders sent from home. Anita's spine stiffened at the thought of the song playing tonight, and she clutched Porter's arm tightly. She looked away from the men and up at her date.

Lottie and Joseph were to be announced first, and Lottie handed her card to one of the ushers.

"Louise Taylor and Old Southpaw," his voice boomed, and Joseph bent over with laughter. "Thank you for that, Lottie," he said as they made their way into the room.

"Anita Hemmings and Porter Hamilton," the usher's voice called out and the pair walked in arm in arm.

"I couldn't be happier," Porter whispered, and Anita relaxed her tight grip.

After the first and second promenades, Caroline motioned to her friends and said, "Come! Let's go try the ices. Gratia said they have tutti frutti ice cream and cake." They left for the parlor, all still with their escorts, though they had changed partners and had different names on their cards for the third dance.

"You're in love, Anita, and it's such a splendid thing," said Belle, walking with her friend, ice cream in hand. "And from my observations, it's requited."

When the first square dance started, Porter led Anita to the center of the room. The girls had begged for years for round dancing, but the faculty had stayed firm, sure that dancing closer than several feet apart was improper.

"You look ravishing," said Porter, as they took their positions. "Have I already said that?"

"You have," said Anita. "But it's not something one minds hearing more than once."

He smiled. "Good. You, Anita Hemmings, will be hearing it for a lifetime."

A lifetime, Anita thought as she moved in time with the other girls. That's what she wanted. A lifetime with Porter Hamilton.

Anita added several other names to her dance card but made sure to give ten out of the fifteen dances to Porter. Even though such coupling up was frowned upon by the faculty, no one protested. Their affection was apparent, and the professors monitoring the dance knew Porter's family name as well as the Vassar girls did.

With everyone out of breath from the fast promenade down the hallway, where bodies were much closer together than when the faculty was watching, the group of eight retired to their box, separated from its neighbors by velvet curtains.

"What time is it, Arthur?" asked Belle, still radiating excited feminine energy. "They'll chime the bell at midnight, and I'm hoping we still have hours yet."

"I'm afraid it's already eleven," said Arthur, a good-natured young man with three brothers and a reputation for awkwardness around women—though this group seemed to put him at ease.

"I wish we were in New York," said Lottie. "Then we could stay out all night."

"Grand idea," said Caroline. "In the newspaper the next day it would say: 'Miss Louise Taylor out all night long in the company of strange men.'"

"I think you mean, dashing," said Porter. "Dashing, robust young men."

Lottie shrugged. "It's only bad if they *don't* talk about you, isn't that right, Joseph?"

"Of course," he replied, handing her his handkerchief. "Back in Boston I am constantly fawned over in the society columns of the *Globe*. You're from Boston, aren't you, Anita? Surely you've read about me? Old Southpaw dining with Mayor Quincy yet again."

"Of course!" Anita responded cheerfully, hoping Lottie would take back the reins of the conversation.

"Is your family in Back Bay or on old Beacon Hill, Anita?" asked Joseph.

Anita's family lived in Roxbury, the Negro area of town. Everyone around them was Negro, and the whites from Boston knew what Roxbury meant. Back Bay and Beacon Hill were dotted with imposing brownstones and ornate mansions, all redolent of money. Roxbury was not.

"I live in Back Bay," said Anita, choosing the slightly less fashionable of the two.

"We're most likely neighbors," said Joseph, smiling. "For years my father's family was on Beacon Hill, but when they filled in the bay, my grandfather was one of the first to have a house built. Now my family is at 148 Beacon Street, right next to the Gardners." He paused as Lottie said something to Belle about Isabella and Jack Gardner's ever-growing art collection. Joseph turned to Anita and pressed, "So, Miss Hemmings, are you my neighbor?"

"Not quite," said Anita, confidently, having memorized the Boston streets and feeling thankful that she knew of the grand limestone house where Isabella and Jack Gardner lived. "I'm on the West Side of town. On Marlborough Street."

"That's still not too far. Perhaps I can call on you over Christmas. Lottie said you have a very charming brother whom she is in love with but that I'm rapidly changing her mind about. See, your brother is not the child of a deceased geisha, so as wonderful as I'm sure he is, he is not me."

"I didn't say that, Anita! I never said such a thing," said Lottie, while the rest laughed.

"I do have a brother," Anita said, regretting Frederick's visit to Poughkeepsie more and more every hour.

"Oh, good. What is his name? I'll be sure to call on you over the holidays."

"His name is Frederick Hemmings," she said. "Though he is up at Cornell and I'm not sure if he'll be returning for Christmas.

"That name sounds familiar," said Joseph. "We must have met before."

"Wonderful," said Anita. But she was starting to panic, and Porter noticed her face change. "I'm sorry," she told him. "I'm feeling a slight chill. I'm just going up to my room to find a shawl. I'll return in a moment."

She stepped out of the box and didn't turn around to see Porter's face again, letting the crowd of mingling students envelop her. She took the elevator to the senior floor, hurried to her room, and sat on the bed. For five minutes she just sat, watching the snow fall outside, thinking of how foolish she had been. Why did she think she could braid her two worlds together again and again? What had she and Frederick done, letting him visit Poughkeepsie?

She had felt so shielded from stares and comments for the past three years, but this year was different. She was at the heart of Vassar, part of the newly coined "Gatehouse group"; she was Lottie Taylor's roommate and sudden best friend. And now all the wires were crossing. She stood up quickly and took a thick shawl from her dressing table so she wouldn't forget it and return really looking the fool. She picked up her mirror, quickly rearranging her hair, and prepared to go downstairs and not utter another word except to Porter. With the mirror still in her hand, she suddenly heard the parlor door open. She ran out of her bedroom and gasped as she saw Porter, closing the wooden door behind him.

"Porter! No!" Anita cried. There were to be absolutely no men anywhere but in the designated parlors and the dining room, and if one were to be found in the bedrooms, it would mean not only expulsion for the Vassar student, but an enormous scandal.

"You must leave at once," she said, rushing toward him. "It's grounds for expulsion. You have to go immediately. Please!"

"It's all right, Anita. No one saw me come up. Lottie helped me."

"No, Porter," she said, standing panicked in front of him. "Please, I beg you. I can't risk this infraction."

"I couldn't sit downstairs alone anymore," he said, placing his hand on her arm. "I was concerned about you. You seemed suddenly unwell."

"Porter!" Anita said, pulling her arm away. "Leave at once, I insist. I cannot have you here in our parlor. You're putting me in a terrible position."

"I will leave," he said, taking her arm again, "but please tell me what upset you downstairs. Was it me? Am I not acting correctly here with you? Should I not speak so plainly about my feelings for you? Or was it the dancing with Lottie? Was that the concern? Anita, I never want to upset you. As long as I live, I never want to upset you. I want to spend my life watching your face light up with joy."

Anita let him take her other arm and stood paralyzed with both fear and delight.

"I know we've only been acquainted with each other a short while, but I already know that I can make you happy," he said, his face flushed with desire. "I can give you a life full of love. And I had no doubts over your feelings for me until a few minutes past. Your wounded expression suddenly gave me doubt. So tell me what is worrying you, what I did wrong, Anita, and I will leave at once. No one will see me. If I have to leave by way of the window and the roof, I will."

"We have been on the roof," said Anita, overwhelmed. *He wanted to make her happy. To live a life full of love.* "Lottie and I. We opened one of the fifth-floor windows, and the two of us ran across the roof looking down on the school. It was wonderful. But unless you can fly," she said finally, looking at him, "you will be stranded there."

"Good," he said holding her close to him. "I want to be stranded there. Then I will come to the senior floor at night and watch you sleep."

"And then we will both be expelled and bring great shame on all who know us."

"Together?" he asked. "Then I'm prepared for the worst. As long as it's the two of us. I want our lives to move in a parallel line, Anita. I want you to be next to me. I want . . ."

He moved her closer to the open door of her bedroom and she didn't protest when he took her in and sat her down on the bed, his knees touching hers.

"I want us to become engaged. We can wait for marriage, after we both have graduated, but I want to have the certainty that you will be my wife. Will you say that you will? Can you grant me that joy? I want to leave tonight knowing that we can start our life together after school. That you'll come to Chicago. I know you want to study in Greece for several months first, but I will come visit you in Athens, and when I'm not there, I will write you the most romantic letters, they will put all the Greek prose you're reading to shame. Then we will come home. You and I. Say yes, Anita, please."

Without letting her answer, Porter took Anita into his arms and kissed her, pressing his chest to hers. He stopped, looked at her face, watched her nod yes, and embraced her again, all talk of expulsion forgotten.

In the next room, the parlor door opened.

Lottie walked through quietly and stood at Anita's bedroom door with a coy smile on her face. She waited a moment before disturbing them.

"My, my, what am I interrupting here?" she said, rapping her knuckles on the door frame.

Anita and Porter jumped apart.

"Lottie, thank goodness it's only you," said Porter as he reached for Anita's hands again. Instead, Anita pulled her body away in shame.

"The only thing you're interrupting is our exciting announcement," said Porter, standing up. "We've been discussing our engagement, and that seems to have warmed Miss Hemmings. She is not in need of her shawl, after all. Isn't that right, Anita?" he said, turning to her.

Anita looked up at Lottie, her joy having flipped back to fear.

"I'm so pleased for you both," said Lottie, rushing over to embrace Anita. "Such news for celebration!" She reached for Porter's hand, too. "But it looks as if you were engaged in that already, celebrating as two, and little old me interrupted so rudely. My apologies." She gave them both another congratulatory embrace and promised that their secret was locked away with her for good.

"No one else will know about the engagement, or the passionate way you chose to mark the event, either," she declared. "But you better get on, Porter. Joseph is asking for you, and if you are caught in our rooms, we will all be on a train home." Porter turned to leave, but Lottie exited first to make sure the halls were empty, followed by Porter and, minutes later, Anita.

"Anita," Lottie whispered when they were together again, walking back to their box in the dining hall.

Anita looked up at her, unable to hide her emotions.

"You're engaged to Porter Hamilton. Engaged! Your life is splendid and perfect and full of love."

Yes, Anita, nodded, looking across the room to Porter. It was.

CHAPTER 12

Boston was wrapped up in Christmas. Anita had been on the train from Albany for six hours, and the cold air felt restorative, stinging her face and hands, when she disembarked in Massachusetts. She was back home for the winter holiday, and for the first time since she'd been a student at Vassar, she was nervous about seeing her family. She was engaged to a kind, intelligent man, and she could not tell them. All she wished to do was go to her mother, put her arms around her, and say: *I've done it. I'm going to be a Vassar graduate, and I'm going to marry a wonderful man whom I love and who loves me in return.* But she could never tell her mother about Porter, and she could never tell Porter about her mother. She had been very careful in her daily letters not to mention her family. She sometimes spoke of her brother Frederick, so that it didn't seem as though she'd sprung from a cabbage patch, but that was as far as it went. She knew that to marry Porter meant she would have to hide her family, cut ties with them, perhaps even with Frederick, and live as white forever. And in saying yes to Porter, a sliver of her heart had felt prepared for that.

Anita waited in the Boston train station for thirty minutes, sitting on a well-worn wooden bench reading her

Greek for the next semester. It was a routine she always followed upon arriving in Boston from Poughkeepsie, to make sure there were no Vassar girls who could connect her to the school left at the station. After the half hour had passed, instead of taking a hansom, she walked alone with her small case to the streetcar stop to wait for the car to Roxbury.

She boarded ten minutes later, apologizing as her bag grazed passengers' legs, and moved to the center of the cold, crowded car.

She was staring out the window at the city's slushy streets, thinking about the younger siblings she hadn't seen since September, when a familiar voice rang out.

"Miss Hemmings! Is that you there in that pretty plaid coat? I glimpsed you boarding at the station and said to myself, that girl with the noble profile looks just like Miss Anita Hemmings!"

Anita looked and saw that it was indeed the voice of Lillian Peoples, a prominent Negro member of Trinity Church, where she had been a communicant since her childhood.

"Hello, Mrs. Peoples, how nice to see you," she croaked. "I'm just returning from school," she added, letting her eyes make a circle around her. She did not want to be seen talking to a Negro yet. She started to turn her back, though she knew it was a slight, but she couldn't risk it until she was safe within the confines of Roxbury.

"I'll see you and your family at church on Christmas morning?" said Mrs. Peoples before Anita could turn around fully.

"Of course," she replied, still angling her body away from her yet showing her face slightly so as not to be overtly rude.

"And will you be in town until then?" the woman said, oblivious to Anita's unease. Anita wished for just one moment that there were segregated sections on cars in Boston.

If someone who knew her from school saw her speaking colloquially to Mrs. Peoples, she would be in a terrible position. Next time she would have to save her money, or take on extra tutoring hours, so she could hire a hansom.

"I'll be in Cambridge a few days," Anita replied softly, accepting that this conversation with the dark-skinned Mrs. Peoples was not ending soon. "My friend Elizabeth Baker of Cambridge is marrying—"

"Mr. William Henry Lewis!" Mrs. Peoples shouted for the whole car to hear.

"Yes, William Henry Lewis," said Anita in a faint whisper, starting to sweat from dread.

"One of the best and the brightest," said Mrs. Peoples with pride, as if she'd raised the man herself. "Amherst football star, Harvard football star, captain of the Harvard team, all-American, beloved coach—the first one they ever paid, mind you—famous lawyer, good friend of the esteemed Mr. W. E. B. Du Bois, and so very handsome, too. What a lucky girl Miss Baker is. They'll be moving over here, I hope, very soon."

"Elizabeth still has a year and a half left at Wellesley, Mrs. Peoples. She's a year behind me. Class of 1898," Anita corrected her.

"Oh no, Miss Baker won't be finishing up at the college," said Mrs. Peoples, shaking her head with conviction. "She's to be married, so she's left Wellesley now. Didn't you know, Anita?"

"Of her marriage, of course," said Anita, surprised. "I am her only bridesmaid. But not to finish Wellesley, I suppose I had hoped—"

"But marrying Mr. Lewis is ever so much more important than a Wellesley College degree," Mrs. Peoples cut in. "Elizabeth was at Wellesley College for several years. I'm sure she's become quite an accomplished young lady. Strong in mathematics, they say. That should help with the housekeeping. She'll be able to calculate the perfect cleaning timetable and how to divide the food and income among their future children. I do hope they'll have many; he's such a smart and handsome man. He has to pass along those good genetics. And Elizabeth, she's a beautiful girl, too. That exquisite straight hair, just like yours, dear. She'll make an excellent wife for that remarkable man. One of our true people. It is too bad she became acquainted with him before you did, Miss Hemmings."

Mrs. Peoples continued speaking, but Anita had ceased listening. She had heard the news about Bessie and William's engagement just two weeks before from her brother, who had passed on Bessie's request that she be her bridesmaid. And while she had been overjoyed for her friend, she was under the impression that Bessie would be staying at school, since Wellesley was so near Cambridge, where Mr. Lewis coached the Harvard football team.

To leave school for marriage, even for a man like William Henry Lewis, who had pulled himself up from a family of former slaves in Berkley, Virginia, and gone on to Amherst College and Harvard Law, was unfathomable to Anita. She was sure a good man would wait for you to obtain a degree when you were so close. Bessie had turned twenty-seven that year, well past what society deemed the suitable marrying age for women, but Bessie was not like other women, thought Anita. She was far more intelligent. Why couldn't they have a long engagement? It was true that Mr. Lewis was one of the most prominent men in the Negro community and a legend at Harvard, where he coached the football team—he had even authored a book on the subject. But surely a man with such an education would appreciate education in a wife?

"Isn't this your stop, dear?" said Mrs. Peoples loudly, knifing through Anita's thoughts.

Anita looked around. She saw the intersection of Tremont and Hammond streets on her left and picked up her bag. "Thank you for alerting me, and Merry Christmas, Mrs. Peoples," she said as she stepped off the car, thrilled to have shed her surprise companion.

Alone. Anita was finally standing three blocks from home, safely in her neighborhood and ready to slowly become the Negro Anita Hemmings again. She had been told at a young age that fewer than 1 percent of Negro children attended high school and almost none went to college, but that her family knew she was going to be exceptional. And it wasn't just her family. It was her community, her church—women like Mame Marshall—her pastor, her teachers. In the Negro community of Roxbury, everyone knew that Anita Hemmings attended Vassar College, and that she was there as a white woman. A necessary evil, it was agreed, the price they had to pay to send one of their own to the best. But Anita was eager to shrug it all off for several weeks. She wanted to see her family, to spend Christmas in Boston, and to sit by a window and dream about Porter, about Chicago and the life that was waiting for her there.

The way Porter continuously spoke about his parents had made a great impression on her, and made her just as hopeful about her life with him as Porter's sterling character had. He called them "very modern." And his mother was active in the suffrage movement and a firm believer in women's education. The women who were behind the vote were often the same ones who believed in equality of the Negro.

Anita imagined Chicago as a place where she could continue her education, perhaps even work as a professor, but also be a wife and mother with the full backing of Porter and his family. And perhaps one day, she could even tell them the truth. She had often thought during her first semester what it would be like to tell Lottie her secret, but she knew she never would. Lottie, even with her contemporary ideas, was from New York, and adhered to the city's social mores. Porter did not. He was a world apart. And he loved her. *One day*, she thought, *perhaps*.

"It's you!" said Elizabeth when she opened the door. Anita's sister was twenty now, and though she didn't share Anita's academic bent, she had the kindest heart in the family. Her gray wool day dress, which had been Anita's, was too loose on her frame, and Anita knew that with her delicate bones, she would never fill it out.

"I've been waiting by the window all day looking for you. I'm so glad you're home safe," she said wrapping her thin arms around her sister's shoulders and humming a carol. Anita and Elizabeth had the same rolling soprano voice and wide, beautiful faces, but Elizabeth could not have passed for white. Anita had once overheard a woman in church, a light-skinned woman, say, "It is almost a blessing that Elizabeth isn't as clever as her sister," and since that day, Anita had fought to remind everyone that she was.

"You're home," came another voice from inside the house, and out walked Robert Jr., the youngest Hemmings. At fourteen, he had just started high school and was looking more like Frederick every day, though he was already taller. Unlike Anita—who had the lightest skin in the family, along with her father—he would never be mistaken for anything but a Negro.

Robert Jr. helped Anita with her case, and the three siblings went to the back of the small, two-story brick row house, where their mother was in the kitchen.

"Anita!" she said, turning from the stove to hold her oldest child tightly. "I wasn't expecting you until very late." The fabric of their voluminous sleeves was pressed down by each other's arms, and when Anita finally pulled away, she stayed within arm's length of her mother to look at her. Anita's mother always appeared blacker to her when she had been away for several months.

"Are those tears on your face, Anita? Don't cry, now. You must be simply exhausted. Eat something to warm you," said Dora Hemmings, wiping her hands on a towel and taking bread and cheese from a shelf. "We are all so happy to see you. And we'll all be together soon, so stop this crying. Your father isn't home yet and neither is Frederick, but it shouldn't be too long now."

Anita knew her mother was used to Elizabeth crying, but never her steel-spined eldest, and she worried for a moment that Dora might suspect something was wrong. In truth, it was the torrent of guilt about envisioning her blissful life in Chicago with Porter just moments ago that had her in tears. For if she were to have that, she would never be able to have *this*. Porter, a new city, it could mean never visiting her family, her home, again. For even if she told Porter the truth one day, that day was years, maybe even decades away. Her stomach turned at the thought. How unfair, the choices that faced her. How horribly unfair.

"Yes," said Anita, speaking of her father. "Frederick mentioned he had taken another job. He's working two shifts as a janitor now, as well as being a coachman?"

"He is, but it's all right," her mother said. "He likes the work fine. It just means he isn't home as often, but we've all gotten used to it."

Anita thought about her father, a bighearted man with

the work ethic of a penniless new immigrant, but who she worried lacked the strength to work two jobs now that he was in his mid-fifties.

"Now sit with me, and tell me everything about college," said Dora, drying her daughter's tears and leading her into the living room to join Elizabeth and Robert Jr. In her small hands, she carried a tray with tea and Anita's favorite cinnamon cake. Dora, with her extremely limited schooling, had never been able to help her daughter with anything academic, but every time Anita came home from college, Dora looked at her in greater awe. Her beautiful daughter, able to speak Greek, Latin, Italian, and French; who looked through telescopes at stars and spent evenings in chemistry labs, meeting women as intelligent as she was. Her husband came home with an aching back every night from sweeping school floors, cleaning windows, and driving ungrateful men around town. And she herself spent the summers making extra money running a small boardinghouse on Martha's Vineyard. And each year, Anita returned a little more worldly, and increasingly different from her mother.

"Frederick says that you're rooming with one of the richest women in America," said Elizabeth, as her mother handed her a cup of tea.

"Don't you dare say Frederick said this or Frederick said that," Dora warned. "You know better than to gossip about your siblings."

But the face she showed Anita when she handed her a slice of cake and a cup of warm tea meant that she wanted to hear about her daughter's wealthy roommate, too.

"Yes, I am," said Anita. "Louise Taylor—we all call her Lottie—she is a part of the Taylor family of New York. It's true, she's exceptionally rich, but more importantly, very charming and intelligent. She's quite a strong chemistry student, like Frederick, and loves the Orient. She's even sailed all the way to Japan."

"Japan is in the Pacific Ocean and is shaped like a string bean," Elizabeth piped up.

"Yes, that is somewhat correct," said Anita, pleased.

She leaned back in her curved wooden chair, not bothering to adjust her traveling dress, and let her body mold to it. She had missed her family deeply, she realized. It wasn't something she let herself think much about at Vassar, but these faces were always with her, in everything she did.

"And how are your studies?" asked her mother. "Did your first-semester examinations go well?"

"Very well," said Anita, putting down her empty plate. Her mother quickly put another slice of cake on it before she could protest. "I had the top grade in Greek for the fourth year in a row."

Dora Hemmings put down her china to clasp her hands together with evident pride. She had grown up in slave quarters in Virginia before the Civil War and had lived in not much better after the war ended. She was married at eighteen, had Anita a few months later, but somehow, by some miracle, God had turned her daughter into *this* woman. Watching her mother, Anita thought of what she had told her when she passed the Vassar entrance exam: "I had one hundred hands guiding me to school. But the two most important were yours."

At that moment, as Dora was studying Anita's pensive face, the front door opened and in walked Frederick with Robert Sr., letting the winter inside with them.

"Look what the snow blew in," Anita's father said when he saw his eldest.

"Father!" said Anita, a warmth of feeling taking her completely over as he came into the room. She stood and embraced him and Frederick. His body felt spare, even in his layered winter clothes.

"You've been working until now?" A clock somewhere in the house had just struck 9 P.M. Anita loved hearing the sound of clocks rather than bells.

"Everyone appreciates a clean school, I imagine," he said with a smile. "I'm cleaning at Frederick's former high school. Not a bad place. And look at everything that institution did for my intelligent child. I should be giving it something back."

Frederick smiled and put his hand on his father's left shoulder, which had started to slump unnaturally.

That night the family stayed up later than they should have, and when Elizabeth and Robert Jr. went upstairs to bed, the Hemmings parents and Frederick and Anita sat by the fire in the small living room and watched the snow create a scene of undisturbed perfection outside.

"Look at you two," said Robert. "Six more months, and you'll both have college degrees. How did my children turn out so intelligent?"

"You told us we would sleep outside in the hail and snow if we ever came home with poor grades," said Frederick, laughing.

"Did I say that?" asked Robert, his light gray eyes smiling along. His thin face, different from Anita's and Dora's rounder ones, was covered in well-groomed whiskers, cut in the popular English style. Despite his evening of janitorial work, he had changed into a wool lounge suit before coming home to greet his daughter properly. "I'm so pleased I said such an awful thing. It seems to have been effective. Perhaps I should threaten Elizabeth and Robert, too."

"Anita," said her mother, when her father had fallen quiet. "Are you lacking for anything in school?"

Anita knew this was the way her mother had of asking: Do the others still think you are a wealthy white student instead of a poor Negro one?

"I'm not lacking for a thing, Mother. I'm still tutoring in Poughkeepsie twice a week," she said. "And I earn enough from that for my clothes and outings. You both do enough by paying the expensive tuition; I can manage the rest. As for the other matter, everything is as it should be."

"I'm so glad to hear it. We do worry so much about you there, hiding certain realities, and for what? To have the education you're entitled to, I suppose. I wish things could be different for you."

"But they might never be," said Anita, reaching for her mother's hand while trying to keep Porter Hamilton out of her thoughts.

"Don't say that," said Dora. "Just finish your year, come home to us, and be my daughter again."

"I'm still your daughter," said Anita, feeling tears of guilt building in her throat.

"Of course you are," said Dora.

Anita got up from her chair and went to sit by her mother, folding her body onto the floor and letting her head fall into her lap.

"You're my brave girl," said her mother, smoothing her daughter's straight black hair, identical to her father's. "You're my smart, brave girl."

For another hour, the four of them sat in the sparsely furnished living room and spoke about the Christmas holiday, about Anita's and Frederick's studies and what the two of them hoped to do after graduation. Knowing that her parents could not pay for any more schooling, as they had to save for her two youngest siblings, Anita did not mention her plans for graduate school and instead maneuvered the conversation toward her brother. Frederick wanted to start work as a chemist immediately, and was aware that his chances of obtaining employment were best in Boston, where the MIT professors could assist him.

Anita looked at her father flush with pride as he listened to Frederick speak of his future. Robert Hemmings Sr. had never been able to make plans or weigh choices the way his two oldest children were now doing, brimming with optimism. His mother, Sarah, was illiterate her whole life. Impregnated by his white father as a young woman, she had never married and had little to offer her son in their tiny wooden dwelling in Virginia. She gave him love, rags for clothes, and a strong head for independence, but that was all. His children had been given so much more.

In Robert's rural southern town, there hadn't been a school for Negroes until 1866, and by that time he was twenty-three, had seen the horrors of the Civil War and had dreams to leave the South forever. He and Dora had married at twenty-eight and eighteen respectively, and had left Virginia without a backward glance. Anita had come along shortly after their arrival in Massachusetts. Robert and Dora Hemmings had made it plain to their children that they had no fondness for the state of Virginia but refrained from speaking about their childhoods past that. Massachusetts hadn't brought them wealth, but it had brought them hope. Their children went to fine integrated Boston schools; they weren't scared for their lives. They were only scared for Anita.

Before Anita went upstairs for the night to the room she shared with her sister, and Frederick to the one he shared with Robert Jr., her brother stopped her at the stairs and put his finger to his lips. He led her quietly by the arm into the cramped kitchen.

"We need to talk about Phil Day," he whispered, trying to get close to the heat still coming from the open fire.

"Lottie hasn't forgotten you," Anita whispered back, "but she's starting to. The man we found as her escort for Phil, Joseph Southworth, he was perfect for her. Amusing, too. Everybody was pleased with him."

"And you?" asked Frederick, firmly. "Whom were you pleased with?"

"Not Porter Hamilton, if that's what you're implying," said Anita. She hated to lie to Frederick, but it was four days before Christmas and if she told him the truth, she feared their holiday would be ruined. She would confess everything to him in a letter when she was back at school. She wanted to give him time to think about it away from their family; she couldn't risk him confiding in her parents now. If they knew, they wouldn't let her return to Poughkeepsie.

"He was not your escort at Phil?" Frederick probed.

"No. He was present, but I didn't share one dance with him. We exchanged a few polite words and I spent my time with others. But not one longer than the next."

"Good," said Frederick, relaxing. "That has been weighing on me, Anita. I understand the temptation, but you cannot. You never can."

"I know," said Anita. "I understand that now." She gave her brother a kiss on the cheek and said, "Good night, Frederick. I'm so happy we are both home." Anita felt her face contorting with her lies, but Frederick, appeased, didn't appear to notice his sister's strained expression or the tension in her step as she walked up the creaking wooden stairs to the top floor.

CHAPTER 13

Three days after Christmas, Anita had just finished getting dressed to stand by Elizabeth Baker as she married William Henry Lewis at St. John the Evangelist Church when her friend took her by surprise. Bessie walked into her bedroom in her parents' small Cambridge house and closed the door quickly behind her.

Like so many Negroes Anita knew, Bessie had been born in the South and had come north as a child. Her family was from Halifax, Virginia, a small town on the Tennessee border. Her father, Eldridge Baker, had been a laborer there, but in Cambridge he worked as a salesman and as a waiter in a hotel. Bessie had left Virginia as a baby and had never returned. One night in their shared room at Northfield, Anita and Bessie had looked out their large window over the campus, down the hill to Dwight Moody's white cottage with its double chimneys, and had agreed to never travel to the state their parents had fled. That same night, Bessie had confided in Anita that she had been born when her mother, Caroline, was still unmarried. She sometimes thought—though she felt sinful for entertaining such thoughts—that Eldridge, the only father she had ever known, was not her biological one as she was so much lighter-skinned than her siblings and was born before her mother married him.

But all of that was forgotten now. It was her wedding day, and to Bessie, and by extension Anita, the world was perfect for one afternoon.

Bessie was wearing her wedding dress of brown and gray camel's hair, topped with a coat basque, the front a beautiful heliotrope silk. Her wide hat, with black velvet trim, matched her gown and gloves. Anita looked down at Bessie's long, slender hands; instead of holding flowers, she clutched a white leather prayer book. Anita opened her arms wide to embrace her friend.

"Oh Bessie, you're getting married!" she said. There was no one, not even her family, whom she missed the way she missed Bessie. Bessie had been with her when she was living as a white student. In their shared room, Anita was able to let her guard down every night, something she sorely missed at Vassar.

"I am," said Bessie, embracing her friend, her prayer book pressed tight against the back of Anita's blue silk and lace dress. "And to the most wonderful man. I can't wait for you to meet him properly. He's primed to do important things in his lifetime. He already has, but I think all this— Harvard and football—is just the beginning. There's much more coming for him."

Even though William Henry Lewis was already a legend in the Negro community in Massachusetts, and one with strong ties to local white political leaders, he and Bessie had decided to keep their wedding intimate. There were but forty guests in the pews, and most were prominent Negroes from Cambridge, Wellesley, and Boston. Anita and Bessie watched from the carriage as their families entered the church. Along with them were respected Negro men, friends of William, and whom Bessie pointed out to Anita as they made their way in through one of the three front doors.

"That is Dr. Samuel Courtney," she noted as one man walked from a hansom to the church. "A renowned physician. Oh, but more importantly, the older man behind him with the closely cropped hair and whiskers is the famous Archibald Grimké. He is the nephew of the abolitionist Grimké sisters and a fellow graduate of Harvard Law School. He currently serves as American consul to the Dominican Republic. A noted writer, too. I've never made his acquaintance myself, but William was telling me he would make time in his travels to attend, and here he is. How kind of him."

"Of course he did," said Anita, watching the parade of distinguished men with interest. "William is marrying the most beautiful woman in Massachusetts. Who wouldn't want to attend?"

After an emotional moment a few minutes later in which Bessie pledged that her marriage would do nothing to change their friendship, Anita walked her down the aisle to William, who was standing with his best man, J. Howard Lee of Newton, Massachusetts.

Anita and Bessie had been so alike until they went to Northfield together. From the day they had filled out their short applications, Anita had made the irreversible decision to be a white student, foreseeing passing as the only way she could gain admission to Vassar, and Bessie, though physically she could have done the same, chose not to. But on Bessie's wedding day, Anita felt as if they were the same girls again, from similar backgrounds and on a shared path.

She had often wondered what her life would be like if she had not decided to study for the Vassar entrance exam, but had remained a Negro and tried to gain admission to Wellesley. Harriet Alleyne Rice had been the first Negro to graduate from that notable school, in 1887, but she and Bessie knew that Wellesley was not likely to admit two in two years. Bessie was only the third Negro to be granted admission, and nearly ten years after the first and second. Anita hadn't wanted to take Bessie's place. That's what she remembered telling herself at the time. But the truth was, she had wanted to go to Vassar since that day in church; she just wasn't sure how. Yes, Mame Marshall had suggested passing, but that did not take care of the paperwork. Northfield—a boarding school that bright women of little means attended after graduating from less demanding high schools—made it a possibility. The school, which some entered for only a year or two, was excellent at preparing women for college entrance exams and provided her with distance from her Boston high school, which had her in its records as Negro. But Northfield did much more than that. To live in a place where differences were embraced and genuinely Christian principles trumped prejudices taken as God's truth elsewhere, gave Anita the confidence she needed to fill out her Vassar application and to say yes when she was accepted.

It was not until well after the ceremony that Anita was able to properly speak to William Lewis, and she quickly understood why not just the Negro community of Boston, but white, educated Boston, had fallen under his spell. He had eyes with a rare depth and brightness, a firm build and broad face with a soft wave of black hair parted elegantly in the middle. He was almost as light-skinned as she and Bessie were, though not enough to disavow Negro heritage.

"Thank you for being part of today," he said, bowing to Anita. "Bessie is fonder of you than you'll ever know."

"And I of her," said Anita, taken aback by William's commanding presence.

"Good," he said, watching Anita change her casual posture to match his formality. "She is a woman who should be loved."

Anita nodded and looked around the room for her friend, but she was busy greeting other guests. She glimpsed Bessie's sister, Gertrude, whom she had already spoken with, mentioning nothing about her trip to Radcliffe. Feeling a familiar wave of shame about her behavior that day, she turned back to William and changed the subject. "Bessie told me that it was W. E. B. Du Bois who introduced you, when you were a student at Amherst."

"That's right," said William, speaking informally about the great Negro leader. "Elizabeth and W. E. B., along with the other Boston-area students—Harvard's William Monroe Trotter and others—they all attended my graduation. I was not the only Negro graduate that year; my Virginia Normal classmate William Tecumseh Sherman Jackson and George Washington Forbes of Ohio graduated, too."

"Three Negroes graduated in the same class?"

"Yes, class of 1892. Life opened its gates for me at Amherst, Anita. It wasn't like Elizabeth's experience has been at Wellesley. I was not alone."

"I can't imagine," said Anita, who had never been in a class with three Negroes.

"No, you can't," he said, softening slightly, his words coming slower. "But I will tell you one anecdote and maybe you'll have a better idea of my school. In my early days there, the president of Amherst College handed me tuition money while I was working as a horse groomer. I was standing in a barn brushing an Appaloosa, and he came and put a stack of notes in my palm. It was quite a bit more than I would have made in six months of grooming horses and he said it came straight from God himself. Can you imagine that?

According to President Merrill Gates, God was set on my graduating as an Amherst man. And then I captained the football team. It was a memorable four years." He allowed a small smile to show on his broad, proud face.

Anita could barely comprehend what William was describing. She knew he had been a football captain and star at Harvard, the first Negro all-American as a law student and then a coach, but she had not known of his happiness at Amherst. It was painful to realize that there were academic communities that embraced the Negro scholar, but hers was not one of them.

"I didn't know that Bessie was acquainted with W. E. B. Du Bois back in '92," Anita said. "We were still at Northfield together then."

"Yes, she was," William confirmed. "And is even more so today."

"I feel foolish that I didn't know," said Anita, trying not to sound like a mere acquaintance of the bride.

"Well, Miss Hemmings," said William, "it is hard to keep up with the actions and friendships of the pioneers of our race when you are living among Caucasians as one of them. Things will change for you after you return to Boston, as yourself."

Anita said nothing, but her throat tightened. She was in a room full of people who were considered the very best of the Negro race, those destined, perhaps, to help transform the country, and she was the only one who had chosen to duck the obstacles of being a Negro college student. French and English descent—that's what she had written on her college application. But it was for Vassar, she told herself as she said goodbye to William and watched him walk over to his bride. She had wanted that more than this.

As the evening wound down, Anita found herself alone

with Bessie for the first time since the ceremony. She stole her friend away and wrapped her arms around her.

"Promise me again that I won't lose you to marriage. I don't know what my life would be without your friendship, Bessie. We are such a part of each other."

"Of course you won't lose me," said Bessie. "You'll never lose me."

Anita let her friend go, and looked at her, a wife.

"Do you think I made the wrong decision?" she asked. "It's horrible to ask you such a question now, on your wedding day, but it was something your husband said to me, and now my mind is racing to the past, questioning everything I never stumbled over then. Should I have done what you did? Taken the entrance exam for Wellesley or Radcliffe and not Vassar?"

Bessie didn't hesitate.

"No, Anita," she said, firmly. "You took the exam for Vassar because you knew you could pass it. You're more intelligent than I. You always have been. You had to take it, you had to prove to everyone—our everyone, their everyone— that a Negro could soar through their exam and be accepted to Vassar just as well as a white woman. They don't know you're there, but we know. That is the most important part. You're so clever, so worthy; it would have been the great shame of your life if you never tried."

"You're braver," said Anita. "You may wrongly think that I'm more intelligent, but you are braver. It is the Negro walking as a Negro through a white world who is braver. Always."

"But now I'm not so brave, am I? I won't be returning to Wellesley, I won't be granted a degree. So now you have to obtain your A.B. for both of us. You'll think of me when you walk for your diploma. Promise?"

"Yes, I will," said Anita, reaching for her friend's hand.

"Northfield was so different from Vassar and even Wellesley, wasn't it?" said Bessie, holding Anita's hand tight. "I miss standing on the tower of Marquand Hall with you and looking down on the campus, on the farmland, all those beautiful stone and brick buildings." She smiled momentarily at the memory but grew serious again as the concern lingered in Anita's face. "Sometimes I wish we were still there."

"I've always wanted to ask you something, and now that I've started speaking like this, let me just ask it plainly," said Anita. She knew she had to let her friend return to her guests, but she wanted to hold on to their intimacy a moment longer.

"You are not speaking inappropriately—"

"Am I a coward?" asked Anita, interrupting her. "Did I apply to Vassar because I'm intelligent and wanted to attend the very best school, or was it because I was afraid; because I no longer wanted to live as Negro in a white world, because it was too difficult?"

Bessie shook her head vigorously. "You did not do it because you were afraid," she said. "I've never seen anything frighten you. As for being Negro in a white world, you were one until Northfield. That's almost all your life. And you are one now, even if you're the only one there who is aware of it. But think of this, Anita: Negro or not, you've been top of your class again and again. So no, you are not a coward. That school, those people, they are the cowards."

CHAPTER 14

It was after the New Year when Anita and Frederick Hemmings had a most unfortunate encounter. In Cambridge to tutor Greek and chemistry at the home of two Negro high school students preparing for their college entrance exams, the siblings crossed the street to the side where the stately Magnolia Inn reigned. Anita had always liked the Queen Anne–style building, with its five rounded windows and bell tower, and today she wanted to observe it more closely. When she walked past the first lower window, Frederick by her side, she saw reflected there, without question, the beautiful flushed face of Lottie Taylor.

"Frederick!" she hissed at her brother. "We have to make ourselves scarce. Now!"

He looked at her trying to jump behind a carriage, but it was too late. Lottie had seen them. She clasped her hands together and ran across the street to them, waving excitedly.

"Anita and Frederick Hemmings, can that really be the pair of you?" she said through the fur collar enveloping the lower part of her face. "I thought of you both on the train to Boston, but I never did think that I would see you. And here you are, a belated Christmas present to me! I'm always the lucky one. What are you doing here in Cambridge? And right outside the hotel where we stayed, Anita."

"Lottie!" said Anita, wrapping her arms around her. "This is such a surprise. A most welcome surprise." She had no idea why Lottie was in Cambridge, and she was terrified what Lottie might be able to find out about them in that city, even in a short amount of time. It was highly likely that they could run into an acquaintance from Negro Boston, or one of Frederick's classmates from the Institute of Technology. The campus was in the Back Bay, but many students hailed from the Cambridge area. Anita had to get rid of Lottie fast. "What on earth are you doing in Cambridge?" she asked, genially.

"It was an absolute surprise of a visit!" Lottie said, her face as animated as ever. "Father is up from Tennessee and had work to attend to here, and I was growing awfully bored in New York. Yes, I know, how does one get bored in New York, especially during the season? But you see, I can get bored anywhere. I bet I could get bored sitting on the moon. So I decided to come up and pay dear Nettie a visit because she's such fun, but I didn't dare telegram you, Anita, so close to Christmas. That's just not done. And besides, I don't have your home address. But now here you are, so maybe it was a sign that I should have."

"Well, it's just a joy to see you, regardless of the circumstances," Anita said smoothly. "It was starting to feel strange not to have you just a wall away."

"Wasn't it!" said Lottie, hugging her friend again.

While Anita and Lottie fussed over each other and the chance encounter, Frederick stood there wordlessly. Finally he said, with forced warmth, "Lottie Taylor, I'm so pleased to see you again. What a fortuitous coincidence. We are just here in Cambridge paying a New Year's visit to an aunt who lives near the Yard."

"Are you? I didn't know you two had an aunt in Cambridge," Lottie replied. "As I said, I'm paying a visit, too. Anita knows the lady in question. Nettie Aldrich, née DeWitt. She lives just off the Yard as well. Are you headed in that direction? You should both come call on her with me. I know she would love to see you again, Anita."

"Oh, no," said Frederick quickly. "We couldn't impose. It wouldn't be right."

"And we've just come from that direction," said Anita. "We were just taking some air until we headed back to Boston."

"May we walk you toward Mrs. Aldrich's?" asked Frederick, both he and Anita praying they could lead her away quickly. They were less likely to see familiar faces in Nettie's sophisticated residential neighborhood.

"You must have been walking circles then. The Yard is this way," Lottie said, pointing behind her. "Unless this is all a lie, Frederick Hemmings, and you're actually having an illicit romance at the Magnolia? Maybe Anita is covering it all up for you?"

"Lottie!" Anita exclaimed, as she scanned the face of every passerby, fearing the worst.

"I most certainly am not," said Frederick, the corners of his mouth twitching a little. Anita glimpsed his expression and knew his intention immediately. It was far better for Lottie to think that he had spent the day indulging in an affair at the Magnolia than that he was heading to a Negro home.

"You know, I'm in no real rush to get to Nettie's," said Lottie. Her face made it plain that she thought she'd touched on the truth. "Both of you are so much more interesting. And Frederick, I was awfully disappointed that you were not able to come to Phil. It would have been so much more memorable a day if you were there with me."

"Come now, I think you enjoy flattering me," said Frederick, shepherding Lottie away from the hotel, Anita trailing behind them, still in a state of alarm. "I'm sure you had far more pleasant company."

"Not at all!" she protested. "A Hemmings is as good as it gets."

The three walked quickly, leaving the hotel full of holiday patrons behind them. Frederick and Anita were extremely thankful that their overcoats hid the plain clothes they were wearing underneath, as they were dressed to tutor, not to visit with Lottie Taylor.

"Come to think of it," said Lottie, looking around her, "why don't we all sit at the Magnolia for a while and catch up on all the holiday gossip? There's nothing very interesting this way, and I have plenty of time. Besides, now that I've run into you together, I feel rude and foolish for not having tracked down your address and called on your family. If you give it to me now, I can call on you tomorrow and finally meet the rest of the charming Hemmings family."

"I'm afraid our younger sister, Elizabeth, has come down with a terrible bronchitis," said Frederick instantly as Anita tried to calm her pulse. "We are not having visitors this week, but I'm happy to ask Mother if she thinks Elizabeth will improve later in the week."

"No," said Lottie, thinking. "This week I am very taken with the occult and an illness is never a good sign. Plus, I am due to train back home with Father tomorrow evening. But I'm so glad fate intervened to correct my social misstep and I was able to see the two of you today."

Frederick saw Anita close her eyes in relief. "But let us all have something to eat at the Magnolia," he said. "We must enjoy the pleasure of your company a little while longer, Miss Taylor."

For the next hour, Anita and Frederick not only had to miss their tutoring appointments, which meant they would lose their positions, but they also sat rudely with their coats on, making excuses about the chill and their fear of spreading Elizabeth's illness.

"Frederick Hemmings, as you tortured me by not attending Phil Day, I shall torture you by telling you about all the fun we had," said Lottie between bites of Viennese chocolate cake.

Anita had been so shaken by Lottie's sudden appearance that it hadn't occurred to her that her roommate might tell Frederick about her attending the dance with Porter Hamilton. She looked at Lottie in a panic but was unable to catch her eye.

"Caroline and Belle, our two closest friends, attended with charming Yale men, and Anita—" She paused midsentence as Anita kicked her hard under the table. "And Anita . . ." she continued, "had a most amusing time, also, even though she was without a formal escort."

She looked at Anita and gave her a knowing smile. "Yes, your sister is quite a wonderful dancer. Though she danced alone! Completely and utterly alone. Just her practicing steps with the wall."

"That's enough talk about Vassar," said Anita, standing. "Please excuse me for a moment. I will leave you two to speak on different subjects." She wound her way through the large room toward the powder room. Anita was used to being in cahoots with Frederick, not conspiring with Lottie to hide something from him. She hated lying to her brother, but she knew he would not be able to contain himself over Porter. He would have erupted right in front of Lottie, with an intensity that was unexplainable.

When she returned, she saw Frederick sitting alone, his

face stony. She looked around the room for Lottie and saw only the back of her coat as she hurried out of the hotel.

"What did you say to Lottie that upset her so?" she asked in alarm.

"What did I say, Anita?" said Frederick angrily. "I explained to the aristocratic Lottie Taylor that we could never be romantically involved. That I would be a great disappointment to her if she knew me better. I told her to give up hope with regard to any sort of romance, that she had to forget me at once."

"You didn't!" said Anita, choking out the words. She was quite sure that no man had ever spoken to Lottie Taylor that way and that she would be furious. "How could you do such a thing?"

"I had no choice, did I?" said Frederick coldly. "We are but a short journey from the institute where I attend school as a Negro, she asked for our home address to call on us later this week—don't you realize how dangerous this all is?" he said, motioning to the hotel's sumptuous lobby. "Do you realize what I do for you, Anita? To protect you? The things I should say to you now, the things I could!"

"I have no notion what you are talking about, Frederick," said Anita. "Just speak plainly."

Frederick looked at her, anger etched on his face. "I don't have a thing to say. You seem intent on ruining your life despite my advice, so please, Anita, continue to do so."

CHAPTER 15

On their first day back in January, Anita left her room in the afternoon for her required exercise. When she returned a half hour later, Lottie was reclining on the couch in their parlor, her head on a velvet pillow, waiting for her.

Taking barely a second to greet Anita, Lottie launched into a riff on her plan to eat all of Belle Tiffany's dinner along with her own because Belle was in the infirmary and being forced to starve away her fever.

"The dear doctor must have taken part in the Salem Witch Trials," said Lottie, her legs kicking the couch rhythmically.

"Dr. Thelberg is two hundred years old?" asked Anita.

"She might have been reincarnated a few times since then, but she was there, I assure you. Only witches require seniors to starve. And tonight they're serving lamb! I stopped by the carving room on the way back from the messenger room and it looked divine." Lottie rolled over to face the wall and said carelessly, "Oh, the post arrived. You had a letter from Frederick. I think I put it on the card table. Or was it your desk?"

Anita looked, angry with herself for not getting to the mail first, and spotted the letter on her wooden desk, where her papers had been pushed aside to make it the focal point.

She turned the envelope over, put it in the pocket of her dress, and stood up. "I think I will visit Belle in the infirmary. Perhaps I can sneak in some food to her. Would you like to come?"

"Are you going to torture me by not opening your brother's letter here and now," said Lottie, pouting. "You know I still hold out hope for us."

"Do you?" asked Anita, shocked. Could Lottie still be so fond of Frederick after what he had said to her in Boston? She knew that Lottie became easily fixated on things, on people, but her affection for Frederick had to have its limits. "I was sure that Joseph Southworth had replaced my unremarkable little brother in your eyes," she said.

"Unremarkable! He is nothing of the sort. He is extremely dashing, your brother. But it is true, so is Joseph. I suppose I'm still choosing," said Lottie with a dramatic wave of her hands.

"Ah," said Anita, taking the letter out of her pocket to appease her friend. She picked up Lottie's sterling silver letter opener from her desk and passed it through the fold of the envelope. She sat on the rocking chair from Uncle Fred and silently read the one-page letter.

> *Dear Anita,*
>
> *I know everything. Lottie disclosed the details of Phil Day with me, from your dancing ten times with Porter Hamilton to your shameful behavior with him in your bedroom. End your relationship now and prove to me that you have, or I will tell Mother and Father about Porter. It is a terrible threat for me to have to make, but I know it is the only one that will prompt you to act as you should. I await your letter, but I won't for very long.*
>
> *Your brother Frederick*

Anita looked up, unable to hide her emotion. So Lottie had revealed everything to Frederick. It must have been the day at the hotel when Anita had slipped off to the powder room, leaving the two of them alone. She wondered why he had not confronted her then, now remembering how angry he was. She guessed that part of him knew how much she needed to be with her family, to enjoy her time at home. Their mother must have told him of her tears on her first night back. But he was not holding back his words, or threats, now.

"Anita! What's wrong?" Lottie demanded, jumping up and coming over to her. But Anita ripped the letter apart before her roommate could take it from her. "I hope it's not about me," Lottie said, and Anita shook her head firmly no.

"No, it's about Porter," she said, determined to say very little to her roommate. "Frederick doesn't approve."

Anita took the pieces of the letter and left the room. She rushed down the stairs to the empty senior parlor, dropped them in the roaring fire, and hurried out the door. She would visit Belle, she would shake off the horrible thoughts in her mind, and then she would go to the chapel and pray.

If she did not end her engagement with Porter now, her parents would force her to as soon as they learned the truth. They might even do it for her, go so far as to tell him the truth about her race. With her brother's solution, she would lose Porter; with his threat, she would lose Porter, her secret, and perhaps Vassar as well.

When Anita returned to her room late that night, having skipped the lamb dinner, Lottie was still awake. Anita sat down on her friend's bed, knowing no excuse was needed for her absence that evening.

"I didn't tell your brother because I don't love you," Lottie said. "Or you and Porter together. I just wanted to feel close to Frederick, to share something with him. And I wanted you to have his blessing. I was sure he would give it if I could explain how happy you were."

"He did not," said Anita, thinking about her swift kick to Lottie's shin, which had made no impression except a physical one. She closed her eyes and let the tears stream. And because she didn't have another shoulder to cry on, she cried on Lottie's.

The following day, before the sun came up, Anita sat in the reading room of the library, her oil lamp so close to her face that she felt her skin prickle with the heat. She pulled out her finest paper and wrote a letter woven of lies.

My dear Porter,

   My heavy hands and heavier heart have to do the most awful thing I can imagine: put an end to our engagement. I misled you. I must marry someone else. I am devastated, and I am sorry.

                                        Anita

CHAPTER 16

I am awash with guilt, Anita," said Lottie as the two were ice-skating on the steely gray Vassar lake, the gelid day silent around them. It was the depth of winter in New York. No bird streaked across the sky, no pine tree stirred, the natural world lay frozen. But Lottie's personality had no such season: happy, exhausted, penitent, she overflowed with life.

She took her hands out of her fur muff, throwing it onto the stiff grass beside the pond, the better to work up speed on the ice.

"I feel such regret!" she shouted, coasting back to the center. "I shouldn't have told Frederick; I can see that now. I simply had no idea he would react so. Who wouldn't want his sister to be engaged to a Chicago Hamilton? They are one of the most renowned families in the Middle West. And Porter is handsome, brilliant, and scandal-free. I know Frederick is tucked away in remote Ithaca, but even he must know that's a rare combination these days at Harvard. All those badly behaved heirs from chip-chop arriviste families. Porter is one of the only ones without rumors of this or that bubbling around them. Frederick should have been thrilled."

"Yes, Frederick should have been, but that is not his way.

He thinks I handled myself very badly," said Anita, her arms extended for balance. "In fact, he is sure I've embarrassed myself beyond repair."

Lottie stopped, gouging the smooth ice with her sharp blades, and looked at her roommate, still a little unsteady on the ice after three years of skating. "I didn't know your brother was such a traditionalist about women. How could I! Besides, it's just not right. Even the most proper woman could not deny Porter Hamilton one little kiss." She made a little moue of apology. "I was aware, by the application of your toe to my leg, that you did not want me to discuss Porter in front of you, but I was quite sure that if it were just Frederick and I, that I could make him understand. I thought I could be a help to you."

Had Frederick told Lottie she had no hope of him after she had told him about Porter, or before? Anita would never know. And it was too late to try to deduce who had acted in retaliation; it was already a fait accompli. She looked down at the frozen lake and couldn't help but think about Chicago— their lake, the elevated trains, the pulse of the city, the man no one wanted her to be with. She swallowed the pain that was feasting on her body and steadied by digging her toe in the ice, too.

"No, Frederick's correct," she replied. "I acted inappropriately. He is right to disapprove. But it *was* very hard to say no to Porter. I do . . . I did . . . have so much affection for him."

"I should have had more foresight," said Lottie, starting to loop around her friend to keep her close. Every Vassar student was required to complete three hours of exercise a week, but in winter, one of those hours could be spent on the frozen lake, and Anita and Lottie had made it a Friday tradition.

Anita licked her chapped lips, her skin raw from the January cold, and watched Lottie circling her like a child desperate to be loved again.

"You know me, Anita, I just can't hold my tongue. It should really have been cut off years ago," Lottie said, swaying winsomely from side to side on her blades. "I am truly sorry. I wasn't using my head. Now, what can I do? Tell me, please, I beg of you. I miss my dear friend Anita Hemmings. She's been replaced with an empty, dispirited impostor. I'll do anything to have the old Anita back."

"This is me we are speaking of?" said Anita, cutting away from Lottie when she circled behind her.

Anita had come to realize that ending her engagement with Porter was unavoidable if she was to save herself in the here and now, but she refused to think of the break as permanent. Somehow she would find a way to put things right again. And this time she wouldn't make the mistake of announcing their relationship publicly. She had to send Porter another letter explaining everything, without revealing the real reasons behind her rash decision, and she had to accomplish it without Lottie intervening, an increasingly difficult task.

Lottie skated past Anita and planted herself in front of her, hands on hips, lips still in a pout. For the first time in the three days since she had written her heartbreaking letter to Porter, Anita gave in.

"Oh, Lottie," she said, her anger trumped, at least for now, by the urge to confide in her friend. "I'm so grief-stricken about it all. I don't know what to do. I know you weren't telling Frederick about us maliciously, and if Frederick was of a more liberal bent when it came to women and morality, it might have been different. You could have been helping me. But Frederick is as old-fashioned as they come, and if news about Porter and me had spread, you can imagine the scandal. It would have left me unmarriageable and caused a terrible scandal for the school. I could have been expelled."

"But word of the romantic—yet unfortunate—incident will not spread, Anita," said Lottie gliding over to retrieve her muff. She picked it up and sat on the white, frozen grass, pulling her wool skirt tight around her legs. "I'll never breathe a word of it to anyone."

"I believe you made that promise once before," said Anita, sitting down next to her. She pulled her skirt tight, as Lottie had, her legs quite numb. There was a smell of snow in the air, and Anita hoped it would start falling while they were on the ice.

"But it was only to your brother!" Lottie protested. "I assumed you were planning to tell him about Porter before the winter holiday ended. Haven't you told the rest of your family about the engagement? Your mother? If I were engaged to a Hamilton, my cries of excitement would have beaten me home."

"Porter and I agreed to wait until after graduation," said Anita. "I thought I had told you."

"You did not," said Lottie, accurately. "But you should have. I wish you had! Then we wouldn't be in this awful position. I feel as if we're pinned to a wall and we just can't be ourselves because of this misunderstanding. The last few days have been miserable. I just can't have you so cross with me. It's our final year here, and there are too many wonderful things to do together. But you'll see, Anita. We can make the world all right again." Lottie stood up, skated to the middle of the pond, and started spinning so fast she grew dizzy.

"You're going to fall!" said Anita, chasing out after her.

"And what if I do?" said Lottie, slowing down and putting her hand on Anita's shoulder for balance. She threw her head back, and Anita did, too, watching as two bright red northern cardinals flew across the sky, a rare sight on campus. Lottie pointed at them, then said, "People sometimes do."

Anita shrugged off her roommate's arm and watched as Lottie spun off like a falling snowflake in the other direction, then came back to lean on her again. Both girls, after a very tense beginning to their second term, were finally growing calmer.

"You never know which way the wind will blow when it comes to these sort of things," said Lottie, rubbing her hands together for warmth. "Porter may not be lost to you forever, and even if he is, the world's men do not begin and end with Porter Hamilton. I was crazy about Henry Silsbury, but I forgot him in a flash when he proved unworthy of my affection. Now I am wild about—"

"Do not say my brother Frederick, not after all this," said Anita, looking out across the frozen campus. Anita had always loved the silence of winter. When she was at Northfield, colder even than Boston, she had loved the way the weather would blow through her skin. Here in Poughkeepsie in January, that familiar feeling of a frozen world was starting to sink in. Anita watched as three other girls, lowerclassmen, arrived at the lake in their skates and stepped tentatively onto it, as if it might suddenly crack and pull them under forever. Once reassured, they held hands and sped off across the ice, shouting with delight as they reveled in their first winter as college women.

"I wasn't going to," said Lottie. "Not after he turned you into this doleful creature. I was going to say Old Southpaw."

"Oh, good," said Anita, relieved. "I like Old Southpaw."

"So do I," said Lottie. Still, Anita sensed that despite Joseph Southworth's amiability, good looks, and deep pockets, Lottie was not yet convinced that he was worthier of her affection than Frederick.

"What did you once say about the borings?" Anita mused. "That you need someone dripping with charm, to cure them? Joseph is that. He's bathed in charm. Every girl who had him on her card at Phil said as much."

"Yes, he is. And very rich. *And* Japanese. I'm so taken with the fact that he might have been born to great scandal in the Orient. Do remind me to look into that story, won't you? I like it too much for it to be made up."

Anita nodded, closed her eyes, and let Lottie ramble on. Though she didn't want it to, the veil of her sadness had started to slip a little.

Anita didn't doubt that Lottie had meant her no harm when she told Frederick about her and Porter. And she had to admit she was happy she still had Lottie in her life. She thought of Alberta Scott at Radcliffe, and how Lilly had crossed the street to avoid her. She even thought of Gertrude and her own Bessie, living in a single room at Wellesley, set apart at the school from the beginning. But she, Anita, got to spend afternoons skating, holding her friend's hand, with freshmen calling out to her by name and watching her with envy. She was lucky.

"Anita! I have the most perfect idea!" said Lottie all of a sudden, spraying up ice like a hockey player. Anita looked at her with amusement. She knew that Lottie Taylor never shared her ideas while standing still.

"What is it?" she asked. She was starting to feel more confident that she could mend things with Porter. If Lottie was so sanguine about life, then why shouldn't she be?

"Let's go to New York!" Lottie said. "Just you and me. Or

you and me and Caroline and Belle. Mother is in and out of the city house, as it's the season, and Father is in Tennessee for months at a time. They won't be a bother, and John is up at school. There's nothing terribly exciting going on here this month, as the third hall play isn't until February. You promised when we started rooming together that you would come down to New York, and now is the right time. It will cheer you up, I just know it will. And if you do meet Mother, it will prepare you for the tornado she will surely be at commencement. Do say yes. Please!"

New York. A weekend at the Taylors' house. It was the kind of idea Frederick would have forbidden Anita to even consider, but she dismissed him from her thoughts, grabbing Lottie's arm and letting herself be pulled across the ice.

"I would love to go," she said. "And let's bring Caroline and Belle, too. The Gatehouse group in New York, what a wonderful idea."

CHAPTER 17

Anita had been to New York City twice before, both times as a guest at another Vassar student's home, and it had left a deep impression on her. She already knew she wanted to live there one day, not just pass through as a visitor. But nothing could have prepared her for the golden New York City of Lottie Taylor.

The new year had brought even more wealth to the Taylor family, as Clarence Taylor had been recruited to work on an expansion of railroads through Tennessee and the Carolinas, now a part of the Southern Railway company. He was headquartered in Charleston, but the money he was amassing with the speed of the locomotives shooting across the hills was being sent straight up to New York to Lottie's mother. A woman obsessed with appearances, and particularly the appearance of her palatial Fifth Avenue residence, Mina Taylor was just as quickly taking the wealth and turning it into rooms full of paintings, sculptures, custom-made furniture, and other fin-de-siècle luxuries. If she wasn't already a fixture of the *New York Times'* society columns for her dinners or connections, she was well aware that her latest acquisitions were always good for a few inches. Her home also gave her an occupation in the absence of her husband and children: as patron and friend of some of the best artists, architects, and interior designers in the country.

The Taylors' home—fit for a European royal or the American equivalent, a magnate with humble Pittsburgh origins—occupied half a New York City block. Anita's whole house would have fit inside Mr. Taylor's bedroom, a matchbox dropped inside a railway station. But she had resolved not to fret about such things. Since their little group decided to make the trip down, she had read descriptions of Lottie's home in past issues of the *Times* archived in Vassar's library, and she felt fully prepared to keep her composure. Caroline had seen more of the world than most people would in their lifetimes, while Belle had grown up amid moneyed ease in Fredonia, New York. They will be impressed, Anita thought, but they certainly won't appear rattled, and I won't, either.

After a two-hour train ride down the east side of the Hudson and a short trot along the busy city streets, their hansoms pulled through the towering iron carriage gates in front of the Renaissance-inspired Taylor house on Fifth Avenue. When the horses were still, several maids rushed out to help the girls with their luggage. Though they would be staying just three nights, Anita, Belle, and Caroline had packed enough for a weeklong trip, anxious about being able to dress correctly. At school, modest, simple dress was encouraged, so Anita's homemade wardrobe had never caused many problems, but on outings away from campus it did. Anita lacked suitable clothes for even the most casual occasion spent in New York society, but Lottie had taken to dressing her like a paper doll, so in the end she was the best supplied of the three.

The enormous house, which the three guests tried their best not to gawk at, had been designed by the much-in-vogue architect Richard Morris Hunt. It boasted four square chimneys and a Florentine exterior, though it had a French Renaissance–style roof. Mixing architectural styles may have been frowned upon in Paris or London, but it was au courant in New York as the turn of the century loomed. And while Lottie often referred to her family's Fifth Avenue home as a cottage, the house was just over seventeen thousand square feet in size.

"I have never in all my years entered a home this way," said Caroline as the driver helped her down from the hansom and she stepped onto the granite-paved driveway. "It's so regal, it might just ruin me for life."

"It's almost as much fun as tumbling through a window," said Lottie. Anita knew that Lottie far preferred slipping inside the windows of Main after a night lying on the roof than coming into her own home through the front door, but now she couldn't imagine why.

The girls walked into the dramatic hall where the Taylors' guests were greeted, a two-story atrium with Tuscan columns of forest-green Connemara marble imported from Ireland. On the towering walls hung four paintings on canvas by New York's most fashionable decorator and painter, James McNeill Whistler. The furnishings were handmade in the style of Louis XIV, and on the farthest wall from the entry door hung Mina Taylor's two prized Gobelin tapestries, purchased three years before in Paris. Even with the room's finery surrounding them, Anita, Caroline, and Belle first craned their necks and looked up. Above them, turning the gray light of day into a stream of greens and yellows, an expanse of intricate stained glass was bolted into the high ceiling. Anita bit her lip to keep her jaw from dropping in wonder.

"Who is home, Mr. Eaton?" Lottie asked the butler, who

had greeted her with practiced respect. A woman in a servant's uniform ran up behind him and collected the girls' coats, hats, and gloves, moving without a word toward the drawing room.

"No one, I'm afraid," he responded, though the house was clearly filled with servants. "Did you not notify your mother of your arrival, Miss Taylor?"

"I did not. I wanted it to be a surprise," she said, leading her friends through the massive room.

"And that it will be," Mr. Eaton said, nodding to another servant to remove what was left of the girls' luggage. "I'm afraid the flowers are a day old," he added, motioning to a large arrangement of crisp white roses and purple angelonia on the hall's entrance table. "They're to be changed in the next hour. And if you had alerted us you were arriving, we would have sent the carriage to meet you at the station. Your mother would be appalled if she saw you stepping out of a hansom from Grand Central."

"She would have fainted," said Lottie. "There has never been a woman more worried about appearances than my dear mother. Luckily she has me to appall her around the clock."

While Belle and Caroline peeked around corners, looking into the drawing room with its panels of sculptured relief, gilt, marble-topped tables, and Belgian tapestry-covered chairs, Anita stood back and watched Lottie. An expert observer, Anita had acquired much-needed layers of confidence over the years by quietly studying women who knew how to command a room.

"You may bring those to the third floor," Lottie called out to the maid who had taken their coats, gloves, and hats. "We will be staying in the east chamber and the park room. And we may want to use the plunge bath this afternoon. Please see that it is heated properly."

"Everything in this house is always heated properly," said Mr. Eaton. "Have you been away so long that you forgot your mother's ways?" He smiled at them only with his eyes, his mouth straight as a pin.

"I must have blocked it all out on purpose," Lottie said. Lottie had told them on the train down that to help the house run properly, her father employed three parlor maids, a linen maid, a scrubbing maid, a separate laundress, four footmen, a porter, and two chefs along with a butler to oversee them all.

The group watched as the butler withdrew, and when they were alone in the drawing room Caroline cried out, "This house!" Anita looked at her with relief, pleased that Caroline had shown her feelings and that she had managed to hold back.

"It's beautiful," said Belle. "It must be the most magnificent house in New York."

"It's not," said Lottie, pointing to a window.

"Is that the Vanderbilt mansion in the distance?" asked Caroline, following her gaze.

"Two blocks down on the opposite side," said Lottie. "It's hard to miss, with those extravagant gates and the stench wafting over from the stable. Even their thirty-seven servants can't seem to control that."

The four girls moved to the windowed alcove to look at Cornelius Vanderbilt II's house more closely. It had been a frequent topic in the papers in 1893 when the favored grandson of the Commodore had destroyed his large town house to make room for the block-long, ninety-thousand-square-foot residence.

"They have it all there," said Lottie. "A five-story entrance hall, a two-story ballroom, a fireplace by Augustus Saint-Gaudens, a mosaic by La Farge, a Moorish smoking

room, and one hundred and twenty-seven other rooms
besides. It's the biggest house in New York City and the
second biggest in the country after George Washington
Vanderbilt's Biltmore Estate in Carolina. *That* place is
just too much. It's downright Brobdingnagian." She stood
shoulder-to-shoulder with her friends and surveyed what
they could see of the monumental house. "If this one ever
burns down, my mother, a long match, and her envy will be
to blame. Sometimes I think her thoughts alone could cause
it to carbonize."

"Have you been inside?" asked Anita, squinting to catch
a glimpse through the far-off upstairs windows of the house.

"Only once," Lottie admitted. "But I haven't forgotten
a thing."

The house they were standing in hadn't been built
until 1886, and Lottie had spent her childhood in a less
lavish, though far from humble home many blocks down
the avenue. Neither she nor her mother ever shared that
fact with new visitors. But it was a futile precaution, since
everyone who paid attention to such things had read about
the construction of the Taylor mansion, of the eleven bathrooms and porcelain tubs with platinum-plated fittings,
the indoor swimming pool, the art gallery and music room
with a handmade Italian piano and a crystal chandelier, the
high-speed elevator, the speaking tubes and bells and the
ballroom with its white marble mantel and wainscoting
nearly as tall as Lottie was. Still, the Taylors comported
themselves as if they had all been born in the house and
lived there among generations of family ghosts.

It was after the building of the Taylor mansion and
many other impressive homes on Fifth Avenue that Cornelius Vanderbilt II had built a house so colossal that no one
else could afford to outdo him.

"Come, let's change our dresses and then ride through the park," said Lottie, backing away from the cold window. "There's no use coming to New York if one doesn't see the city. I also heard a rumor that Nettie Aldrich is in town, and she would love to hear the Vassar gossip, I'm sure."

"Nettie DeWitt Aldrich?" asked Belle. "I've heard stories of her at school. Let's do call on her."

After they had changed out of their traveling clothes, their skirts muddy from the weather, the girls were helped into the family coach by the Taylor staff and set off through and around Central Park, as much to be seen as to see the lively city. In the summer they would have been paraded in an open carriage past a line of oglers, but as it was nearly freezing outside, they were safely enclosed as they headed to the park's East Carriage Drive. At four o'clock they started slowly down Fifth Avenue, with Lottie naming the occupants of each house and recounting what lay behind the limestone façades, even if she hadn't been inside herself.

Finally, Lottie directed the coachman to take them to Nettie's family home farther up Fifth Avenue. A long twenty blocks later, the girls were all gathered in the De-Witts' foyer on the corner of Seventy-Ninth Street and Fifth. The DeWitt residence was not nearly as large as the Taylors', but at ten thousand square feet, it still qualified as grand. Elevating the family's status even further was the presence in their drawing room of not one but two oils by Ferdinand Roybet, an artist also collected by Mrs. Astor.

"Misses Louise Taylor, Anita Hemmings, Belle Tiffany, and Caroline Hyde Hardin to see Mrs. Nettie Aldrich," said Lottie to the maid who opened the door. The three others stood behind her in the foyer waiting, as Nettie was alerted of their visit. The servant returned quickly and nodded to the group to follow her. Before they had taken more than a few steps, she paused and said something under her breath to Lottie, who promptly exclaimed, "Goodness, my mother is here! Of all the things."

She turned and gave her friends a warning look. "Well, this was certainly not planned, but I'm afraid you will be meeting my mother momentarily, the one and only Mrs. Mina Taylor. Keep your wits about you."

The girls murmured that it was a lovely chance coincidence and followed Lottie into the main parlor, which was half the size of the Taylors' palatial room.

The first to jump up and greet them was Nettie, her black hair piled onto her head like a nesting animal, in line with the latest New York fashion. Her maid had even taken to collecting the stray hairs from Nettie's brush to create a tangled doughnut of natural hair that she embedded into her employer's mane for added volume. The finished effect was certainly dramatic.

"Lottie! Aren't you the most wonderful surprise?" said Nettie, walking over to her friend. Lottie and all the Vassar girls still wore their hair parted in the center and arranged tightly on the crowns of their heads, a more old-fashioned look, but one favored by college women. "And Anita!" Nettie added, embracing her. When she pulled away, she greeted Belle and Caroline. "A pleasure to meet you both," she said warmly.

"I can't possibly be seeing my daughter in front of me," came a voice from the corner of the room where four middle-aged women were playing a round of whist at an ornate French card table with a black marble top. "No daughter of mine would arrive in New York unannounced, to the great shock of her aging mother. But now, come to think of it, that does sound like my child."

Mrs. Taylor, who shared her daughter's petite build

and blond hair, though she was starting to show streaks of gray, rose from her chair to embrace Lottie. It was the dead of winter, but her dress was a brighter blue than the Mediterranean.

"You are the queen of mischief makers," she scolded. "And the house is in disarray, I am sure. Have you already been there? Of course you have. You didn't travel in those clothes. What an embarrassment when you bring friends down from school unannounced and the staff has no time to prepare. I'm sure the flowers looked funerary."

She paused and surveyed Lottie's friends, falling first on Anita. "Now, dearest, I have no doubt in the world who you are. You are Anita Hemmings. I can tell from that beautiful face. Lottie told me you've been the school's reigning beauty for four years now, and she wasn't off the mark. Such loveliness. Those dark eyes, big as a dollar coin. Do introduce yourself to the others, dear," she said, ushering Anita and her daughter to the whist table. "And you must be Miss Tiffany and Miss Hardin," she said, taking the other girls' hands. "Wasn't one of you raised by godless men in Africa?" she asked, looking from one to the other.

"That would be me, Mrs. Taylor," said Caroline, not taking offense. "But I was raised by my parents. Christians. Americans. My father is a reverend and schoolmaster, so I spent much of my life in Syria."

"My poor child," said Mina Taylor, her deep-set eyes examining Caroline as if she were checking an orphan for lice. "Syria, that's near the Congo, is it not? I read a report that the Belgians are colonizing it rapidly. Thank goodness for that. You must be traumatized by the experience. And all that sun at a young age eats at the skin like leprosy. No wonder your hair went red. You will have to wear a hat every day now or you'll die young. Come, come now, you must be hungry," she said looking from Belle to Caroline. "All of you, such thin girls. I thought there was mandatory exercise at that ladies' college to build sturdier physiques. Mrs. DeWitt, please feed these starving birds."

"Oh, Mother, we're not hungry," said Lottie from over by the window that looked onto Fifth Avenue. "But I could use a spot of something strong to drink, if you don't mind, Mrs. DeWitt. Just to fight the chill."

"Louise! Please! I can't take your awful manners so early in the day," said Mina Taylor, fanning herself rapidly. The girls all looked to the window, where the sky had gone completely dark. "First a surprise visit, and then you want to take to the drink without a thing in your stomach. And put down my new Japanese fan," she said, looking at the one Lottie had picked up from the whist table. "You should have been a pickpocket. Who knows, perhaps you are. Girls, is my daughter known for thieving around your college? Does she run through the halls at night picking out the prettiest things from your possessions? Please let me know if she has. I'll have Clarence send a check up to Poughkeepsie at once."

"She's known for quite a bit of fun, Mrs. Taylor, but not that," said Caroline.

"We can have both food and a little brandy," said Mrs. DeWitt diplomatically, nodding to the servant who had opened the front door. "Ladies, your timing is impeccable, because we were just speaking about suffrage, and I imagine you all have very interesting, modern views on women taking to the ballot box. So why don't you join us and tell us about the talk up there at Vassar?"

"Yes!" said Nettie, excitedly. "I've just become involved with the National American Woman Suffrage Association and was telling Mother all about our work. In fact, I went to my first meeting soon after our visit in Cambridge, Lottie, and of course, Anita."

"It's the most important cause of our day," replied Lottie. "As you know, we've been staging votes at Vassar since the school opened. This year it was mostly everyone for McKinley."

"I don't imagine there are many silverites among you," said Nettie's mother, whose dark hair was puffed out like her daughter's and highlighted with painterly strokes of red.

"It is quite a passionate time at the school, Election Day," said Anita. "This year many of us participated in the political campaign, with the Republicans, the silverites, and the gold Democrats all holding their own parades and meetings. We dressed up as the candidates and other important men—Governor Morton, Governor Bushnell, Senator Jones, McKinley, of course—and there were elaborate receptions on campus. It was very entertaining."

"It was quite," said Caroline from her seat on the sofa. "We all attended the reception for Major McKinley, played by Miss Rosamond Brevoort, and watched as some of the other girls paid homage to her dressed as members of the New Women's Gold Standard Brigade and the Gold Bugs of Chappieville—that group was led by my roommate, Miss Hortense Lewis."

"I do miss all that fun," said Nettie. "But all the voting I do in my lifetime better not take place in Phil Hall at Vassar College."

"We'll win the right," said Lottie. "And you'll be there helming the charge, Nettie."

"I'd like to see it before I pass on, Nettie," said a voice from the whist table. It was a Mrs. Hewitt, who told the Vassar girls that she had no daughters, only ungrateful sons who considered suffrage just another woman problem. "So do hurry on, dear."

The four girls stayed at the DeWitts' to dine and spent the evening discussing not only the right to vote, but women's education and their own hopes for better employment opportunities. Only for a few moments did the subject of men or marriage come up, when Mrs. DeWitt mentioned her and her husband's recent trip to Chicago, their first since they traveled there for the World's Fair in '93.

"Anita Hemmings is well acquainted with the city, even though she's never journeyed there," said Lottie, reaching for an oyster. "She is a dear friend of Porter Hamilton's up at Harvard. I'm sure you know the family, the lumber Hamiltons."

"You don't say," said Mrs. Taylor, a note of surprise sharpening her tone. Anita suspected that Mrs. Taylor studied significant last names the way her husband followed the stock market and that the Hemmings name meant nothing to her. She flushed with embarrassment at Mrs. Taylor's noticeable shock. "Quite a friend to have, Miss Hemmings. I do worry about Lottie, never time to look for a husband. Too dedicated to her studies, my girl." Mrs. Taylor made a disappointed face.

Caroline, Belle, and Anita sat bemused at the picture of Lottie as the ardent academic.

"Lottie," said her mother, suddenly lighting up with a smile. "I have just had a wonderful idea, as most of my ideas are, and you, my insolent child, will not protest when I share it with you." She put her silverware down on her plate, nearly chopping off the head of her whole filet of sole with her fish knife. "I insist that while your beautiful visitors are here, you attend tomorrow evening's opera at the Metropolitan. It will do you good to be seen out socially. Those women's colleges do keep you so hidden during the season. How do they expect you to meet eligible gentlemen when you are in Poughkeepsie reading all day in Greek?"

She sighed and looked down at the gold DeWitt monogram peeking out from under her fish. "Is my daughter going to marry a Greek? Is that what it will come to?"

"No, that's a more likely fate for Anita," said Lottie, chewing her bread noisily. "She's very strong in Greek."

"From the sound of it, she is also well versed in the art of finding a proper husband," Mrs. Taylor responded forcefully.

"Yes, I've met the Hamiltons," said Nettie, whose husband, a Harvard professor, was acquainted with Porter in Cambridge. "Fine Chicago people. An exceptionally good match for you, Anita."

"I should have had you as a daughter," Mrs. Taylor told Anita, gesturing to the maid to take away her plate. "Instead I have insolence wrapped up in an amusing package—and when did that ever help find a husband? Have you ever seen a newspaper headline saying, 'Lord this or that marries most amusing girl in America'? No, you have not."

Lottie tried to protest but her mother quieted her with a prod in the ribs. "Now, girls, I insist you go to the opera in my place. Lottie, your father is in the Carolinas, and Mrs. DeWitt and I had plans to attend, but you won't be cross if we do not, Mrs. DeWitt, will you? If we let the young ladies go in our stead?"

Anita and Belle exchanged an excited glance. They had studied an impressive array of arias in Glee Club, but Anita had never attended a professionally staged opera and Belle had never in New York City.

"How terribly boring it will be for them, Mother," said Lottie. "Though I do suppose it will allow me to point out all the dreadful women who do nothing but chase husbands to the sounds of powdered sopranos screaming. That will be entertaining."

"You will do nothing of the sort," said Mrs. Taylor. "You will wear gloves, fix that frightful hair, greet everyone courteously, be polite to the young men, and listen to *Mefistofele* with an expression of interest on your face, all four acts *and* an epilogue. That is, if your guests do not mind," Mrs. Taylor added.

"As members of the school chorus and Glee Club, Anita and I would be delighted," said Belle after she had patted her mouth with a starched napkin.

"Yes," Caroline added. "We are lacking an opera in Syria. I know I will enjoy it. Thank you for the invitation."

"Nettie, will you join us?" asked Lottie.

"I'm afraid I'm heading north in the morning," said Nettie. "One can't keep away from one's husband for too long or he might start to enjoy the solitude."

"Young love is beautiful, isn't it?" said Mrs. Taylor, smiling at Nettie. Her own husband had been in the South for three months and counting, only returning for two days at Christmas to drop off gifts, give her and the children a kiss on the cheek, and make an appearance at his club, but it didn't trouble her at all.

Anita's heart was in her throat as the four girls glided back to the Taylor house in the velvet-enclosed warmth of the family's Brewster carriage. It was in vogue for noted families to adorn their carriages with their house color, as the Vanderbilts did with their signature burgundy shade. The Taylor family, though widely whispered about as too new to engage in such a ritual, had chosen a deep evergreen as their house color, and the bottom half of the carriage was painted in that hue, the driver in livery to match. Anita's eyes grew heavy as she listened to the four horses clip-clopping down the avenue and thought about herself the summer before, cleaning a boardinghouse with her mother, wearing her oldest dresses, wondering what a person facing so many limitations could ever really do in life. Perhaps, thought Anita, more than the world would like.

The next morning found the girls stepping out as tourists, despite the glacial cold and a light snow, stopping in at the Metropolitan Museum of Art to view the Cesnola Collection of Cypriot antiquities acquired by the institution twenty years before. As much as they enjoyed showing off their knowledge of Greco-Roman style, the conversation kept turning to the evening's entertainment. None of them had brought dresses suitable for an evening at the opera, and the taller Belle and Caroline did not fit into Lottie's clothes, but Mrs. Taylor had arranged to have gowns delivered for them early in the morning, apologizing profusely to the two girls that they had to wear store-bought clothes.

"Perhaps Vassar is not the most wonderful place on earth," said Caroline, twirling in front of the mirror after she had changed that evening. "Maybe the Taylor house in New York is."

"Take it from someone who has lived in both," said Lottie. "The school wins every time."

But that evening, for her guests, the fabled Metropolitan Opera House on Broadway and Thirty-Ninth carried off the prize. To the girls, the Italian Renaissance–inspired structure represented the apogee of architecture, music, and society—and they were given a grand introduction. Unlike the general public, who had to enter on Broadway, their carriage dropped them on Fortieth Street, and they went in through the door reserved for box holders.

"It's larger than La Scala in Milan," said Lottie as they

weaved through the clusters of men in capes and top hats in the box holders' lobby.

A footman in a red tailcoat accompanied them through their personal ladies' dressing room and the private men's smoking room to the Taylor box. Anita, Belle, and Caroline stared in wonder at the gilded auditorium with its tiers of ornate boxes—the stockholders' boxes being the most notable—taking in the grand tier, the dress circle, the parterre circle, the Vaudeville Club in the Omnibus box, a society exclusively for men; and the large orchestra floor. In all, the theater accommodated more than six thousand patrons. Anita looked out at the gold proscenium, designed to replicate an ornate square picture frame, and imagined what was about to unfold on the vast stage.

The women took their places in the Taylor box, which was draped in gold and red, with a partition that could be removed if need be. They sat as upright as they could on their mahogany chairs with not-too-comfortable black rattan seats, but they would have been happy to sit on the floor.

Anita studied every corner of the hall, without making it too apparent that she was, so she could tell her mother and sister everything about it one day. She wasn't sure when that day would be, what with Frederick's current grip on her life, but she would find a way. Her mother and sister, as passionate about music as she was, had to know that such a place existed.

"I take back every negative thing I have ever said about Lottie Taylor," Belle whispered to Anita as the two gazed down at the audience below. Even at the orchestra level, the women had diamond ornaments dotting their coiffures and were wearing burgundy and silver brocades, ivory satins, and even navy velvets trimmed with otter fur.

"Agreed," said Caroline from Anita's other side. "She can dictate my comings and goings all she wants after this." Anita nodded, though she had never doubted that the good that Lottie effected far outweighed the bad.

When Lottie had returned from greeting several women in a neighboring box and had finished arranging her dress around her chair, she motioned for them to lean in and covered her mouth with a fan.

"Ladies, do you see across from us in the east box, with the most direct view of the stage, the woman in the Prussian blue and black silk, diamonds everywhere? That is Mrs. Lucretia Montgomery Schotenhorn, very much the gatekeeper of all this. The man sitting with her is Thornton Force, newspaper columnist. Paid to do, well, you can imagine what."

"I don't think I can imagine," said Belle, trying not to stare. "Carry on a scandalous affair with Mrs. Schotenhorn?"

"Oh, Belle, not with the old horn," said Lottie, covering her face with her fan. "Don't even say that. It's well known that her breasts hang all the way to her waist when she's not wearing a corset. Her maid has to roll them up every morning like slices of salami."

"Lottie, that is vulgar! And it is no way to speak about—" said Anita, but Lottie waved her and her kindness away.

"Plus, it is also well known that Mr. Force prefers the company of men. Young ones, if possible."

"Is he a homosexual?" asked Caroline, turning her opera glasses on him.

"Do not stare!" Lottie hissed. "My mother will behead me if we end up in the newspaper as impertinent spies rather than elegant attendees. And of course he's a homosexual. Only a homosexual could enjoy both the opera and the company of Mrs. Schotenhorn in such large quantities."

"I don't know that I've ever seen a homosexual before," said Anita, taking the lorgnette from Caroline.

"Anita, of course you have," said Lottie. "Rumors do fly about some of the teachers at our dear ladies' college. I dare say Miss Salmon could be one. I've heard it whispered that her friendship with Adelaide Underhill is of an intimate nature."

"You're just fabricating scandal," said Anita, frowning. Miss Lucy Maynard Salmon was a history teacher at Vassar who was doing her best to replace the practice of rote memorization in her field with primary source research and criticism. She was one of the students' favorite professors.

"I wouldn't dare concoct such a rumor! And think about it a minute, Anita. The great majority of our female professors are unmarried, even the most beautiful like Miss Wood. Our dear physician is one of the only ones who is and she had to marry a Swede. More advanced in their thinking over there. Let's just state the facts, even the most modern men fear a woman who works. Homosexual women, on the other hand, do not," said Lottie. "Now everyone stop and speak of something more civilized or we will be in terrible trouble. The opera walls absorb everything, and they report directly back to my mother. I think they know how to send telegrams. And my poor dear mama, one of her main dreams in life is to sit in that box there, where the old horn is so well settled." They all turned to look at it again, sandwiched between the Morgan and Whitney boxes.

"But surely you have enough money for that one," said Caroline.

"Money has nothing to do with it," Lottie said. "It is the Schotenhorn box, and it will always be the Schotenhorn box, even if no Schotenhorn ever chooses to sit in it again. They reigned over the old Academy of Music opera house, and though they were loath to buy into the Metropolitan at first, they bit and now hold court here, too. The faces in New York change, but the last names seldom do."

"New York is an odd place, isn't it?" said Caroline, looking across at the ample shoulders of Lucretia Schotenhorn. "She's a horrible-looking woman."

"I think New York is magical," said Anita. "I'd sit under the stage of the Metropolitan Opera if I were invited to. Or in the attic pulling the ropes. I've never seen a more beautiful room. Such a shame that some of the boxes are empty."

"I'm glad you like it so," said Lottie. "Because we will be stuck here for the next four, long, painful hours. As for not using things one owns, that is the sole purpose of owning things in New York. Half of the houses we passed today are unoccupied. And it's only worse up at Newport. Mother is looking into purchasing a home in California to store her art collection, not that she would ever live there. They're a wasteful bunch, these women. That's why after Vassar I'll be fleeing New York in favor of the world."

"Here's to seeing the world," said Anita, though she was thinking that if there was one place that could keep her in America, it was New York.

Lottie turned around to see if anyone might be coming to greet them in their box, then spun back in horror.

"Ladies, do not look up. I repeat, do not turn around. Mr. Wallace Peters is approaching us through the smoking lounge with the eyes of a madman. He has been pestering me since birth. For several years I had him convinced that we were first cousins and shouldn't marry, but he produced papers proving otherwise. Can you imagine! Hired a man and everything—Oh, hello, Wallace!" said Lottie, pivoting gracefully in midsentence. "What a most welcome surprise."

She held out her hand to him and introduced her companions.

"Ladies, it is my pleasure to make your acquaintances," said Wallace, with a strong lisp. His opera tuxedo, waistcoat, and white tie were crisper than the air outside. "Louise is always surrounded by such beautiful women."

"Yes, I do pride myself on the company I keep," said Lottie, trying to bat Wallace away with her fan. "And the company I don't keep. Do tell me, Wallace, how is your mother?"

"She is most well, indeed, thank you for inquiring, Miss Taylor. Now, am I wrong in thinking that you should be at school? Up in Poughkeepsie?"

"Yes! I should be. In fact, I must be getting back. Ladies, let us go at once," said Lottie, standing up.

"Lottie!" said Caroline, shocked. "She's such a wit, isn't she?" she said, glaring at Lottie, who finally sat back down. Caroline turned to their new companion, whose light hair was worn center-parted to show off his natural wave, and explained that they had taken leave for a long weekend.

"Then you are all students at the college?" Wallace said with interest.

"Yes, of course they are," snapped Lottie. "In fact, you will find Miss Caroline Hardin of most interest to you as she spent her entire childhood as a prisoner in Syria and you are so passionate about the Phoenicians. I do remember hours of conversations with you about antiquities where I had to amuse myself by staring at the wallpaper."

"A prisoner in Syria!" Wallace stuttered, nearly pushing Anita over the railing to move closer to Caroline. "How ever did you escape?"

"You'll have to do her chemistry for the next week to make up for that lie," Anita whispered to Lottie, who could barely repress her glee.

"I don't mind. Did you see his expression? Imagining poor Caroline locked away in a dungeon. Besides, now the pest is busy, and we still have ten minutes until curtain. Let Caroline swim in his sea of saliva for a change. I've done my part."

Belle edged closer to them, and Lottie sat up, visibly pleased to be holding court again.

"Who is that gentleman there?" said Belle, looking straight across at a man with jet-black hair who had been gazing their way since they arrived.

"That one, there?" asked Lottie, taking her glasses. "I believe that's, oh, of course, that's Marchmont Rhinelander. Whatever is he doing here? It's shocking of him to attend."

"Why?" asked Anita, squinting to see him. "Should he be off living in exile?"

"You can live right in New York and be in exile," said Lottie. "I imagine the New York exile is the worst kind of all. But no, Mr. Rhinelander should not be in exile, exactly. I'm just surprised to see him at the opera, as he very recently jilted Lucretia Schotenhorn's homely daughter, Estelle. She has the face of a horse and no personality to speak of, so it wasn't surprising when he broke their engagement, but it was only a month ago. It's in very poor taste for him to appear in public so soon."

Lottie put her lorgnette back on her lap and said, "Ladies, we can do all we want now, there won't be one inch of room in that newspaper column of Force's to talk about a thing but Marchmont Rhinelander's appearance. How impertinent of him to come! Maybe he isn't such a bore after all."

"I think he's the most handsome man I've ever seen," said Belle. "I've been taken by his profile since we arrived. He looks like a Spanish dancer."

"Luckily for your parents, he's nothing of the sort. He hasn't worked a day in his life. Perhaps we can make introductions after this interminable performance is over," said Lottie. "Anita, what language is this dreadful opera in?"

"Italian," said Anita, smiling. "Four hours in Italian."

"Do wake me when it's finished," said Lottie, closing her eyes.

As the lights dimmed, Wallace Peters stood up and said his goodbyes.

"Leaving us so soon?" said Lottie. "And I was just starting to memorize the wall coverings. Do give my fondest to your mother. Tell her I will call on her soon."

"Does he not catch on that you're ridiculing him?" asked Anita, after he had left.

"Not everyone is as clever as you, Anita Hemmings. I think he truly believes that I feel passionately about wall coverings."

The four hours of opera, including two intermissions, passed, and Belle and Anita, the music lovers, were in tears when it concluded.

"Don't tell me that this nonsense brought you two to this state!" said Lottie, looking at their pink faces when the lights came up.

"Lottie Taylor, you have no appreciation for the arts," said Belle, dabbing her eyes with her handkerchief. "Anita and I have more elevated minds than you."

"I prefer my art on paper," said Lottie. "It doesn't take as long to appreciate it."

After the four had stepped daintily out of their box, they were helped into their coats by the footman and moved with the small crowd downstairs.

"There is that man again!" said Belle, spotting Marchmont Rhinelander entering the box holders' lobby, where patrons were waiting for their carriages. The girls followed her gaze, and Lottie pinched her.

"Belle, you have all the subtlety of a foghorn. One false move in this company and you will be a headline for a week."

"You should invite him to Founder's," said Anita, watching him cross the room.

"A man like that at Founder's Day!" said Belle. "But he must be nearly forty years old, Anita. He would never bother himself with one of our little school dances."

"It's not just any dance," said Anita, "It's famous. I'm sure he's familiar with it, since it makes the *Times* every year."

"It would do him good," said Lottie. "At least he would be in the newspaper for something other than jilting old pony-face."

"Let's speak to him," said Belle, moving forward. Anita watched her admiringly but stayed where she was.

"Why not?" asked Belle, seeing her friends stuck to the floor like houseplants. "No one else is. It's terribly sad to see him alone."

Lottie sighed and motioned for them all to catch up with Mr. Rhinelander before he left the building. She reached him first and placed her hand on his arm, her fingers stroking the sleeve of his cashmere coat.

He stopped and looked down at Lottie and her pleasing face. "Miss Taylor. What a welcome surprise. Aren't you kind to come and say good evening?" Marchmont removed the hat that had just been brought to him. "None of the other young ladies in attendance would dare."

"It's not that they don't desire to," said Lottie. "It's that their mothers don't want them to. Or not quite yet. The brush-off you gave Estelle made a stir that's going to keep on stirring until another scandal trumps it. If I were you, I'd pay off one of these men to do something unforgivable. Preferably in the presence of Mr. Force and his venomous pen."

"Now there's a grand idea," said Marchmont, smiling for the first time that night.

"Why did you come this evening?" asked Lottie after she had introduced her guests. "If you don't mind my speaking so. You looked quite a sad sight all alone in your box like a ghost. It will obviously cause a sensation."

"Quite honestly, Miss Taylor, I wanted very much to see *Mefistofele*. It just came here from Italy. That's truly the reason. Art beckoned me to my death. And between you and me, I've stopped caring about the rest of it." He indicated the patrons around him.

"I found it wonderful," said Belle, blushing at the sound of her own voice.

"Belle is quite a talented singer herself," said Anita, as Marchmont nodded, though he was looking at Anita rather than Belle.

"Miss Hemmings, did you say it was?" he asked. "Have we met before and I've rudely forgotten? Your face is familiar to me."

"I don't think so," said Anita, nerves sweeping over her. She looked down and tried to recall if they had ever met.

"She is from Boston," Lottie offered, to Anita's annoyance. "From which part, Anita?"

"I am—I—I'm from the Back Bay," said Anita, damning herself for her flustered hesitation.

"That could be it," Marchmont said, smiling. "I do quite a bit of traveling up and down the coast. Perhaps I was introduced to you or passed you on the street and never forgot."

"Perhaps," said Anita shyly, thinking of the people she had walked through Boston with. If he had seen her there, and if she hadn't been alone, it was certain she had been in the company of a Negro.

"Belle, I would like to hear you sing one evening. Lottie will help arrange it," Marchmont said, recovering his manners. "Now, I must be off before these other women have me shot for social impropriety." He put his hat back on and escaped through the crowd.

"He's fascinating, isn't he?" said Belle giddily, watching him climb into his carriage. "I would love to marry a man just like that."

"Just marry that one then," said Caroline as they headed to the Taylor carriage.

As Anita tucked the carriage blanket around her, she chided herself for the freedom she had felt in Boston over Christmas. She had walked all over the city with her darker-skinned sister, Elizabeth, and hadn't thought a thing of it. She needed to remember that all roads led back to the world of Lottie Taylor.

"Do take the newspaper for the train, Louise," said an exhausted Mrs. Taylor from her perch in the drawing room the next morning as the girls were preparing to leave. "You are mentioned, which is astonishing considering the appearance of Mr. Rhinelander. How impudent of him."

"What does it say about me?" asked Lottie, taking the *Times* from her mother's hand.

"It says you were asleep, dear," said Mrs. Taylor, her face in her teacup.

"Does it really?" said Lottie, holding the paper in two fingers as if it were poisonous.

"No, it does not, but I know you were. Nothing will change you, not even that college. Mr. Force compared you to a gardenia. Or was it a cactus? You'll just have to read it for yourself."

Lottie tucked the paper under her arm and gave her mother a kiss. "It could be worse, Mother. Let's try to remember that."

"Who was Mr. Rhinelander with, dear?" asked Mrs. Taylor. "The one night I leave the box to you I miss the most scandalous event of the season. I am very surprised Mr. Force did not mention it in his column. I suppose it was the discreet thing to do, but Mr. Force and discretion tend to go together like your brother and sobriety."

"He was alone, Mother," said Lottie. "Sitting in the Rhinelander box very much alone."

"Scandalous," said Mrs. Taylor, waving goodbye to the group. "Just scandalous."

The four returned to Vassar on Monday evening, three of them confiding in one another that the visit had opened their eyes to a new, appealing world. This, they decided, could be what awaited them after college. Not the opulence—only the very few could obtain that—but the activism, the conversation, the art. They did not have to turn into their mothers, because many in their mothers' generation wanted to turn into them.

CHAPTER 18

When Lottie joined Anita and the others for breakfast the following morning, their senior table was decorated with twisted pink streamers, elaborately inscribed name cards, and large balloons. It was tradition to decorate the hall for birthdays, the labor done by the students who shared a table with the honoree. The decorations, this time in honor of Hortense Lewis's birthday, would stay up for lunch and dinner, too, and a party was planned in Caroline and Belle's wing of the senior hall after classes and chapel.

On that festive morning, Anita felt closer to Lottie, Belle, and Caroline than she had all year. The trip to New York—seeing the city from the Taylors' carriage, hearing Nettie Aldrich speak about her work, taking in the opera— had left her with the conviction that these women would be her lifelong friends. She would always have Bessie, but now she felt that she wouldn't *only* have Bessie. She wasn't as afraid of life after Vassar. She wasn't even afraid of losing Porter Hamilton. She felt a reassurance that she hadn't felt since she received her Vassar acceptance letter. If she made the right decisions—difficult, but right for her—she could have what Caroline, Belle, and Lottie were looking forward to: a career, intellectual stimulation, a husband and family who supported her, the opportunity to make a difference in society. She was sure she could find a way to enter that world—with them, with Porter—while also holding on to some part of her true identity.

During the days that followed, tension mounted at the school as the students began preparing for the midyear examinations at the end of January. Lottie and Anita agreed that their minds had benefited from their taste of freedom in New York, and both passed their tests easily.

It was in the early February lull that Lottie let her academic studies go in favor of a life of hobbies. She had taken up ikebana, the art of Japanese flower arranging, and had stems sent in by the dozen, turning their parlor into a living preamble to spring. But Anita clung to her books. She may have disobeyed Frederick by traveling to New York, but she would not let her grades go anywhere but up. Studying also proved to be the only way she could stop herself thinking about Porter and the fact that he had not yet responded to her letter. She understood his anger and had penned numerous follow-up letters, but she did not dare send them until she had word from him first.

On the Friday before Valentine's Day, as she tried not to dwell on the holiday that the campus was planning to celebrate with gusto, Anita headed to the library, where she planned to stay until the dinner bell rang. She was hurrying, eager to find a good corner table, but she slowed her steps when she saw Sarah Douglas and her roommate, Alice Sawyer, in the hall outside the library entrance. They both looked at her with interest as she approached.

"Anita! What are you doing here?" asked Sarah when Anita was in close enough range that she did not have to shout. "Didn't I see Porter Hamilton disembark at the Poughkeepsie station this afternoon? I was sure he was coming to see you. Did he leave already?"

Anita couldn't hide her confusion, and both girls knew immediately that Anita did not have plans to see Porter. He must have been in town to visit another girl.

"Are you sure it was he?" asked Anita. "Porter Hamilton from Harvard?"

"Absolutely," said Sarah. "He's not one you miss, is he? I was on the three o'clock train from Albany. I was in the capital visiting Mary Mumford. Perhaps you remember her from the class of '94? Beautiful red hair, a bit darker than Caroline Hardin's, and president of the Shakespeare Club during her days here. She is teaching near Albany now, making quite a name for herself at the Emma Willard School in Troy."

Anita looked at her blankly and said nothing.

"But I am going on about something you have no interest in," Sarah said, collecting herself. "It was certainly him. I recognized him from Phil Day. Porter Hamilton. The rumor at school is that you and he are engaged. Is that not the case?"

Anita looked into the library at the clock. It was almost five. The dinner bell would ring in an hour, and she did not have permission to miss the meal.

"Do you have an idea why he came to Poughkeepsie?" Alice asked Anita.

"I don't," she said honestly, though it must have been to see her. Maybe he had tried to surprise her with a visit, to plead his case, but none of the maids or students could find her when he came to the visitors' parlor. She had been in the chapel earlier that afternoon practicing her solo for the Easter concert. Perhaps no one had thought to look there.

"I imagine he has come to see me," Anita said. "I must have missed a letter or telegram from him saying as much."

"Of course he has," said Alice, kindly. "You are lucky in love."

"And much better off than your roommate," said Sarah. "For all her money and that pretty face, she does seem to find an incredible number of scandal-ridden suitors."

"Lottie does?" asked Anita, every comment from Sarah more bewildering to her than the last.

"Of course, Lottie," said Sarah. "Can you believe the news about Joseph Southworth?"

"They're engaged?" asked Anita.

"Engaged!" she said, putting her hand on her chest and laughing. "Anita! Have you been ill? They are anything but engaged. Have you not spoken to her at all this week?"

"I suppose we've both been rather busy with midyear examinations," said Anita, hoping her excuse sounded plausible. The truth was that she and Lottie had been inseparable that week, and had been ever since their return from New York.

"It is high time you had a little chat with her," said Sarah. "She confided in Caroline Hardin that the story Joseph Southworth told about his mother being a deceased Japanese geisha is true, the deceased part being the exception. Benjamin Southworth, Joseph's father, paid thousands of dollars to get Joseph's mother, who was sixteen at the time, out of her contract in the geisha house in Kyoto because he was madly in love with her. Then he married and impregnated her! Hence Joseph Southworth's arrival, not on American soil, but Japanese. Yes, he was born there. Sounds terribly dangerous, doesn't it? Of course the Southworth family was outraged, so Benjamin fabricated some story about this woman's death and brought Joseph back to the United States. Lottie told Caroline that she had tea with Joseph at the very end of Christmas vacation in Cambridge and that's when her feelings for him truly developed. But then, when the two were speaking about his family in Japan, Commodore Perry and all, he told her this story! She didn't believe him, of course, but Lottie's father did a little prying, and it turns out it's all true. The geisha woman is still alive, and Benjamin and Joseph make routine trips to the Orient to see her. Joseph even admitted that when his American grandparents die, his father plans to bring her to America."

"And how did you come to know this?" asked an increasingly disturbed Anita, suddenly understanding why Lottie was in Cambridge in late December.

"Lottie told Caroline the whole story in the middle of the senior parlor with the dividing curtains all thrown open. One has to think she did so on purpose. It only took a matter of hours for it to fly through the school like a carrier pigeon. Had you really not heard?"

"I really had not," said Anita. "But that sounds like the type of story that Lottie would love. I would think she would be more attracted to the prospect of Joseph after hearing it, not less."

"Anita, dearest. Let's be realistic," said Sarah, her smooth southern inflection taking her vowels for a ride. "She's a Taylor! Her father might let her marry a Japanese man from the royal family—though none would ever marry her, their culture won't allow such a thing—but she would never be permitted to consider a child of a common prostitute!"

"Are geishas really prostitutes?" asked Anita. "Lottie described them as talented entertainers who—"

"Anita, you know Lottie romanticizes everything. Joseph's mother is no better than a brothel woman in New York."

"Have you ever heard anything more scandalous?" said Alice. "It's the gossip of the year, that's for certain."

"It's amazing that Joseph has managed to remain so popular at Harvard," said Sarah. "Though I suppose northerners care less about such things. It's all very shocking."

"Lottie has cut off contact with Joseph now?" asked Anita.

"Of course she has," said Sarah. "What choice did she have? He is very handsome and as charming as a man can be—he was on my dance card at Phil—but he's the child of a common whore," she said, whispering the last word. "The venerable Southworth name means nothing after hearing about such a lineage, doesn't it?"

"It's a pity. He was very handsome and good-humored at Phil," said Alice. She swatted at the hair falling on to her forehead as if it were a fly and rearranged the expertly cut plaid shirtwaist she was wearing. After Lottie, Alice was the senior with the most expensive clothes, though she didn't seem to care a thing about fashion. She wore, like all the other girls did, what her mother sent up. Alice was a girl who was happy to follow, even if her soft, measured personality was often stamped out by those bolder and louder than she, like Sarah Douglas. "He was on my card, too," she added.

Sarah gave Alice a stern look and then smiled at Anita. Anita could sense that she was thrilled to be the one recounting the story to her.

"She'll have no trouble finding a new love interest, though, will she?" she said to Anita after a moment. "She's Lottie Taylor."

"The rich win at everything," added Alice.

"Not everything," said Sarah, who was known to be competitive on every level.

"Of course, Sarah. I didn't mean—" said Alice, but Anita, uncharacteristically, cut them both off.

"So Southpaw, I mean, Joseph Southworth, was really born of Asian parentage? Through his mother?"

"Yes, Anita. Haven't you been listening?" said Sarah. "Lottie must be beside herself. She loves to say shocking things, Crown Prince of Japan this and that, but she would never, she *could* never, marry someone like Joseph South-worth."

"I appreciate your telling me," said Anita, backing away, all her plans for the library forgotten. "I must go and find her."

Turning quickly Anita rushed upstairs and checked her shared rooms for Lottie, but they were empty. She walked briskly down the hall to Caroline's room, which already had her Valentines from the freshmen taped to the door, and knocked loudly.

When she heard Caroline's voice, she opened the door and saw her friend sitting in her rocker with a volume of Stendhal's *Le Rouge et le Noir*.

"Is it true what Sarah Douglas is saying about Old South-paw?" said Anita, still in the doorway. "That his mother was a teenage . . . courtesan?"

"Yes, it is. Can you imagine? Lottie is in shock," said Caroline, putting down her book. "Did she not tell you?"

"Not yet," said Anita, so worried about her friend that she had even forgotten Porter Hamilton was in Pough-keepsie. "She must be devastated. Is she . . . have you seen her?"

"She said she was having tea at the Nelson House Hotel. She had permission to leave campus and to miss dinner this evening."

"She did?" She had said nothing to Anita. "Was this something she had planned for several days?"

"I think so," said Caroline, shrugging. "Perhaps she's already found a replacement for Joseph. You know Lottie: she doesn't mourn for long. Or at all."

Anita nodded her thanks and backed away from the door. A replacement. No, she thought to herself, it was impossible. She ran back up to her rooms and opened the door to Lottie's bedroom. She opened the drawers of her nightstand and went through the papers, but found nothing but letters from her mother and father. She closed the drawer carefully and looked through Lottie's desk and in her wardrobe. She had gone through every coat pocket, looked under her mattress and behind pillows, but it wasn't until she reached Lottie's favorite school dress that she found what she feared. She pulled the thin duplicate of a telegram out and searched for the recipient's name. It was to Porter Hamilton.

WRITING ON BEHALF ANITA. IN NO STATE TO RESPOND TO YOUR LETTER. DISTRAUGHT. HER DECISION FINAL. MEET ME FRI. FEB. 12 POUGHKEEPSIE LOBBY NELSON HOUSE HOTEL 4 P.M. WILL EXPLAIN ALL. MUST CLOSE HEART TO HER. IS ONLY SOLUTION. L. TAYLOR

Anita combed through the rest of Lottie's things frantically, but she found nothing else. Where was Porter's letter to her? Had Lottie hidden it? Could she have destroyed it? Not knowing what else to do, she plucked her coat from the hook on the back of their parlor door, took the elevator down, and hurried out of Main toward the Lodge. With her leather boots heavy from the slush and snow, she rounded the corner to Market Street, aware and uncaring that she did not have permission to leave campus or to miss dinner.

The building across from the Nelson House Hotel on Market Street housed Smith Brothers, where just a few months ago she had joined Frederick for afternoon tea. She thought of how happy she had been when she first saw her younger brother, of the warmth of being able to speak with someone from home who knew her every secret, who had to love her. Then she remembered his warning about her conduct. Should she have listened to him then? Had she been wrong to let her feelings for Porter escalate? She stopped to catch her breath and looked in the restaurant window, which was fogging slightly at the corner from the windy February day. She put her hand on the pane and looked at the table where she had sat with her brother. No, she thought, she hadn't been wrong.

Anita removed her hand and crossed the street to the hotel. She hadn't been inside it that year, but its name, printed in large white letters on the brick façade, was a familiar sight to all the Vassar students. The double doors were opened for her and she walked in, immediately stepping to one side of the heavily draped room, behind the commotion of the front desk.

"Excuse me, miss. May I be of service?" said one of the men at the desk, and she shook her head, embarrassed. "I'm waiting for my mother," she said, hoping that would deflect further queries. She stepped even closer to the oak-paneled wall and looked carefully around. There were ten separate seating areas in the lobby, full of men and women engaged in tête-à-têtes or taking refreshments.

In the middle of them all were Lottie Taylor and Porter Hamilton.

Anita put her hand over her mouth, desperate to scream Porter's name, to run to him and explain that there had been a horrible misunderstanding. She wanted to tell him she had been forced to write what she did and that she had never received his letter in return. That she didn't want to call off her engagement. That she loved him.

She let herself steal another glance at Porter sitting in the middle of the room. His light eyes were full of emotion as he spoke to Lottie, who was leaning toward him familiarly as she listened. It couldn't be the first time they had been alone together, Anita thought suddenly—their intimacy was palpable. She watched them, uncaring about the strangers around them, succumbing to their senses like they were alone in the world. Perhaps what Porter had said in his letter to her had been expressions of relief. Or a confession of his true feelings for Lottie over his muted ones for her. She watched them again, their bodies, leaning over the table into each other, blind to the periphery, looking nowhere but into each other's concerned faces. No, this friendship, this more than friendship, must have been building for weeks, even months.

She looked as Lottie put her hand on Porter's, ungloved and for all to see, and he did not pull away. He looked emotional, but Anita interpreted that as a display of his feelings for Lottie. She closed her eyes and leaned her head back against the wall. She had made a terrible mistake. Porter may have been interested in her at one time, but not the way he was with Lottie. Not like this.

Why had she let herself think of their life in Chicago together? That word. *Modern.* It had let her dream about a romantic pairing with him that society labeled as unnatural, ungodly. Even her own brother was horrified by it. She had made herself believe that Porter was different, that even if she did reveal her race that he would love her, but she had let her emotions cloud reality. He had clearly never loved her like he did Lottie.

For the first time since Anita had been observing them, Porter let his eyes drift away from Lottie, and Anita turned around quickly, thankful she had worn a hat and a simple, unrecognizable black coat. She stood there, staring at the wall for several minutes, then allowed herself the quickest of glances back at them. Porter was looking into his lap, and Lottie was speaking to him gently, encouragingly, both still unaware of Anita's presence.

Her heart raw, she rushed out of the hotel and steadied herself against the building. It was only thirty degrees that afternoon, but the newspapers had announced that spring was arriving early in the Hudson Valley and soon the world would be alive and blossoming again.

Anita was sure everyone was wrong. The bleak, frozen landscape would never thaw. How had she been such a fool! Falling in love with Porter Hamilton, who had probably never even entertained the idea of a true engagement with her—he had just wanted to kiss her in her bedroom. More than kiss her. And Lottie! She couldn't be the friend Anita had assumed she was, the friend she had loved. Anita had just been a convenience for her, too. Someone she was happy to cross whenever it pleased her.

"A fool," she said under her breath. "I am such a fool." She wiped her eyes with the back of her hand and walked slowly back to school, pausing in front of the handsome red-brick gate and looking down the long dirt road to Main. This was why she was here, she scolded herself: for her mind, not for romance or friendships. She hadn't asked to be part of the Gatehouse group, or for Lottie Taylor to take to her as she did.

It was only four months until graduation, and she would not be embarrassed again. She would not mention what she had seen to Lottie or Porter. She would back away from both of them, leave behind this new sought-after, self-assured Anita Hemmings, and return to the one she had been for the first three years at Vassar: studious, reserved, and determined not to be remembered.

CHAPTER 19

Anita was wrong about the world not coming to life again. It did, for everyone, including her. In mid-March, when Lottie finally confessed to exchanging letters with Porter, even to seeing him in Poughkeepsie, Anita told her she was free to act as she wished. By Lottie's surprised face, she was sure she was displaying the equanimity she hoped to, but inside her chest, everything burned against Lottie. She had decided not to confess to her roommate that she had found the telegram duplicate, or that she knew about Porter's letter to her. Their faces at the hotel made that confession unnecessary. They desired each other—and because of who they were and who she was, they could have whatever they wanted. It was quite clear that neither of them was bothered about her happiness. But since the day she read Lottie's lying words, she was filled with a skepticism and mistrust that she doubted would ever diminish.

"But it's awful!" said Lottie as the two walked by the lake. The lake that had been frozen two months before was alive with small silver fish darting in bright layers over each other. "I'm too impulsive and terribly selfish. I wish someone in my life had kept me from being that way, but I was spoiled from the moment I sprang to life in my mother's womb."

"We are all selfish," said Anita, thinking about her own choices. "We sometimes set singular goals, and we do everything we can to achieve them, even if it means hurting people along the way."

"But no!" said Lottie, stopping abruptly. "You must understand. Porter Hamilton was never a goal of mine. His letter came to me soon after our return from New York. He was naturally upset about your ending the engagement, and we started a correspondence. I know I shouldn't have responded to him, but I was still in shock about the news regarding Old Southpaw. I think my ego was crushed and I needed male reassurance. I'm much weaker than you are. No one ever voted me the class beauty."

"But your ego shouldn't have been crushed upon learning the news about Joseph. It would have been his that was," said Anita critically, her heart cracking like old china as Lottie continued to lie.

"I suppose his was, too," said Lottie. "But I'm sure I'll never know. He wrote three or four letters after I alerted him that I knew the truth about his disgraced family, but I threw them into the stream on the farm, unopened."

"The stream on the farm?" said Anita, thinking about all the torn-up letters to her mother that she had let disintegrate in that water, unsent.

"Yes, quite dramatic, I am aware." Lottie shortened her stride and looked out at the stone wall that kept them safe inside. "I wish I was more like you, Anita, I truly do. You're my friend despite it all, aren't you? Say you are. I'd be heartbroken without your friendship."

"Of course I am," said Anita, biting down her anger. "And I'm actually glad I've been able to devote myself to my studies again. I really would like to travel abroad after school and to earn another degree. I lost sight of those

goals in the last few months with Porter, but I'm now looking single-mindedly ahead to graduation and an academic
life." The truth was that Anita had not lost sight of her academic goals when Porter was in her life. She was sure that a
man like Porter would have let her pursue her career while
building a life at home. Perhaps she would have taught in
Chicago rather than at Vassar, but that was something she
was willing to sacrifice for marriage. But her dreams of a life
with him were nothing now. All she had to look forward to
was the expansion of her mind, no longer her heart. It was
the more important of the two, she told herself, the reason
she pursued Vassar, and took so many risks in the first place.
But it didn't make the reality less painful.

"Miss Macurdy has recommended me for a scholarship to
travel to both Italy and Greece in August," Anita explained.
"After that, I will look into graduate programs. Perhaps
Yale, so I can be near New York. Or Cornell, like Frederick.
That is all I care about now, a continued education."

School was what she could have so she was going to
throw herself fully behind it. She needed to work twice as
hard as she had that year so that she was certain to obtain
a scholarship. Then she must prove herself with her work
abroad so that the coed graduate schools did not see her as
just another college woman who wanted to go into teaching. She would be more than that.

"Anita, it's perfect for you, it really is. You'll graduate
from here a cum laude, I'm sure of it," said Lottie excitedly.
"It would be such a shame for an intellect like yours to be
wasted on marriage. You *should* travel and continue your
studies. I'm thrilled for you, I really am."

"And you? Will you still go to Japan?" asked Anita.

"Of course," said Lottie, smiling. "I'll just try to stay out
of the geisha houses."

CHAPTER 20

It was always at the end of March, when spring could be felt arriving in the valley, that the Vassar campus was at its most joyous. One exam period felt long past, the next was a long way off, and the outdoors was fragrant and welcoming again. It was in that spirit that Lottie, Anita, Belle, and Caroline found themselves quite drunk one March day when they had promised each other they would have only apple cider, brought to them by their hallmates who had hiked to the nearby cider mill.

"Hand me the apple cider, will you, Caroline dear," said Lottie, her eyes glazed. "I'm going to mix it with this half-drunk glass of champagne. It will help me see straight again."

"How diplomatic of you!" pronounced Caroline, handing her the jug from the side table in Lottie and Anita's parlor. "That's not really the correct word, is it? How levelheaded of you. Responsible."

"She is not responsible," said Anita, laughing. "She's intoxicated."

Caroline swatted at the bottom of her green silk dress. "This thing is terribly in the way. Anita, do you have any scissors? I am going to cut this skirt off."

"You should have worn my basketball costume," said

Belle, laughing at the sight of Caroline trying to rip apart her skirt. "You would be much more agile in bloomers."

"What I would be much more agile in is a dress that did not weigh ten pounds. I detest being a woman sometimes."

"Why on earth?" said Lottie. "All men ever talk about are themselves and the weather." She refilled Anita's glass and suggested she drink it all at once. "Makes your nose fizz. Very pleasant."

Anita sneezed and thanked Lottie for the advice.

"Anita, I have never heard you sneeze before," said Belle. "You must have superior nostrils, it was such a quiet sneeze."

"No, it's definite," said Caroline, speaking over Belle as her hem gave way. "I loathe being a woman."

"Why ever so?" asked Lottie again, languidly, as she looked out at the gatehouse with her monocles. "The Gatehouse group," she said aloud. "I like our name. I should thank whoever gave it to us. It has a much more glamorous ring than those other groups. The Nine Nimble Nibblers. The Gobblers. What dreadful names for eating clubs. They sound like turkeys. And the society of the grandmothers club. That one is the very worst. Dead before their time."

"They're the granddaughters, not the grandmothers," Anita reminded her. "The Society of the Granddaughters of Vassar College. I always have to correct you." She hiccupped loudly.

"Anita!" said Lottie, laughing.

"Excuse me," said Anita. "I don't think I've ever been this intoxicated before."

"Does anyone care why I hate being a woman?" Caroline shouted. "Are you not all terribly curious?"

"My mind is in a frenzy over it," said Belle placidly, refilling her glass. "Do you really want to be a man and have to walk around all day in a plain sack suit and smoke cigars that smell like dirt?"

"That actually does sound fun," said Anita.

"It really does," said Lottie. "Who has a cigar? I bet Kendrick smokes them in secret. She did live in the South and has been widowed since '89. What else does she have to do? Let's sneak into her quarters and steal them all. I bet she sleeps with her eyes open, the college handbook clutched to her heart."

"Listen to me!" Caroline cried out, loudly enough for the lady principal, whose quarters were on their floor, to hear. "I have a real grievance, and my friends aren't even interested. Such ill-mannered company I keep."

Lottie put her hand over her mouth, and the two others followed her lead.

"Finally," said Caroline. She tilted her head back, her red hair down around her shoulders, and tossed off the rest of her drink. "The reason I hate being a woman is that these dresses are oppressive."

"So take it off—" Lottie interrupted before Anita threw a pillow at her. She put her hand back over her mouth.

"And," said Caroline, raising her voice, "all I've ever wanted to do is become a lawyer, and what will I do after graduation? Probably marry and end up a housebound woman with thirteen children."

"I didn't know you were seriously interested in the law," said Anita admiringly.

"Why would you be housebound?" asked Lottie, laughing. "Do you lose your legs in this grand vision of yours?"

"You could take the exams for law school," said Belle. "Harvard and Yale don't admit women—well, Yale did once accidentally and then the poor girl died before she could ever practice—but there are schools that do. The University of Pennsylvania does."

"How many have graduated from there?" asked Caroline, refilling her drink.

"I don't know," said Belle. "Four? Five? A few at least."

"But why shouldn't I be able to attend Harvard if I qualify?" said Caroline. "My brother graduated from Harvard Law and now he practices in Washington. He tells quite good stories about it. He once had to defend a man who cut off his mother's head with an axe. He said he thought she was a tree."

"More than five women have graduated from the University of Pennsylvania's law school," said Anita.

"But not many," said Caroline. "Two dozen at best."

"So you will be lucky number twenty-five," said Anita, who had never let difficult odds dictate her life. "And twenty-six and twenty-seven and twenty-eight and so on will have you to thank."

"I just want to sing and write music," said Belle, belting out a quick scale.

"And I just want to repose by a Japanese palace while someone feeds me little orange fish," said Lottie. "That will be my profession, fish connoisseur and cultural surveyor."

"Will you write to me from Japan, Lottie?" asked Belle, fashioning a never-before-seen cocktail and watching Lottie trace the outline of her woodprint with her eyes closed.

"Of course I will. I'll write to all of you in golden ink, with a paintbrush."

"Is it true they write only with brushes in Japan?" asked Belle, trying to focus on Lottie's face.

"Perhaps we should telegraph Joseph Southworth and ask," whispered Caroline.

"Oh, stop it, you ignoramuses," said Lottie. "It isn't his

fault that his mother was a child prostitute who wooed the senses out of elder Southpaw with her minuscule waist. Anyway, I think it's quite charming that he's Japanese."

"You let him go rather quickly despite that opinion," said Belle. "And found someone else very quickly."

"Well, I didn't want to, really. But what choice did I have? I suppose everything worked out as it should," said Lottie, her back turned to Anita.

"Yes, you'll eat fish in Japan with Porter, and I will mother my thirteen children," said Caroline, raising her glass.

"No," said Anita, her heart stinging at the idea of Lottie and Porter together for good, "you will be a lawyer."

"Your father is a lawyer in Boston, isn't he?" asked Caroline.

"That's right," said Anita. An image of her father cleaning classrooms and bathrooms, always the invisible employee, lingered in her mind.

"Is he with a large, prestigious firm in an ornate building filled with leather-bound books?" asked Belle.

"No. He's privately employed," said Anita. "In an ornate building filled with leather-bound books."

"We, too, have an ornate building filled with leather-bound books," said Lottie. "It's called the library. Perhaps we should sneak in there now and write our names in all the volumes. Then we'll never be forgotten. I'm truly afraid of being forgotten once I walk out of the Lodge for good."

"Anita, you would make a fine lawyer but a terrible judge," said Belle, looking down at her drink. "You forgive too easily."

"Agreed," said Caroline, looking at Lottie. "And Lottie, no one is ever going to forget you, so stop fretting. But they'll remember all of you, the bad as well as the good."

Lottie laughed and refilled her drink, raising it to her

friends. "Your own personal hurricane, ladies. That's what I am."

"I think one can still be judicious with a forgiving heart," said Anita, who despite weeks of anger toward Lottie, had fallen into her old ways, their friendship flourishing again. "My father, Robert, he was considered for a judgeship. An old Harvard friend recommended him, but he decided against it."

"Harvard?" said Lottie, lowering her drink to her lips. "If your father went to Harvard, why did your clever brother run off to radical Cornell?"

"I'm not sure," said Anita, too quickly. "If I remember correctly, he didn't pass the Harvard entrance exam."

"Smart as he is?" said Lottie, doubtfully. "That can't be true."

"Some people just want time away from home," said Anita. "For a few years."

"But Ithaca over Cambridge? No one would ever make that choice," said Lottie.

"My father never even attended college," said Belle, shrugging. "I think it's wonderful that your family is so cerebral, Anita. You'll make a very good professor. And yours too, Lottie." Belle stood up and picked one of Lottie's hats out of her closet.

"Enough of this intellectual talk!" said Lottie, watching her. "Let's do something dangerous. Who is brave enough to follow me to the fifth floor and onto the roof?"

"The roof?" said Belle. "How do you do that? Kendrick will surely catch us. And the maids are on the fifth floor."

"Oh, no," said Anita, who had been to the highest points of the roof with Lottie many times before. "It's very possible. And we won't disturb a soul."

"It's simple, really," said Lottie. "We just enter the empty maid's room, the one who was caught stealing a watch and was banned from campus and jailed, open her window, and fling ourselves out. There is a small chance that we will fall to our sudden deaths, but it is very small."

"Caroline, do you want to die tonight?" asked Belle.

"Absolutely not," said Caroline, her hair wildly protesting as she shook her head.

"Fine, you two," said Lottie. "You can watch us and imagine what a daring life might feel like."

"I'll take boring over deceased. Miss Caroline Hyde Hardin, found in pancake formation on the manicured grounds of Vassar College. I don't think so," said Caroline.

The four girls stepped quietly out of the room, padded upstairs to the fifth floor, and tiptoed into the empty maid's room.

"Far better to be caught by a maid than the lady principal," said Lottie. "We can always pay them off."

"Anita, you go first," said Lottie.

Belle and Caroline stared with horror as Anita opened the latch on the window, pushed both panes open, and deftly slid herself out. She shifted her backside out first, then swung her legs around, inching herself up the inclined roof—which fell straight down five stories—until she was close to the building's flat-topped east wing. Then she rose to her bare feet and curtsied.

"Anita! Don't! You'll fall!" cried Caroline in panic. Anita took a few graceful steps that brought her up to the flat walkway. She did a little jump up, drawing a scream from Belle.

"Sound the alarm, why don't you?" said Lottie before positioning herself on the window frame. "Or maybe just invite old Kendrick for tea." Lottie followed Anita's exact routine, and soon they were both standing on the roof of the long east wing, looking at their friends at the far-off open window.

"They didn't really believe us," said Lottie, resting her weight against Anita's shoulder. "That we come out on the roof at night."

"I know," said Anita. "Maybe if you had said you did it alone they would have believed you. But it's the idea that the two of us dare to do it, that they didn't believe. It was me." She would never have dared put a toe on the roof before Lottie persuaded her to, but that was Lottie's way, opening the doors to a brilliant world, then closing them whenever she wanted to. Anita had decided she would refuse to have the doors closed on her for good.

"They don't understand our friendship," said Lottie, watching Anita walk confidently along the roof, stopping to take in the bright stars hovering above the dark earth. "I know what everyone says about me—that I love someone and then tire of them. That I drop them and leave them to rot after a few months. But you have never bored me." She looked at Anita and leaned on the railing next to her.

"You have never bored me, either," said Anita. "Quite the opposite. You have your flaws, Lottie, let's not pretend you don't. But so do I. And you're the most interesting person I know. And I'm sure the most interesting I will ever know."

"Has this been your favorite year at school?" asked Lottie. "Despite everything that has happened in the past few months. Despite my mistakes, my flaws as you say. Has it been?"

"Of course it has been," said Anita. "You know that."

"Good," said Lottie. "Because I love you. I always will." She paused for a moment before grabbing Anita's hand and pulling her farther along the roof. "Let's run to the other side and really terrify them."

They raced down the horizontal footpath, built for workers who needed to access the tower roofs, and turned to see their friends white with terror. Belle was jumping up and down with her hands on her mouth to keep herself from screaming.

"Come," said Anita, "let's go back. I think Belle is going to faint."

"But first, just look out at the gatehouse, at Strong and Raymond," said Lottie, pointing to the new dark red-brick dormitory identical to Strong Hall. "Look to the west. You can see the observatory and the alumnae gymnasium. And the outline of the lake if you really squint." She put her head on Anita's shoulder. "I never want to leave this beautiful place. I know there are great things waiting for us, but if it were up to me, this would be forever."

"Me, too," said Anita. "Vassar for the rest of our days."

Lottie smiled as she blinked away tears.

"It will be, in a way," said Anita, sensing Lottie's distress. "I promise." But in that moment, June felt very close. Anita seized Lottie's hand again, and together they ran back across the roof, praying not to be spotted by the tower watchman. The two hopped back through the rounded wooden window frame, silently, one after the other.

"I told you, Anita," said Belle the next afternoon. Both girls' heads were pounding after the night's revels, and she and Anita were struggling through their Latin assignment. "You would make a most unsatisfactory judge. You've forgiven Lottie already, and you will every time."

Anita smiled at Belle, and looked back down at her translation. Belle was right. Anita had forgiven Lottie without reservation when they had been together for those few minutes high above the campus, just the two of them in their own private world.

CHAPTER 21

I f Anita's anger toward Lottie had nearly vanished, as she admitted to Belle, her resolve was cemented by a letter she received from her old friend Bessie Baker Lewis a week into April.

The letter was delivered to Anita by one of the maids. Just one letter, placed directly in her hand in the hallway, which was not school protocol.

"I'm afraid some of the mail has been going into the wrong hands, miss," said the maid, curtsying. She hailed from the depths of the Catskill Mountains and was only one year into her employment. "This one wasn't in the right stack. I wanted to give it to you myself." Anita thanked her and walked up the grassy slope to the farm, letting the fragrant spring air warm her face. She paused for a moment on Sunset Hill, between the blooming crab apple trees and daffodils, looking down at the school she felt increasingly terrified to leave. She tore open the letter, looking at the familiar postmark from Ithaca and the handwriting of their go-between, and was shocked to see it was from Bessie Baker. Frederick must have helped her by sending it via their special route, Anita thought, her hand unsteady at the sight of the writing.

She read it with her back against a tree, trying not to cry at the feeling of Bessie's familiar, lilac-colored paper in her hands.

My dear Anita,

I have been worried about you, so worried in fact that I am writing to you for the first time in your four years of being away. I hope this letter makes its way directly into your hands and does not compromise you in any way. Frederick told me not to be anxious, that with his help it would, but I'm still fretting over it.

I imagine you are a mix of relieved and angry to see my handwriting, but I must tell you the reason that I took the risk of writing. William and I had dinner with Frederick in Cambridge, and he confided in me about your relationship with Porter Hamilton. Anita, I don't understand it.

It was always agreed that after Vassar you would return home and that you would be you again. If you entertain a flirtation with a man like Porter Hamilton, you will have to hide everything about your past—your parents, Frederick, Elizabeth, and Robert. Me. You could never see me again, unless I passed for white when we were together. Now that I am the wife of William Henry Lewis, that is impossible. It was different when I was younger and could go between the black and white worlds almost unsuspectingly, but now, I could not. What is more, I have no desire to. Do you? Do you really want to marry someone white just for the sake of opportunity? Frederick says it is for love. That you fell in love with him. And if he believes that, then I know it to be true, because you've always been terrible at hiding such things. I remember at Northfield after an assembly at Mount Hermon, when one young man struck your fancy. You denied it because of his race, but it was written like a verse upon your face.

Please do not be upset with me for writing such a candid letter. I sat upon it for weeks before mailing it, knowing what could happen to you if someone else read it. I hope that you don't feel I've penned it out of disrespect.

There are great men and women in our community, Anita. We are doing things that could change the world. The voices of men like William are rising. In three years, it will be a new century, and the Negro men who are leading our race into it are right here in Cambridge and Boston, around me. Don't you want to fall in love with one of them? Don't you want to be a leader here? I can't think of any woman as intelligent as you, or as suited for such a role.

Your future has me panicking, Anita. I worry that you've lost perspective about the way the rest of the world works. Vassar has been a great thing for you, but you cannot forget what life is like outside her walls. Do you remember the man we saw at my wedding? The distinguished Mr. Archibald Grimké? A few years back, he married a white woman, and they had a daughter together. The couple soon separated, and his wife took their daughter, Angelina, back to the Midwest. Years later, she returned her to Boston, to Archibald, before moving home and committing suicide.

The rumor now is that the daughter is a homosexual at the age of seventeen. I am not saying that I am against unions between white and Negro—after all, you and I are products of such relationships, though they weren't quite the same back then, were they? Perhaps one day a marriage like the Grimkés' will be celebrated, and a love between you and Porter will be accepted. I hope it will be so, but do not deceive yourself now. We do not live in such a time, and

you are as aware as I am, Anita, nothing good can come
of such a marriage.

Enjoy your final months at Vassar. I know how fond of
it you are. Then come home to me, come home to Boston,
and be the Anita Hemmings that everyone here loves.

Your Bessie

Anita ripped the letter into pieces so small that she couldn't rip them anymore, then dropped them into the stream, followed by a shower of pebbles, tossed in one by one. How, Anita thought, had Bessie dared write her such a letter! If the wrong hands had opened it, her secret would have been exposed, and just before graduation. Who was to say that the maid hadn't opened it and sealed it again? Anita wasn't sure how literate she was, but even someone with a primary school education would recognize the word *Negro.* Bessie was well intentioned, but she had never lived in the world Anita had. Northfield was different. There were students from thirty different countries there. There were Chinese students and Native students and Negro students. And at Wellesley, Bessie had not formed the kinds of friendships Anita had at Vassar. She didn't know how white people treated you when they thought you one of them. She did not know what it was like for a man like Porter Hamilton to love you.

Anita left the farm flooded with anxiety. She walked down the hill, the art gallery, with its undulating roof, coming into view. At Northfield, Bessie had sympathized with her; now she was chastising her. What would Anita have if she went home? Could she be the person Bessie believed she was? Is that even what she wanted?

No, she thought. Not yet. She still hoped to travel, to study, to soar beyond what she had been so often told were her limits.

As she passed the gallery and headed into the rear of Main, she thought of the rift that might open between her and Bessie after her graduation. She thought about the possibility of a life without her. Bessie had made it clear in her letter: if Anita chose to live permanently as a white woman, they would no longer see each other. Anita chewed on her lip, biting back tears at the prospect. It wasn't fair of Bessie, she thought. She didn't turn a blind eye to her now, while she was living as a white woman at Vassar. Why should she after graduation?

Anita brushed the dirt from her dress and hurried inside Main in time for her Greek class with Miss Macurdy.

At thirty-one, Grace Macurdy was one of the youngest professors at Vassar, having graduated from Radcliffe in '88 and joining Vassar when Anita came in '93. This semester, Anita's last, she had shared with her students one of her deepest passions, the history of Hellenistic queens in Macedonia, Seleucid Syria, and Ptolemaic Egypt.

After forty minutes of translation work, so difficult that one of the students had tears of frustration smearing her pen marks, Miss Macurdy switched to the lecture format she most enjoyed. Anita listened, fascinated, as the professor spoke about Berenice I of Egypt and her lack of royal blood. Miss Macurdy looked directly at Anita, who had previously confided in her teacher how much she enjoyed the subject, and said, "Berenice's end was like her beginning. She knew how to live dangerously and how to die bravely, and she had a pitiful heart."

"I could listen to those stories all afternoon," Hortense Lewis, Belle's studious roommate, said to Anita as they stood up to leave together. Hortense and Anita had never been great friends, as Hortense was the kind of person who could only be great friends with a book, but they shared a passion for Greek history, which gave them fodder for conversation after class. Anita was poised to respond when Miss Macurdy approached her.

"Miss Hemmings, please stay a minute. I'd like to discuss something with you, briefly before the dinner bell."

Anita nodded, said goodbye to Hortense, and tried to shake off the dread filling her body faster than a well in a rainstorm. She had not been asked to stay after class since Miss Franklin had kept her to share her complicated views on the Negro race. Miss Macurdy placed a pile of papers in front of Anita and pulled out the chair next to her. She gathered her skirts and sat next to her devoted student, her face unsmiling.

"Applications for graduate scholarships awarded by Vassar are on the top. The paperwork for the Babbott Fellowship and for the fellowship for four hundred dollars given by the class of '87 are underneath. Anita, we will get you to Greece so you can continue your studies, I am sure of it."

Anita looked at her professor and wanted to cry out with delight. Miss Macurdy, Anita knew, refused to see a passion for the classics wasted. She had told Anita her freshman year that she hailed from Vermont, a state she described as feeling farther from the riches of Greece than the sun. "I myself will be in Europe this summer," she added now, "at the University of Berlin. Perhaps we will have a chance to meet."

"I would love that," said Anita, flipping through the application. "I'm so appreciative that you thought of me. That you recommended me." Her eyes fell to the Babbott Fellowship paperwork and the space where an applicant was required to fill in her race. French and English, Anita thought to herself. And nothing more.

She thanked Miss Macurdy profusely and headed up to her room to spend the hour before dinner.

Before she reached the top of the staircase, she collected the mail, three letters, all for Lottie. Two of the stamps indicated that the letters had been sent from New York. The other was from Cambridge. Anita looked at the handwriting and recognized it as Porter's. Desperate to open the letter before Lottie did, she looked around the hall, trying to work up a nerve that did not come naturally to her. But before she could persuade herself to tamper with it, to read it, Caroline stepped out of the elevator.

"Anita, I was hoping you'd be about," she said. "Let's go and sit and do absolutely nothing in your parlor before the dinner bell rings. I've had such a day. I'm coming from a Phil meeting, and I swear to you that Vassie James is more demanding than the head of the Metropolitan Opera. I have nearly one hundred lines to learn. And you should see the program design for the next play. It's in the shape of a small black coffin, isn't that ghastly? My character is not moribund, she's quite in the prime of her life."

"But isn't the play about death?" asked Anita. Lottie had been reciting her lines for the play all week.

"It is, but why must we be so literal? The last program was in the charming shape of a teakettle, and the play was not about tea."

The girls walked into Anita's parlor room and found Belle and Lottie already there, Belle strumming her mandolin idly as Lottie rested, a book on her face.

"Your Shakespeare is upside down," said Anita, picking up the book to reveal Lottie's closed eyes. "And I fetched the mail. All for you." She handed Lottie the letters, and Lottie immediately put Porter's down and out of sight. Sitting up, she opened the first one from New York with her ornate silver letter opener, which boasted a large *T* at the top with a pearl-encrusted loop.

"Can I try my hand at that?" asked Anita, reaching for Belle's mandolin. As she took the neck of the instrument in her hand, Lottie let out a gasp like a punctured bicycle tire. They all dropped what they were doing and gathered around her.

"Why, we've been invited to Clavedon Hall!" said Lottie, as she continued to read.

"The four of us?" asked Caroline. "How delightful. What is Clavedon Hall?"

"Moreover, where is Clavedon Hall?" asked Belle.

"It's the Rhinelander estate in Lenox, Massachusetts, in the Berkshire Mountains," said Lottie, still looking down at the letter embossed with the family's intricate monogram. "Marchmont Rhinelander has invited us all to visit. He says we could come during our spring vacation in just two weeks' time!"

She looked up, seemingly as surprised as everybody else. "He writes here that he appreciated our kindness at the opera and would like to see us all again. He's encouraged us to come for at least a weekend, but preferably a week."

"Did he write that? All of us?" said Anita.

"He did," said Lottie, pointing at the line. "There will also be a musician, no, a composer, from France as a guest, and he says that Belle will have many opportunities to showcase her voice." She looked up at Anita and added, "You, too. I'm afraid we forgot to mention how well you sing. Won't that be a surprise?"

"Do you think it's a good idea?" asked Anita, thinking about what Marchmont had said to her. She had managed to deter him once, but could she block his scrutiny for a whole weekend? She didn't want him to have time to study her face. And what if Frederick were to find out? He would cross Massachusetts to drag her home by her hair and lock her away in Roxbury forever.

"I don't know," said Lottie. "I'm not sure we can go. The Rhinelander family is one of the most highly regarded in New York, but Marchmont is very much its black sheep—"

"But we must!" said Belle excitedly. "I'm already half in love with him, and a week at Clarendon Hall—"

"Clavedon Hall," Lottie corrected her.

"A week there will certainly make the other half surrender, too. Please respond yes, Lottie. My parents expect me home, as does your mother, but we don't need to be there for more than a few days, and spring vacation is nearly two weeks long."

"I planned to remain at college," said Anita, "and Caroline, too."

"Even if my mother does approve, we'll never be allowed to make the trip without a chaperone," said Lottie from her sofa. "It's just not done. And my mother as companion is out of the question."

"What about Nettie Aldrich?" asked Belle, sitting down with her and taking the letter from her hands. It was written on the thickest paper either had ever seen. "Nettie is married and close by in Boston."

"Of course!" said Lottie. "And Harvard has its spring vacation in April, as well. Perhaps Talbot can accompany her. That would appease my mother."

"It has to happen!" said Belle, turning pink. "You will come, won't you, Anita? Caroline?"

"If Lottie's mother approves, and our families consent, then yes, we will," said Caroline, answering for both of them. Anita knew she would have to lie to her parents and say she was staying at college for the entire spring holiday. But she couldn't worry about that now. She was too busy wondering how she could alter her appearance in two weeks' time so that Marchmont did not bring up the subject of Boston again.

Mrs. Taylor more than approved. Marchmont may have been the pariah of New York that spring, but he was still a Rhinelander, and when the scandal had blown over, he would again become one of New York's most eligible bachelors, even at forty-one. Lucretia Schotenhorn had already approved him for her young daughter, and that meant everything in New York.

CHAPTER 22

When the four girls disembarked from their train at Pittsfield on the first Friday in April, the Rhinelander coach was waiting for them. And when they were helped down from it in Lenox, where the Rhinelanders' stone mansion sat on 128 acres, the first person they saw was Nettie Aldrich. She ran toward the large carriage, the sleeves of her light blue dress billowing. Lenox was full of white-blossoming trees, but between them lay open fields, cleared by farmers, which let the wind through.

"Nettie!" Lottie cried as the girls spotted her.

"Aren't you all a delight to ask me here?" said Nettie. She was wearing her hair in an even more voluminous style than the last time they had seen her, and they all admired the way it puffed out under her straw sporting hat. "The weather is too beautiful to be in the city," Nettie said, patting her coiffure lovingly. "And to kick off the spring season at the Rhinelander estate, it's just marvelous. We've already been here three days."

She turned to Lottie and said, "I was shocked when I received your note. How ever did you acquire an invitation to Clavedon Hall? It's the grandest house in the Berkshires."

"We were polite to Marchmont," Anita explained before Lottie could. "When no one else was."

"When no one else was!" echoed Nettie, laughing. "Of course no one else was, Anita. He called off his engagement two days before his wedding to Estelle Schotenhorn! Seven hundred oysters had to be thrown out, three hundred live quails had to be returned—can you imagine the embarrassment?"

"Oh, no, not the live quails," Caroline whispered to Anita, making them both laugh.

"Enough, you two," said Lottie. "Hailing from the middle of nowhere, both of you. You just don't know the power of the Schotenhorns in New York. They run society, and society runs the city. I'm surprised they still allow Marchmont to live there. He really should be banished to this Berkshire cottage."

"The Rhinelanders are one of the original families," Nettie reminded Lottie. "They can't run him out of town, even if they want to. He can trace his roots in New York back two hundred years. That's earlier than the Schotenhorns, though they don't like to admit it."

"Still, I hear Estelle Schotenhorn hasn't appeared in society since," said Lottie. "The poor bucktoothed little thing. That man turned her into a recluse, forced to live a life of solitude like Henry David Thoreau. And with summer on the horizon, too. She's spent every summer since she's been out in Europe or Newport. But not this year."

"Luckily for us!" said Belle, grabbing a golf club from the ground and swinging it with all her might.

"You remind me, I need to tidy those up," said Nettie. "Marchmont, Talbot, and the Frenchman Xavier de Montmorency are in town," she added, leading them inside where a maid was ready to help them unpack. "They'll return shortly. The Frenchman is very regal indeed, descended from one of the grandest noble houses in France. He's a composer, but he still has an air about him. He's charming and plays the piano wonderfully. You'll enjoy his company. Come now, I'll show you the drawing room. You're going to fall in love with this house."

"I already have," said Belle, looking into the first of forty-one rooms.

When the men returned from town, the women were gathered in the drawing room, dressed for dinner. The tall windows had been thrown open, and the sheer curtains fluttered in the fragrant breeze of the early evening.

"Well!" said Marchmont, striding in. He had had a new spring suit cut for the occasion of hosting four unmarried women in his family home, and all the ladies looked admiringly at him as he approached. "It looks as if you're holding a party for ghosts in here. Everything blowing every which way," he said, taking Lottie's hand in greeting.

"Marchmont Rhinelander," she said, standing to meet him. "You're one of a kind, aren't you? Inviting us here after we spoke to you at the opera. I don't know that it's proper, but we are all very glad to be here."

"I'm happy you could get away from your studies, devoted academics that you are," he said, turning to Belle next and kissing her hand with familiarity. "It will be an amusing weekend, most notably because I will be in your company, but also because we have Monsieur de Montmorency here," he said, indicating the fair-haired Frenchman, who appeared closer in age to the girls than to Marchmont. "We became acquainted on my second long tour in Europe when I was taking in opera after opera and he was Paris's musical prodigy."

"We must hear you play," Anita said politely. "And if you'll allow us, Belle and I would love to join you for a song."

Anita knew that one of her greatest social assets was her voice. And perhaps, she thought, it would help persuade

Marchmont that she was not the girl he had seen walking the streets of Boston.

Xavier promptly complied, and the rest of the group sat mesmerized as he played, and Anita and Belle sang, the flower duet from *Lakmé*. The girls had trained in the same choir for nearly four years, so their voices blended well, Belle's strong mezzo holding its own against Anita's soaring soprano.

"Such beauty!" said Marchmont, standing up and clapping when they had finished. "And *Lakmé*, of all things. Anita, you sang Lakmé's role superbly, and Belle, your Mallika was just as it should be, engaging and fresh, with all the power of a mezzo. I was in the audience in Paris when *Lakmé* was first performed at the Opéra Comique. The angelic Marie van Zandt and Elisa Frandin debuted your roles. It is to this day one of my fondest memories. And you both sang it so well."

"Lovely," said the Frenchman from his seat on the piano bench. "For two American students, I am most impressed. But now, for a little something *plus dramatique*!" he said, before launching into Chopin's exceptionally difficult Sonata No. 3.

When he was finished, Marchmont rose again and said, "The three of you, please do join us in New York next season when I am no longer banished from the ladies' drawing rooms. Your talents would make it much more bearable. So many of the young women in New York have voices like cats and play the piano as if their fingers were sewn together."

"I can't imagine why you've been banished," said Lottie slyly. "You'd think all the hostesses of New York would be competing to be worthy of such compliments."

"At least there is Lottie Taylor," said Marchmont, moving to sit next to her as Belle's face dropped. "You've never bored anyone."

"I don't want a thing to do with New York society," said

Lottie, as Nettie closed the windows next to them. The sun had just started to sink behind the rolling hills, and her husband, Talbot, turned on the lamp beside him, illuminating Lottie's face.

"I've seen its effects on my mother," Lottie went on. "She threatens suicide through poisoning if there is a notable event and she's not invited. It's ridiculous the things intelligent women become worked up about: tea trays and china, balls and parties, the nip in the waist of a gown. Marchmont, we here represent a different generation of women, the first girls in our families to attend college. And we won't succumb to the same fate as our mothers. We have minds formally molded to do important things. Splendid things."

"Well said!" commented Nettie from the sofa she was sharing with her husband.

"And what do you intend to do after your graduation from Vassar, Miss Taylor?" asked the Frenchman, still perched on the piano bench.

"Me? Nothing but the greatest adventures that money can buy. I plan on traveling back to the Orient—Japan specifically—for a good deal of time. I'd like to study the language, the culture. It's so much more interesting to see a country that has been open to trade with the West for only forty years. France and Italy, England, too, with so many Americans already established there, they don't attract the pioneer in me," she explained to Xavier. "So off I will go, chaperoned, of course. But I've been skilled in shaking off a chaperone for decades now. Who knows, I may stay forever. I may even marry one of them."

"And Porter?" said Anita suddenly. "What will become of him then?"

"Porter Hamilton is a student at Harvard," Belle clarified for the others, a firmness in her voice hinting at her sympathy for Anita on this particular subject. "He's finishing at Cambridge in June, and then it will be back to Chicago. Lottie and he are . . . what would you call it, Lottie? Flirting? Or that modern term, dating? Or perhaps more?"

"Flirting with a man from Chicago, Miss Taylor?" said Marchmont, teasingly. "Then you may become your mother yet, just in a lesser city."

"I most certainly will not," retorted Lottie. "I plan to sail for Japan immediately after graduation. If a man loves me enough, he can follow me. Or wait."

"Yes, your affections do change so quickly," said Belle, saying what Anita did not dare to. "Just a few months ago you were so taken with Joseph Southworth."

"Then I discovered that his mother was a teenage prostitute in Japan when she gave birth to him," said Lottie. "You can all imagine why I had to abruptly throttle my emotions."

"Is that true?" said Talbot, looking at his wife. "Doesn't the family reside in Cambridge? In that handsome house on Beacon Hill?"

"This is the son of Benjamin Southworth we are discussing?" asked Marchmont.

"Yes," said Lottie, "Joseph Southworth. Or Southpaw, as we call him."

"I know the family well," Marchmont replied. "They have a cottage on Walker Street, one of the largest in the Berkshires. They don't stay there often, but I have met Benjamin and remember him as being very respectable, as well as amiable."

"This sounds like a very American scandal," said Xavier. "If this Southpaw—"

Anita opened her mouth to correct him, but Caroline shushed her. "Please don't. I'm enjoying it too much," she whispered.

"If he were residing in Paris and had found a lover, he would still be welcomed everywhere, even if she was with child," said Xavier.

"His son, too?" asked Anita.

"*Mais bien sûr*, his son, too," said Xavier. "Just think of Alexandre Dumas. He was half-*nègre*."

Anita had read two of Dumas's works in their original French at Northfield, but no one had ever mentioned his race. She was shocked to hear Xavier say he was a Negro, knowing his place in the French literary canon.

"I wasn't aware of such a scandal in the Orient," said Marchmont. "But I suppose a man will be a man, no matter which country he is traveling in."

"That is such a preposterously male thing to say," said Lottie. "You and your freedoms, able to do what you please, the world always bending to your whims. As women, we cannot make our choices so lightly, since the consequences are far graver."

"I think that's often your own faults," said Talbot from his comfortable perch. "It is the women who run society and the women who judge each other. We as men may tell you what you can and can't do professionally, but personally, socially, women make the rules."

"I think American men would be much happier if their female counterparts had more sexual freedom," said Xavier, causing every woman to blush except Lottie. "And I agree. It's the women who keep each other from it, who impose their idea of morality. Now in France—"

"I think that's enough of this talk!" said Nettie, springing into action as their chaperone.

"Come, gentlemen," said Marchmont, standing up. "Let us leave these women to their plans for changing the world. How about a game of billiards before we dine?"

"With cigars," said Talbot. "You're right, Marchmont, I should change rooms. I can see my wife is desperate to denigrate me and my rigid ideals to her charges."

"That's right," said Nettie, blowing her husband a kiss.

The following morning found the group in good spirits as Xavier had woken them all up with a delightful piano piece he had recently composed.

"That's certainly more pleasant than a bell," said Lottie, walking into Anita's bedroom already dressed.

"It's wonderful here," said Anita, looking out at the hills and the dogwood trees in bloom. During her entire career at Vassar, she had behaved as she assumed a woman passing as white should. Blending in, disappearing into the middle, was her main objective. But now, she realized, she was throwing caution away and doing exactly as she pleased. She no longer heard Frederick's voice every time a man spoke to her, or shared her mother's concern when she attracted attention for doing something outstanding. She was finally just letting herself be who she was, indeed, discovering who that was, and she relished the feeling.

After breakfast, served in the vast dining room at a table that could easily seat twenty, the group retired outdoors, where lawn badminton was set up. The new game had become a craze at Vassar since the girls' freshman year. Anita and Lottie were pitted against tall Caroline and the athletic and even taller Belle, and appeared headed to certain defeat when Marchmont came to the net after the first set and asked Anita to take a walk with him.

"There are the most beautiful flowers to be picked near the stream. It runs all along the edge of the property," he said, leaning on a golf club in his sporting costume. "I think you would enjoy it."

The other women stared at Anita, their faces blank with

surprise, since it had been obvious to all that Belle was the one who had set her cap for Marchmont.

"Yes, I would like that very much," said Anita, feeling it would be rude to decline outright though she was terrified of being alone with him. She guessed he wanted to speak about Boston, though she knew the others would not think so. "Lottie has become a passionate horticulturalist this spring. She spends many afternoons engaged in the traditional Japanese art of ikebana. Perhaps she—or Belle—would like to—"

"If you don't mind," said Marchmont to the other girls, "I think Miss Hemmings would most enjoy this particular walk."

Anita nodded a stiff yes, put down her racket, and looked at Belle apologetically. Belle looked hurt, but there was nothing Anita could do. She reached for her hat, which was resting on the outdoor glass table, and followed Marchmont.

"This is such a beautiful house," said Anita, when her schoolmates were out of view. "I was in preparatory school not too far from here, and this view of the orchards reminds me of the one I woke up to there."

Marchmont nodded approvingly, and the two walked in silence until they reached the stream. Anita leaned down and placed her hand in the cool water. She swished it about, then placed it on the back of her neck. She bent down again and plucked several flowers from the bank, turning to look at her host to make sure it was allowed.

"I find your quiet nature very arresting, Miss Hemmings," Marchmont said, watching her hands. "So many women tend to screech. They remind me of canaries having their feathers plucked. Not you."

"It must be because I don't hail from New York. Every-

thing is louder on Fifth Avenue," said Anita, becoming increasingly nervous in the older man's presence.

"That's right, you are from Boston," he said, studying
her soft features as she looked up at him from under her
straw hat. "The Back Bay. Or was it Beacon Hill?" He leaned
down to take the flowers from her hand.

"Miss Hemmings, I am sure I have seen your face before," he said, his eyes fixed on her as if she were a scientific
specimen. "I have a very good memory for such things, because I am an only child. I had very little to do when I was
young but watch the faces of New York go by my window.
To this day I never forget a face, and certainly not one as
pretty as yours. Now, when did I see you?"

"I don't know," said Anita, turning to face the water so
he couldn't scrutinize her. "I don't remember seeing you
before we met at the opera. I'm sure of it."

"No, I've seen you before, I am certain," he said, reaching
for her face and bringing her chin toward him. "Such a delicate appearance, nothing Roman-nosed about you. I think
it was in Boston around the New Year," he said, letting her
face go. "Were you in Boston then? And could you have been
walking through another part of the city, not the Back Bay,
with a . . . a younger woman?"

Anita thought of the many times she had walked in the
snow with Elizabeth. They hadn't left Roxbury, but still,
how could she have been so callow as to think she could go
wherever she wanted, even there, as if the city had gates
separating the color lines? The rest of the world lacked the
safety she took for granted at Vassar. White men were often
in Roxbury. She had walked past many of them when she
was home; she could easily have walked past Marchmont
Rhinelander and never known.

"I spent most of my time indoors this holiday," said

Anita. "I am not one for the cold. But when I did get outside, it was only around the Back Bay."

"Not a fan of winter," said Marchmont, ignoring her last claim. "Then you must love this." He kicked the tall grass as the two moved farther from the stone house.

"I more than love this," said Anita, praying he had dropped the subject of Boston. "Every spring is like walking into a world you've never seen. Because it is, isn't it? Everything changes, takes on new forms, new growth, new air."

"Yes, I've always liked change, too," said Marchmont. "I often think about change when I make my trips to Boston. You see, I make them quite frequently."

"Why is that?" asked Anita, crouching down to pick one perfectly formed spring daisy.

"My father has a child there," said Marchmont abruptly. He bent down to help her uproot the flower without crushing the stem. Anita looked up at him, her face a picture of shock, and appeared about to lose her balance. Marchmont took her arm and helped her stand up.

"I'm sorry, I didn't mean to seem so shaken," said Anita.

"It's perfectly fine," he said, letting go of her arm. "I would expect you to be. Come, let's walk a little way, it's good for nerves."

He offered her his arm as he led her over a patch of high grass and fallen branches. "His daughter—my father's daughter—is illegitimate, as I am sure you assumed. Her name is Carrie, and she lives with her still very young mother in Boston. I look after them financially. I visit her when I feel it's appropriate. She's young herself, just eleven years old."

"Was her mother a servant? Or—"

"No," said Marchmont, cutting Anita off before she had to say something uncomfortable. "She was employed in a less fortunate way in New York's Tenderloin district. I know now that my father has had a penchant for such women for decades."

"And your mother?" asked Anita, thinking of what she might do if she were in her place.

"She is aware of his bad habit, she stays, and she ignores. And she prays, of course, but it doesn't do much good."

"Does she know about his daughter?" asked Anita, lifting her skirts higher than she should have as she walked, as the girls did at Vassar.

"She does know there is a child in Boston," said Marchmont, his eyes drifting to Anita's slender ankles encased in her small leather boots. "But she doesn't know that she lives in the Negro area of town. She doesn't know that her mother is a Negro."

"A Negro!" Anita said loudly. If Marchmont had not steadied her, she would have fallen in the grass. "The mother of this poor child is colored?" asked Anita, not realizing how hard she was gripping her escort's arm.

"She is," said Marchmont calmly. "She is from New York originally, but she went to Boston after she learned she was with child. She has a forgiving aunt living there who took her in. She and Carrie still live with her."

Anita was stunned into silence. If Marchmont had been in Boston after Christmas visiting this Negro child, he was most likely in Roxbury. He certainly could have seen her. She looked up at him and prayed that if he *had* glimpsed her with her sister, he would have the decency not to say a word about it to anyone but her. She bent to pick another flower and said, "That's very surprising."

"It is surprising," said Marchmont, his voice still flat. "But it's a fact. And though it surprised me at first, and I disapproved of my father's behavior, I've become very fond of Carrie. I don't plan to abandon my support of her, either financially or emotionally."

"Does your father know her?" asked Anita, focusing on the mossy ground rather than her host.

"No. He's never met her, or even seen her mother again after she announced she was with child. He didn't believe it was his and sent her back to the brothel house. In her state, it was unforgivable. I only learned about Carrie six years ago when he confessed everything to me on my thirty-fifth birthday. He figured me man enough to know then. It was a lecture given so I would not make the same mistakes he had, but instead it brought me to Carrie. My father has always thought of me as a man just like him, but I will never be that sort of man."

"What is the area of town called?" asked Anita, finally looking up at him. As soon as she said it she knew, and he knew, that she should know the name. "Where she lives. Which neighborhood is she in?"

"Roxbury," he said, looking at her intently, reaching for her face again, but stopping short. "It's called Roxbury."

"Is this why you called off your engagement with Estelle Schotenhorn?" Anita asked quietly.

"That's partly the reason. Estelle is a lovely girl, despite her mother's steel will pushing her this way and that. She doesn't deserve to be mixed up in a scandal, if it ever broke. I've made many mistakes in my life, but scandalizing a young woman has never been one of them."

"Why did you tell me this?" Anita said, wishing that he touched her face again. There was something about Marchmont that she liked tremendously, not in a romantic way, but in every other way. "I assume this is something almost no one knows?"

"Very few people outside my family know," he said. This time he did put his hand on Anita's cheek, and left it there longer than was proper. "But there is something about you." He let his hand slide down her face and placed it on her shoulder, and looked at her respectfully. "I know you'll keep my secret."

When they finally returned to the house, everyone was sitting in the drawing room, cooling off after their sporting endeavors.

"These are for you," said Anita, handing Belle the little bouquet of wildflowers she and Marchmont had picked. "From Marchmont," she added.

"Oh!" said Belle, clutching them in surprise.

Anita watched Marchmont as he bowed, and her heart swelled with relief. Yes, he had guessed her secret, but in exchange for knowing hers, he had confessed his. *See*, Anita wanted to shout at Bessie and Frederick. There are men like this in the world. There are people who think this way, who act this way. *Look at me at Clavedon Hall, allowed to stay here even though he knows the truth. Look at me!*

"Belle, I do hope I can call on you in Fredonia once you have graduated," said Marchmont when he accompanied them to the train station in Pittsfield two days later. "That is, if you're not off to Italy straightaway."

"Of course," said Belle, blushing to the roots of her hair. "You would be most welcome."

The porters carried the girls' suitcases onto the train and they settled into a wagon with strong gaslights and a tea tray already set up. Within an hour, Lottie and Caroline, who were seated in front of Belle and Anita, had their heads resting on each other in deep repose.

Belle pressed her face to the window, watching Massachusetts become New York, and said, "Do you like Marchmont, Anita? Do you think I should allow him to write to me? To call after graduation?"

"I do," said Anita. "And you should. I like him very much."

CHAPTER 23

Back at school after their surprising trip to the Berkshires, Anita made it one of her first tasks to collect the mail. She separated her letters from Lottie's, which were all from Porter Hamilton, and hurried up to their shared parlor room.

She tossed Lottie's mail onto her disorganized desk and closed the door loudly behind her, heading to Caroline's room. Opening the door, she found Caroline with her head on her table, her writing papers scattered around her and all over the floor.

"You're just in time to keep me from checking myself into the infirmary for mania," she said, not lifting her head.

"Why would you do that?" asked Anita, coming in and starting to straighten Caroline's things. "Sane as you are."

"Because of Founder's!" said Caroline, handing Anita an opened letter. "Raymond DeGroot can't leave Yale so close to finals; he's too nervous about them. He says if he comes to Founder's, he'll fail. Have you ever heard anything more absurd?"

If Phil Day had possessed the minds of the Vassar students for weeks, Founder's Day riveted them for months. It was a favorite day on campus, featuring not only celebrations for the birthday of school founder Matthew Vassar, but also the other large annual dance. And because Founder's fell so close to the end of the school year, and the end of the Vassar experience for the seniors, it was a day full of nostalgia.

"We can find you another date for Founder's," said Anita, patting her friend's bent head. Caroline's hair was unfashionably down, as it often was when she was in her room alone. "It's not for three weeks. I don't yet have an escort myself."

"Of course you don't, because Lottie Taylor and Porter Hamilton broke your heart," said Caroline, sitting up. "Poor Anita. If I were braver, I would tell Lottie exactly how I feel about what she did to you. And Founder's is not three weeks away, it's but two and a half."

"That is still ample time for us to find escorts," said Anita. "As for Lottie, she's not entirely to blame for my current state. I'm the one who broke off my engagement with Porter, so he was technically Lottie's for the taking."

"Any true friend would not have taken," said Caroline. "I don't mean to say that she's not fond of you. She is. She prefers your company to that of every other girl at school. She was never close to Dora the way she is to you, and they roomed together for two years. The problem with Lottie is that above all else, she loves herself."

When Lottie and Anita were together in their parlor that evening, the wide-open window letting in the buzz of talk and laughter from outside, Anita told Lottie about Caroline's plight, and how upset she was to still be dateless. Lottie put down the flowers she was arranging and looked at Anita.

"Poor Caroline, she shouldn't fret yet." Then, appearing as uncomfortable as she was capable, she added, "Do *you* have an escort for Founder's? I've invited Porter, but if you find that inappropriate, as he said you might, I am happy to attend alone."

"No, Lottie," said Anita, her mouth rigid. "I expected you would invite Porter. And if you do not mind, I would like to invite Joseph Southworth."

"You intend to invite Joseph!" said Lottie, dropping backward into the rocking chair, her flowers falling to the floor. She swept them up, placed them in a wastebasket, and picked up fresh ones. "Do you really? Even after that scandal?"

"I don't mind," said Anita. "I would be more comfortable with someone I already know, and you have to admit, he is very amusing."

"Indeed he is. Such a pity about his mother." Lottie picked up a shawl and arranged it over the light shirtwaist she was wearing. "And you're sure you are not upset about Porter attending? Will you promise me? It's your last Founder's, and I want you to enjoy it to its fullest."

"I promise," said Anita, finding she was able to lie with a smile on her face. "If you don't mind about Joseph, then I am fine with Porter attending."

Joseph Southworth accepted Anita's late invitation with alacrity and notified her that he would be taking the train down with Porter Hamilton, as he had done for Phil. For the next two weeks, Lottie asked Anita repeatedly whether she approved of her attending the dance with Porter, and Anita continued to reassure her that she did, though she finally added one caveat.

"I have no ill will toward you about bringing Porter," she said, three days before the dance, "but I imagine we would both feel less awkward if we were not in the same group."

"Do you think so?" said Lottie, practicing her hat face in

her mirror. "I detest the way this hat cuts so low on my fore-head." She placed it on her head and sucked in her cheeks to make them look thinner. "Absolutely not this one. I look like a hippopotamus wearing a bonnet. Would you like it?" she asked Anita, holding it out to her.

"Founder's?" Anita reminded her.

"Oh, yes, Founder's," Lottie repeated. "Though I have held my tongue this time around, I have been thinking the very same thing. I doubt Old Southpaw is dreaming of a place on my dance card, and he might still feel some animus toward me. Perhaps you should group with Belle, as you are performing together with the Glee Club before the lecture, and I will group with Caroline. We can request boxes at opposite ends of the parlor."

"But surely Belle and Caroline will want to be together on their last Founder's," said Anita. "They're as close as you and I."

"I think they'll understand," said Lottie, throwing the hat in the wastebasket, too.

On the afternoon of the event, Anita was already dressed in the simple rose-colored satin gown she had purchased from a dressmaker on Noxon Street when she looked out the window of her shared parlor to watch the carriages come through the gatehouse. Japanese paper lanterns had been strung from the Lodge to Main, and she felt a twinge of distress as the first few visitors were brought down the long, illuminated road.

Anita hated having to prepare for the dance alone, but she had agreed to meet Joseph earlier than usual so they would have plenty of time to make their way to the chapel without encountering Porter and Lottie.

When her hair was curled and arranged at the nape of her neck and she had smoothed her dress just so, she walked down the hall to Belle's room for reassurance about her plain costume.

"Anita, you would be breathtaking in a gown made of cleaning rags," said Belle, who was just starting to dress for the evening. "There is nothing that could diminish the beauty of your face. And the dress is very smart. Its simplicity brings one's eye up to your neck, which is without comparison on campus."

"Thank you, Belle," said Anita, looking down at her unembellished dress with embarrassment. She knew she could have borrowed one of Lottie's expensive Parisian gowns, as she had done for important occasions all year, but in this instance it did not seem right. Porter wanted Lottie, Anita thought to herself. He did not want her impersonating Lottie in her clothes.

"You've always been such a staunch friend," she said to Belle, overcome with gratitude. She put her arms around Belle's neck and promised to save her two seats in the senior section of chapel. "And Belle?" she said, before leaving the room.

"Yes?" Belle looked up at her from her mirror.

"I'm sorry you and Caroline won't be in the same box for the dance. I feel wretched about it."

"Do not worry about that," said Belle. "You, Anita Hemmings, should never feel you are a second choice. I'll still see Caroline, as will you, and we will have a wonderful evening. Let's make it so."

Anita slipped downstairs to the visitors' parlor to wait for Joseph. When she arrived, she was the only student in the elegant room.

"Old Southpaw!" she said, standing up when Joseph joined her ten minutes later. He was just as handsome as she remembered, and he had lost none of his sophisticated air.

"You were brave to say yes to my invitation," Anita said, taking the bouquet of white roses from his hands.

"I was happy to receive it," he said, perfectly at ease with her, just as she had hoped. "We are first, I see," he said, with a glance around the empty parlor. "Lucky me. More time spent with you." He offered her his arm and they headed to the chapel.

"I'm honored to be your escort, you know," he said when they had sat down, he a proper distance from her, she clutching her flowers. "I assumed, when I received your invitation, that there is no ill will between you and Hamilton or you and Miss Taylor. Am I correct in thinking so? Hamilton said as much on the train down, but who believes a Hamilton? I thought I should ask the more intelligent party."

"None at all," said Anita, her heart fluttering along with her lie. "They are happy together, and I am content on my own. I've come to appreciate that academics are the reason I am here, not to fall in love with Porter Hamilton. And in any case, life would not be interesting without twists and turns, would it?"

"Not mine, anyway," said Joseph with a broad smile. "My life has been on a path shaped like a figure eight since birth, and frankly, I think I'm a better man for it."

Soon afterward, Belle came into the chapel to collect Anita for their warm-up with the Glee Club and Professor Gow before their performance. "We will return soon," she said to Joseph, whom she had greeted like an old friend. She left her date, a Columbia man she'd been paired with by Nettie Aldrich, and the two girls retreated behind the organ to meet with their group.

Anita was performing one of two solos that evening, singing "O Saving Victim" by Berthold Tours, as she had done two weeks earlier at the Easter concert, also in the college chapel. To her delight, it went off beautifully, and the crowd's faces blurred comfortingly before her. But when she walked back to sing with the group, she couldn't help but search the rows for Porter. Neither he nor Lottie was anywhere to be seen. When they sat back down, Belle whispered in Anita's ear that Lottie and Porter did not seem to be present, or if they were, they were not in the senior section.

Anita tried to peek behind her at the upper level, wondering if they had sat with the freshmen, but Vassie James, the fair-haired president of the Students' Association, stepped onto the stage and Anita had to turn her eyes to the front. Vassie introduced the evening's speaker, a Columbia philosophy professor who was to address them on the education of public opinion.

The lecture over, the crowd flooded out of the chapel for refreshments in the hallways before moving on to the dining room. As Anita and Joseph approached the tables of glass pitchers filled with lemonade and teas, she saw two seniors looking at them questioningly and exchanging whispers. When they caught Anita's eye, they stopped mid-sentence and moved away quickly.

"Don't worry," said Joseph, looking down at Anita. "I am sure they were speaking about me, not you. I imagine Lottie spread wild stories about disgraced Old Southpaw all over school. I must be something of a cause célèbre around here."

"Does it not bother you that people gossip about you? About your mother?" Anita asked.

"Yes and no," Joseph replied. "I've known from childhood that people were going to gossip about my birth, my race, my parents. My father's money helps quiet the rumors a bit, but women like Lottie Taylor will never let me forget.

I knew that from the start with Lottie, but she amused me, so I thought I'd push it as far as I could. I don't regret it, really. She's like a pleasant breeze that you enjoy while it's there, knowing it won't last."

"But why did you tell her your mother was deceased?" Anita asked. They had moved to a corner of the hallway, a little removed from Belle and the rest of the students.

"That's been my story for quite a while," Joseph explained. "Less scandalous that way. I'm sure it will continue to be my story once I move out of these school circles. Scandals come and go, Anita. They don't just follow you like a stray dog."

"I hope that's true," she said, looking up at him. "For your sake," she added quickly. "You are too entertaining, too kind, to have the circumstances of your birth haunt you forever."

"Aren't you a truly modern woman?" said Joseph, motioning to a waiter to refill their drinks. "And to think you're Lottie's very best friend. Oil and water. I can see why she is so fond of you."

Anita looked down and thought how unfortunate it was that Founder's couldn't be just like Phil Day, and all because of Frederick barring her relationship with Porter Hamilton and Lottie leaping across all boundaries to take him for herself.

"Don't worry so much about people like Lottie," Joseph advised, as Anita remained silent. "Wealth will only get one so far if they don't have the wealth of heart to match."

"Some men may feel that way," said Anita. "But their mothers will care about her bank account."

"Luckily for you, my mother barely speaks English," said Joseph, finishing his drink.

When Belle and her date, Lawrence Foster, had joined them, Anita took the opportunity to slip away. She badly wanted to find Caroline, who had stopped to say hello as they were taking their refreshments, and ask her where Lottie and Porter might have gone. Anita had been sure she would see them before the girls were announced with their escorts, but she had yet to spot them in the large crowd. Was it possible they had chosen not to attend?

"Caroline went outside with a few others," said Hortense Lewis, when Anita questioned her. "Lottie and Sarah Douglas and their dates, I believe."

"Lottie and Sarah in the same group?" asked Anita, surprised.

"I'm quite sure of it," said Hortense. "They went down the main staircase. I assume they just wanted to take some air before the dances start."

"Thank you," said Anita, taking off down the stairs herself.

Outside Main, she found several groups standing about enjoying the twilight, but Caroline, Porter, and Lottie were not among them.

Anita was about to turn to go back inside when she saw a man in a black tailcoat walking away from Main in the direction of the farm. From his gait—long steps favoring the outside of his shoes—she knew it was Porter. Without stopping to think, she ran toward him, briefly losing sight of him as he walked down the slope toward Sunset Hill. She lifted her skirts, ran faster, and called his name when he was in view again. He turned around as soon as he heard her voice.

They looked at one another for a long moment, and it occurred to Anita that this was the path they had walked together when he first came to the campus. It was where he had asked whether his affection for her was misguided. It wasn't then, and if there was any left, it was not now.

Porter looked behind his shoulder up the empty hill, then turned back to Anita, and held out his right hand to her. That was the only signal she needed to approach him.

Her eyes fixed on Porter, Anita did not at first notice Lottie Taylor appearing at the top of Sunset Hill in a daringly low-cut ivory dress. When she did, it was clear from her horrified expression that Lottie had seen her first.

"Porter!" Lottie called, watching Anita.

Porter tensed when he saw Anita's gaze shift and her expression change. He turned and looked up the hill, as well.

"You were to meet me on Sunset Hill," Lottie called down. "Did something keep you? I'm growing awfully lonely here. Fresh air can keep a woman entertained for only so long."

"I will be there shortly," said Porter. He turned back to Anita and started to walk toward her.

Anita had never seen Lottie look so angry. If she were a hurricane, her face was its terrible eye. Anita made a lightning calculation: she could never have Porter, but there was a chance she could still keep Lottie. She looked at Porter walking rapidly toward her, his hand no longer extended but his desire to join her showing plainly on his face. She was desperate to go to him, but instead, she turned away. With Main now in her sights, Anita took off running and never looked back.

CHAPTER 24

"It was a mere confusion," Lottie declared to Anita later that week. Porter and Lottie had not come into the dining room for the scheduled fifteen dances, as all students were instructed to do, after Anita had seen them. They had stayed on the farm, Lottie explained, so as not to put Anita or Joseph in an uncomfortable position.

Anita had her own explanations ready. "I did not leave Main looking for Porter," she said from her perch on the divan. The girls had rearranged the furniture in their parlor as the weather grew warmer, and the divan was now centered under their window. They had taken to kneeling on it and looking down the drive to the gatehouse at night when the lights were low and the stars were out.

"It doesn't matter. I have much bigger things to think about," said Lottie, brushing her long hair in front of her mirror. "I'm not cross with you about that trivial business."

Anita, who knew the cadences of Lottie's voice as well as she knew her own, was unconvinced. She tried again.

"I had a wonderful time with Joseph," she said. "He has a maturity about him that I admire. He's already been exposed to so much, and his perspective is a refreshing one."

"I doubt he has been exposed to more than you," said

Lottie, turning around from her mirror and smiling sweetly at Anita. "For who has seen more than Anita Hemmings?"

"Just about everyone," said Anita, laughing. "Certainly you have."

"Me?" said Lottie, letting out an odd little chortle. "Most definitely not. I, it turns out, am the naïve one. You are the one running the show."

"You're not naïve, Lottie," said Anita, looking away from Lottie to rest her head on the windowsill. "Your appreciation of life, your thirst for it, is my favorite thing about you."

The room was quiet for several minutes as Anita took deep breaths of the spring air, in and out, in and out; it was like a pharmaceutical for the soul, she thought. When she looked at Lottie again, she was surprised to see her in the same place, still facing away from her mirror, watching her.

Anita smiled and turned back to the window, delighted to see the guard's lights go on inside the Lodge. She liked to catch that nightly ritual and always felt a pleasing shiver down her spine when she was looking out the window at the right time. She turned around again to beckon to Lottie to join her, but Lottie was still sitting in the same position, still watching her.

"Do you know how I found out about Old Southpaw being the son of a prostitute?" Lottie said finally.

"I thought the correct term was *geisha*," said Anita from the window.

"It is," Lottie replied. "But tonight, I think the word *prostitute* sounds just fine." Her tone had altered, but her expression remained studiedly bland.

"I see," Anita replied. "But no, I can't say I remember how you found out about Southpaw."

"And I don't know that I ever explained it," said Lottie. "But now seems the right time."

She put her brush down and tilted her head, examining Anita. "You see, Anita, how I did it—how I found out the truth about Joseph—is I asked my father to hire a private investigator. Resourceful, I know. Papa is often involved in sensitive business affairs down in the Carolinas and has to work with men from quite a different class than . . . us. These men have the most colorful backgrounds, and some of them may or may not have been engaged in questionable business practices. So Father, who is an enterprising man, has them investigated first. He's been doing it for years, and has stepped up his investigations as he's expanded the southern railroads into the mountains. It's wild out there, as you are aware. Or," she said, taking a step away from her desk and toward Anita, "maybe you are not aware."

Anita felt her body shrinking down into the sofa as Lottie spoke, but she couldn't bring herself to say a word.

"What Father does," Lottie continued, "is he hires a man to trail these aspiring employees, and that man sets out to find the unfindable. Scandals, embezzlements, anything that would make them untrustworthy, that's what he's after. I told Father that I had grown interested, romantically, in Joseph Southworth but that a story he had told was keeping my affections from growing, and I asked him to have his investigator look into it."

"And it was the investigator who confirmed that the geisha was still alive?" asked Anita in a small voice.

"That's right," said Lottie, moving from her desk chair to the larger couch. She fluffed the pillows and propped herself on them, reaching for her favorite blanket and draping it on her feet. She took a cigarette from the small silver case on her left and lit it, ignoring the stringent college rules. "The investigator, a very thorough man, looked into legal documents, and even had a man in Japan search for this geisha's death certificate. It does not exist. The young woman is alive and well and waiting for Benjamin Southworth's poor parents to die off so she can come here and ruin Joseph's life even further."

"I'm glad you found out before it was too late," said Anita, now able to hear her heart beating. "Though Joseph did admit to the half of it on Phil Day. The only discrepancy was that in his telling, she was deceased. He didn't deny her existence."

"That discrepancy is enough, don't you think?" said Lottie, exhaling smoke in one long line. "And then there's the way he told me his story, as if it were all in jest. I didn't really believe him until Father's hired man provided the evidence. Then it turned out not only to be true, but worse than he said."

"I understand your anger," said Anita, sweat forming along her hairline despite the breeze. "It was surprising. And I'm glad you were able to discover it all before your heart became . . . before you became too involved. You seem more at ease now."

With jerky movements, Lottie nodded her head yes, giving the impression of a wounded bird. "I *am* happier now. Much happier. And severing my association with Joseph was just the beginning. I am about to do so much more."

Anita felt panic creep into her body like a sudden illness. She flushed and fought back the urge to be sick, remaining stock-still while Lottie continued to recline comfortably on her couch like Ingres's *Odalisque.*

"There are some unfortunate situations you can avoid with the proper footwork, but others are just thrust upon you, and you are none the wiser," said Lottie, relighting her cigarette. She inhaled deeply and blew the smoke in Anita's direction. "Until you are. Then everything just begins to make sense. Has that ever happened to you, Anita dear?"

Anita said nothing, allowing only her eyelashes to flit, then shook her head no. Anxiety had her pinned to the couch. Her limbs felt leaden, her vision tunneled.

"It took much longer than it should have for me to suspect something, Anita," said Lottie, maintaining her indifferent tone.

Anita looked at her the way one might watch a woman pulling a loose thread on a dress. The effect of the action could be minuscule, or it could unravel the whole garment. Anita prayed that what Lottie knew would unravel only a tiny corner of her world.

"I was sure you were just like me," said Lottie, finally sitting up to look at Anita. "I knew you weren't as well-off as most of us here, but I've never been one to judge a woman on her wealth. A man, perhaps, but not a woman."

Lottie looked at Anita, still unmoving, and let out an exasperated sigh. "Your silence is bothering me immensely. You have to respond to me," she ordered. "This conversation will not be a one-sided one."

"In many ways, I am just like you, Lottie," Anita said at last. "We are both students here, and at school we lead nearly identical lives."

"At school we do, nearly identical, as you say," said Lottie. "But what about the rest of the time? See, I did believe that we came from similar stock, but I was wrong, wasn't I?"

"I have no idea what you're speaking of," said Anita, turning to look out the window again. She felt bile rising, and her heart constricted painfully. She closed her eyes and imagined herself falling out the window. Four floors down, then gone, just another part of the endless earth.

"Yes, you do, Anita Hemmings, and don't you dare look away from me again," Lottie threatened. Anita did not turn back around to see Lottie's face. She knew what she was about to hear, but she refused to see it being said. She leaned out the window a little farther, remembering her old dream. A dead Negro whose secret everyone knew.

"You've known that I've been suspicious of you for some time," Lottie went on. "For months you had me fooled, you had all of us fooled, but then you started to falter. I could tell there was something amiss the night we climbed out on the roof to the shock of Caroline and Belle. Something was wrong with you."

Anita could just make out the gatekeeper sitting at a table inside the Lodge. She thought about the kind of man who had that job, one who was willing to stay up all night for a meager paycheck. She tried to think of everything except what Lottie was poised to say.

"That night," said Lottie, "there was something very dishonest about you. All the time we had spent together, and this was the first night you mentioned your father's supposedly impressive career. His Harvard Law School days. Why would you wait so long, I thought to myself. Caroline had spoken of her interest in a legal profession many times before, but you'd never said a thing about Papa Hemmings. Then that night, when you'd had too much to drink, you suddenly felt free to tell us all about him. Yet even that wasn't the greatest cause of my suspicion."

Anita felt Lottie's eyes locked on her back, waiting for a reply, but she still refused to turn around. In her dream, she used to fall from one of those majestic red cliffs in the West. But maybe that detail was wrong. Perhaps she was really supposed to fall from a window, and the small hand that pushed her would be the hand of Lottie Taylor.

"What did it for me, ultimately," Lottie continued, "was the story of your brother at Cornell. *That* was your gravest mistake, Anita. That terrible fib is what inspired me to alert

Father. It's very easy to check a school record, you know. When you said that your brother had chosen Cornell over Harvard, it made no sense at all. No man in his right mind would make that choice. You forget that I know Frederick, and he is very much in his right mind. So what did little Lottie Taylor do, you want to know? I may not be able to see your face, Anita Hemmings, because you are looking away from me like a mouse, but I know that you are desperate to learn how I proceeded."

Anita finally turned around, and the room seemed like a blank. The beautiful things they had hung on the walls together, her small picture of Greece in the corner—all had disappeared. All she could see was the pure hatred on Lottie's face.

"I wrote a letter to Frederick Hemmings, Cornell University, not using the address I had used before, which was provided to me by you. And do you know what happened? Of course you do, but I'll recount it anyway. Anita, the letter came back to me. It said, no such student found." Lottie flicked her cigarette ash, letting it fall onto Anita's best school shoes placed next to the couch. "That, my dear, is why Father sent his man on a little voyage to Nine Sussex Street, Boston. Are you familiar with that address?"

"You sent him to my parents' home?" said Anita, flooding with anguish.

"Why, yes, I did," said Lottie, adopting an innocent tone. "For a handsome sum, the investigator was more than happy to take a train up to Boston and take a little peek around Sussex Street and the large family residing at Number Nine."

She looked Anita up and down, her eyes lingering on her old shirtwaist and her indoor slippers that needed replacing, and said, "You do know that you slipped, don't you, Anita?"

"I'm afraid I don't know—"

"Just stop saying that!" screamed Lottie, cutting her off. "Do not cheapen yourself any further. You know what I am speaking of! If you need me to speak plainly, I will."

All Anita could see at that moment was Lottie's large pink mouth, her top lip curled with rage.

"Look at you, with nothing to say now about your deception," said Lottie, throwing her cigarette to the floor. "You are very lucky that all the various races in your pathetic form blended so attractively for you. That pretty face hides it well, doesn't it? But you can no longer fool me. I know everything about you now, Anita. Your mother is a Negro. Your father is a Negro. And he is no Harvard-trained lawyer. He is a janitor. That's right, isn't it? He washes bathtubs and toilets for the wealthy in Back Bay just as the janitors do here. That's who your father really is. Sometimes he even works two jobs, shuttling through the city at night as a coachman."

She picked her blanket up from the couch, clutched it to herself, and shouted at her roommate. "Say I'm right, Anita! Say it!"

"And what will that accomplish, Lottie?" asked Anita quietly. "Will that make you hate me any less?"

"Say you are a Negro," Lottie shrieked, ripping at the satin edges of the blanket. "Say it!"

"I am a Negro," Anita said loudly, watching Lottie's face light up like an evening fire.

"I knew it," said Lottie. "I think I have always known. You're a Negro, and what's even worse is that you are a lying Negro. You deceived me and everyone else at this school."

"I never denied my race," said Anita, torn between fighting back and maintaining her silence. "I never said I was not a Negro."

"But you never said you were!" Lottie shouted.

"Why should I have?" asked Anita, taking advantage of the moments before the tears she knew would come flooded her face. "How was that relevant to my time here? To our friendship?"

"Relevant!" Lottie screamed. "That is the most relevant thing about our friendship. This, us, all this is completely dead to me now. You have become my curse."

Anita put her face in her hands, trying to push her tears back in. She did not want to let a single one slide down her cheek, giving Lottie one more cause for smugness.

"I did not notice it before," said Lottie, surveying her. "But now when I look at you I see it. I see the Negro in you. It's all I can see." She looked straight at Anita and said, "I look at you, and a dirty, ugly, lying colored face looks back at me. That's the face of Anita Hemmings now."

Lottie fell back on the couch, running her hands through her hair and pushing her bun to one side. "How could you do this to me? The devastation it could wreak on my reputation, Anita! Phil Dance with the child of a prostitute and now rooming with a Negro. Best friends with some Negro janitor's child! Was anything you said to me the truth, Anita? Or has everything from the first day we moved into this room been a fabrication?"

"Nothing has been a fabrication," Anita said quietly. She could not erase what Lottie knew; all she could do now was try to pacify her. "Nothing except what I was forced to say to make it through school."

"You let me fall for your brother!" Lottie shouted, as if she had just remembered her self-avowed unwavering love for Frederick Hemmings. "A Negro! Can you imagine? I could have embraced a Negro. I could have—" She lay back down, apparently overcome.

Anita felt as if a cord were tightening around her neck.

She knew that how she handled Lottie at that moment would determine whether she would graduate or not.

"You should feel such shame, Anita Hemmings," Lottie said when she had her breath back. "I am not just any room-mate from anywhere. I did everything for you. I took you home to New York. I took you to Harvard." She rolled her head back as if it were too heavy for her neck. "I have no idea what to do."

Anita turned away from Lottie and thought back to the night on the roof and the stories she had spun. Of course Lottie had grown suspicious. This disaster, thought Anita, was her own doing.

"Does Porter know?" asked Lottie suddenly. "Does he know who you really are?"

"No," Anita whispered.

"Of course he doesn't," Lottie said. "If he knew, he would never have fallen for you. He would have shunned you." She shook her head. "The shame he would feel. The utter shame." She looked up at Anita, who finally had tears on her face.

Anita took a step toward her. "I will tell him when—"

"You will do nothing of the sort," said Lottie, cutting her off firmly. "You've done quite enough. If you ever felt any-thing for Porter, you will not want him living with the fact that he shared a kiss with a Negro. Worse still, was engaged to one."

"When we were at Radcliffe," said Anita slowly, "and we saw the Negro student Alberta Scott, you did not speak ill of her, or insult her, as your cousin did."

"I do not share rooms with Miss Alberta Scott!" Lottie bellowed. "Separate but equal. Not 'equal and in my parlor'!"

"You've always seemed very modern to me, Lottie. Your views on different races, on women, you've—"

"Do not dare to go on about what I am and am not," said Lottie, her body rigid. "You don't know a thing about me."

"But you wanted to marry the Crown Prince of Japan," Anita whispered, unable to repress her sobs. "You're so different—"

"Of course I want to marry him! He's the crown prince, not a Negro!" Lottie took a deep breath and shot a hard look at Anita's shocked face. "I am modern, but the world around us is not. And to room with a Negro, Anita, that is unthinkable. It could cause me irreparable social damage. And with your brother on top of it. What would people think? It would render me unmarriageable, despite my money. Do you remember how scared you were when you thought you could be ostracized and left to a life on your own? Now you have put me in that very same position, and I do not want to be alone!"

"You will never be alone," said Anita, thinking that she herself now certainly would be.

"You don't know," said Lottie, shaking her head. "You're pretending to be a part of this world here, lying to us all so you can be a part of it, but you're not. You have no notion how our society operates." A tear ran down her face, and she seemed to be as surprised by it as Anita was. She flicked it aside. "Why did you do this to me? To everyone? Why were you so tremendously selfish?"

"But what choice did I have?" asked Anita, daring to take another step toward Lottie. "I passed the Vassar entrance examination just as you did and wanted to attend just as you did."

"You don't deserve to be here," Lottie said flatly, drying another tear. "You will be known as a shame to this school from now on."

In that moment, Anita thought very carefully about how

she should proceed. If she could just succeed in calming Lottie, her time at Vassar might not be over. Lottie would hate her, would shut her out forever, but Anita—who knew her roommate well—prayed she might at least recognize where her self-interest lay.

"I think I will tell President Taylor about you," said Lottie, voicing Anita's greatest fear. "But perhaps I will not. I know what will be the most amusing for me; I'll make you agonize over it. That's what you deserve after what you have done to me. But one thing is for certain: I will be going to Kendrick and asking for a change of room first thing tomorrow morning."

"So close to the end of the year?" asked Anita, wishing something might go her way. "But Kendrick won't—"

"Of course she will," shouted Lottie. "And if she knew why, she would do so this instant. Right now! I will never sleep in rooms with you again, Anita. We, this," she said, pointing around the room, "is over."

Lottie stood up, walked to her bedroom door, and closed it loudly enough to rattle Anita, but not loudly enough to disturb their neighbors. That was the only thing that could save Anita. The fear Lottie had for her own reputation.

CHAPTER 25

For the next week, it was just rumors. Lottie stayed true to her word and moved into a large single room the next morning, but Anita had no idea what she had told Mrs. Kendrick. She would have had to give some explanation for why she needed to move a month before graduation, but she could have used illness or any number of other credible excuses. She was Lottie Taylor, and everyone was in the habit of saying yes to her.

In the days after Lottie's relocation, the students were scarce in the college's common areas as final examinations crept up on them. But Anita could barely see the words on the pages she was studying. In the quiet of her room, as she tried to prepare for her tests, all she could feel was panic. She was unable to sleep without waking up crying, her bed soaked in sweat. The walls in her parlor room were bare, except for the small picture of the Artemis statue still glued up in a corner. They seemed to Anita to be closing in on her, caging her. She made excuses not to see Belle or Caroline, floated through her classes in silence, and somehow never saw Lottie Taylor closer than thirty feet away. Even in the dining room, where Lottie had switched tables, Anita only saw the back of her head.

Among the seniors who lived in the same hall as Anita and Lottie, rumors flew fast, but it was Sarah Douglas who first told Anita what the women of '97 had been saying since Lottie moved out of room 21.

After the final meeting of the Federal Debating Society, Anita found herself one of the last two people in the room. Lottie wasn't there, having dropped the only club in which the two had overlapped. Distracted as always by the hell that had shattered her happiness, Anita looked up and realized that she was alone with Sarah.

"I have to say, Anita, you are quite the stoic," Sarah said, picking up her books. "I've always thought there was more to you than your quiet, reserved exterior suggested. Your cold presence, as some describe it. There must be, if Lottie Taylor had such affection for you."

Anita opened her mouth to protest, but Sarah held up her hand to stop her. "I know we're not close, Anita, but if I were in your position, I would want to know what everyone was saying about me."

"I would like to know," said Anita, alarmed. "What are they saying?"

"The gossip is that it's all about Porter Hamilton," said Sarah, unable to disguise the thrill in her voice. "That you and Lottie are desperately in love with him. Everyone says that you both were rather physical with him and that now a war has erupted between you."

Anita flushed with relief. A love triangle involving Porter Hamilton—was that what the students truly thought? Perhaps she had been wrong. It was not Lottie's concern for her reputation that might save her, it was her affection for Porter.

Anita's extreme panic started to ebb after her conversation with Sarah. Lottie, she was sure, appreciated the rumor about Porter as much as she did. She could imagine the satisfaction she took in being seen as the victorious party in a love triangle. If they were still rooming together, they would have laughed at such a rumor. Anita could see the two of them kneeling on the couch under the window, looking down at the gatehouse, Lottie's sentences tumbling out at their usual rapid-fire pace. But that world, as Lottie had said, was gone.

The dreams that sent her into a pool of sweat and despair every night started to subside, too, and she was able to sit in the empty parlor without crying or thinking of the blissful times she had experienced there. It was now two weeks since Lottie had confronted her, and nothing had happened. No student had looked at her strangely. No one had ostracized her. She was starting to feel dangerously safe. Lottie would never speak to her again, but it appeared that she would have the decency to keep her secret, to let her graduate.

Belle and Caroline split their time between the estranged roommates and told Anita they were trying their best not to take sides.

"But of course we're actually taking your side," said Belle one day when Caroline had gone. "Lottie is the most selfish girl who will ever graduate from this school. I like so much about her, but increasingly, there is more to dislike. I will never forgive her for what she did to you. You were right to exile her from this room. It would have been too much for me to handle, as well."

"You shouldn't be angry with Lottie," said Anita, terrified of saying a word against her. "She isn't all bad."

"Sometimes, Anita," said Belle, standing up to leave Anita's bare parlor room, "she is."

It was just two days later, as Anita was walking to chapel with Belle for choir practice, that she heard the low-pitched female voice so many students feared. This time, it was saying her name. Repeating her name.

Anita turned around to see Mrs. Kendrick approaching, her skirt taut on her ankles as she walked swiftly and with purpose. She wanted to whisper to Belle to jump with her out the nearest window and run until they were far from the campus, never to return.

Instead, she simply said, "Hello, Mrs. Kendrick."

Belle also greeted the lady principal, who was still wearing a high-necked winter shirtwaist though the air outside was scented with spring, then put her hand supportively on Anita's back before slipping into the chapel to give them privacy. Anita knew Belle assumed that Mrs. Kendrick wanted to speak with her about her feud with Lottie and the gossip they were generating around the school, distracting other girls in the midst of their finals. Mrs. Kendrick was known to abhor distractions. But there could only be one reason why Mrs. Kendrick would single her out, and as the reality of it set in, the nerves in Anita's body felt like they were being split, one by one.

"Miss Hemmings, would you mind stopping by President Taylor's office this evening after chapel?" Mrs. Kendrick said evenly. "Something has come to our attention that we need to discuss with you promptly. I imagine you know what it is I'm speaking of, but I do not want to bring such a sensitive matter up at an inappropriate moment."

"Yes, Mrs. Kendrick," said Anita quietly, her eyes cast down. She wanted desperately to close them, to keep the room from spinning, and to shut out the lady principal's stern face. But that would not be possible. From that moment on, Anita knew, she would have to comport herself as the most dignified student Vassar had ever known. She had to be the good Negro, the exceptional Negro. "Maybe then," she prayed, "they will let me graduate."

"Thank you," said Mrs. Kendrick levelly. "I'll let you get

to choir practice now. I assume that's where you were going with Miss Tiffany?"

Anita nodded.

"You have a beautiful voice," Mrs. Kendrick said, even her compliment devoid of emotion. "I will greatly miss hearing it next year." She gave Anita a nod and walked off down the hallway.

Anita felt that her heart had started pumping twice as fast, and she longed to be far from campus, but she could not run from her fate.

At choir practice, she sang flatly, her high notes breaking. During chapel, she feared she might hyperventilate. She wanted to stand up and denounce Lottie to the school at the top of her voice, but instead she bowed her head along with the other students, in silent, despairing prayer. Then she stood up and walked to the president's office.

Except for a polite hello in passing, Anita had never spoken to President Taylor. At that moment, she wished she had. If they had developed a rapport, then maybe she would be more than a word on a page to him: Negro, the school's only Negro.

His secretary guided her to his office, knocking on the door and ushering her inside. The president was seated behind his simple wooden desk, his short silver hair parted on the side, his mustache trimmed and neat. Seated on a chair to his right was the lady principal, next to her was Lottie, and surprisingly to Anita, across from the desk was Miss Franklin, her Latin professor.

"Miss Hemmings. Come in, and please have a seat," said the president, with a look on his face that Anita interpreted as friendly. But of course, she thought to herself, firing squads were never in tears. "I assume Mrs. Kendrick has already informed you what this meeting is about?" said the president, superfluously. The presence of Lottie Taylor told everyone what the meeting was about.

"She has," said Anita, politely. She would remain calm, unshaken. She sat down in the empty chair and thought of her father, putting money away week after week for her and her siblings' educations. Sweep the floors, clean the toilets, scrub the windows, wax the building until it gleams like a glass palace. The faceless Negro janitor. She thought of that. For him, she had to persuade the people in that room to let her graduate with the class of 1897. For him.

President Taylor lifted several sheets of paper from his desk and glanced through them. "Miss Hemmings, I'm afraid a sensitive matter has arisen for us all. Are you aware of what I'm implying?"

Was she aware that she was a Negro? Up until two weeks before, she had been the only one who was aware. Her nerves were jumping, but she managed to look squarely at the president and said, "Yes, sir, I am aware."

"Good," said the president, picking up the first paper in his stack. "Then this delicate matter with Miss Taylor is what I want to address first. This document here represents the findings of a private investigator hired by Miss Taylor's father. It states that he traveled to the Boston home of Miss Anita Hemmings in the Roxbury neighborhood and discovered that her parents are both Negroes. Light-skinned, it says, gray eyes, whiskers, nearly able to pass as white. Nearly." He looked up at Anita and said, "This refers to your father, I presume?"

Anita nodded, trying to keep her expression perfectly compliant.

"It was presented to me two days ago by Miss Taylor herself," said the president. "Very unusual to approach me directly, but I suppose in this case it had to be done."

Anita looked over at Lottie, but Lottie kept her eyes fixed smugly on the president.

"While I think this is certainly crossing a line into personal matters, the hiring of an investigator and so on, it is something we have to address," said President Taylor. He looked at Anita and said, "So this is true, Miss Hemmings? Your parents, and therefore you, are Negroes?"

The moment Anita had dreaded for four years had arrived. The cold fear of it had governed her life, causing her to wake up in plashes of sweat, to destroy her unsent letters to her mother, to forbid Bessie Baker to write to her or Frederick to visit her on campus. Full of sorrow and regret, she took a breath so deep that it made her stomach swell and said, "They are, I am. We are Negroes."

"I see," said the president, still looking at her for an explanation.

"I was never asked whether I was a Negro, so I never addressed it. If I had been asked, I would not have lied." Anita looked down at her hands, half-shocked that she was still breathing after such a confession. But there she was, alive, and now at the mercy of the people in this room.

A sigh of protest came from Lottie, but Mrs. Kendrick silenced her quickly. She handed a few more papers to the president, who read them slowly. Anita immediately recognized her handwriting.

"Miss Hemmings, the application to the school asks specifically about a family's origin. Mrs. Kendrick has pulled your record here, and I see that you wrote French and English in response to that question. Why did you claim such?" asked the president, without looking up. President Taylor was known to be conservative in his views on women but also deeply religious. Anita prayed that his conscience would sway him her way in this instance.

"I am French and English," she replied simply.

"Fine," said the president, now studying her light complexion. "But if you are a Negro, there must also be African blood."

"I suppose there must be," she replied.

"So you are not denying the accusation," he said.

"I am not denying it," Anita replied. "My mother is a Negro, though light-skinned. My father is a Negro, though very light-skinned, with gray eyes, as the Taylors' detective mentioned. And until I went to Dwight Moody's Northfield Seminary to prepare for the Vassar examination, I lived as a Negro."

Lottie's smug smile widened.

"I have known for many months now that Miss Hemmings is a Negro," said Miss Franklin suddenly. "That is why I'm present. When Mrs. Kendrick approached me a few days ago, since it was I and Miss Macurdy who had recommended Anita for several postgraduate scholarships, I told her that I had suspected it for some time and had had my suspicions confirmed in December."

"And you never spoke up?" asked President Taylor. "Why not, Miss Franklin? You certainly should have. The school must always be first and foremost in your considerations."

"It didn't seem the Christian thing to do," said Miss Franklin, stealing a quick glance at Anita. "She earned her place in the school. She is a well-liked student with excellent grades. Who was I to disturb such an equilibrium? It did not seem right. And if I may raise my voice now, all of this does not seem right, either. Should we really be entertaining the findings of an investigation done out of malice?"

Miss Franklin had known. The day she had approached Anita after class, she had known the whole truth. She had not been supportive then, even of the idea of Anita rooming with a Negro, but perhaps time had softened her. Anita let her head fall back, thankful to have one person speaking on her behalf.

"But how did you come to know when the rest of us did not?" asked President Taylor. "We did not know, did we, Mrs. Kendrick?" he asked. The lady principal was supposed to be his eyes and ears on campus regarding everything to do with the students.

Mrs. Kendrick shook her head no, and everyone in the room looked at Miss Franklin expectantly.

"I have a friend, a Latin instructor at Northfield, where Anita was a preparatory student. Because of Miss Hemmings's close friendship with a quadroon woman there in 1892, this instructor always suspected that Miss Hemmings was a quadroon, as well. She shared these thoughts with me last year when I mentioned Miss Hemmings by name. I was speaking of my most gifted students. Miss Hemmings is certainly one of them."

Miss Franklin folded her hands in her lap.

"I'd like to add one point that supports Miss Hemmings's argument that she never tried to conceal her race," she said. "In December, there was an article in the *Boston Daily Globe* that stated that Vassar College's Miss Anita Hemmings was bridesmaid in a wedding between two prominent Negroes in Massachusetts. The bride was Miss Hemmings's roommate at Northfield. This article stated plain as day that Miss Anita Hemmings of Vassar College was the bridesmaid during a ceremony with only Negroes in attendance."

She cleared her throat and glanced at Anita, who had never seen such an article. Had Bessie's wedding been reported in the newspaper, she wondered? Had her family simply never mentioned it because they worried about alarming her? "But I suppose no one but me ever saw the article. Our school staff is too learned to be reading New

England society sections. Especially when they concern Negroes," Miss Franklin added.

"I certainly do not bother myself with those pages, Miss Franklin," said the president. "They are written for consumption by you ladies."

"My point is simply that Miss Hemmings was not purposely misleading the school," Miss Franklin said. "She did very little to conceal her race. It is we who simply failed to see it."

"Very little to conceal it!" Lottie burst out. "I beg your pardon, Miss Franklin, but she did everything to conceal it, starting with the fact that she excluded the word *Negro* from her Vassar application. What could be more duplicitous than that? Furthermore, she concocted an intricate story about her father practicing law when he is nothing but a Negro laborer, a mere janitor."

She paused, reassumed her ladylike position, and lowered her voice, which was huskier than usual from emotion. "We must think of the good of the school. Imagine how our esteemed founder, Matthew Vassar, would feel knowing a Negro was about to graduate from his institution. He would turn over like a barrel in his grave."

"Negroes have graduated from other women's colleges," said Miss Franklin, moving straight to the decision that the president had to make. "Radcliffe has two now, Mount Holyoke one, and Wellesley has had several. Should Vassar not follow in the footsteps of the other women's colleges?"

"Miss Franklin, you know as well as I do that Vassar does not follow the actions of other women's colleges," the president said sharply. "We lead. Our position in this is that we do not admit Negroes, which extends to graduating them as well."

Anita's throat closed, her eyes beginning to well up.

President Taylor selected a sheet from the papers in front of him and said, "Now, let me be the authority on this matter, Miss Franklin, if you please. There is nothing spelled out in our bylaws that forbids Negroes from attending the school, but I did find in our minutes from 1865 that the school was not authorized, nor did it feel prepared, to admit anyone but white students. That is written plainly, as you can see here." He took the sheet of paper, covered in large cursive script, and thrust it toward the Latin instructor.

"But does Miss Hemmings's success here not show that the founders may have been wrong in thinking that?" asked Miss Franklin.

Anita, grateful for her ally, looked at her and prayed that she would have the courage to continue arguing with the president, as she herself was certainly not in a position to do it. She had to remain quiet, deferential, like a person who would never cause a problem for the school again.

"There will never be other Negro women at Vassar, Miss Franklin," said Lottie, her voice severe. "This school was not founded to educate women like Anita; it was founded to educate women like me."

Miss Franklin sat back, shaking her head at Lottie's insolence.

"There is truth in that, Miss Taylor," said the president. He looked down at his papers and again at Miss Hemmings and her pleading, pleasing face. He inspected it carefully and Anita was sure she knew what he was thinking, what they all were thinking. It was certainly hard to tell she was a Negro. She watched him looking at her, plainly searching for Negroid features. She regretted walking so much in the sun that spring. Did she look darker than usual, she wondered. Would that be the pitiful thing that kept her from being allowed to graduate?

"We have never graduated a Negro, and do not plan to admit any in the future," said the president, still looking at Anita. He paused. "However, we will be making an exception this year. Our board met yesterday, Miss Hemmings. We have discussed it and have agreed that it is in the best interest of the school to allow you to graduate on June seventh. We do not need any negative press when our school is still so young."

"Yes, so young and in need of funds, is that it?" broke in Lottie. "You wouldn't want anyone to hear about this embarrassing scandal and stop donating so generously to our campus? Well, I can tell you which family will never give you another cent, President Taylor. The Taylor family. *My* Taylor family. I will have nothing to do with this institution when I have graduated from here."

"Your rudeness is shocking, Miss Taylor!" Mrs. Kendrick exclaimed, breaking her silence. "You are still a student here and will cease speaking to the president like this at once."

Lottie apologized and looked pleadingly at President Taylor.

"I hope you will change your mind in time," the president said stiffly. "Until then, I ask all of you in this room not to mention this matter to anyone. I assume we are the only ones at school who are aware of this situation besides our board—is that correct? Miss Taylor, did you speak to anyone of this matter besides myself and Mrs. Kendrick?"

"I did not," said Lottie. "I do not want to be known on my graduation day as the girl who roomed with the Negro."

"Very well," said President Taylor. "As we are the only five on campus who are aware of Miss Hemmings's race, we will remain the only five at Vassar who ever know. No one will speak of this until after graduation. I would implore you never to speak of this matter, but I understand that my authority extends only to current students and faculty, not graduates."

He looked at Anita again, this time as the respected college president and not as a man scrutinizing her face for answers. "You will be graduated with the rest of your class, and you will keep your head down until then. The same applies to you, Miss Taylor. Despite what you said, I know you care about this school and are willing to make sacrifices for the good of the institution."

"Of course," said Lottie, her contempt audible.

"Then it is decided," he said, pushing the pile of papers away from him. "Miss Hemmings, I hope you are pleased, but I must make one additional stipulation. Your association with this school must have its limits. Miss Franklin informed me that you have applied for several scholarships for continued study and to travel abroad this summer. I'm afraid that even if you have been found a worthy candidate, you will no longer be considered for those. If news of your race was ever revealed, it would be ill-received that the school had continued to bolster you after graduation."

He pulled Anita's transcript toward him again and turned the pages. "You have excelled here academically, and I have no doubt that you will continue to do the same after graduation."

Turning to Lottie, then back to Anita, he said, "Good luck to both of you as you finish your time here with us. I trust there will be no other reason to see you again before the semester concludes, so I will see you both at commencement."

He stood up and walked out of his office, leaving four stunned women behind. Despite the Lottie Taylors of the world, Anita Hemmings would graduate from Vassar College.

CHAPTER 26

I can't believe this day is finally here!" said Belle, taking Anita by the hand as the two of them hurried toward Main the morning of commencement exercises, trying to stay out of the rain that fell disruptively. Anita may have been rooming alone and a magnet for gossip, but she would never lose Belle.

Belle clutched Anita's arm, which was holding a large umbrella, but both stopped walking when Lottie passed them without a word.

"What a pity about you and Lottie," said Belle, opening her own umbrella. It was being said on that June day, their third day of rain in a row, that '97 had entered college with a storm, kept the college in a storm, and left the college in a storm.

"It's just a misunderstanding," said Anita, trying her best to smile.

"Everyone is still gossiping about it," said Belle, pressing her friend's hand. "They're calling it the Hamilton scandal, and Sarah Douglas has become the official mouthpiece for it, since neither of you will say a word. Scandal presented with a southern inflection. It doesn't sound right."

Anita gave a little, knowing look and replied, "I have never been fond of Sarah Douglas."

"She's a lot like Lottie," said Belle. "But not as cruel. I suppose Lottie is difficult to say no to, but I know Porter was in love with you. I'm sure it was just his family, pushing him to be with her. Louise Taylor, if available, will be chosen over any other woman, even one as good as you. They are just after her money. It's been said in the papers that when she marries, she will bring with her a dowry of nearly two million dollars."

"I just don't want to be talked about anymore," said Anita, folding her umbrella and handing it to a maid as the girls entered Main Building. She twisted to fix the wide ribbon running around her waist and down the back of her dress.

"It's almost over now," whispered Belle, helping Anita. Like the other women poised to graduate, they were wearing starched white dresses with high formal necks and lengths of ribbon nipping in their waists. Black robes were draped over their shoulders, and they wore the flat, tasseled graduate's caps that were newly in use at the school.

When they walked up the staircase, crowded with soon-to-be graduates, and stood in front of the still-closed doors of the chapel, Belle whispered, "And wasn't it so very gauche of Lottie to announce her engagement to Porter right before graduation? Yesterday's Class Day was supposed to be about unity, about us being together for the last time as seniors. But Lottie Taylor found yet another way to make it about her."

Anita looked at Belle with surprise. She had attended Class Day, but her peers had clearly succeeded in keeping the news from her. If she had known as she watched the ten carefully chosen sophomores parade into the chapel with the traditional daisy chain, carrying almost a hundred pounds of fresh flowers, that Lottie was at that very moment engaged to Porter, she would barely have seen what was taking place. Members of Vassar's first classes, '67 and '68, had been there, and one of the most prominent of them had told the girls: "Our appearance here will forever destroy the fallacy that a college education unfits a woman for matrimony. The college woman is not handicapped for life in mind, body, or estate." Those words, thought Anita, must have caused whatever was left of Lottie's heart to swell with pride. She was about to be one of those educated married women.

Belle looked at Anita sympathetically. "Lottie may be engaged to Porter, but we have the rest of the world, don't we? You'll be off to Greece, and I to study music in Italy or Austria, and all this will feel very small to us then. We'll always love it, of course, but it will feel very small."

"It doesn't feel that way yet," said Anita, looking at the large '97 woven out of daisies hanging on the chapel door. She tried to remember that in a matter of hours, she would become a true graduated member of the class of 1897.

"Of course not," said Belle. "But Anita, promise me that even with all that Lottie has done, you will not forget about the rest. For most of the year, life was extraordinary, wasn't it? You, me, Lottie, and Caroline. The Gatehouse group. Who did coin that phrase?"

"Probably Lottie," said Anita, thinking back. "It sounds like her."

"I feel guilty saying it now, after what happened between the two of you," said Belle, hesitating, "but it was the best year of my life. I loved every minute that we spent together, did you not, Anita?"

"I did," said Anita honestly. "In many ways, it was the best year of my life, too."

"Oh, I'm so glad," said Belle, beaming. "I know you and Lottie will work out your differences. Your time abroad will do you both a world of good, and you'll meet someone else, someone much better than yellow-hearted Porter Hamilton."

"I'm afraid I'm not heading to Greece after graduation," said Anita, unable to keep her disappointment from showing on her face. "Financially, it just isn't a possibility anymore."

"Is it not?" said Belle. "But I was under the impression that the school had recommended you for a scholarship."

Anita shook her head no. "They recommended me, but I did not come out the victor, I'm afraid. The Babbott Fellowship was awarded to Misses Ellery, Bishop, Clark, and Hotchkiss, and four others won the graduate scholarships. Even Sarah Douglas was awarded the Barringer Prize."

"That's such a pity," said Belle. "There is no senior stronger in Greek and Latin here than you. Can there be no way—"

"I'm afraid not," said Anita, interrupting her. "I'll be going back to Boston and will continue my schooling on the East Coast. But I still intend to become a professor, Belle. I think I'm more committed to that goal now than I ever was before."

"Oh, good! Good! Do not give up on education, Anita, don't you dare. You are far too intelligent. I am sure that one day you will be teaching here. Then you'll go to Greece. And I'll meet you there. You have my word."

"It's time to march in as a class," said Medora Higgins as she passed them. "Do line up, please."

"Are your parents not here, Anita?" asked Belle before they moved to comply. "I didn't keep you from them, did I?"

"No, I'm afraid they aren't able to attend," Anita lied. "Frederick is graduating from Cornell this very same weekend. I told them to please make the trip to see him, as we also have family in Ithaca. I'm happy to be here simply surrounded by friends."

"That you are, Miss Hemmings," said Belle, looping her arm through Anita's. "Come and say hello to my mother and father after we are awarded our diplomas. They remember you and your voice so well from our choir concerts."

"I will," said Anita, and the two ran over to Medora to be placed in the proper alphabetical order.

As Anita stood between fellow seniors Mary Hecker and Rose Heywood, she watched as Lottie approached her, gliding past the beginning of the alphabet, heading to the back near Belle Tiffany. Anita wanted their eyes to meet, just one last time before they were separated for good. Maybe there would be something in Lottie's expression that showed remorse, or even friendship. Just a glimmer of the old Lottie, thought Anita as her roommate approached, something of the girl that made Vassar come so alive for her. But she didn't even receive a glance. Lottie walked by her section with her head high, and turned it away from Anita as she moved past. Anita looked down at the wooden floor, embarrassed, as the other girls straightened their spines proudly and prepared to march in the chapel. At that moment she became quite certain that Lottie Taylor would never utter another word to her for the rest of their extraordinary ordinary lives.

After the academic papers were read and Anita had sung an aria from *Le Cid* backed by the choir, President Taylor addressed the gathering on the supreme importance of conservatism. Anita closed her eyes and for a moment thought only of the diploma she was minutes from possessing.

"Avoid the dangers of notoriety, emancipated thought, and forgetfulness of soul," the president advised as he concluded his oration. "Commune much with the Invisible, seek simple faith, true life, and fidelity to duty. Keep yourselves, and keep the trust."

Anita squeezed her eyes tighter as the room erupted in applause. She had sacrificed so much for her diploma, more than any other girl present, and had earned what she was about to hold in her hand.

CHAPTER 27

Y ou're home. My girl. My graduate," said Mrs. Hemmings, hugging her daughter as soon as she walked in the front door of the Sussex Street house. "You did it! My smart, smart girl."

Anita smiled and allowed herself to be hugged again, so soothing were her mother's plump arms. She had done it. Only five thousand women in America had obtained college diplomas that year, and almost none of them were Negroes. But she was one. She was Vassar's one.

"Tell me all about your graduation day. What a pity it rained," said her mother, ushering her farther into the house. "I wish circumstances were different and we had been able to come. Though even if they were, we wouldn't have been able to afford the trip. But never mind that. I just want to hear about the whole splendid affair. They say rain is good luck. Unless of course you are hungry? You must be, after such a long journey. Let me prepare something for you. Your brother is in Cambridge tutoring, and your father is at work, but—"

"Anita!" came a cry from the stairs. Elizabeth came flying down the crooked staircase and enveloped her sister in a tight embrace, nearly knocking her over.

"Elizabeth, please," said her mother, laughing. "Dignified young women do not run down the stairs like horses."
She turned to Anita and put her hand on the back of her
hair. "As I was poised to say, Elizabeth is home."

"Yes, she is," said Anita, kissing her younger sister.

"Are you staying now? Forever?" asked Elizabeth, her
face still pressed into Anita's shoulder, which sagged a little
with fatigue after her journey.

"Not forever," she replied. "But for now. The short now
and the longer now."

"I'm so glad," said her sister. "I want to sleep next to you
and listen to you exist."

"All in good time," said her mother, peeling her youngest
daughter off her oldest. "First, I would like to see Anita's
diploma. Is it buried deep in your trunk?"

Anita knew what a relief it was for her mother to have
her graduated. Dora Hemmings had survived in a state
of controlled panic since Anita had left for Vassar four
years earlier, constantly voicing to her family her terror
that someone might guess the truth. She was the one who
counseled her daughter to always wear a hat, to stay out of
the sun, to never act in a way that was unbecoming a lady.
Before Anita had left for her freshman year, her mother had
cried on her shoulder and said that if someone did guess
that Anita was a Negro, it would be because of *her* family—
the Logan blood, not the Hemmings. Anita thought of that
day as she reached for her mother's hand, so glad that her
years of worry were over.

When Dora eventually released her, Anita opened her
trunk and took out the carefully wrapped paper that lay
on top. She pulled out her Vassar diploma, walked into the
dining room, and laid it on the simple pine table where the
family took their meals.

"Here it is!" said her mother with pride, leaning down to examine the black letters. "How formal the writing is. Will you read it to me, Anita? My eyesight is slipping away from me this year." She bent as close to the paper as she could without her nose touching it and said, "Is it not written in English?"

"It's in Latin, Mother," said Anita, pushing away the thought of her lost summer trip. "It's the custom of the school. But it says I'm a graduate. Do you see my name, there?" she said pointing. "Anita Florence Hemmings. And those words, right under it, indicate that I graduated with honors."

"With honors," said Dora, moving her finger across the diploma. "I am so proud of Frederick for graduating from the Institute of Technology, but there's something different about my daughter being graduated," she confessed. "My little girl, who I watched study after the rest of us fell asleep. Who can speak different languages and make sense of everything. My Anita, a college graduate." She wiped her tears before they fell on the diploma. "My own blessed mother was still illiterate when she died. But here you are despite it all, my exceptional child."

Anita had decided on the train ride home, which she had made with several other Vassar students traveling back to different parts of New England, that she would not say one word to her family about Lottie and what she knew. Now, looking at Dora's tears of pride, her resolve hardened. This moment was what her mother deserved, she thought. She must never hear about the day her daughter sat in the college president's office, humiliated and terrified.

When Frederick came home late that evening, he placed his diploma next to Anita's, and brother and sister stood and examined them together, disbelief on their faces.

"I'm very proud of you," said Frederick, patting his sister's hand.

"And I of you," she replied. "Father told me you already have employment with a chemist in Boston."

"I do," said Frederick, smiling as if he were the most surprised of all. "I'll be working with Henry Carmichael, an analytical and consulting chemist. His office is on Federal Street. Number 176. I found the work with the help of one of the faculty at the institute, a man who was very kind to me. He helped me obtain my three scholarships after I was admitted to the chemistry program."

"I had a professor who sounds similar," said Anita, thinking about Miss Franklin.

Frederick left to go upstairs, returning moments later with a slim bound volume that he handed to Anita. "My senior thesis," he said. "I'm afraid it won't make much sense to Mother and Father, but perhaps you would like to read it."

"'The Change That Glucose Undergoes During Fermentation,'" Anita read aloud. "Frederick, as hard as I tried, I never became the chemistry prodigy that you are. That was Lottie's domain—"

"Let's not talk about her now," said Frederick, cutting off his sister. "Just read it, even if you don't fully enjoy it," he said. "It would make me happy."

"Of course I will," said Anita. "My brilliant little brother."

Anita spent her first few days back in Boston with her family, but on Sunday, as was the custom of the devoutly religious Hemmingses, they walked to the Episcopal church where Anita had worshipped since childhood. It was no shock to Anita, or her parents, that the first person they saw standing outside the door was Mrs. Lillian Peoples, chief gossip of not only the Negro community of Roxbury, but also that of the Negro community of Boston's Trinity Church.

"Anita Hemmings!" she shouted, clasping her pillowy hands together as if she were already praying. "And the proud parents! I knew you would all be at church today, I just knew it. I've been reading all the newspapers, as I always try to do, and I read about last week's Vassar graduation ceremony. I said to myself then, this is when the famous Hemmings girl makes her journey home. Vassar's Negro angel. Come here, Anita, give me a kiss. I want to applaud the most intelligent girl in the commonwealth of Massachusetts."

Anita prayed silently for Mrs. Peoples to lower her voice, and she knew the rest of the family would be praying, too. The church community of course knew her as Negro, but the white parishioners did not know she had gone off to Vassar, and many were just entering the building as Mrs. Peoples spoke.

"Our Frederick also graduated this June," said Robert Hemmings. He put his hand on his son's shoulder. "A chemistry graduate from the Massachusetts Institute of Technology. And he's already found employment with Henry Carmichael on Federal Street."

"Of course you have," said Mrs. Peoples, beaming at Frederick, though with a shade less animation. "Such a brilliant family, and the highest honor for the community. Come now, Anita, we must show you off. A graduate! There are girls here in the church who know all about you. Young schoolgirls. And not only do they know about you: they hope to become you. You must speak to them, guide them, shake their hands. Let them worship you as they should." She turned to Dora. "Perhaps we can have Reverend Donald say a few words about Anita's triumphant return?"

The Hemmings family stopped as one, a shared panic shooting through them.

"That won't be necessary, Mrs. Peoples," said Dora. "Anita does not need any recognition. And it probably wouldn't be wise, given the mixed company." Reverend Brooks had passed away in '93, and while he had been very familiar with Anita's education and how she had achieved it, Reverend Donald was not.

"Of course, of course, the mixed company," said Mrs. Peoples, clearly not caring who her company was as long as she had their attention. Anita Hemmings was her trophy. She took Anita by the arm and marched her inside.

"Lord give you strength," Dora mouthed to Anita as they watched her go. The family walked in and sat in a pew toward the back of the grand church and observed Anita being guided around by the effervescent Mrs. Peoples. She held up Anita's hand as if she were a boxing champion.

"A graduate!" they heard her loud voice echo. "And one of us! The Negro who graduated from Vassar College. It's unprecedented! It's only happened twice before at Wellesley and never at Vassar until today. Be sure your hearts are welling up with pride for Miss Hemmings, welling up to the point of bursting," she warned her friends in the congregation, in case they weren't sharing her immense joy.

"Now you, Miss Mable March," she said, singling out a young girl sitting in a pew in a starched yellow dress. "Are you going to study hard so you can have the same distinguished fate as Miss Hemmings? These ladies' colleges don't open their doors for just anyone. One has to prove oneself the best of one's race, just as Miss Hemmings did."

"Yes, Mrs. Peoples," the girl responded obediently. And that was the chorus that followed, as Mrs. Peoples cross-examined every Negro girl sitting near her about their commitment to education and to becoming the next Anita Hemmings.

"I suppose it's all right," said Robert, pride battling concern on his face. "What is the risk in gossip now that she has graduated?"

Anita wondered if Mrs. Peoples was unaware that she had passed for white at Vassar. She had never told her herself, assuming instead that her parents had, since almost everyone in her Roxbury community knew. But Mrs. Peoples seemed to think that Vassar had willingly invited a Negro into its halls and would happily do so again. Anita decided to let Mrs. Peoples maintain that belief. She made her way back to her family, and Elizabeth moved over to make room for her.

"They have it all wrong," Elizabeth whispered in her ear. "It's me who wants to be the next Anita Hemmings."

"No, Elizabeth. You're already so much better," said Anita, squeezing her hand. "Just stay exactly as you are."

CHAPTER 28

It was in late June that Anita decided to prepare for the entrance examination for graduate study in Greek and Latin at New Haven's Yale University, which had recently started accepting female graduate students. The family agreed that she would live at home in Boston while she studied, since Frederick was moving to his own quarters on Pearl Street, and there would be more room. Anita was to work as a tutor in foreign languages for the summer, as she had done in Boston every year since starting at Vassar. Dora would spend much of the season in Martha's Vineyard, running her small boardinghouse in the Highlands of East Chop, part of Cottage City, the only town in Martha's Vineyard where Negroes could buy property. Unlike many of the boardinghouses in the area, Dora's house did not cater to Negroes, and because of it, she was able to charge a higher rate, a decision she had made with her children in mind. A portion of her wages would go toward Anita's future schooling.

"As a graduate student," Anita wrote in a letter to Bessie, whom she had not seen since returning to Boston, "I know I'll be able to make the journey to Greece and perhaps even Italy. My scholarship to study abroad did not materialize while at Vassar, but I feel that it will at Yale. And to be even closer to New York, Bessie! Have you and William made the trip together? I imagine you have, with the Harvard football team traveling there so often. I visited in January and fell more in love with it than ever. My trip was made at a time where everything felt so right in my life, and I'll always associate the city with that rare sentiment."

The summer was a busy one for Anita. With her Vassar degree, she was in much higher demand as a tutor than she had been as a mere student. Life at home soon resumed its normal pulse, and she slowly began to feel a sense of peace she had forgotten was possible.

"But of course you feel that," said William Henry Lewis one evening when Anita was dining with Bessie and her husband for the first time since returning to Boston. "You are where you should be. You must always have pride in being a Negro, Anita. For if we do not, why should *they*?" he asked rhetorically. "You and Bessie, you are destined to lead a whole generation of Negro women who long to be educated as you both were, who dream of opportunities our mothers could scarcely imagine. My parents were slaves. They lived in terrible conditions in Virginia. But my father, after serving as a sergeant in Virginia's First Regiment for colored troops, worked his way up from a dockworker to a Baptist minister, all because he could read and write. He pushed me in the right direction and now I am a Harvard-educated lawyer and paid to run their football team. Bessie came into this world in difficult circumstances, and now look at what she has done. Look at all the other Negro women gaining college degrees. Alberta Scott at Radcliffe was raised right here in Cambridge. Her family moved from Virginia to Massachusetts, like both of yours. Martha Ralston at Mount Holyoke is from Worcester. All these bright, young Negro women are here in this state, Anita. Massachusetts will be the force driving Negro rights going into the new century. This is where you need to stay."

"I'm in touch with the National Association of Colored Women, the group formed last year in Washington," said Bessie, when her husband had finished. "There are strong women at the helm along with the founder, Miss Ida B. Wells. Harriet Tubman is involved. Mary Church Terrell, who graduated from Oberlin in the eighties. And Boston's own, Josephine Ruffin. We could join them, too, Anita, especially you. Your graduation from Vassar will interest them greatly."

"Bessie is right," said William. "I know you've lived differently for four years, but you'll see. You will gain a renewed sense of pride working with other Negroes."

"I have a great sense of pride in being a Negro," Anita replied. "Just as much as you do. I did not want to attend Vassar just for myself; I wanted to attend Vassar to show that a Negro woman is just as intelligent as a white woman. That we deserve to be at Vassar, that we deserve to be in every school that admits white women. In my own way, I did that. But William, if I could have attended the school as Negro, I would have."

"I'm glad to hear it," he said, raising his glass to her.

What Anita was afraid to tell him and Bessie was that she would have to apply to graduate school as a white student. If she didn't, she would expose the secret President Taylor had urged her to keep. She felt she had no choice but to continue passing, at least until her education was complete.

"You've done very well, Anita," said Bessie, taking her friend's hand. "We are all," she said, glancing at her husband, "*all*, very proud of you."

By August, Anita's entire family was on Martha's Vineyard helping with the boardinghouse. Bessie and William had promised to come up to stay with them in a few weeks, and Anita, surrounded by the tight-knit Negro community on that crescent of beach, started to shed the layers of anxiety she had built up over the past four years.

Cottage City had been established decades earlier as a place to summer by white Methodists and Baptists who came year after year for revival meetings, at first pitching tents, then gradually building small, colorful houses. When the revivalists moved their fervor elsewhere, tourists gradually took their place, Negroes as well as whites. When Anita told her Vassar classmates that she spent the summers in Cottage City, it wasn't a locale black enough to cause alarm, but if anyone had been paying attention, it might have given them pause. The area was part of the Vineyard, but in many ways it was a private town, which not only accepted Negroes but largely let them run their own community.

Anita found herself walking on the Cottage City beach on one of the warmest days of the year feeling as if the wrongs and worries she had endured were behind her. It was mid-August, and she was strolling for the sake of strolling, Elizabeth and Robert Jr. running on ahead. She trod in the wet sand by the water's edge, not caring about her shoes, and thought of the hard lessons she had learned about kindness. The world was kinder to the educated, and kindest of all to whites—and she knew that in a way that almost no Negro ever would.

But that was all over for now.

As the morning slowly rolled into afternoon and the boardinghouse was miles behind them, she called out to her brother and sister to turn around. They had to return by two o'clock to help their mother prepare dinner. Cooking for fifteen people took many hands and many hours.

"But there is Bessie!" Elizabeth called suddenly, running even farther ahead. Anita looked and saw her friend hurrying toward them. She must have just arrived on the Vineyard, thought Anita. She started to run, too, her long bathing costume scratching her legs.

"Anita!" Bessie exclaimed, grabbing her friend when she reached her.

"I didn't know you were coming today!" said Anita, laughing. But Bessie took her by the shoulders and started to cry.

"Anita, oh, it's just horrible," she said, her eyes full of tears. Elizabeth started to cry because Bessie was crying, and Robert Jr. implored her to compose herself and listen.

"It's in the paper, Anita," Bessie said. "The *Boston Daily Globe*. The very front page. They know. Someone told them. They know you're a Negro."

Anita cried out, and the four of them ran for the boardinghouse on Wayland Avenue. Walking as composed as they could past several white guests, the group bowed their heads and moved to the back of the house, to the cramped quarters where the Hemmings family slept. Dora cried out at the sight of her daughter, panting for breath after her run to the house, and Frederick motioned to the paper they were reading, his face more panicked than Anita had ever seen.

"It can't be. It just can't be," said Anita, her voice cracking as soon as she saw the unfolded paper. Though she glimpsed her name in the body of the article, she couldn't take her eyes off the headline. Elizabeth moved past Bessie to Anita's side and held her hand as tightly as she could. Anita knew that Elizabeth, the most sensitive of them all, could not bear to see her sister upset. She was the sister she had shared a room with for years, the one she called Lillybug.

Anita let a tear fall onto her cheek but wiped it away before her mother could see. It was worse for them, she thought to herself. The notoriety, their names in a newspaper. It was worse for them.

The family and Bessie stared at the bold headline at the very top of the paper, centered on the front page—DARK, BUT BEAUTIFUL—in a size they had seen when important men had died. How could a story about Anita merit the same size print?

"'Globe Extra! Five o'clock. Dark, but beautiful. Colored girl went through exclusive Vassar College,'" Bessie read the three-tiered headline aloud.

"What is this, Anita?" her father asked, distraught. "What is all this?"

"They knew," Anita confessed, crying now. "The president, the lady principal, even my Latin teacher, Miss Franklin. They all found out the truth just weeks before commencement." Frederick led her to a chair. "I didn't want to tell you. I didn't want to upset you. I was graduated, that is all that's important."

"But this, Anita!" said Bessie, holding up the paper. There was a large likeness of Anita, drawn from her official graduation portrait, which must have been provided to the *Globe*.

"Lottie knew?" said Frederick, guessing correctly.

"Yes," Anita said, barely able to say the word. "My roommate Lottie was aware of my race. She discovered it first, and she told them all." As she recounted what had unfolded those last weeks at school, her mother took her hand and held it against her heart. "But the president asked us all to keep quiet," Anita told them. "He implored us not to share the story."

"But someone certainly did share it. Your roommate. It must be your roommate who told the papers," said Robert Jr. "The story of 'the roommate' takes up half the article. Look." He took up the paper and read to Anita. "'The denouement came in the senior year and was directly traceable to the girl's roommate.' It goes on from there about her suspicions and her father hiring a private investigator. Anita, she must have been the one to tell the newspapers. And not just the Boston papers; it's already been printed in New York, too. Read this," said Robert, pointing. "It says 'Historic Vassar College is in a state of ferment over an announcement in a local paper that among this year's graduating class was a colored girl.' That means Poughkeepsie."

"Lottie is the one who exposed your secret. And who would dare question her?" said Frederick, his voice bitter. "How could she act so wickedly?"

"My poor Anita," said Bessie, wrapping her arms around her friend. "What you must have gone through those final days. And not confiding in any of us. You are so brave. You've always been brave, but this, I can't imagine what it must have taken to endure it."

"I didn't want you to worry," said Anita, her face flushed with emotion. "What would you all have thought? I had only two things to accomplish in college: hide my race and graduate. And I only succeeded in one."

"The important one," said her father, resting his hand on her head. "The other you were only doing for them, their school, their rules."

"They cannot take back your diploma, can they?" asked Dora weakly.

"Of course not, Mother," said Frederick. "As Anita said, the president allowed her to graduate. They may not have admitted her knowing she was a Negro, but in the end, they approved of her being there or they would not have awarded her her diploma. It was just this hateful roommate."

"It won't just be her now," said Anita quietly. "Now that this news has broken, I won't hear from any of my friends again. I knew the administration might not be pleased if I returned to campus, but now my classmates will surely forbid it."

"Don't say that yet," said Bessie. "I know I'm always welcome at Wellesley. I've been back to campus once already."

"It's a different school," said Anita. "A different circumstance. You know that. And attending graduate school as a Negro woman who was in the newspapers," she croaked. "That will be extremely difficult."

"Anita," her father said sternly. "You have already proved that nothing is impossible. Look at you, you have already accomplished the impossible."

Anita glanced down at the paper. The story about her, with the enormous headline, took up a quarter of the front page. She scanned the words, certain passages leaping out and dealing hammer blows to her confidence.

Anita Florence Hemmings, "a colored girl—beautiful it is true, but nevertheless colored."

Colored. She would now forever be known as Vassar's colored student. The Negro. The only one.

"'It is an outrage that the imposing institution founded by old Matthew Vassar should have sheltered within its ivy-clad walls a real, true colored woman. Such is the prevailing sentiment of the townspeople.'" Anita tried not to cry out again as she read this, knowing that her tears were directly causing her mother's.

"'The faculty sat, so it is said, in secret conclave, and decided that, as the girl had completed her course satisfactorily, a diploma could not very well be refused her,'" Bessie read aloud over her shoulder. "Oh, Anita, how do the news-papermen know all of this?"

"She was there," said Anita. "Did I fail to mention that before? I'm so overwhelmed I don't remember what's been said and what hasn't. Lottie was present for the meeting. It was myself, President Taylor, the lady principal, my Latin instructor, Miss Franklin, and Lottie. President Taylor stated during our meeting that the board had met before he spoke with the four of us. Lottie must have remembered and shared that detail with the *Globe*."

"What a hateful girl," said Bessie. "If only you'd had another roommate. There are students there who would have protected you, I am sure of it."

"Yes, there are women of integrity there," said Anita, remembering how lucky she had felt being the roommate of Lottie Taylor, a member of the sought-after Gatehouse group. She thought about how for so many months Lottie had been one of those women of integrity. With her fascination of Japanese culture and the way that she had told her cousin that skin color wasn't worth fussing about, Lottie had seemed to her the most modern of women. But it had been only in speech, it turned out, not in action.

Bessie, who had started reading the paper again, pointed to a section down the page. "'Prexy' Taylor, whose kindness of heart is a byword in the college, was appealed to, with the result that the girl was awarded her diploma. The girl took a prominent part in the exercises of Class Day, and no one who saw the class of '97 leave the shades of Vassar suspected Negro blood in one woman voted the class beauty." She looked up with a reassured expression. "See, Mrs. Hemmings, Anita will not lose her diploma. There is no talk of that at all."

Dora Hemmings shook her head disbelievingly. She

looked toward the door, prompting Frederick to assure her
that no one was going to burst through it demanding Anita's
diploma. "I am unable to listen to all this any longer," she
said, standing. "If you will all excuse me." She walked back to
the kitchen to continue kneading dough through her tears.

Bessie sat in the chair that Mrs. Hemmings had vacated
and kept reading, focusing on Lottie, who was not named
in the paper, referred to only as "the roommate." "'This girl
began to suspect the dark beauty, whose statements, freely
made, as to the wealth and position of her family soon
passed the bounds of credence.'"

Frederick turned and looked at Anita. "If you could have
just spent time with different students, if Lottie Taylor—"

"I'm sorry," she whispered to him. "I should have listened to you, I should have—"

"You didn't do anything wrong," he said, and Anita was
thankful he was able to hold his tongue about Porter. "*They*
are doing something wrong. *They're* wrong. All of them."

"Yes," said Bessie firmly. "No one could expect you to go
four years without making friends. You had to grow close to
people. Living without a community would have done real
damage to you. You did what any of us would have done.
You have nothing to be ashamed of."

"But I do!" Anita cried out. "Now I do. What will become
of me? Of my life? I won't be accepted into any graduate
programs now, certainly not Yale. They will know my true
race. It is hard enough to be admitted as a woman to their
graduate programs, and impossible as a Negro woman."

"What about one of the universities for Negroes?" Bessie
suggested softly.

"Most are far down south," Anita said, looking up at her
friend in desperation. "Plus, I fear . . . who can say how the
educated Negro community will feel about me now knowing

I passed for four years. They might shun me as well." She looked away from Bessie and down to the ground, which seemed to be wobbling back and forth like an anchored boat. "Even a high school or grammar school teaching job will be out of the question now. Who will want me, a woman who was in the newspaper for her deception?"

"Don't say that, Anita—" Bessie started but Anita, growing hysterical, cut her off.

"All my work, the reason I went to Vassar in the first place was so that I could better myself and become an educator, and now that is entirely impossible. It was all for nothing. My efforts, my secrecy, have only achieved shame and public humiliation!"

"Anita, that may not be the case," her brother said, putting his hand on her bent-over back. "There could be schools that, after a certain amount of time passes, won't remember this."

"Frederick, you know as well as I do that I will never be able to shake this notoriety," she said without looking up. "The liar. The Negro girl from Vassar. It will bar me from employment for the rest of my life. And Lottie knew that being a professor was all I aspired to. She knew what the consequences of this article would be. I was such a fool. Forgive me, Frederick," she said, looking up finally. "I made a terrible mistake."

Anita thought back to Mame Marshall, the woman who had first told her that even though Vassar barred Negroes from attending, she might make herself the exception. She cringed at the thought of Mrs. Marshall reading this article and the embarrassment she would feel for Anita, the guilt she might endure for having placed the idea of passing in her head in the first place. Mame had moved to Canada after Anita's freshman year at Vassar and had not returned to

Boston since, and for the first time, Anita was glad. Perhaps she would not see American newspapers where she lived. But others would. Cora Shailer, Lillian Peoples, the members of her church. She had been such a source of pride for them. What would she be now?

Frederick didn't respond to his sister, instead rereading the article, his eyes lingering on the passage that mentioned him as a graduate of the Massachusetts Institute of Technology. He took the paper from Bessie and read it aloud. "The other children, while they are fine looking, are not quite as light as Miss Hemmings. But this fact must be taken into consideration, that in colored families the children are likely to be graduated in tints from a dark brown to a very fair white, or the reverse."

The paper did not name the writer, but Frederick was quite certain that whoever this sensationalist, cowardly reporter was, this man who had followed his family around without their knowledge, was no Negro and no expert on the Negro race.

Elizabeth looked down at her dark, bare arm and started to cry again "Should we stay here for the rest of the summer?" she asked, burying her face in Anita's lap. "I don't want to go back to Boston. They'll be chasing us."

"No one will be chasing us," said Frederick, hugging his sister. "You'll be safe at home in Boston. You'll be safe with us."

But he was wrong.

CHAPTER 29

When the Hemmingses returned to Boston some days later, they were immediately faced with newspaper reporters knocking on their door, clamoring to see Anita, to interview her and, Anita thought, to gawk at the shade of her skin and that of everyone else in the family. Robert Sr. did not let any of them past the stoop.

Anita watched from her small upstairs bedroom window, but she never made herself available, choosing to stay locked inside for more than a week. She would not pose for a photograph. She would not discuss her days at Vassar. Instead she mourned losing her future educational possibilities, her career, and the identity that she had had for four years.

One morning at the end of August when Robert Sr. left for work at his usual hour, rather than very early to avoid reporters as he had been doing, he was cornered by a man from the *Globe* who refused to leave him without a statement. Anita watched the scene from her window, unable to intervene. Her presence would only make things worse.

The next morning, her father's words were featured in the paper in another two-column story topped with an illustration of Anita.

Frederick read it to the family in their small dining room.

"Here is Father's quote," he said, pointing. "It's rather long, Father. I do hope they leave us all alone after obtaining this much from you." He moved as Anita leaned in to look at her likeness, a sketch that was far less flattering than the first one she had seen. "First, Father denies that Anita told her professors that she was a Negro. He also denies that her tuition was paid by a white benefactor. Where that rumor came from, I don't know."

"Is that circulating?" asked Anita in horror, thinking about her father working two arduous jobs to send her to school. After the first article they had all read in Cottage City, Anita had been guarded from the ones that followed. This was the first she had read since that afternoon.

"In several articles it has stated such," said Frederick. "As if we were unable to send you to college because we are Negro. A white benefactor, such an offensive assumption. Father had been saving for our educations for decades."

"These reporters will invent anything to make us appear unworthy," said Dora, with tears leaking from her brown eyes, her permanent state for the past week.

"They will, and they have," said Frederick. "But Father's quote is very strong. Here is what he says about Anita and Vassar: 'We know she went there as a white girl and remained there as such. As long as she conducted herself in a manner becoming a lady, she never thought it necessary to proclaim the fact that her parents were mulattoes. Anita was always a quiet, studious girl, and from the time she first went to school, books were her chief pleasure. She did not care for the play of other children, but much preferred the companionship of her favorite authors. Vassar was always her favorite college. She always wanted to go to college when she went to the girls' high school [*sic*] in Boston, but there never seemed to be any doubt in her mind as to which college she desired to enter most. Vassar it was, first, last, and always.'"

Anita tried to listen, but she could not stop looking at the illustration that accompanied it. She was in a newspaper, her likeness and her story, but for the worst reasons. For deceit. For lying. And not just once, but for years, to hundreds of people. She bent down and took her mother's hand, crying with her.

Later that day, Robert Sr. decided that to better shield Anita from the reporters, she would go to stay with Bessie and William in Cambridge and not be allowed to read the newspapers.

The Lewises were happy to take her in, and Bessie tried her best to keep Anita from crying and sleeping her days away. She came in to check on her every morning, and every morning Anita had to apologize for her state, her bed a tangle of sweaty sheets, her eyes bloodshot.

"I'm terrified," she confessed one morning to her friend, while pulling her knees to her chest, still in her nightclothes. "I don't know how to proceed. Who can I become now? School is out of the question and I am unemployable. I don't recognize myself anymore."

"But I know how you should proceed," said Bessie. "You are very hirable, Anita. You are. You are still a model for education in the Negro community. Even if that hateful girl shouted out your secret in the end, you still accomplished what you set out to. You, a Negro, graduated from Vassar College on your own merit. Don't ever forget that."

Anita looked up at her with gratitude. She had already begun to forget it.

"Now, a woman William knows quite well is employed at

the Boston Public Library," said Bessie brightly. "That would be a perfect job for you. Perhaps you have the strength to go and see her about possible openings. They have a foreign cataloguing department that would suit you well, with your strength in languages. Once they hear you are highly competent in not only Greek and Latin but French and Italian, as well, they'll take you at once."

"Do you really think so?" asked Anita slowly, letting go of her legs. "Even with this notoriety? They wouldn't. Would they?"

"Mrs. Greenwood, the woman William knows, is a Negro and active in Negro education. I imagine she will be sympathetic to your story. I hope very much that she is."

The two decided that Anita would go to the library the next day to meet with Mrs. Greenwood and that Bessie would accompany her. It had been nearly a week since Mr. Hemmings had given his lengthy statement to the *Globe*, so they waited for the streetcar without making any special effort to avoid attention. Surely Anita's story no longer held the public's interest. But within minutes, two newspaper reporters from the *Boston Post* had approached them.

"What should we do?" said Anita in a panic. She recognized both of the men from their numerous visits to her parents' front door.

"Let's speak to them," said Bessie firmly. "We each give one short statement, and then perhaps they will leave you alone for good and go on to the next story. I hope they will find one worthy of printing instead of trying to ruin another woman's life."

After Anita had put off the reporters as best she could, with Bessie speaking on her behalf, they took the streetcar into Boston, changing twice to reach the library.

"I'll wait for you here," said Bessie looking up at the

McKim-designed building that had graced Copley Square for the past two years.

Anita entered the library with timid steps, asking the man at the front desk for Mrs. Greenwood and praying that no one would recognize her face from the newspapers.

"And who should I say is here to see her?" the man asked Anita.

She looked down and murmured, "Miss Anita Hemmings," letting him see only the top of her head.

He left to fetch Mrs. Greenwood, and Anita took a seat near the entrance. She looked up at the vaulted ceiling and marble mosaic and thought about Lottie's house and the one and only time she had slept in its marble halls. She knew now she would never sleep in such a place again.

"Are you Miss Hemmings?" a middle-aged woman said, interrupting her reverie.

Anita stood up at once and extended her ungloved hand.

"I am, and you must be Mrs. Greenwood," said Anita, following her through the middle one of three wide aisles.

"That I am," she said, her head and neck straight as a pin as she moved. "Come, we will walk to the Abbey Room and discuss your potential employment as a foreign language cataloguer. You would work mainly on translation and bibliography. Do you feel you have the competencies to do so?"

"I do," said Anita, hastening to keep up with her. "I just graduated from college and am competent in seven languages, including Greek and Latin."

After Anita had spent two hours with Mrs. Greenwood, writing and translating in several foreign languages, the woman seemed pleased and took Anita on a short tour of the library, pointing out the impressive mural paintings of the Quest for the Holy Grail.

Anita nodded, excited to be near such artistic and architectural beauty again. This was not the dream she had nurtured since she arrived at Vassar and fell further in love with her Greek and Latin studies, but it might be the only place open to hiring her.

After Mrs. Greenwood had finished her tour, she asked Anita if she had any questions. Anita had but one.

"Do you not mind what has been written about me in the newspaper, Mrs. Greenwood?" she asked plainly. "That I am the subject of a story which has traveled from coast to coast, and not a flattering one at that. Are you not embarrassed to have me here?"

"Your story?" said the woman, moving closer to Anita to let several patrons pass. "That you are a Negro? Is that even a story? I have been known as a Negro my entire life."

"Of course," said Anita. "What I meant was not my race, but that I attended Vassar under false pretenses. That I have been branded a liar, publicly humiliated."

"What other choice did you have?" Mrs. Greenwood asked, not missing a beat.

"None," said Anita, the word feeling soothing as she said it. "To attend Vassar, I had no other choice at all."

"No, you did not," said Mrs. Greenwood. "And from what Mr. Lewis wrote about you, they have educated you properly at Vassar and I am sure you will do quite well with us. I will see you on Monday, Miss Hemmings. Eight o'clock sharp. And please wear a dress you can carry books in. This job requires one to have one's arms full."

Anita, shocked by the stranger's open-mindedness, remembered to thank her and hurried out of the library, back to the safety of Bessie's home.

The next day, as Anita and Bessie expected, their statements to the reporters who had accosted them appeared in the newspaper.

Anita's was terse: "I have been unnecessarily drawn into public notice and refuse to say anything about the matter."

But Bessie had done her best to defend her friend, and the paper quoted her in full. "Miss Hemmings is entitled to all the honor of having obtained her education at Vassar, which has not reflected an atom of disgrace on that college nor upon any other pupils," she said. "She is good and true, brilliant in many things, refined and always ladylike in her actions. Her reception at college tells the story in itself. She was admired there and put forward in all things. They loved her, no matter what you may hear, as to know her is to bow to her pleasing ways. She is an honor to her race and she is an honor to Boston, and, I must say it, she is better than many other American girls. Because her face did not tell her secret, why should she go about placarded 'I am colored' or, for that matter, what difference should color mean to one like Miss Hemmings, who could enter society and be not only an ornament but prove her wealth of refinement?"

When she and Bessie finished reading, Anita glimpsed a newspaper she hadn't been shown resting in the large book Bessie had been pretending to read. She had left it open accidentally to come over and console Anita. The paper was another issue of the *Boston Post*, and Anita could see it contained still another article about her, this one accompanied by a sketch of her parents' home as well as another one of her face. MOST BEAUTIFUL WOMAN IN THE COLLEGE AND CHUM OF ARISTOCRATIC GIRLS, the headline read, followed by a subheading: THE DAUGHTERS OF WEALTH ARE SHOCKED. Anita could imagine Lottie writing that herself.

She stood up and reached for the paper.

"Oh, Anita, no!" cried Bessie. "Do not read that nonsense, please! It was obtuse of me to have left it out."

Anita ignored her. She read the headline again, then the first column, and started laughing until she bent double.

"What is it?" said Bessie, smiling. She hadn't heard her friend laugh since the day she ran to her on the beach in Cottage City.

"'Young men students had paid court to her. The flower of Harvard's young manhood had eagerly asked for an introduction to the beautiful Vassar girl, and after the introduction had become her willing slaves, enchanted by her beauty, her refined manner, her air of aristocratic distinction, and the soft tones of her voice,'" Anita read aloud. "'Not only among Harvard men was she a society idol, but Columbia men, Princeton men, and the democratic sons of Yale all alike fell under the spell of her charm.'"

Anita's laughter rang out again, and she dropped the paper onto the table. "Have you ever heard anything more ridiculous, Bessie? They make me out to be Helen of Troy! The only man who was ever enamored with me was Porter Hamilton, and now I have my doubts that he ever really was."

"I firmly believe that many men were desperately in love with you," said Bessie, thrilled at this flash of her friend's old lightheartedness. "As I told those reporters, to know you is to bow to your pleasing ways. Perhaps all these sons of Yale wrote to the paper en masse to declare their love for you just yesterday."

"Despite my race," said Anita, serious again.

"Despite your race," Bessie echoed.

In the days that followed, the Boston papers reported that the story about Anita was also appearing in dozens of publications across the country, from the *New York Times* to a newspaper in Hawaii. All of America was seeing her likeness and reading how she deceived the nation's top women's college and its elite community.

Once Anita realized the reach of her story, she fell into her depression again, wanting only to shut herself indoors, but Bessie wouldn't allow it. She saw her off to the street-car on her first day of work at the library and didn't turn around when Anita called her name from the road.

Though it took several weeks, the library helped keep Anita afloat. Negro and white employees alike were kind to her, keeping reporters at bay and treating her as if she were not the eye of a page-one scandal, but simply another intelligent college graduate who had joined them in their important work.

When Anita came home one evening after two weeks at the library, surprised to have made it to that milestone, Bessie greeted her and dropped several letters in front of her, only smiling when Anita looked at her in alarm. "I am hoping for the best from these, Anita. I don't think people would write if they had hatred toward you. They would just ignore you," said Bessie. She explained that she had been in Boston that day, as well, visiting Anita's family to find out whether the flood of reporters coming to Sussex Street had started to thin. She assured Anita that it had, and left her alone to open her mail.

The first two letters were from Belle and Caroline, both declaring their unfailing support. Anita held them to her chest for a moment before she opened two others, one from Miss Macurdy and the other from Medora Higgins, the former president of the Federal Debating Society. To Anita's surprise and pleasure, they both expressed similar sentiments.

But the last letter she opened came as a much bigger surprise.

Dear Miss Hemmings,
 As you know, I guessed your true race the evening we were formally introduced at the opera, as I was certain I

had seen you in Roxbury as the New Year approached. You also have similar coloring, similar striking features, to my sister Carrie. I do consider her my sister, if you wondered when we spoke, and not just someone I care for financially.

Miss Hemmings, I want you to know that you will always be welcome at Clavedon Hall, and rest assured that Miss Taylor will not be.

Do stay in touch and call on me when you are in New York. I would very much like to see you again, especially now that we can speak candidly. That will be delightful for us both, I'm sure of it.

Yours faithfully,
Marchmont Rhinelander

CHAPTER 30

It was two months later, when she was concentrating on acting with the utmost decorum in order to keep her new job, that Anita made an unexpected acquaintance. Busy with her cataloguing one morning, she looked up as a fashionably dressed man with a long, confident gait approached her, carrying a large book.

"Are you Miss Hemmings?" he asked, gripping his hat firmly with his other hand.

"I am," said Anita, happy to speak to someone who did not already recognize her from the newspapers. In the months since she had been employed at the library, there had been many who, in recognizing her, gave their unsolicited opinions on what she had done, and through those interactions, Anita had grown even more reserved and hesitant in her demeanor.

"My name is Dr. Andrew Love," said the man, his voice deep but amiable. "I was told you might be able to help me with this physiology book. It's been mental gymnastics for me for the past few hours, as I'm afraid my Greek is not what it used to be before I took up my medical studies. It has been quite a few years since I did undergraduate work and read more than a line or two in Greek."

Anita took the book from him, sat down as it was quite heavy, and flipped through the pages. The medical terminology was daunting, but she gestured to him to join her at the table by one of the library's large windows.

Anita helped him for just shy of an hour—she translating the small print aloud, he taking dictation—before he paused and laid down his pen. Feeling his eyes on her, she continued reading, not sure what else to do.

"Miss Hemmings," he said, interrupting her. "Please pardon my ill manners but I must confess something to you," he said as she lifted her eyes from the book. "I came here to the library with the intention of meeting you. I have been reading about you in the newspapers, and I told myself that I must make the acquaintance of this brave, intelligent woman."

"I'm sorry," said Anita, standing up quickly. "But I do not wish to speak about the stories in the newspapers, and it would be most inappropriate to do so at my place of employment. I'll have to ask you to leave my section at once. I'm sure you can find someone else to help you with your translation." Anita knew it wasn't correct to speak to a patron this way, but she could not bear one more conversation about her passing at Vassar, even if the man in question was congratulatory of her actions.

She turned to leave, but Andrew Love moved with her, closer than a shadow.

"I apologize for upsetting you," he said quickly. "I shouldn't have spoken so forthrightly, or even come here seeking you out. But you see, I wanted to meet you, and I thought it might be helpful for you to meet me, because I—" He took a step back as Anita moved as if to sprint away from him.

"I have a great amount of respect you for, Miss Hemmings," he said changing his approach. "For what you did to receive the best education you could. And furthermore, what I should have disclosed initially is, I am the same as you, Miss Hemmings. I am a Negro, like you," he said in a whisper. "And I thought to myself, this bold young woman might not have met anyone like herself before. A well-educated Negro who knows what it is to live as colored and as white." He looked down while fiddling with the brim of his hat, suddenly seeming as nervous as she was. "You see, I am in Boston readying myself to attend Harvard as a Negro student, but at times I have lived otherwise. I have practiced medicine both as a Negro and as white."

"You are a Negro?" Anita asked softly, bending her head, too.

"I am," said Andrew Love, who though clearly several years her senior, still had a youthful roundness to his face. "If you would please sit back down with me, I will be happy to tell you more about myself. If you might find that of interest. But if not, I will leave at once and apologize for my impertinence."

Anita gestured to the table and sat down with him again, now anxious in a very different way.

Situated at a respectable distance from Anita, and speaking with half the volume he had before, Andrew said, "My full name is Andrew Jackson Love. I was not born in Massachusetts, nor have I been here for very long." He cleared his throat and dropped his voice even more. "I was born into a family of twelve children, by two different women, my mother and my father's second wife, in Canton, Mississippi. That's right in the heart of poverty-stricken Madison County, north of Jackson, east of Yazoo City. Have you ever been to Mississippi, Miss Hemmings?" he asked, taking small glances to his left and right to make sure they were still alone.

"I have not. I have never been further south than New York City."

"And I had never been north of Tennessee until this year," he explained. "My father was, and still is, a farm laborer down in Mississippi. But he always said we, his children, should amount to more. Sadly, that wish is difficult to make a reality when you are poor and Negro in Mississippi. He was born in Virginia like your parents, but he went south instead of going north like he should have."

His mention of her parents reminded Anita how much the newspapers had printed about her private life and she felt a stroke of panic flush through her body. Still, she could not bring herself to stop Andrew from speaking, and she looked at his pale face with more interest than she hoped to show.

"My brothers, many are farm laborers," he continued, "yet I knew I would do something different, something with medicine, even if it took me a long time to find my way. And as you can see, I was light-skinned enough to pass as white if I chose to. Many of my siblings are not."

"Mine, either," Anita explained, though the newspapers had already made that clear. "My nearest brother Frederick is able to, though not as easily as I, and for the two younger ones, it is out of the question."

Andrew nodded in understanding and said, "Still, like you, I didn't pass for many years. I was a schoolteacher down in Tennessee and Louisiana at Negro high schools. That was before I scraped together the means, and the confidence, to attend medical school in Tennessee. And I'm glad I did. It changed my life, even if it meant giving up seeing family for years now. That's probably the most important place to start."

"Your story sounds much like my family," said Anita. If

he had not told her, she would never have known he was a Negro.

"I read in the newspaper that Vassar had been your singular goal for many years," he went on. "It was the same with me, Miss Hemmings. I've been aware since childhood that I wanted to pursue medicine. In the community where I spent my early years, there were no doctors for miles, just terrible suffering."

Anita nodded her head in understanding, though it was hard for her to fully understand the poverty of the rural southern Negro. Black Boston was not the South and her parents had made her aware from early on how lucky she was to be born in Massachusetts.

"'Doctor' meant a mother, a prayer, never a licensed physician," Andrew explained. "I watched people die around me, people who could have been so easily saved. So, like you, I focused on one goal: in my case, attending medical school. And I did. I eventually enrolled as a student at the medical department of Central Tennessee College, a medical school for Negroes only."

"Our doctor in Roxbury," Anita interrupted, "he too attended a Negro medical college. Perhaps it was the same school."

"Perhaps," said Andrew. "But he was intelligent enough to come north, if so. It took me much longer to do the same. After I graduated, I worked as a doctor—a colored doctor for the colored community—in Chattanooga, Tennessee. It was rewarding work, but one that also gave me a new goal, to attend a medical school in New England. So I came to Massachusetts with my sights set on Harvard. If Harvard becomes a reality, they will have me on record as a Negro, as you can't lie about your race if you come from a Negro school. But that may change in the future."

Anita thought about her luck with Northfield, and how true that statement was. "In what circumstance would that change?" she inquired. "If it is not too rude of me to ask."

"I don't know precisely," Andrew answered honestly. "The world works with you sometimes and against you at others. Passing isn't a future goal of mine, as I know, from experience, what one has to give up in the process. But sometimes, to obtain what you think you deserve, or to advance your studies or career, the world forces you to live that way. Wouldn't you agree, Miss Hemmings?"

"I do, of course," she replied quietly, looking around as Andrew had done to see if they were still alone. "But when I passed at Vassar, I did not have to give up my family. You say you haven't seen yours in many years."

"That's right," he replied, moving his hat around in a circle with his right hand. "But it's not because of passing. It's economics. I'm afraid I haven't had the means, or the time, to travel back to Mississippi, as saving for Harvard has been my priority."

"Of course, a journey north is very expensive."

"It is," said Andrew slowly. "But I see what you are touching on. Many people like us, who do not see their families for an extended period—it's a by-product of passing."

"Yes," she whispered. "That's something that has always terrified me. At Vassar I was able to have both. It ultimately worked against me, but for four years, I could pass and I could be with them, my family, during the holidays. I'm afraid that now, outside of a college existence, that would not be the case. It would be the choice of one or the other. Or at best, I would have to visit with them in a very different, limited capacity."

Anita had heard stories of it before, Negro women who went on to live otherwise and had to pass off their mothers and fathers as servants, forcing them to use the maid's entrance, the back door. When she was with Porter Hamilton, she had considered being one of them.

"I hope I never have to fully make that choice," said Andrew. "But as it stands now, my family understands what a person has to give up to pursue a career in medicine. A Negro person, that is. Which is time and money, and occasionally, dignity."

"My family understands, too," said Anita. "To a point."

"I think only someone who has lived as we have can truly understand our positions," said Andrew. "And that's why I wanted to meet you, Miss Hemmings. I never attended school as a white person like you did, but I have lived as one. I am familiar with floating between both worlds, to be treated as white. I know what it's like to leave behind your identity as a Negro and be confused about whether you are doing so willingly or unwillingly. And I understand the guilt that can come with securing a better life by passing. The shame. You may think, am I doing this because I am not brave enough to live as a Negro? Or am I living this way because it is the only way to pursue a career I deserve? Perhaps it is an act of bravery? Tricking them into treating you like one of their own. Have you had thoughts like these, Miss Hemmings?" Andrew paused and looked at Anita with an intensity that should have made her uncomfortable, but his words, his presence didn't disquiet her at all. "Still," he said, moving his body farther away from her, "I acted indiscreetly, and I apologize, but I hope you can understand. I had to meet the Negro woman who had graduated from Vassar. This brave woman."

Anita let the smallest of smiles form on her face and then backed away from him, too, when she spotted another cataloguer looking at them with interest.

"My apologies," he said, seeing Anita's colleague. "I'm making you uncomfortable. I will go. I do hope you will allow me to call on you in the coming days. I'm afraid all of Boston knows your address after the papers published it so many times, but I do not want to come unless you would like to see me again."

"I am not staying at home for that very reason," said Anita, standing up. "But I would like to speak to you again."

No one had ever put into words so plainly the emotions she had felt for four years at Vassar. A decade ago, Mame Marshall had tried to prepare her, but Anita was still many years from understanding fully. Andrew Love was the first man she had ever met who passed for the sake of his career, for his intellectual betterment. He hadn't passed to shed his Negro identity. She couldn't help but feel a jolt of energy as she thought of the way he had articulated the things she had never spoken—not to Frederick, nor Bessie, not even to herself.

Anita walked to the front desk and came back with Bessie and William's address written on a slip of paper.

"If you would like, you can call on me here," she said, making sure her hand did not brush his as she gave him the note.

"I will call on you tomorrow," he said, placing his hat back on his head and leaving Anita as quietly as he came in.

CHAPTER 31

Andrew did as he said and rang the bell at the Lewises' house the following evening.

Bessie, who had heard only briefly about Anita's encounter with a light-skinned man at the library, opened the door and was shocked to see someone who looked even whiter than Anita standing there, holding flowers for both her and Anita.

"Mrs. Lewis, please excuse me, I do believe I'm ringing your bell near dinnertime. Miss Hemmings, whom I had the pleasure of meeting yesterday, told me you and Mr. Lewis would be so kind as to allow me to call on her today."

"Of course, of course," said Bessie, trying to mask her surprise at his skin color as she let him in the door. "And this is a perfectly good time. If you do not have plans, you could join us for supper."

"Oh no, I could not impose," said Andrew, walking into the large, comfortable house. "I would be glad to another evening, when it's not an inconvenience."

"Nonsense," said Bessie, showing him to a chair in the sitting room. "I will just fetch Anita upstairs." She turned to her right and called for her husband, who was around the bend in the dining room, introducing the two men before she went upstairs so that her visitor was not alone.

"I heard him come in," said Anita as Bessie walked into her bedroom door where Anita was penning a letter to her mother. "Andrew Love."

"Yes!" Bessie said excitedly. "Anita, you said he was light, but this man looks positively white."

"But he's not," said Anita defensively.

"No, of course not," said Bessie, not having meant to offend. "What I should have said is that he is very handsome and exceedingly polite."

"Isn't he?" said Anita, her excitement matching to rise Bessie's. Since meeting Andrew the day before, she hadn't been able to think of anything except the man who in so many ways seemed like a carbon copy of herself. Throughout her time at Vassar, no one in her Boston community had fully understood her challenges. Andrew Love did. It was as if she hadn't realized just how alone she was until she met him.

"Come, Anita," said Bessie, interrupting her thoughts. "Re-pin your hair and let's go downstairs. I've already invited him to stay for supper, but if it turns out that you don't want him to, then we shall send him away at once."

"I don't think it will come to that," said Anita, smiling.

"No, me neither," said Bessie, crossing the room to leave. "I think we will all fall a little bit in love with Mr. Love after this evening."

She didn't turn around to see Anita blush, instead leading the way downstairs, where the women greeted the two men who were speaking animatedly.

Anita and Andrew greeted each other politely and familiarly, as if somehow their private, personal words exchanged the day before had helped them cross the boundaries into emotional intimacy very quickly.

"Thank you for allowing me to call on you," said Andrew,

standing a respectable distance from Anita and not offering his hand to her. "I very much wanted to see you again."

"Of course," Anita replied politely before William and Andrew took up their conversation on the Negro community in Boston.

The Lewises spoke animatedly about the people they knew in the area who were leading the charge in social change, and Andrew nodded at the familiar names.

When they sat down to dinner a few moments later, the conversation switched to the ways of Northeastern colleges and what Andrew might expect as a Negro at Harvard, but William swung it swiftly back to social change after the main course was served.

"We do hope Anita joins Bessie as a voice for the educated Negro woman," William explained to Andrew after Bessie had finished describing her work with Josephine Ruffin and the Boston chapter of the National Association of Colored Women.

"I have no doubt that she will," said Andrew before he complimented Bessie on the meal.

"Yes, of course that is something that interests me," said Anita, though she had not attended a meeting with Bessie yet. She intended to, but she was still too afraid of the possible judgment on her character by such smart, proud Negro women. Not everyone thought the way Mame Marshall did. She worried they might sneer at her choice to attend Vassar as white, not look upon her with pride as they did Bessie.

"I am sure Miss Hemmings's commitment to the Negro community is just as strong as mine," said Andrew. "We were able to speak at some length yesterday and I found that we have very similar values."

"That's all excellent to hear," said William, pushing

aside his empty plate. "I believe there was also some talk of passing?" he said, looking at his wife.

Shocked, Anita also looked at Bessie, whom she had confided in the night before. Clearly, Bessie had turned around and told her husband the details of their intimate conversation.

"Yes, like Miss Hemmings, I have passed before," said Andrew quickly, guessing the circumstances and wanting to break the tension before it could mount. "But only for brief periods of time, and only out of necessity."

"What sort of necessity?" William asked, moving his eyes from his wife to his guest. "When is it ever a necessity?"

"To practice medicine," Andrew replied matter-of-factly.

"Am I incorrect in thinking that you ran a practice for Negroes in Tennessee?" said William, who had clearly been relayed Andrew's entire life story by his wife.

"You are not wrong," said Andrew, looking briefly at Anita, who was sitting rigid and uncomfortable. "But for a time I learned my profession beside an extremely gifted white doctor. He was far older than I and compared to my dedicated instructors at Central Tennessee, his schooling and training were far superior. I firmly believed that learning from such a man would enable me to save more lives in the future. Negro lives." Andrew cleared his throat and folded his napkin in his lap. "Working with him," he explained, "I only treated white patients, so my need to disguise my race was essential. You can imagine what the reaction would have been if they knew they had colored hands on them."

"They would have died right there on the table, from your touch, not from disease," said William, causing everyone to laugh and relax slightly.

"The poison some think exists in Negro hands," said Bessie, shaking her head.

"In Negro everything," said William. "They think the foundations of religion, of country, will all start to crack if the Negro is looked at as even fifty percent worthy of the white man."

"Some believe that," Anita said, coming out of her shell and correcting him.

"Yes," said William, agreeing. "Not all. But many."

"In my life, I've had to ignore most of that hateful talk," said Andrew. "If I hadn't carried forward with shatterproof optimism, I would never have come out as I did."

Bessie looked across the table at Anita apologetically, but Anita smiled at her. It was clear that Andrew could handle himself very well with William, and did feel great pride in his work.

"You and I," said William, pausing to collect his thoughts, "we come from very similar circumstances. Bessie moved up north from Virginia when she was very young, and Anita, though her parents are Virginians, was born in Boston, but we spent our childhoods in the South, didn't we."

"Yes, indeed. I've spent my whole life in the South," Andrew said respectfully.

"I was in Virginia until I was twenty years old," William explained. "Started out my college education at Virginia Normal, aged fifteen. But I had a helping hand moving me up north. The president of the school gave me the idea of Amherst and helped make it a reality. Once there, I had to pay my way working as a waiter and a stable boy, but I had help, I'll admit that. Negroes helped me. White men helped me. But you didn't have such a step up, did you, Mr. Love?"

"Call me Andrew, please," he said, looking squarely at his host. "I'm afraid that in the South there's the South and then there's Mississippi. And I believe that like mine, your parents were born slaves, but your father became a literate, highly esteemed minister. Or that is what I have read about you."

"That's correct," said William between bites of the cherry pie that his wife had served for dessert.

"I don't doubt that it was just as difficult for you to move on to college as it was for me," said Andrew carefully, "but I, as you say, did not have a step up. My father works as a farm laborer; most of my family is still illiterate. But he gave me drive, maybe more than any other parent in the South did. He wanted me out of Mississippi and out of the fields."

"And you made it," said William.

"Eventually. I wasn't fifteen in college, I was thirty years old when I graduated from medical school."

"But you're here now, and we are all very glad to have you," said William, finally looking approvingly at Anita.

When dinner was over and the women were clearing the table, Bessie pulled her friend over to the corner of the kitchen, looking like an excited schoolgirl.

"He's extremely handsome, Anita. And coming from absolutely nothing, becoming a physician with not a soul to help him. Even William had mentors. You and I had Northfield. He had no one. I have great admiration for him already. Please tell him he's welcome back anytime. No, better yet, I will deliver the message."

"He is elegant, isn't he," said Anita, unable to repress her smile. "And his ambition is so honorable."

"He," said Bessie quietly, taking her friend's hand, "reminds me quite a bit of you."

The following evening Andrew Love called again, and the next week, Anita and he made the short journey to Boston so that he might meet her parents. The reporters had finally given up on the family, and Andrew and Anita were free to move between Sussex Street and Bessie's home in Cambridge without scrutiny.

"My darling girl," said Mrs. Hemmings, after Andrew had gone. He had just dined with the Hemmings family for the third evening in a row. Dora clutched her daughter's hand and said, "A horrible thing happened to you, and from it sprang something good. That is a handsome, remarkable man. Imagine, a Negro becoming a doctor with his sights set on Harvard. God is great."

"He does seem both those things," said Anita, her pulse steadying for the first time in weeks thanks to her mother's healing presence.

"And he doesn't seem to be coming to dine here just because he enjoys my cooking. I think he far prefers my daughter's company."

"It is all happening very quickly," said Anita, resting her head on her mother's soft shoulder.

"Is there a timeline to love?" asked Dora, stroking her daughter's piled-up hair.

"No, there is not," she replied, thinking back on Porter and how after their first kiss she had known that love would swiftly follow.

With her weight still leaning on her mother, she let her thoughts of Porter multiply. She was no longer in love with him, she was sure of that, but her fondness for him remained unshakable. He would always be part of that one magical year of school, when Anita didn't feel hindered or limited by her race or her sex. When everything, even a life with a man like Porter Hamilton, seemed like a possibility.

But that year was long over and the stone walls of Vassar College would never safeguard her again. But perhaps Andrew could.

In the weeks that followed, Andrew's courtship continued, and Anita, three months after their initial meeting, confided in Bessie that she knew she could grow to love Andrew, perhaps even more than she did Porter, because together they could live a genuine life together, full of confidences and shared goals. He, just as Bessie said, was very much like her. And with him, she thought, she could be the best version of her true self. Not Anita Hemmings passing; Anita Hemmings living.

Soon after that declaration, Andrew must have sensed the change in Anita's heart, for he felt confident enough to utter the word *marriage*. When he did, he confessed it had been on his mind since he first caught sight of her in the library.

"But you want to move back to Tennessee," said Anita. "After Harvard." She thought about that distance and how awful it would be to leave her family, even with a man like Andrew by her side.

"I do," said Andrew. "Chattanooga feels like home and I have an established practice there. My patients are expecting me to return."

"Do you think I would be content there? In Tennessee?" Anita asked, her voice laced with doubt.

"I hope so, but I can't be certain," said Andrew. "It's a very different world. Perhaps you wouldn't take to the South. As you are aware, things can happen to the Negro there, awful things." He turned to look at her and kissed her hand. "But Anita, if you were not happy in Chattanooga, we would leave. We could start a new life together somewhere else if you did not take to the lifestyle there."

"My parents said they would never return to Virginia," said Anita. "To have their daughter go even further south, I don't know how they would feel. And I've disappointed them enough this year." She looked at his downcast face, and added, "But I would be willing to try. For you, I would try anything."

"Would you?" said Andrew hopefully. "And what if we left Tennessee and had to establish ourselves somewhere else one day? Anita, if that were the case, and we had to pass as white, is that something you think you could do again?"

"Even if I was open to it, I don't think I could, with my notoriety," she replied nervously, her eyes darting around the tree-lined Cambridge street. "My story was printed everywhere from New York to Hawaii and back again. I even, recently, received a letter from the colored writer Paul Laurence Dunbar," she disclosed. It was something she hadn't been sure she would share with Andrew, but with the subject of passing back in the conversation, she felt that she had to. "He intends to include me in his new musical work," she said, her voice unstable. "I'm going to be the subject of a song entitled 'The Colored Girl from Vassar.' He sent me a verse, and the lyrics are just awful. I'm called a poor dusky maid in the presence of millionaires. I'm so disturbed by it that I don't dare write him back. I—" She wiped a tear from her face and looked up at Andrew, feeling the same brokenness to her heart as she did when the newspapers first came out.

"But think," said Andrew, putting his hand on her worried face. "If we were to marry, your name would change. You would no longer be the Anita Hemmings of the newspapers or of a play like Mr. Dunbar's. You would be Mrs. Andrew Love. Anita Love. Now, I think we both look at passing as a very last resort, something we would be forced to do, not something we would choose to do again, but we have to discuss it before marriage. For Anita, I never want anything to come between us. We share such similar views and values—I think that's what brought us together initially—and I always want it to be such."

"I do too," said Anita, her eyes drying. "And of course, Andrew, it is something I would consider, with you. If we had to, we would."

"Perhaps if Tennessee did not prove a safe place, we could go to New York?" Andrew offered. "That is where you said you hoped to live, is it not? If you did not like the South, or if we were forced to leave, we could settle there."

New York. Anita thought about gliding through Central Park in the Taylor family carriage, taking in the opera with Lottie by her side, glimpsing Marchmont Rhinelander across the gilded room for the first time. No, her New York would never be like that again, but it would still be New York. And perhaps it could be just as good.

"I know you've decided not to apply to the graduate program at Yale because of your notoriety," said Andrew, interrupting Anita's colorful memories. "But I can promise you a life of the mind, Anita. I can. I want to be married to a woman more intelligent than I am, better than I am, kinder than I am, and that person, without a doubt, is you."

"Is it me?" Anita asked, reaching for the comfort of his hand. "I want to be all those things, Andrew, but sometimes I'm not. At times, I think I am built of horrible things like fear, apprehension. That confidence I had built up at Vassar still feels stripped from me. You are helping to bring it back, but I don't know that I can ever be like I was again. Or even like you."

"Of course you can be," said Andrew, gripping her small hand tightly. "Intelligent as you are, beautiful as you are, and now strengthened from what you've endured—of course you can be."

"But passing again, the idea terrifies me," said Anita, her voice shaking. "What would become of our families? Would we ever see them again?"

"Anita, you are speaking as if we are going to start passing as white tomorrow. I hope we never have to. I pray the world changes and that no one has to. It's just something we need to be realistic about, aware of. And as for your family, if we did have to live as white, we would never lose sight of them. It might have to be different, especially when our children are born, but we would still see them. I will make that promise to you."

Anita nodded, relieved. She did not fully understand the realities of Negro life in the South, but she did know that Andrew's career in medicine would be far more lucrative if he passed as white. But could she really do it again? If necessary, did she have the strength to wipe away her history, lose her identity through the practice of stepping out of one's skin and into another's yet again?

Anita leaned against Andrew's strong shoulder and thought about her sister, Elizabeth. Lillybug. She had the darkest skin of them all. How cruel it was, Anita thought, that they had to have this conversation at all, when speaking of something as joyful as marriage.

When they had walked back into the Lewis home, and straight through to sit on the ornate iron bench in the small backyard, Anita sat close to Andrew, their legs just brushing each other. She pictured her ailing father, her mother who had sacrificed so much, her brother who had looked after her during her Vassar years and thought about how happy they would be if she said yes to a marriage with Andrew. But she considered herself, too. She had thought Porter Hamilton could never be surpassed, but she was slowly coming to realize that with Andrew, she could have a deep, generous love—an honest love—and it was what she wanted. She would say yes to him not for her family or her community, but for herself.

"I want to marry you," she said as the sun had finished setting and a chill was spinning its way into the early spring air. "I would like very much to be your wife."

"You would?" said Andrew, taking Anita in his arms. "You'll never know how happy that makes me," he said, his voice full of joy. "I couldn't go on without you now. We need each other, Anita. We will have a wonderful life, I promise you. I will do everything I can to make sure you are the Anita Hemmings, the Anita Love, you want to be."

"I'll hold you to that promise," she replied, falling into him, letting him kiss her, thinking how nice forever sounded.

Just two days later, as Anita was organizing her room at Bessie's, thinking of how memorable a year 1898 had already become, her friend knocked on her door, holding the day's mail. She handed her two letters, which had been dropped off earlier in the day. Anita was bursting to tell her friend the news of her engagement, but she had to wait. It was the respectful thing to tell her parents first and she had not yet had time to travel to Boston.

She took the letters in her hand and blinked back her surprise. "But these are addressed to me at my Boston address," said Anita.

"A neighbor brought them by this afternoon," said Bessie. "A man who works with your father and had customers to drop off in Cambridge. Frederick asked him to do so. He told him they were important." Bessie left Anita alone to read her letters and retired to the kitchen to begin making supper.

Anita looked at them both. One, she was sure, was from Porter Hamilton. She recognized his large script, and it had a Chicago postmark in the right corner. She held that one in her hand, turning it over a few times, before she decided to open the other.

She looked down at the signature before she read it. It was from Sarah Douglas. It read simply, "Anita, though I am sure you would think otherwise, you have a friend in me," followed by her name.

Anita had heard many times from Belle and Caroline since they first wrote, but she had never expected to hear from Sarah. She refolded the short note and put it in the envelope. So she had a friend in Sarah Douglas, former Vassar College Southern Club president. Perhaps, with so many other girls, and now Sarah, as allies, she would be able to return to campus one day after all. Maybe even in the company of Andrew Love.

Heartened by Sarah's words, she opened the letter from Porter, and the sight of his slanted handwriting, scratched onto the paper in thick black ink, brought a rush of memories: their meeting at Harvard, their first walk on campus, the maids bringing her letter after letter postmarked from Cambridge, the kiss. That wonderful kiss. Holding the pages, her feelings surged back in full force, but she pushed them down quickly. With steady hands, she put the unfolded letter on the table and read it.

Anita,

To the world, and to me, you are a Negro. I understand now why you put an end to our engagement so suddenly: You knew you would have to marry a colored man. From that moment forward, you were acting in my interest, and I thank you for that. You put me before yourself, when you could have carried on your charade much longer.

Will the world ever change? I wonder. My mother, who was raised in a family of abolitionists, thinks it will. But that is not the reality now. The world does not want the races to join together. If you hadn't told me, and your race had been made public while you were my wife, we would have been ostracized. We are not people who could thrive in such a pitiful state, so you saved both of us from great humiliation.

I do not agree with what Lottie did. She should have kept your secret for you. She owed you that, certainly, as it is you who made her a true, whole person. Without you in her life, Anita, she would have remained a girl with not very much to offer but money and imagination. You can't live a life based on those two things alone, even if you are a Taylor.

Marrying Lottie will certainly keep me on my toes. And I do love her. Don't doubt that. But you, Anita, I will never forget.

Fondly,
Porter Hamilton

Though she didn't have to, though she could have kept it and looked at those words for years to come, she walked into the kitchen where Bessie was bustling about and dropped the letter, folded in its envelope, into the fire. Porter Hamilton would stay part of her vanished college life, of the Anita Hemmings she had been when she existed safely under a mansard roof, hidden away from the rest of the world.

"It wasn't important after all?" asked Bessie.

"It was once," said Anita, watching the pen marks fade into black ash, the edges of the letter curling like a child in repose. "But it no longer is."

CHAPTER 32

1924

E llen Love walked out of Rockefeller Hall, the cold air jolting her out of the mental haze that had overtaken her during her demanding two-hour English class. Though she had finished just one semester at Vassar, there was something about coming back after a break that made her feel she was now a proper member of the college community. She wasn't nervously arriving for the first time; she was proudly returning.

"Ellen Love! There you are!" said a girl with a haircut identical to Ellen's. As the 1920s had crept in, all the students had had their hair uniformly shorn so that it just grazed their cheeks, never long enough to pull back. "Can you believe there is more snow than when we left? It looks pretty, but it's a terrible pain to get around in."

Mary Elise Watts also hailed from New York City, and in one short semester had established herself as a leader of the freshman class.

"I know!" said Ellen, shaking the snow out of her hair. She had been standing outside the building daydreaming and hadn't realized the amount that was accumulating on her head. "It could be knee-high by this evening, that's what the newspaper said. I wore the wrong shoes, and now my feet will be soaked on the walk back to Joss. I didn't have time to change them before Macurdy's Greek class. You know what an axe she is about tardiness."

"Don't I?" said Mary Elise. "Well, good luck to you and those darling, if inappropriate, shoes. I must run," she declared, sending Ellen an air kiss. "I have to put some time in at the libe or I'll fail everything and have no chance of a Phi Beta Kappa key."

"Are you thinking of that already?" asked Ellen, laughing. "It's freshman year!"

"I know, it's ridiculous, but if I don't snap up that key, my mother will—" She made a cutting motion at her neck with her index finger. "I'll come by your room this afternoon!" she called back as she ran off.

Ellen watched Mary Elise hurry into Thompson Memorial Library, the beautiful Gothic building made of Germantown stone and named for Frederick Ferris Thompson, a former college trustee. Students past had known him, from his many appearances on campus, as Uncle Fred until his death in 1899. Whenever Ellen was in the library, she tried to find a seat under the stained-glass Cornaro Window, which depicted a young Venetian woman being awarded her doctoral degree, the first woman to earn the honor. Ellen had written to her mother her first week at school from her favorite spot under the large window and said she couldn't imagine college without such a building to study in.

But books were not on Ellen's mind after she had run across the quad to escape the cold in her building, Josselyn Hall, one of the campus's newer dormitories. As soon as she was inside the foyer, she smoothed her bangs, which were damp from the snow. Her dark hair was fashionably bobbed but was so straight she didn't bother to give it a wave, as many of her friends did. She had tried first semester, but it fell every time, like attempting to crimp cooked spaghetti.

Once in her room, she kicked off her shoes and threw her coat on the floor, placing her beloved Irving Berlin record on the phonograph. She hummed the words to "What'll I Do?" as she pulled on a heavy-knit cardigan, changed her wet tights, and reached for a cigarette. She let the ashes drop in a small glass tray next to her picture of her family, which stood in a silver frame on her desk. As she was about to move the phonograph needle to hear the song again, there was a knock on the door, and an older woman, with yet another identical haircut, stuck her head inside.

"Ellen, there is a telephone call for you downstairs. It's your mother. Would you like me to take a message or can you come take the call?"

"I'll come down, Mrs. Morris. Thank you," said Ellen, putting out her cigarette. The woman shut the door, and Ellen pulled her brown saddle shoes on and ran downstairs to the dormitory telephone. There were plans to expand the phone lines, but in 1924, only a few were available to the students. The messengers, and sometimes the dormitory warden, as Mrs. Florence Morris was for Josselyn Hall, alerted the girls when they had a call. Ellen smiled at Mrs. Morris when she reached the phone; unlike many of the girls, she was fond of her building's warden. Mrs. Morris was a member of the class of 1898 and had overlapped with her mother for three years. She loved reminiscing about the school before the turn of the century and had only admiring things to tell Ellen about Anita Love in her college days.

Ellen sat down in the comfortable armchair by the telephone and pressed the receiver to her ear. "Mother? Mother, is that you?" she said, addressing a symphony of static. "The connection is terrible," she shouted.

"Yes! It's me. Can you hear me?" Anita Hemmings Love's middle-aged voice came over the wire from her comfortable apartment on Riverside Drive in New York City.

"Now I can hear you fine," said Ellen, kicking her feet onto the nearby desk. Mrs. Morris gave her a look, and Ellen brought them down apologetically, crossing her calves in their gray wool tights. "I'm happy you called. Just checking in to see if I made it to school all right?"

"Yes," said Anita. "That, and it's just nice to hear my eldest child's voice." Anita often called Ellen her eldest, though she was really the Loves' second child. Ellen had a sister born a year before her in 1904, but baby Dorothy had died from diphtheria on Valentine's Day in 1907. Ellen had one younger sister, Barbara, and a rebellious younger brother, Andrew Jackson Love Jr., named after their father.

"Was the train ride bumpy?" asked Anita. "I worried with all the snow and wind. It's still warbling through the buildings here."

"It was just fine. I quite liked the excitement, and the Hudson looks so pretty when it's frozen," Ellen replied, wishing she had brought her cigarettes down. "But I'm happy to be back on campus, and the semester is starting off well. Oh! And Evelyn Colgate, who I took the train up with, said that my new coat with the fur trim was just perfect for school. Snappy, even. What else?" said Ellen, fiddling with her tights, which had twisted. "Well, classes have started, and I'm taking Greek with Macurdy just like I promised. I am doing very well so far, though we are only two days into the semester. And I absolutely love my English class. So many complain about the expository writing requirement freshman year, but it's by far my favorite class, Mother. As our text proclaims, we must learn to convince our audience that they have come to a certain conclusion themselves, even if we are the ones convincing them. Don't you love that notion?"

"I wish your generation would avoid words like *snappy*," said Anita, after she had applauded Ellen for her interest in her required course. "But I suppose we had our fair share of strange vocabulary when I was up there."

"Oh, Mother, I almost forgot," said Ellen excitedly. "Take a guess who was on my train up the Hudson?"

"I don't know. I imagine many excited Vassar women who use dreadful words like *snappy*," said Anita drily.

"Well, yes, but we were joined for a moment by Mr. Rhinelander! Marchmont Rhinelander. He was making the journey to Hyde Park to call on Mr. Frederick Vanderbilt. He'll be staying in that magical house on the bank of the river. Can you imagine ever going inside such a grand house? Mr. Rhinelander told me and Evelyn that there is an Italian garden with two thousand rosebushes dotted all around. That must smell heavenly, especially with the breeze up the river. He promised he would call on us to tell me about it over Easter."

"What a wonderful coincidence," said Anita. "He's always been such an elegant man."

"I agree," said Ellen, who had been acquainted with Marchmont all her life. "And how's Dad? And everyone?"

"Your father is well," said Anita. "There's an outbreak of measles in a building on One Hundred and Tenth Street, so that is keeping him plenty busy. And he's doing a fine job harping at your brother to listen to music less and spend more time on his studies and devotion. Don't write and tell Andy, please, but we are considering sending him to Mount Hermon, the brother school to Northfield, where I went."

"Yes, I know it, Mother, you talk of it often enough," said Ellen, who had attended high school in the city. "But why?

Andrew loves New York. Don't send him away." She was protective of her younger brother, who had never known anywhere but New York City. "He's not even thirteen."

"He's not like you, Ellen," said Anita. "And it wouldn't be for this year. You've always been studious. You did wonderfully at Horace Mann, but he is not excelling in school. Music is taking over his life and greatly interrupting his academics. He listens to so much jazz I'm waiting for a trumpet to fall out of his ear."

"Music won't rot his brain, Mother. Just give him time to grow up."

"I'm trying," said Anita. "But you know your father, he expects perfect grades every year, and no growing pains allowed."

"Daddy can't have everything he wants all the time," said Ellen, waving to two of her friends as they came into the dorm, snow slowly melting into the shoulders of their coats.

"No, not all the time," said Anita. "Though he is thinking of changing offices. There is a bigger suite available and he might move up a few floors. There is a beautiful view of the south end of the park from the higher levels."

"As long as he doesn't change buildings," said Ellen, half-listening. "East Fifty-Fourth Street is so lovely, and all the wealthiest people live on the Upper East Side."

"I didn't say he was going anywhere but up," Anita replied, sure her daughter was thinking about many other things besides her parents.

"Come outside, Ellen!" said Helen Tweedy, who was hovering around her friend, pulling on the phone cord. She was one of the most attractive girls on campus, and always managed to keep a perfect wave in her blond hair. "There's a snowball fight about to start, and we need your arms."

"I must go, Mother," said Ellen, signaling to her friends to wait for her. "There is a snowball fight in the quad, and my muscles are in high demand."

"And you won't even get in trouble for it," said Anita, cheerfully. "In my day, we would have been in the lady principal's office and given a lecture on female gentility."

"Lucky for me they've done away with that position," said Ellen, as her friends waved at her to hang up the receiver.

"I'm so glad you're there," said Anita before Ellen hung up. "I'm looking forward to visiting you on Class Day in June. I know that plenty of '97s plan to attend. And I will talk your ear off about all the nice times I had, even if we did have a lady principal."

"I'll be glad to hear it, Mother," said Ellen. "Thank you for calling. I love you, and send kisses to Daddy, too. And Barbara and Andy!" She hung up and ran outside with her friends, not caring that she was about to run through a foot and a half of snow in saddle shoes.

"Shoulder-to-shoulder, march we forth, twenty-sev'n!" yelled Helen, making a snowball and lobbing it at a group of fellow freshmen walking to Thompson Library.

"Don't you dare attack us from behind, you traitors!" shouted one of the girls. Ellen and her friends quickly cornered them against the back side of Rockefeller Hall and dove into the accumulating powder to make snowballs as fast as their cold hands would let them. The other group, knowing they were unprepared, screamed to a trio of sophomores coming out of the library who quickly ran to their aid.

"Now we're outnumbered!" yelled Ellen as she wiped the snow off her face. Her right cheek was numb from a fastball hurled by her hallmate, but she was still grinning.

"Come," said Helen, packing snowballs with machinelike

precision and handing them to a girl from Wyoming who was an excellent shot. "That sophomore there is frightfully rich and can barely use her delicate hands," she said, pointing at an elegantly dressed girl. "And the other one is constantly eating marshmallows. We can take them."

"Perhaps," said Ellen, grabbing snowballs from Helen's pile and lobbing them at the girls. After thirty minutes, half the students were lying in the snow on their backs, trying to catch their breath and calling for a truce as loudly as they could.

"Here, Ellen, your own personal snowfall," said Ellen's friend Virginia Heard. She stood above Ellen and sprinkled snow onto her face like powdered sugar.

"Stop it, you pest!" said Ellen, laughing until she started coughing from the cold air. She pulled her friend onto the ground by her ankles.

"You two are going to be soaked," said Helen, standing above them. "And we have the Granddaughters meeting in half an hour. Stop wrestling and come back to Joss with me. I have to change out of these wet rags and curl my hair again. Why have a bob if it ends up looking like a dead octopus attached to your head after a little fun?"

Helen's mother, Grace Landfield Tweedy, had graduated in 1897 like Ellen's mother, and Virginia's mother had been class of 1901. Ellen and Helen often talked about how they would walk for their diplomas exactly thirty years after their mothers did and already had grand plans to carry the ribbons from their mothers' graduation dresses on their day.

"Did you hear me?" said Helen, leaning down and wiping the snow off Ellen and Virginia's faces. "Granddaughters! We have to go now or we will all be sitting on the floor in the parlor, and I refuse to do such a thing in winter. The floor is too cold."

There were eighty-eight members of the Granddaughters club, fifteen in the class of '27 alone, so many that they
had to meet by class rather than as a group. Ellen loved the
way she felt when she walked in to the parlor to discuss Vassar history and alumnae with her branch of the elite club.
She felt part of a family tradition, rather than just another
freshman.

On the agenda for the meeting was a luncheon for the
granddaughters and their mothers scheduled for the Friday
before Class Day the following spring. It was a ways off, but
as the main event of the year for the Granddaughters club,
preparations lasted for months.

"I'll have to tell my mother the date now," Helen whispered to Ellen, "or she won't be able to make the luncheon.
You would think Vassar was always her first priority, but
she's been the head math teacher at our school in Bingham-
ton since 1898 and her allegiance, I'm afraid, lies there. And
you know how long those high schools stay in session."

"Mathematics? Isn't that your sore subject?" asked Ellen.

"Don't remind me. I have to get my grade up or my
mother will force a tutor on me. Some whiskered woman
who hits me with a ruler," she said, laughing.

"Well, I think it's wonderful that your mother worked
through your childhood," said Ellen, making sure to whisper. "My own worked at the Boston Public Library as a
foreign language cataloguer until marriage, but then it was
goodbye employment, hello babies and housekeeping. You
know how most of that generation was. Even the intelligent
ones. All that schooling just to tend house. A real pity."

"Not like us," said Helen, closing her mouth quickly
when the club president caught her eye.

No, not like us, thought Ellen, who had been considering
a career on the stage since she was in high school. Her par-

ents constantly urged her to pursue medicine like her father, to do something academic with her life, and she worked hard in school to appease them, but even at eighteen, she knew where she would be after graduation, and it wasn't an operating room, or tending house and raising children.

"At least your mother made her way down to New York City after graduation," Helen whispered when she was sure the club president was no longer watching them. "We have to move there after school. I am not going back upstate."

"Don't we, though," said Ellen. "I can't imagine living anywhere else. I was born in Tennessee, but we moved up when I was little. And then we darted around New York a bit, from Broadway to One Hundred and Forty-Second Street and now on Riverside Drive. That's where I like it best. With a view of the water and a city all around."

"You lived in Tennessee?" said Helen, surprised.

"Briefly. For my father's medical practice. But they weren't happy there. My mother does not like the South but she adores New York. She loves the opera and the museums and lately, with me, the Broadway revues, though she pretends not to. She spends a great deal of time being supportive of my father's office since he works independently, but she was always very good at making the city come alive for me, for all of us."

"After graduation," said Helen, "it will be your turn. You can make it come alive for me."

"I promise," said Ellen, thinking that while she knew she wanted to go back to New York eventually, she hoped her four years at Vassar would go by very slowly.

When the meeting had ended, the girls left the parlor together, ready to part ways for their late afternoon classes.

"I have zoology," said Helen, the leather soles on her new boots tapping their way through Main Building.

"Come to my room after class. I have the greatest record to listen to, 'Riverboat Shuffle.' My brother gave it to me over winter break. You'll go crazy over it," said Ellen.

"I don't think I can like anything better than 'King Porter Stomp,'" said Helen, whistling the song.

"If you keep whistling that tune, I swear I will tape you to your desk chair and never set you free," said Ellen, putting her hands over her ears and holding her breath.

"Good, then I won't have to go to zoology," said Helen, twirling into a wall.

Giddy from the start of the new semester, the two girls made their way to the second floor, where many of the classrooms and administrative offices were located, and passed President MacCracken's office on their way to the back stairs. Both looked inside as they walked by and paused when they saw the dean of the college, C. Mildred Thompson, sitting at the desk in the president's reception room.

"I live in fear of being called in by Prexy or Thompson," said Helen, after they had smiled and walked by the dean. She was a much-admired woman who had marched in the second suffrage parade in 1911 and was now actively involved in Democratic politics, helped by her close friendship with Eleanor Roosevelt. Despite that, the students hoped never to have to meet her alone.

"Me, too," said Ellen. "Though my mother admitted she had to meet with President Taylor her senior year and said it wasn't all bad."

"What was it about? Academic probation?"

"I'm not sure," said Ellen, looking out the window at the snow falling on Taylor Gate. In 1913, the original gate to the school had been torn down and replaced by a Gothic Revival building and handsome stone entrance. It was one of Ellen's favorite buildings on campus, though her mother said the

old gatehouse was superior. "She graduated a cum laude, so
it couldn't have been that. Whatever it was, she survived."

Ellen said goodbye to her friend and ran down to the
first floor and out the door, across the quad again, greeting
the freshmen she had not said hello to since returning from
winter break. Ellen had loved growing up in New York City,
and had spent a good deal of time in high school sneaking
out to music clubs and theaters. But as she walked past
Strong and toward her own residence hall, she was glad that
her mother had pushed her to Vassar. She remembered how
when she was barely fourteen and had just started thinking
about college, her mother had said to her, "Vassar. There's
no other school to consider."

Ellen was beginning to think she was right.

The sight of Ellen Love walking past the president's door
startled Dean Thompson, since she was waiting to speak
to President Taylor about that very student. When Ellen
had dawdled by, the dean stood up and positioned herself in
the door frame, watching the dark-haired freshman as she
laughed with her friend. Ellen Love appeared to be very
happy at Vassar.

"I've just hung up, Miss Thompson!" President Mac-
Cracken boomed from his office. "Come in, come in."

"This weather!" said Dean Thompson, making her way
into the president's capacious office. On the walls hung pictures of presidents past, and Miss Thompson paused and
looked at the stern face of President Taylor, his thick white
mustache combed and trimmed with precision. She then
pulled an envelope from the brown folder she was holding.
She glanced at the return address, which also indicated the
sender's class year, and placed it on the president's desk.

"This came for you yesterday, but my assistant, Hilda, is opening all the mail addressed to you from alumnae, as you know."

"Saving me much time," said the president briskly. "And this letter is from an alumna?"

"Class of 1897," said the dean, waiting for him to remove the letter from the envelope. "It's from a Mrs. Louise Hamilton. She was Louise Taylor when she was a student here. Hilda said that not only did she send this letter, but she has been telephoning nonstop since the last alumnae reunion at the end of fall term. I'm afraid she's desperate to contact you."

"Class of 1897. Louise Taylor," the president repeated. "I know the Taylor name, her father Clarence especially, but I don't think they've given a penny to the school."

"They haven't."

The president looked up at the dean and raised his eyebrows before diving into the letter.

My Dear Dr. MacCracken,

After serious discussions at the last class reunion and many unreturned phone calls to your office since, I have decided to ask you by letter if it is the policy of Vassar College to accept Negro students, and if so, is it the policy of the college to accept them as white?

Already the South is asking questions concerning the colored girl in the freshman class.

I am particularly interested in the matter because of my own painful experience with a roommate who was supposed to be a white girl but who proved to be a Negress. After rooming with Anita Hemmings during my senior year, I suddenly discovered that she was colored. Terribly upset, I wrote to my father at once, and he, while quoting

*the Golden Rule to me, quietly had a man in Boston
investigate. The report came that the family was colored
and it was considered impossible for a girl from such a
section and family to be at Vassar. But at Vassar she was.*

*In my own case, I learned after Miss Hemmings had
been a guest in my home, that she resorted to falsehood to
cover the distressing truth. I should not like any young
girl to repeat my harrowing experience for it is Anita's
daughter, Ellen Love, who is now at Vassar.*

*Parents of girls in both preparatory schools and
college are giving this matter careful consideration for the
question, we feel, is moral as well as social. I await your
response and am optimistic that it will contain the news
that Miss Love has been removed from school. The class of
1927 does not need the same stain that the class of 1897
will always carry.*

Very sincerely,
Louise Taylor Hamilton

"Not a reserved woman, is she?" said the president,
putting the letter down. "Is what she is saying true, Miss
Thompson? Is this student in the class of 1927 colored?"

"She could be considered that way," said the dean. "I
don't know how familiar you are with her mother's story,
but it caused a sizable scandal in '97."

"I'm somewhat familiar with it," said the president. "I am
aware that we graduated her knowing that she had strains
of Negro blood."

"We did. And while I'm sure for the faculty it felt like
negative press at the time, it's not something that stayed in
the hearts and minds of the alumnae. I'm confident most of
our women—apart from those who were with her in '97—
are not aware that such a person graduated. Just think of

all our current professors, our wardens who were employed while her mother was a student. And the Granddaughters club. Many of those women have mothers who overlapped with Mrs. Love, but it's second semester and it seems no one has informed Ellen. The scandal, I believe, dissipated long ago."

The dean glanced into her file and closed it again, changing her train of thought. "I looked for the minutes from the special session of the board meeting at which it was decided that Anita Hemmings should graduate, but no minutes exist."

"Do you believe they were purposefully destroyed or is that an unfortunate coincidence?" asked the president. He was known around the college for keeping every paper that was ever in his possession, and boxes of his letters were already piling up in storage—everything from personal correspondence to receipts for coffee and a note saying he had left his razor on the train and could he have a new one sent up? No minutes from his tenure would ever go missing.

"I can't be sure," said Miss Thompson. "I hope it's just an unfortunate coincidence."

The president looked down at the letter and read it again. "We certainly don't want a repetition of 1897," he said after a moment. "But we also have to proceed carefully, as this Hamilton woman sounds unbalanced."

The dean watched the president as he studied each line of the letter carefully, then she sat down in the chair opposite him and said, "To be quite frank, if I may, I don't think Ellen Love even knows she's black."

"Is that so?" said the president with interest.

"From what Ellen wrote about her family on her application, I think her mother is living as a white woman now.

You can see her file here," she said, removing it from her folder and placing it on his desk, "that her father is a medical doctor who attended Harvard. Surely he is Caucasian."

"I think that makes our decision even easier," said the president. "If this girl does not know that she's colored, why should anyone else?"

"I'm in complete agreement," said the dean. "And she is in a single room in Josselyn Hall."

"How did that come to be?" asked President MacCracken, who had no say in where the students were housed.

"Many freshmen are in singles now," said the dean, "so it might be a coincidence. Or maybe someone in the housing office paid more attention than we did. But please be at ease as the wardens have assured me that she will remain in a single all four years."

"The thing to do is to turn a blind eye," said the president, taking out his official stationery and uncapping a pen. "If they let her mother graduate twenty-seven years ago, I am certainly not going to hold her daughter back now. We are not a college that goes back in time. We only move forward."

He put his pen to paper and wrote in bold script to his petitioner.

My dear Mrs. Hamilton,

I thank you for your letter dated the 5th of January and have taken your concern as an alumna under careful consideration.

You use the word Negress in referring to her mother, but you probably know that both mother and daughter are more white than black. I may go so far as to say it is my understanding that Ellen Love herself is entirely ignorant of the fact that she has any Negro blood in her veins and that the communication of this fact to her would be a very great shock.

I understand from the wardens that Mrs. Love's daughter rooms alone, and that there is no intention on the part of the department to have her room with anyone during her time here.

My own particular point of view is perhaps not pertinent but I may say that Negro students were my classmates at New York University and Harvard, and that I have taught students with Negro blood in Syria at the American University, and later at Yale. I was never aware that the universities lost caste through the admission of students with Negro blood.

We have no intention of removing Ellen Love from college and thank you for keeping this matter a confidential one.

I am,

> *Very sincerely yours,*
> *President Henry MacCracken*

Though it was nearly dark outside, Ellen and Virginia decided to put off working on their first Greek translation of the year and instead walked up to see the brindled cows on the farm, the smell of livestock mixing with the sweet aroma emitted from the cider mill up the path. The snow had stopped and the sky was glowing purple, in the fleeting state where the stars were visible through the last trace of sunlight.

"Look, the stream is completely frozen," said Ellen, putting her foot on it and letting it slide. "Helen and I walked through it barefoot this fall. It's shallow, though there are quite a lot of pebbles at the bottom."

"I love this part of campus," said Virginia, who had also

spent her childhood in a city, "especially in the snow. I bet fifty years ago it all looked exactly the same."

"I think when our mothers were here, most of it was like this," Ellen replied, looking down at the distant yellow lights of the road.

Ellen had sensed as soon as she walked through Taylor Gate for the first time that she was part of something bigger than herself. She felt it when she sat in the wooden seats of the handsome classrooms; when she lay in the parlors smoking cigarettes, her bangs in her eyes, listening to girls play "Tin Roof Blues" with amateur hands. When she heard the first few notes echoing in the halls of Main, she recognized the melody instantly and felt a mix of excitement and longing. Her brother had played it on their phonograph countless times. She looked toward the four quad dorms, the trees and bushes covered in snow. She felt uplifted as she walked, her posture straight, her head held high. There was something magical about this place, this hour, as snow refracted light from the lampposts and the campus buildings. She felt a glow being there, just as she knew her mother had.

"Tell me we'll never have to leave," said Virginia, tilting her head back as far as she could. "That somehow life can stay just like it is today."

"It will," said Ellen, looking down at the campus as Virginia lifted her arms toward the stars. "Part of us will always be here."

AFTERWORD

The story of Anita Hemmings began for me in 2013, when I came across a dusty stack of Vassar College alumni magazines I kept from my student years. A cover from 2001, with a picture of a beautiful woman wearing a style of dress popular in the Gilded Age, caught my attention and I immediately began to read the article inside. "Passing as White: Anita Hemmings 1897," written by Olivia Mancini, a Vassar alumna, quoted Anita's great-granddaughter Jillian Atkin Sim extensively. The article went on to explain that Anita Hemmings was Vassar's first African-American graduate, but that she passed as white until her roommate revealed her secret at the end of their senior year. What it did not mention was who her roommate was or how she came to know that Anita wasn't just of French and English ancestry as she claimed. I, a loyal Vassar grad, was surprised that I had never heard Anita's story before, but I was immediately taken with it and started down a path of research and writing that would happily consume me for years.

Following the Vassar article, I read an in-depth piece by Anita's great-granddaughter, published in *American Heritage* magazine in 1999, in which Jillian disclosed that it was the death of her grandmother, Ellen Love, in 1994, which led her to discover the truth about her family's race, eventually finding out that Anita was Vassar's first African-American graduate and her daughter, Ellen, the school's second. Jillian stated that after Anita and Andrew Love were married, they chose to pass as white once they moved to New York City. The consequence of that decision was that their children, including Ellen, were cut off from their black relatives. By Jillian's account, Dora Hemmings, Anita's mother, came to the Love residence in New York only once and was made to enter via the service entrance. Yet, according to Jillian, their daughter Ellen was aware of her race during her time at Vassar, as she was able to find her grandmother on Martha's Vineyard in 1923.

Jillian's more recent research extended to the familiar Hemmings name and the fact that Anita's family hailed from Virginia. Could she be related to the famous Hemings clan, the one forever tied to President Thomas Jefferson through his relationship with Sally Hemings, despite their different spellings? Jillian believes, but has yet to confirm, that her branch of the Hemmings family is descended from Peter Hemings, the brother of Sally Hemings and the son of Elizabeth Hemings and an English sea captain. Peter worked as a cook and brewer at Monticello before being granted his freedom in 1827.

While I found Anita's family history and Jillian's premise fascinating, what interested me most as I continued to research was how Anita made her way to Vassar and lived her life as a white woman there, and how her roommate almost derailed her at the eleventh hour. In none of the articles I read regarding Anita Hemmings was her roommate's name ever mentioned, nor was it readily available in the Vassar archives. I did not want the woman who was so happy to stay anonymous in the newspapers of the era to remain so more than a century later, and thankfully, after several research trips, her files were found.

Anita's roommate was Louise Taylor, a girl known by the nickname "Lulu" (rather than "Lottie," as I call her in the book). She was born and raised in South Orange, New Jersey, and lived comfortably, but nothing like the millionaire's Gilded Age life that I gave her in the novel. Her father was not a turn-of-the-century tycoon, but a surveyor, engineer, and postmaster of South Orange. After Vassar, Louise went on to earn her master's degree in English literature at New York University and then taught history and mythology at schools in South Orange until the 1930s. She never married and had no children, which gave her ample time to keep tabs on Anita and her family.

Louise and Anita roomed together for two years, not one, as I write in the book. And though newspapers at the time say that Anita did boast about family and connections, which led to her roommate's suspicion, it was the article about Bessie Baker's wedding to William Henry Lewis in Cambridge that was Anita's ultimate undoing. This article ran in the *Boston Daily Globe* on September 24, 1896, at the start of Anita's senior year, not in January as I have it, though Louise may not have acted on her suspicions until the end of their senior year, as reported by many papers at the time. (All the newspaper articles that I quote in the book ran in

1896 or 1897. The dates are off on a few to make them work in the context of the story, but they are accurately cited.)

I imagine Louise Taylor was none too happy that Vassar allowed Anita to graduate in 1897, and she was still incensed about it when she discovered that Anita's daughter was a student there in the 1920s. She wrote several letters to Vassar president Henry Noble MacCracken explaining what she had to endure and hoping the school would not allow other girls to feel similar pain. MacCracken fought back, explaining they considered Ellen Love's admission as a daughter of an alumna. He told Louise that Anita lodged the statement that her daughter did not know she had "negro blood in her veins" and the school took that as fact. Though it is a shameful point in Vassar's history that they did not admit African-American students until the 1940s, MacCracken and Louise Taylor's correspondence made it apparent that the school chose to admit Ellen despite knowing who her mother was, and that they kept her there in the face of Louise's complaints.

Sadly, as is the case in regard to most women living in the 1800s, very few traces of Anita's life exist, which is why her story was such a good candidate for historical fiction. As beautiful and intelligent as Anita was, I wanted to give her a romantic adventure in the book, but there was no way for me to know the details of Anita's quotidian life at Vassar. The newspapers from the time did carry on about all the Ivy League men who were taken by her beauty, and, inspired by those reports, I created her romance with Porter Hamilton, an entirely fictional character. While I doubt that Anita was ever serious with any man while she was at school, she would certainly have danced and socialized with the many male college students who attended Vassar's functions. As for Louise's love life, she wasn't lucky in love at school or after. And I don't believe she ever met Anita's handsome brother, Frederick, though he reportedly did come visit his sister at Vassar despite his darker skin—darker than I describe in the book—which could have raised suspicions.

Though much of Anita's life at Vassar had to be fictionalized, the way she ended up at Vassar has been documented. According to her prep school, Northfield Seminary (now Northfield Mount Hermon), she started passing as white when she applied and she and Bessie had already selected their first-choice colleges before they entered the school.

At the end of the nineteenth century, only three of the Seven Sisters schools accepted African-American students: Radcliffe, Wellesley, and Mount Holyoke. By the time Anita entered Vassar in 1893, Wellesley had had two African-American graduates, Harriet Rice in 1887 and Ella Smith in 1888. Mount Holyoke had graduated one African-American student, Hortense Parker in 1883, but at the time the school was a seminary (not the college it became in 1888) and the race of Miss Parker was only discovered when she arrived. Radcliffe had not graduated any African-American students when Anita entered Vassar, and would not until 1898, the same year that Mount Holyoke graduated an African-American from its college, but Radcliffe did not have the same restrictive policy as Vassar.

Because of these painfully low admissions statistics for African-Americans, I believe that Anita, her best friend, Bessie Baker, and Bessie's younger sister Gertrude planned together where to apply to college for the best chances of acceptance. As Anita, Bessie, and Gertrude were coming into college in the classes of 1897, 1898, and 1900 respectively, they could not have been accepted to the same school, as even progressive Wellesley had never had three African-American students enrolled at the same time and would not for several decades. Anita, being the lightest of the three, had the best chance to pass as white, and thus by going to Vassar, Anita left spaces open for the Baker sisters at Radcliffe and Wellesley. I also think that the Bakers and Anita knew about Alberta Scott—a fellow gifted African-American student—and her intentions to apply to Radcliffe the same year that Bessie was hoping for admission at Wellesley, since Alberta was from Cambridgeport and grew up close to the Baker sisters.

Anita's decision to attend Vassar was therefore motivated by much more than wanting the best education; it also allowed her equally gifted friends to attend Seven Sisters schools. (Smith, Barnard, and Bryn Mawr did not graduate African-Americans until the twentieth century—1900, 1928, and 1931, respectively—and if you do not count Anita Hemmings or Ellen Love, Vassar did not graduate an African-American student until 1944, the very last of the Seven Sisters to do so.)

Although I do not include much about Anita's life after Vassar in the book (except for my last chapter, which focuses on her daughter Ellen), it was a large part of my research and proved to be just as fascinating as her Vassar years.

Anita and her husband, Andrew, who were married in 1903, did end up living in Tennessee, but were back in Massachusetts in 1905 when Andrew was a postgraduate student at Harvard for the summer. The couple finally settled in New York City, where their children attended elite private schools, including Horace Mann and Friends Seminary. (Their son Andrew later transferred to Mount Hermon in Massachusetts.) Though Anita and her husband desperately wanted their children to be more academically inclined, Ellen and Andrew Jr. ended up inheriting their mother's love for performing. Ellen went on to a successful Broadway career, opening in *Oklahoma!* and testing for

Scarlett O'Hara in *Gone with the Wind*, according to Jillian. Andrew Jr. inherited Anita's voice and good looks and was a successful musician on radio and TV. He sang for band leader Mitch Miller, as well as with his band the Tune Twisters, and wrote many well-known commercial jingles.

I had many unexpected discoveries while researching this book, but one of the most important was the friendship between Anita and Bessie Baker. Bessie may not have finished Wellesley, but she went on to guide her children's educations in Massachusetts and Paris and to support her husband's distinguished career. William Henry Lewis was not only the first African-American all-American football player (as I mention in the book), but went on to be the first African-American appointed as an assistant U.S. attorney and then was appointed assistant attorney general in 1910. He was also a friend of President Theodore Roosevelt and a leading voice for civil rights.

Bessie and William had three children together, and their son William Henry Lewis Jr. followed in his father's footsteps, attending Harvard Law School and practicing with him. Their eldest daughter, Dorothy, graduated from Wellesley in 1920 and went on to marry a Belgian nobleman, while their youngest daughter, Elizabeth, earned a B.A. and an M.A. from Radcliffe, but met a tragic end—hanging herself at her parents' home in 1926 soon after she began working as a teacher at the Cambridge Latin School.

I have yet to discover if Bessie and Anita's friendship was maintained after Anita and Andrew began living as white in New York, but I sincerely hope that it was. With fervency, I will continue to dig into their stories, even as I move on to other books, for after immersing myself in Anita's bright, brilliant, turn-of-the-century world, I know she will never leave me.

ACKNOWLEDGMENTS

My deepest gratitude to Kari-Lynn Rockefeller, my beloved friend, Vassar scholar, and the best research partner one could ever hope for. Kari, your passion and intelligence never cease to amaze me. Mary-Alice Farina, I am indebted to you for your help and constant encouragement. You were my other half at Vassar and always will be. Keisha Nishimura, thank you for lending your wisdom to this book and to my life. Juan Acosta, Marcus Barnes, Rebecca Brizi, Kristin Dailey, Christian Gabriel, Paola Mantilla, Dalia Rahman, Jamilyah Smith-Kanze, Kavita Srinivasan, Rashida Truesdale—your love and support continue to bolster me and my writing.

If it were not for Jillian Atkin Sim, Anita Hemmings's great-granddaughter, Anita would be just another gifted, yet mostly unknown, African-American woman. I am so grateful for Jillian's passion for her family history and for giving Anita a second life.

My editor, Sarah Cantin, yet again made my writing so much better with her superb edits. Sarah, your positivity and excellence in everything you do bring me infinite joy. Also at Atria, a giant thank-you to president and publisher Judith Curr, Tom Pitoniak, Carla Benton, Haley Weaver, Arielle Kane, and Tory Lowy.

Bridget Matzie, my wonderful, always insightful agent, deserves all the credit for giving this book legs and seeing the literary potential in Anita's remarkable life from the very start. I'm also indebted to Elizabeth Ward, the first editor of this book, for her sharp eye and for helping me refine Anita's story. Gilda Squire and Simone Cooper put their powerhouse PR and marketing skills behind me and my writing, and I'm so thankful to have such intelligent women on my side.

My research was hugely aided by the gifts of time and knowledge from Peter Weis, school archivist at Northfield Mount Hermon, who made Anita's pre-Vassar education and the beauty of her prep school come alive for me. Dean Rogers and Ronald Patkus of the Vassar Archives & Special Collections Library deserve a world of appreciation, as they aided me in piecing Anita's Vassar years together. And I'm thankful for the assistance of Patricia Hurley at Trinity Church Boston, Laura Reiner at Wellesley College, Myles Crowley at MIT, and for the research done by Nora Nercessian at Harvard Medical School.

I am indebted to my always supporters—Rebecca Frankel, Georgia Bobley, and the women of the Georgetown Book Club—and to my fantastic parents and my brother, Ken, who founded Loving Day, an annual celebration of *Loving v Virginia*, which struck down U.S. anti-miscegenation laws. I often thought of his tireless work for racial equality as I wrote. My husband, Craig Fischer, deserves buckets of gold for his patience and encouragement with this project. Craig, thank you for loving me as much as I love you.

And lastly, I am grateful to the staff of the Georgetown branch of the District of Columbia Public Libraries, where I scribbled much of this book and where I hope to write many more.

THE GILDED
YEARS

KARIN TANABE

A Readers Club Guide

Questions and Topics
for Discussion

1. At the end of the novel, Ellen Love remarks of Vassar College that "part of us will always be here" (page 372). What is the significance of location in the novel? How do Vassar, Manhattan, and Boston shape Anita and Lottie? In your own experience, are there places that you feel have shaped you in similar ways? Do you think you'd be willing to give up part of who you are to keep those places in your life?

2. *The Gilded Years* depicts a time when the attitude toward women's education and the prioritization of marriage was shifting in the United States. Did anything surprise you about characters' opinions on these topics? Were they more or less similar to your own feelings or goals than you expected? If so, how?

3. "It is not an escape. . . .When one passes for a higher purpose, it's worth it. . . ." (page 50). Do you agree with this sentiment? Why or why not?

4. At Bessie's wedding, Anita considers the paths she and her friend have taken given their similar backgrounds, and wonders what her life would be like if she had made different choices. Do you think she would have been happy living a life more like Bessie's? Why, or why not? How do the decisions they both make impact their friendship? Do you have friends with whom your paths have diverged, or ones who you feel are on a "shared path" (page 168) with you?

5. In what ways does the revelation that Joseph Southworth is half Japanese differ from or parallel the reaction to the discovery that Anita is not white? Do you think these differences are the result of differing attitudes toward Japanese people and black people? The characters' class backgrounds? Discuss these and any other factors you think were contributors (e.g., gender, having a white father, etc.).

6. On page 229, Lottie asserts that "Porter Hamilton was never a goal of mine. . . . I think my ego was crushed and I needed male reassurance. I'm much weaker than you are. No one over voted me the class beauty." Do you believe her explanation and apology in this scene? Why or why not?

7. Did you notice any foreshadowing of Lottie's betrayal? In retrospect, what moments hint at Lottie's eventual actions? Alternately, what moments led you to believe she wouldn't turn on Anita?

8. Anita reflects that Lottie has seemed "the most modern of women" (page 319). What does it mean to be "modern" in 1897? Does the same idea hold true today? In your own experiences, have you come across someone who espouses modern ideas but balks when confronted with situations that veer from tradition? Do you think Lottie was more concerned about Anita's identity or her own reputation? Why?

9. Why do you think that Anita and her husband, Andrew, ultimately decided to pass as white again in New York and raise their children that way? Do you think it affected their relationships with their families? Should it have?

10. Many characters, such as William and Bessie, suggest to Anita that she has a duty to the black community as an intelligent and educated woman, and that her Vassar education will help her be a figure of progress. Did you agree that she owes something to the community she was raised in? Why or why not?

11. Lottie quips, "The faces in New York change, but the last names seldom do" (page 209). The notion of legacy figures prominently throughout the novel, from Vassar's Society of the Granddaughters and wealthy family names, to Lottie's fear of being forgotten. What does legacy mean to you? What is the significance of legacy in the novel?

12. We see only a brief glimpse of Anita's daughter Ellen as she also passes for white at Vassar. Do you think this experience was easier for her because her family also passed? What challenges might have been different or similar to her mother's situation? Were you surprised that Anita allowed her daughter to attend the school?

13. If you haven't already, read the Afterword from Karin Tanabe about her research on the real Anita Hemmings. Are there any distinctions between the true story and the novel that struck you? Why do you think Tanabe made the changes she made?

ENHANCE YOUR BOOK CLUB

1. As a group, look at images of (or consider visiting!) some of the locations in *The Gilded Years*, such as Vassar College in Poughkeepsie, New York; Oak Bluffs (known as Cottage City before 1907) on Martha's Vineyard; or the places Anita visits in New York. Do they appear as you imagined them while reading?

2. Consider reading *A Chosen Exile: A History of Racial Passing in American Life* by Allyson Hobbs as a group for more historical background on the issue of passing. Discuss how Anita Hemmings fits into the large picture of passing in America.

3. When did your alma mater, or the colleges closest to your hometown, start admitting black students? What are their racial makeups today? Have there been any recent controversies with regard to racial tension at colleges in your state? How might things be improved for black students attending college today?

4. Try reading *The Price of Inheritance* by Karin Tanabe as a group, and compare the depictions of wealth with those in *The Gilded Years*. Discuss how Tanabe's writing differs or remains the same in the entirely fictional contemporary novel compared with this historical novel based on a true story.